R J Dillon was born in the North West of England. He taught history and visual culture for over ten years. He now writes full-time, and is the author of five novels, a poetry collection and a book examining the portrayal of history on British television. He is married with two children and lives on the Lancashire coast, where he devotes his time to writing and walking.

For more information, visit rjdillon.com

The Oktober Projekt is the first in a series of novels based around the British Secret Intelligence Service's (SIS), Covert Operations Directorate, CO8.

By the same author
The Fanatic
Hunted and the Damned
Network of Lies
Point of No Return

Poetry
Midnight's Revolution

Non-fiction
History on British television: Constructing nation, nationality and collective memory

R J DILLON

The Oktober Projekt

REVIDION BOOKS

First published by Revidion 2012

Third revised edition published by Revidion 2020

British Library Cataloguing in Publication Data. A catalogue record for this book is available from the British Library.

ISBN: 978-0-9572651-8-9

For Halina, Charlotte, Oliver

A man may learn wisdom even from a foe.

Aristophanes

One

Sally Wynn was in a hurry. Three minutes and fourteen seconds remained for her to reach the public phone outside the Peace & Love Hostel and take the call. Her collar length auburn hair flicked against her neck as she pounded up Katharinenstraße walking fast, and she was blowing hard when she reached the booth on what was already turning into an unseasonably warm day. Sweeping back her hair she inhaled, exhaled, telling herself that she was doing fine, recalling her instructions as she worked through her shoulder bag, engaging in a little piece of theatre in order to claim the booth for as long as required. Stir the nest, nothing more, nothing less, she had been told. Which is exactly what she'd done, and her perseverance had delivered a response.

On the street the midday traffic was heavy as a motorcycle wove in and out of cars, vans and trucks crossing the Holzbrücke towards the booth. When the phone gave its first shrill notes, she snatched it off its cradle.

'Yes, this is Christa,' she answered, her breathing still a touch hard.

A heavy hand slapped the booth's glass, startling Wynn.

Resting his head against the glass, smearing it with his long greasy hair, a bearded beggar demanded money.

'I have no change,' Wynn shouted through the glass, her back to the road.

Drawing alongside the booth, the motorcycle idled. The pillion passenger steadied himself, both feet planted on the tarmac. Then he fired.

• • •

Polizeirat Straelen of Hamburg's *Kriminalpolizei* wearily longed for spring, an opportunity to escape Hamburg, its noise, its climate, its ability to constantly surprise a detective, even one with over twenty-years of experience.

'So, you saw the motorcycle stop?' he gently asked a young woman, the tears down her cheeks dried into black stream beds from her mascara.

'And there was a beggar, sitting right over there,' the woman told him, pointing to a tattered sleeping bag by the Peace & Love Hostel. 'He came to the booth, banging on the glass, scrounging for change.'

'So, where did he go?'

'He ran,' the witness explained, adding that the beggar had seemed too drunk to stand one minute, but suddenly when he'd got the attention of the woman in the booth he sprinted away, as fast as an athlete on the track.

'Then what did you see?' Straelen asked, though he knew this last question superfluous. Over the witnesses' shoulder he watched as a forensic team stepped warily over fine grains of glass mixed with blood and tiny splinters of bone from Sally Wynn's skull. A professional killing, two shots to the head he decided, returning his gaze to the witness though not before he spotted the Range Rover with its tinted windows and diplomatic plates, which he instinctively understood would bring trouble of an altogether different kind.

• • •

If *Polizeirat* Straelen was already preoccupied with the murder of Sally Wynn, an equally testing issue had the attention of Nick Torr, as he entered Latvia for a hastily conceived operation christened SALVAGE. All too familiar with raw deals, Nick's features contained all the maturity he needed for the rest of his life; fair skin ribbed by clawed lines around his blue eyes, a strong mouth and a pronounced line down his right cheek as proof he smiled. Dark hair dropped raggedly over his forehead in a jagged line and a broken nose set badly gave him an aggressive arrangement that Angie, his wife, compared to a tormented Caravaggio figure. On this run into Russia to check out the claims made by one very jittery agent code-named Viper, Nick would be tormented for an entirely new set of reasons.

Of course, hindsight is a wonderful commodity for cynics. And in the dark halls of the Secret Intelligence Service there was an abundance of them, a good portion of them prominent men and women, seasoned officers all, who after the event claimed they knew that Operation Salvage was doomed from the outset. The operation had, or so it seemed to them, possessed a self-fulfilling mandate for disaster. To Nick Torr none of this retrospective soothsaying mattered. What concerned Nick was the indecent haste in which the operation had been cobbled together, that and the fact that his CO8 Directorate was so desperately stretched that he had no option, but to take command of the operation himself with barely a full briefing provided. There was also Alistair Foula.

At forty-six and an agent handling expert, Foula was more accustomed to training new officers in the psychological dexterity of ensuring their agents did not self-destruct or wilt at the first signs of pressure. This had been Foula's main duty for over eighteen months, during which time he had become quite attached to turning his seminar theory into practice in the training facilities at Aspley. Nick had bumped into Foula during refresher courses, so when Nick met up with him at the small provincial Latvian city of Rēzekne, he was shocked at the transformation. For Foula bore the physique of a man too fond of his desk, of which he had indeed become.

A dour Scot originally from Fife, Foula's sandy hair had retreated as much as his paunch had advanced which seemed to have crept into his arms as well as thickening his legs; while his thick flabby neck was topped by a square fleshy face set in a permanent anxious scowl. Their cover, or lack of it, amounted to false passports and visas declaring them tourists.

'Is it reliable?' Nick asked. He nodded at the sturdy dark blue Gaz-3110 saloon fitted with false plates, parked close to the Kolonna Hotel overlooking the river.

'It's the best our representative in Riga could do at short notice,' replied Foula, chewing a fingernail, a poor substitute for the thirty cigarettes that had at one time eased him through the day. 'Is there a problem?'

'No problem,' answered Nick, lighting a cigarette. 'You do have all the documents?'

Letting out an exasperated sigh, Foula nodded. 'They're in the glove box.'

'And the extra plates?'

Foula simply cocked his head towards the boot, setting his jaw as firm as it would go to prove that he wasn't in awe of a CO8 roughneck, regardless of his rank as Director.

'We need to leave,' decided Nick, walking to the driver's door, taking a casual glance up and down the road and pavements on Brīvības iela, checking for unwanted company.

They crossed without incident from Grebnova on the Latvian side of the border, heading north-east along the A-116 to Gavry, before turning south to pick up the A-117 at Opochka.

'What's Viper got that's so precious?' Nick wondered as he drove towards Dubrovka where they would hit the M-9, taking them all the way to Moscow.

'Wasn't told and didn't ask. The blessed Vapour Trail Group has spoken, and I obey. Presumably, so must you, because you're here apparently, to hold my hand.'

'Vapour Trail?'

'Reading group, steering group, knitting circle, book club... Not the faintest. I haven't been baptised into its hallowed brethren, and neither it seems, have you.'

'Why's Viper's handler not making the collection?'

'Far as I'm aware, his or her involvement went only as far as organising the approach,' Foula drawled, a hint of his Scottish roots lurking in his vowels. 'It's a straight in and out, so I hardly think there's much to go wrong?'

'Isn't there?' demanded Nick sharply as they travelled through featureless countryside, a frozen wasteland dreaming of spring. Beside him, Foula chewed a fresh nail.

'Nothing more at the pre-op briefing?' Nick threw the question casually, but for some reason it caused Foula to tense.

'Parfrey was in her most charming Levite mode, warm as a glacier. Seemed sort of rushed, but it was vaguely hinted it carried JIC endorsement.'

Nick heard Parfrey's soft voice echo again at his own briefing. Ruth Parfrey Head of Russian Operations, RUS/OPS, assured him it was a straightforward case of babysitting Foula for the operation. The operation had come at a bad time she observed, they were in the midst of yet another terrorist alert as Nick knew only too well, and the only CO8 people available at such short notice amounted to Nick, who with his exhausted team had just flown in from Libya.

The task as it presented itself to Nick's weary mind, his logic sluggish, appeared simple; ensuring Foula got in and out without encountering problems. There'd be minimal resources available, which meant it would be a solo run with no support and no backup, Parfrey had disclosed; so, Nick deciding that his team deserved a rest, volunteered himself for the operation. As he waited for Parfrey to give her usual in-depth assessment, he sat there in vain. Parfrey for some reason he couldn't quite fathom, was somehow subdued, citing the speed of events for the paucity of her briefing.

He turned on Foula in the passenger seat.

'Have we any insight on the package?' Nick lit another cigarette, and Foula started on the nail on his little finger.

'Obviously a priority, obviously a direct retrieval,' Foula sniffed, spitting a piece of nail into the footwell. 'Other than that, RUS/OPS didn't enlighten me on the material or how it is packaged.'

'That it?'

'As lean as it is, yes.'

'That's not lean, it's non-existent.'

'My opinion? Viper has struck gold and it's hot, normal protocols are off the menu.'

...four for silver, five for gold, six for a secret never to be told, Nick thought, flicking his cigarette out of a gap in the window, watching it curl away in a red trail as Foula sought out a fresh nail.

'Just got back from exotic parts, haven't you?' Foula ventured, changing the topic, hiding his nerves behind small talk.

'Have I?'

'How was it?'

'Exotic.'

'Have it your way,' said Foula, his mood souring.

'I intend to.'

After that exchange, Foula abandoned any attempt at building a dialogue with Nick as they took it in turns to coax the Gaz down the M-9. Three kilometres outside Moscow Nick pulled up and changed the plates again, then let Foula take the wheel. Nick who had barely managed seven hours sleep out of forty-eight after Tripoli, wasn't in the mood for city driving. On their way into Moscow, they'd skirted the city twice against Nick's vehement protests, only for Foula to observe sourly that he was getting his bearings.

The final compass point consisted of Foula turning left and right through high-rise concrete apartment blocks and Stalin's experiments to social housing. A brick water tower rooted to a roof on Upper Zolotorozhsky was plastered white by the snow, and beside it, Nick thought he glimpsed a figure duck down out of sight. Only Head Office knows we're here he assured himself, not for one moment convinced by his logic. Turning a corner, they passed a T-34 tank, a war relic fixed to a slab of concrete, its barrel pointing menacingly at an apartment block. Slumped against its tracks a drunk held on for comfort or support, eyeing them warily as they drove on.

This is the real Moscow, Nick reasoned. Drink, drugs, prostitution, rape, murder, all the hidden buds of communism had blossomed out here where no one gave a damn. Even in the districts you felt the tension, the next explosion waiting to happen; as if the city had held its breath for decades and suddenly it was going to let it all go. On Zolotorozhsky Avenue, light spilled from dozens of unadorned apartment windows, pockets of life in a communal block glowing green from the street lamps. Boom and bust, loss and gain, Moscow promised all the delights of a frontier town during a gold rush. Bright lights, bars, clubs, dancing girls, hustlers, thieves and pimps flourishing after capitalism had rolled into town.

'This is it,' Foula announced and clipped the kerb as he parked the Gaz.

Nick rubbed his eyes and took stock. 'Impressive.' He watched a gang of drunken youths plough their way through a children's play area, setting the swings going as they passed through.

Slowly the night crept around them, a veil for lovers and a mask for thieves. Shallow pools of light shimmered on snow-capped pavements off Krasnokazarmennaya Prospekt. A late evening tram passed them, groaning and squealing in its haste to get home; then nothing. Silence as deep as a scream. Snow pounded the windscreen and tiny curls of steam rose into the cool night air off the bonnet. Across the prospekt, Nick took in the scene; a Georgian baker selling lavash bread shared an island plot with a clearance centre and a fortified store offering cellphones, DVD players and cameras at knock-down prices. No wonder some Muscovites believed they were living in a wonderland, their own personal *strane chudes*, he reasoned.

'I don't like it,' decided Nick.

'What?'

'This place, this address.'

Nick swung his gaze round to rows of communal apartment blocks, their concrete shining thinly to a lost cause; stacked without hope in dismal canyons for a future none of the inmates would ever be able to afford. Behind the children's play area, a row of old *khrushchyovka* housing stood boarded and empty, waiting for demolition. Even the shadows fell in subdued heaps with a touch of rage about them, as though this heady scent of freedom in the air had no right to be there. Starved trees planted in shallow clusters stood in splintered stumps, the remains of a forest ravaged by urban battles. Democracy always thrived on hard cash Nick decided, only here no one had bothered to turn on the tap.

'It's your call whether you make the collection,' Nick reminded Foula. 'I'm not here to make that decision.'

Glaring straight ahead Foula didn't respond. A slight dry cough they both knew to be nerves racked his whole body. A couple in their thirties dragged a sullen child and a pair of suitcases through the snow. At a communal foyer the man read from a scrap of paper in his massive hand. Opposite Foula's door the child pulled towards the car, forcing Nick to a heightened sense of anticipation, wondering if this counted as the FSE's signal to pounce? Nick stared at their blank faces as they passed the car, the mother's small round brittle eyes as hard as beads.

Meeting Nick's stare she turned quickly away. Welcome to wonderland. Welcome to a world gone mad. In another ten years a different team would be waiting for a child like that to pull a stunt, trying to get a trainer on life's up-ramp. All you needed was the right start and guidance, he remembered. Sometimes, depending on the country, they even gave children a helping hand with a grenade, maybe an improvised explosive device or automatic weapon.

'Any reason for this address?' Nick asked abruptly.

'A halfway house. For safety,' snapped Foula, his nerves frayed. 'Wasn't told and my opinion wasn't canvassed.'

'Okay.'

'And no, I don't know who she is either. His sister, mother, lover... Parfrey didn't say.'

'But the contact?'

'Yes.'

Rolling back his sleeve Nick checked the time. 'You ready?'

Something happened to Foula at that precise moment; stiffening in his seat as though he'd been caught by a painful spasm, his shoulders sank, his whole body sagged. 'You do it,' he muttered.

'What?'

'I can't go in... I can't do it... I...,' Foula stumbled over his excuses, unable to look at Nick.

'Stay there,' decided Nick.

'Can we... you know... can we keep this to ourselves,' Foula pleaded, his rapid breath steaming a square on the windscreen.

'Give me ten minutes no longer,' Nick insisted. Leaning forward he peered into the darkness before doing up his leather jacket.

'If things should... you know... if...'

'I'm compromised, rounded up,' said Nick, finishing for Foula. 'You don't wait, you go for the fallback and the escape route.' He hooked a crumpled packet of Capitals from his pocket. Three cigarettes on a loose bed of tobacco that would have to last him back over the border.

He lit another as two cars slowly passed them, driving slowly down a road built for taking tanks abreast, their headlights playing along the shabby concrete, hard searchlights seeking a living target. Nick watched them drive by the family, no slowing down, no sign from the pavement. Then that would have been too unprofessional he decided.

'I'm sorry, I really am...' Foula started, his voice wavering. 'I ... I've been out of operational engagement too long.'

'Listen to me Alistair,' Nick urged him, shaking Foula by the shoulder. 'I'll get us home, but you have to help.'

Beside him, Foula stared at Nick, his blank eyes barely able to focus. 'Don't leave me, you promise, you won't leave me behind,' Foula pleaded, his request drifting out of the window along with the smoke from Nick's cigarette. Nick tasted the sourness of the Latvian brand stick to his tongue.

'No, I won't leave you,' Nick assured him. 'What's the approach?'

'Approach?'

'The entry to make the collection, what was agreed?'

As though speaking on behalf of someone else, Foula uttered numbly, 'You tell her you have a taxi waiting.'

Giving his hands one last nourishing boost of warmth from the car's lacklustre heater, Nick was out beside the Gaz tucking up his collar and crossing the road. The evening air hit him hard after the car's heat. Pellets of snow whirled in his face, dribbling down his neck past the collar on his jacket. Pulling on his fur hat, its brim twisted for effect, Nick continued his long walk aware of the isolation and the distance.

Two

Out and into the night and Nick's focus never faltered, his stride crisp and true, carrying him towards a block as indistinct as the next, tall and glistening against a sky tinted pink. A colour for the mental scrapbook he was compiling; oddments, facts, memories: the outline of a hill, the touch of sea on his skin, what normal people called sanity. All of it amassed for a day when he'd outgrow this dangerous trade and stick to his Devon cottage, where he'd pull all his collected trivia together in paint or words.

As he neared the block, he waited for the hand on his shoulder the rifle butt in his back, but they never came. He saw them before even opening the stiff doors, a gang of seven, four male and three female no older than nineteen. Members of *Nashi* decided Nick, a youth movement loyal to the Kremlin, or another splinter group of young fanatical patriots. Sitting on a banquette its red leather ripped and scarred by knives and cigarettes, they smoked impassively, assessing him as soon as he stepped in.

In one corner someone had dumped an old style large silver framed pram, this one minus its wheels; next to it lay a washing machine and fridge, looking as if as they'd been rolled all the way down the stairs from the top floor. Across from the gang, posters were taped across split green tiles; scuffed, frayed at the edges from the passing of bodies. Monthly communal committee edicts were hung in rows running at eye level to the lifts. One of them advertised the residents' committee, with a much-abused Lefortovo Administrative District logo in its top right corner. Along the bottom a list of absentees from the last meeting, the names printed large by a neat official hand, the red ink already fading. He scanned the list halting at the thirteenth name, matching the one supplied by RUS/OPS. Unchanged and bold, it confirmed the address and bid him welcome. As Nick started up the stairs some of the gang glared at him, but none of them made a move.

Steep and wide, the stairs were stale and in poor repair with not enough air and too little light from strip lights spluttering with age. He came out on a bare landing never quite finished. Somewhere above him he heard footsteps clatter in the gloom, hollow and unwanted. Starting on the next flight Nick came across two drunks blocking his way, sitting shoulder to shoulder. In their thirties, both reeked of cheap vodka, both reluctantly leaning apart to let him pass, the heavier set drunk spitting in disgust, his comrade challenging Nick with a drunk's mean stare. Nick moved on to the sound of babies screaming, and the stunted music of mass entertainment echoing round dull halls.

The name was the same as he'd read down in the lobby, Evgeniya Vrangelya. Written at speed in loose unsteady characters on a yellow sliver of card, jammed carelessly into a slot beside the ninth door along. He pressed the bell once, then twice in quick succession and followed this up by hammering on the faded panel door.

She opened the door in a single movement framed in its shadow, a silk wrap creased with its newness hardly covering her. Evgeniya stood with her hands punched onto her hips, her nose flaring and her lips parted in a hiss. Nick, his Russian firm, announced that he had a taxi waiting. She nodded and he followed her in, into a darkened passage with a hard polished floor, the odour of cooking lapping against perfume worn for the day.

He kicked the door closed, grabbed her forearm and dragged her into the middle of the room.

'Where is it?' He had to shout over the television and radio. She stood square to him, defiant, rubbing her arms, a gauche face lifted up to him burning with hate. The silk wrap strayed open, but she made no attempt to cover her small rounded breasts. Her eyes signalled a determined resoluteness, moist and swollen by tears she refused to release. Plain, without make-up, Nick put her in her late-thirties, and she mocked him with taut brown eyes. Evgeniya Vrangelya lifted her hands and dropped them, too weighty to support. She had a shoulder-length bob parted on the right, and from its wild strands Nick guessed she hadn't long been out of bed. Her lips and nose somehow looked a touch too big for her face, giving her a sense of severity. Around her neck she wore a cross and a medallion on heavy gold chains. Belatedly she clutched at the silk to cover her breasts.

'I'm leaving...right now,' yelled Nick.

Vrangelya inspected him slowly, judging him critically as neither handsome nor ugly. A clean scar over the right eye prompted her to think of a fighter for some reason. Out of a childhood game grown to a habit, she classed people according to the respect they deserved. She took two uncertain steps back, crossing aimlessly to the window, terribly pale against the night.

A door opened and a short, thin figure emerged.

'I am Vasily Lubov,' he announced, taking in the scene.

Christ, thought Nick, this is all I need, Foula over the edge and an asset who supplies his name. Vasily Lubov stepped forward to meet them, his small face cluttered by wire-rimmed spectacles and an old-style walrus moustache. Every inch of him screamed pedantic administrator; an accountant or a bookkeeper of some sort, Nick decided as Lubov proudly squeezed between an upright piano and a walnut bureau loaded down with sheet music. In a tight awkward walk, conscious of his clothes, Lubov seemed as though he'd got himself a new skin that desperately needed to be broken in.

A loose lick of hair refused to stay in place and Lubov brushed it back onto his forehead with practised ease. There was a frailness about him; an inward acceptance that his life thus far, had been marked by failures, of which he had a considerable list. At Vrangelya's side he stood a good seven inches shorter than his mistress and he gripped her hand for support, but this only emphasised the disparity and he stepped forward out of embarrassment or chivalric honour.

'I am ready to leave. I am travelling with you,' he said in a bold declaration.

A hundred things happened in Nick's head at that moment and all of them were mirrored by the shock on Evgeniya's face, how she clasped her hands to her cheeks in the perfect symmetry of Munch's screamer and let out a small sob.

'That's not the deal,' Nick told him wearily.

'If you want what I offer, you will have to take me,' insisted Lubov.

'What about me, Vasily? You are going to leave me?' Evgeniya cried.

For a wonderful moment, Nick thought Lubov and his mistress were going to have a full-on tiff and he'd have to separate them until Lubov's next statement changed everything.

'I am sure, maybe ninety-seven per cent that I am a suspect,' Lubov confessed, launching into his forceful grasp of English as if he urgently needed to polish it. 'My superiors, I think have been watching me,' he added, turning to Evgeniya for support but she simply stared at him, not out of anger but pure surprise, dumbstruck.

Great, thought Nick. Absolutely marvellous news, the best I've heard all month and if we get out of this it'd be a miracle.

'I haven't room for a passenger,' Nick said. 'I'm leaving in one minute and I need the package.'

Lubov's shoulders shrank, his face suggesting he was close to surrender, only his eyes appeared bright and fierce. 'The deal has changed.'

'Changed? How?' Nick demanded.

Lubov stretched for a faded canvas bag, caught at the neck by a frayed cord. 'I must speak to someone I trust in London. There is great danger unless I do this.'

'Passport?'

'It has been taken, the same for everyone in my department.'

Nick shook his head in total dismay. 'Then we go. Now.'

'Evgeniya must come with us,' he insisted, turning his watery eyes on his mistress.

'No.' Nick and Evgeniya declared at the same time.

'Then she will travel later.'

'Sure, why not,' said Nick. 'Invite the whole block.'

'See,' Lubov told her, giving her a long embrace. 'We will be together again soon.'

She touched his arm and in the same movement turned her broad face towards him, a paper lantern burning with a steady blush, watching her lover go, knowing he'd never come back.

'I'll be here,' she called as they moved to the door. Only her eyes told of the lie.

•••

They moved in total silence. Nick leading the way down the stairs, past plaster littered with lover's names boldly hacked in for eternity. A girl's laugh flew past them up the stairwell like a rocket. A door snapped closed behind them with a dull steel echo leaving nothing but a distant hum.

Together they set out for the car, in Nick's mind a thousand things to go wrong. The snow had slackened but not stopped, which for Nick constituted one small blessing. If a car happened to come out of the distance he would pause, sensing Lubov behind him doing the same. They kept close to the apartment walls for what little protection they offered, but in the end, they were out in the open approaching the Gaz fast. Nick bundled Lubov into the back without ceremony and dumped himself next to Foula in the front.

'Go,' Nick ordered, his eyes fixed squarely ahead though Foula was twisted in his seat, his face in a wild grimace, his eyes frozen on Lubov.

'What...?'

'Don't ask,' Nick told him, 'Just go.'

'With him?'

'Yes,' snapped Nick. 'He wants to come along for the ride.'

'How the fuck do we get him across?'

'I don't know. But it's not going to be FedEx, is it? Not in the boot, not without documents. So we lay-up this side of the border and wait for an extraction team. Now drive.'

In his haste to be off and away Foula fumbled with the ignition key, started the engine then messed the gears, the clutch, finally bucking the Gaz clumsily out into the slack traffic.

'Keep it steady,' Nick insisted, 'he thinks he's attracted unwanted attention,' he added, cocking a thumb towards Lubov in the rear. 'Passport's been confiscated.'

'Dump him,' roared Foula, glaring through his rear-view mirror at the uninvited passenger, then quickly swerved as an on-coming taxi driver protested at his erratic driving with rapid blasts from his Skoda's horn. 'We won't make it,' he said, seeming to regain some composure.

Ignoring the chaos unfolding around him, Nick had his cellphone to his ear, providing a status update delivered in an agreed clear code, ending with the suggestion... 'Perhaps you could come to meet us. Will do, you too, take care.'

'Dear God, you're utterly mad,' Foula snapped, his words forced through compressed lips.

'Watch our back,' Nick insisted, slumping back.

'We must make stop first, we collect key to material,' said Lubov, rooting in his canvas bag, looking for something that he couldn't find or maybe had forgotten to pack.

'You don't have it on you?' Nick demanded incredulously. 'Does your mistress know? Back there, is she aware that the product is a separate item?'

'I disclose nothing to her.'

Where did you meet her? Your girlfriend, your mistress, where?' Nick wanted to know, and he wanted to know fast.

'At work, at Defence Ministry, she was transferred nine months ago,' Lubov confessed.

'Great, wonderful.' Through the wing mirror Nick had been tracking a set of headlights from an Audi that had sat on their tail since they'd set off, diligently following each turn they'd made. 'Pull in,' Nick said abruptly, 'I'm driving.'

Flinging the Gaz towards the pavement, Foula did an emergency stop. As Foula got out Nick slid into the driver's seat, already revving as Foula landed heavily beside him. Hitting the accelerator with meaning, Nick cut straight through three lines of traffic. In the Lefortovo tunnel Nick drove recklessly fast, switching lanes to blasts from the horns on cars, trucks and buses. Taking a junction by the Kristall Distillery on Samokatnaya ulitsa at red, a second Audi joined in the pursuit.

'An address,' Nick demanded over his shoulder. 'Now.'

Lubov hunched into a ball on the back seat insisted, 'I will deal only with a senior ex-officer in London.'

'You already told me, but you need to take us to the material,' Nick yelled, watching the leading Audi's headlights stick wilfully to their tail as he cut across a busy intersection streaming with traffic by the Casino Mirage.

'Golyanovo,' Lubov offered, as Nick hit the brakes on Kutuzovksy Prospekt, swerving around a three-car pile-up where an angry crowd had hauled out a driver too drunk to stand.

'Hold tight,' Nick yelled, speeding over the Moskva River on the Crimean Bridge. With Foula gripping the dashboard, Lubov braced in the back, Nick used the handbrake and accelerator to spin the Gaz in the middle of the bridge.

'Out,' Nick ordered them, the Gaz at an angle blocking the lanes of traffic.

Marching towards a red Lada that had pulled up short, Nick snatched the door open, hauling the driver out as Lubov and Foula scrambled in. Smacking the gears into reverse Nick stamped on the accelerator and wove back across the bridge, clipping nearly every car in his way. Using another handbrake turn, Nick faced the Lada down a wide avenue running from Krymsky Val.

'How far?' demanded Nick as shallow bars of fine light from the street lamps played on the windscreens of passing cars, wishing he was in one of them, on his way home instead of having to extract a blown asset who was probably doomed.

'Five kilometres, maybe less,' Lubov stated, positioning his body exactly in the centre of the back seat. 'Then you will see what a profitable exchange we will all benefit from. It is proof of a great secret, and I am trusting you with it,' Lubov added, a glossy sheen spreading out over his skin, as though his mistress had given him a fine coating of baby oil.

Snow hit the windscreen steady and hard, making it difficult to count how many avenues and boulevards they criss-crossed in Nick's race across Moscow.

'Tell me when we're close,' Nick snapped, not in the mood to make it an issue, not here, not in this city. Nick knew enough heroes and most of them were dead.

'Here, just here,' said Lubov by a budget Mapka store in the Golyanovo district.

Leaving Foula in the driver's seat, Nick took the lead and initiative all the way. Striding past a pre-cast fountain no longer connected to the mains, they entered a narrow alley of shuttered daytime stalls and shops that led to a square with wind twisted saplings bent double under frost and snow. At the very core, grey concrete towers with Lubov's block sitting solidly on the corner. An empty Audi was drawn up outside the wide main entrance, which Nick took to be neither a coincidence nor an omen, just a sign they were out of luck.

Tucked against an apartment wall, Nick signalled to Lubov that they were going in.

'You stay right behind me,' Nick warned him, working out a strategy as he went, not knowing whether to laugh or cry, calling on all his considerable experience from other operations fighting unconventional dirty wars.

The address Lubov so badly wanted to reach was ten floors up and Nick insisted they do it on foot; the heavy loud throbbing of drum and base from the second floor following them all the way. Holding Lubov back when they'd reached the hallway to his landing, Nick didn't have to ask which apartment belonged to the little administrator, because stationed outside it, a crop-haired figure in a Puffa jacket.

'Wait,' he ordered Lubov. Jamming a cigarette between his lips, Nick rounded the corner, his pace easy, his shoulders dropped. Approaching the man, Nick theatrically patted his pockets. Strolling brazenly up, he adopted the surly manner of a true Muscovite, and demanded a light. Caught monetarily off-guard, the man instinctively delved into his pocket with a hand, his right. Any punch can be fatal, it depends on delivery and timing; Nick had both, launched as he let the cigarette fall from his lips. Where Nick struck the man is immaterial, but strike he did, rocking the man's head back. Falling in a heap, the man crashed into Lubov's door. As Nick started to drag the body inside by his jacket collar, the little administrator rushed down the hall slipping past Nick.

The apartment consisted of four rooms and everything radiated off a linoleum-floored hallway, as did the wide trail of blood. Lubov tried twice to run on ahead, but each time Nick pushed him behind, and if he'd had time would have walked him all the way back to his car to prevent him becoming a nuisance.

'Know him?' Nick asked Lubov as they stood over the body of a second male in a Puffa jacket, a kitchen knife plunged at a crazy angle into his neck below his ear.

Lubov paused, his face very red, his way lost. He stood open mouthed, his eyes fumbling for somewhere to look.

'No,' mumbled Lubov.

'Who else should be here?'

'Wife and nephew.'

Already Nick knew they were too late.

In a long narrow living room, there were twin sofas in a fawn plain fabric, rugs on polished floorboards and charcoal sketches strung in a well-proportioned line. Nothing was ostentatious just too neat; flat pack utility creating Lubov's hard won paradise where someone had fought and lost, decided Nick. He picked out the splashes of blood, smashed porcelain lamps and ripped cushions. Playing loudly a CD worked its way through a Mariah Carey album, and Nick gratefully silenced her mid note. An oversized tropical fish tank filled a wall, its filter humming away; shoals of bright fish large and small darted out of coral and waving plants unaware of the destruction around them.

Taking a room at a time Nick took the lead with Lubov following, muttering curses under his breath. Every room bore hallmarks of a quick ruthless search; in too many places to count, on the fabric, walls and carpet, there were ominous dashes of blood. The nephew and Lubov's wife must have fought a running retreat after putting up resistance with the knife, thought Nick as each room revealed more destruction. The final bedroom door was closed, and Nick knew this was where the wife and nephew had finally run out of places to hide.

'Wait here,' Nick told Lubov, facing a plain cream door.

'I am not afraid,' Lubov said proudly.

Nick tricked the door from its jamb and stepped in. By his foot, blood formed in a thick circle on a Persian rug at the bottom of a bed too big for the room.

Lubov gasped and Nick guessed he hadn't seen a close relative in such a state. Well this was his lucky day, there were two for him to consider, Lubov's wife and nephew toppled elegantly forward in a last clinch.

'Your family?'

Lubov nodded once for each body, and unable to look again, had folded in a heap on a corner of the bed.

They'd tortured them slowly Nick reckoned, one made to watch as someone had gone quite berserk on the other with cigarettes and razors, which one first really didn't matter. Pieces of cushion were still taped across the wife's mouth and Nick knew why Mariah Carey's high notes had been selected to accompany their pain. Nick guessed the wife must have been a lot younger than Lubov, but from what they had done to her body, age counted for nothing.

Planting his feet either side of the congealing pool, Nick swallowed his bile and turned the nephew's plump short body over, a teenager who hadn't been given a fighting chance.

'What have we come for?' Nick asked Lubov.

For a full minute Lubov didn't move, drained of colour and energy.

'Have they taken it? Did your wife know what it was? Who knew where it was?' Nick rattled off the questions aware that time was running out.

'No one but me, okay,' admitted Lubov, slowly searching the shattered bedroom with his eyes, but never allowing them to stray too close to the bodies.

'Then get it, we have to go... now,' Nick insisted.

And after they'd been tortured for information they couldn't divulge, Lubov's nephew and wife were executed. The nephew's head split by a single shot, his black glasses screwed up in a knot beside him, the wife shot twice, in both eyes. This was getting better by the second thought Nick, right back in messy deaths and secrets never to be told. *One for sorrow, two for joy...*

'Anyone else know you might have stashed something here?' Nick asked, but Lubov had sloped off into the living room, and Nick could hear him quietly weeping.

'Sure, I tell everyone, the whole damn world,' shouted Lubov. 'How should I know?'

'Is it still here?' Nick asked when he joined Lubov.

'Yes,' said Lubov, going to his fish tank, tears and snot running together on his ashen face. With shaking hands he turned off the power, plunging the tank into stagnant darkness. 'They...' but he ran out of breath before completing his pledge and moving pieces of coral, pushing gravel aside, his fingers locked onto a small plastic watertight container that he extracted, his sleeve soaking wet.

Holding out his hand for the container, Nick waited as Lubov clung to his precious cargo, eventually shaking his head in noble defiance.

'They died for this,' he announced gravely, nodding towards the bedroom. 'And I keep it until I'm safe in London.'

'You're going nowhere until I take a look at what you've got,' promised Nick, ready to seize the container by force. 'My rules and that's my last word.' He stepped forward and Lubov sensing what was to come, hurriedly uncapped the container slipping out a SIM card.

'To assist me retrieve my material,' he said. 'It is already in London. I took a precaution.'

Fantastic thought Nick, if you'd booked a flight you'd have saved me making the trip of a lifetime. 'Then we need to take care of it,' he said, holding out a hand and when Lubov dropped the SIM into his palm he hurried into the kitchen.

'Sharp knife,' demanded Nick, unlacing a boot, easing it off. 'And cling film, you got some of that, know what it is?' Nick hopped on one foot pulling drawers open. 'Sharp knife,' he yelled again.

'They make big mistake,' Lubov raged, coming into the kitchen and handing Nick a knife that was anything but sharp, the anger rising through him; a charge too powerful for his demure frame.

Nick heated the knife on a gas ring, a handkerchief wrapped round his fingers. 'Wrap the SIM in the plastic,' Nick told Lubov as he opened a slit along the outer edge on the thick rubber sole of his boot.

Obediently, Lubov folded the SIM in cling film and passed it across. Easing the card into the slot, Nick heated the knife again and sealed it in.

Bending and stretching the sole to check if it held, Nick pulled on his boot and laced it.

'We're leaving,' he said, nudging Lubov towards the door. Lubov needed coaxing and he didn't have time. 'Right now, go,' added Nick.

Outside a police siren tore into the night, an eerie wail moving closer. Glancing out into the corridor Nick pushed Lubov ahead and closed the apartment door. Out into the snow they faded into the shadows, hugging walls and the freezing air as a second police car sailed towards the block. As they crossed an open square Lubov let out a piercing scream, cursing the GRU, SVR and FSB to hell and back, all *siloviki* adding the President and Prime Minister for good measure. Nick had heard enough, and clasping Lubov's arm dragged him at a rapid trot. Weaving into courtyards and alleys, he refused to drop the pace or lessen his grip on the little administrator as big wet chips of snow billowed after them, chasing them all the way to a frantic Foula huddled in the car.

The Lada bumped heavily as Nick pitched Lubov in the back.

'Drive,' Nick ordered, flopping heavily next to Foula.

'What's happened?'

'Carnage. His wife and nephew are dead. Butchered, tortured, not what I'd call a pretty sight. Happy? All the information you need? Now drive,' snapped Nick his patience wearing thin, a weariness settling over him.

Three

Once Nick had committed to recovering Viper, it was inevitable events would run such a bloody course, certain senior dissident voices in the Service asserted not long after the dust had settled. And neither the detractors nor defenders of Operation Salvage were quite so ready to admit how they had the benefit of replaying events from the security of their desks in the Service's headquarters at Vauxhall Cross. Whereas in CO8's own satellite headquarters, which for obvious reasons was kept at arm's-length from the Service's modest, unassuming premises by the Thames, Nick was regarded not as a villain, but a hero.

Nick's CO8 Directorate was housed in a thin narrow building tucked quite sensibly off Vauxhall Bridge Road. Possessing an air of stoic resilience, the small ragged four-storey place of tired stone had long ago accepted its fate as a government annexe, an Edwardian vision surreptitiously avoiding the developers. Trapped between a fast copy shop and mortgage brokers who could be relied on for Wimbledon tickets, it sat proudly aloof as though better times were ahead. Along both floors the blinds were permanently drawn. Traffic dust covered it like a cracked tarpaulin, while two solid doors that had shed their varnish were electronically barred, deterring casual callers. A large notice clearly printed and trapped behind scratched Perspex, declared it to be the SOUTHBRIGHT RESEARCH INSTITUTE, VISITORS BY APPOINTMENT ONLY. And for anyone foolish enough to try the entryphone overlooked by two severe CCTV cameras, they would receive a firm, but none the less specious answer concerning statistical research. If that failed, a frank exchange with two duty door staff usually did the trick: ex-warrant officers from the Royal Military Police not chosen for their conversational technique.

It was known simply to its officers as the Mad House, which some unkind critics claimed symbolised Nick's temperament. Trained in weapon handling, close-quarter combat and other dubious dark arts, CO8's mandate provided the Service with the capacity for operations classed as dirty work, which carried the highest level of deniability.

At six-thirty in the evening, Jill Portland settled in for her second night as senior duty officer. Besides a computer, a television on a stand tuned permanently to a news channel, the decoration in the DO's office ran to political newspaper cartoons haphazardly tacked to the rear wall above secure fireproof cabinets. She flicked on an Anglepoise and a yellow tongue of light spread out across the grey metal desk. From outside on the street against the background hum of traffic, a motorbike sped along leaving a blur of noise in its wake. Why was it always the sound of motorbikes that stood out at night? she wondered, always sounding so sad, so lonely. Maybe it's only the sad and lonely that pick up every sound, she told herself. Approaching her thirtieth birthday, Portland's appearance had a no-nonsense practicality about it; her mid-brown hair swept at an angle off her forehead into a ponytail accentuated a slight oval face with deep intense eyes. In her white shirt and dark business suit she could have passed for an IT manager, and often did.

Clearing a portion of the desk she flicked through the latest edicts to come over the river from Head Office, laying each page on the sheet of glass covering the desk. All the duty officers used it for storing bits and pieces, slipping timetables and memos under the sheet along with theatre tickets and takeaway menus. The latest addition, a donation slip for a marmoset someone had adopted at London Zoo. A soft distant laugh rippled through the labyrinth of corridors as she ate a salad with no real appetite or conviction. Returning to a wad of operational directives that should have been filed, she looked up with a start as Ramsgill the IT team leader knocked and strode briskly in.

'We've got an emergency in Moscow. GRU and FSB are hogging the airwaves,' Ramsgill declared. 'I think you better come down to the cage.'

The cage was not a cage at all, but a long ugly basement room at the back of the building, its barred windows turned dismally to Chapter Street. Portland threaded her way through individual work bays holding flat screen computers connected to their own large servers, electronic voice transcribers, digital recorders, and CD recorders. All of it staffed by specialists who only ever managed formative grunts, none of which Portland acknowledged as she settled in a playback booth, slipping on a pair of headphones as Ramsgill replayed the call Nick had made on his cellphone.

What she did next, she did very fast. Up in the duty room she opened a safe with a key from the duty officer's bunch, a small squat robust cream Chubb mottled by many hands. A slim book no larger than a desk diary lay by itself on the second shelf, along with manuals for handling a string of different emergencies of varying magnitude. An emergency contact log, it listed assigned cellphone numbers to the worknames of specific senior SIS officers. Returning the log, she relocked the Chubb, and began to make a number of calls on the encrypted landline. In order of importance five all told, ending with an acrimonious exchange with a Foreign Office night clerk.

By three that morning her work had begun to bear fruit.

Arriving in a foul mood, Paul Rossan, Director of Production and Requirement, pitched his duffel coat across a chair. A year shy of turning forty, Rossan was much given to wearing comfortable clothes, dressing with the expensive élan few people can afford. His face ran to a point, pulling his shallow cheeks with it, forming a poacher's face, full of cunning. Pinched from the early morning cold it tracked Portland across the room.

'So, what's the damage?'

'Failed collection in Moscow and the couriers are going to hold off on the Russian side until we arrange extraction. They have the asset with them,' she explained, passing over the decoded printout.

'The couriers?'

'Torr and Foula.'

Nothing else?' Rossan demanded, bent over the desk, reading the printout.

Portland shook her head. 'Nothing, but it means the operation has been compromised, and they were not in immediate danger but...'

'It's a probability,' Rossan said, already ahead of Portland. 'Who else have you notified?' he wondered, sitting on the corner of the desk.

'Controller Central and Eastern Europe, Director Global Operations and Resources and the Deputy Chief.'

'Well, I don't know if Jane's going to be available, she was attending some damn conference in Germany the last I heard. Roly, who knows, he could be anywhere, and Teddy's hardly likely to consider a failed collection as an emergency.' He straightened up, rubbing his back, pulling his lank face at the effort. 'What other action have you taken?'

'That's just it, I wasn't sure who...' Portland trailed off but Rossan waited, uncommitted, refusing to help her.

'Then I suppose I'm in the hot seat,' he snapped, setting off to find an office he could call his own.

• • •

Nick would have willingly exchanged Rossan's dilemma for his own predicament, as it was, he was stuck with Foula and the little administrator, doing his damnedest to get them safely out of Moscow. With Foula having selected his emergency escape route completely at random, they lurched through side roads that offered bleary snatches of Moscow as it gradually closed down for the night. A grey sky the colour of fog pressed in low and squalls of snow reduced visibility by half as Foula hit reckless speeds, reinforcing Nick's unspoken sense of urgency. As Foula nursed the Lada towards the M-9, Nick fought the lure and pull of sleep. He shifted in his seat already aware that the little administrator was a liability; a marked man and they'd no chance of slipping him over the border.

'Is this going to work?' Foula asked petulantly, his Scottish burr becoming more pronounced.

'Don't know, haven't tried it,' Nick replied, his breath a misty hand climbing the door glass.

'Yes, well...' Foula broke off then regrouped for another charge, changed his mind, the veins in his temple standing proud.

Nick fought to remain calm as Foula struggled to keep the car on a straight line down the Baltic Highway, running for all they were worth for the border. Squinting through the windscreen Nick could barely make out the road as snow rushed at them distorting distance and proportion, swelling and shrinking the tail lights in front.

In the back, Lubov remained quiet and alert wishing every kilometre to be five, or ten, anything to hasten his departure from a country he had been proud to serve and call home. It took twenty minutes to put Moscow well behind them leaving nothing but a tedious drive to the Latvian border, and each stroke of the wipers beat heavy snow into ice ridges. With the city in their wake Foula fiddled with the radio, his idiosyncratic choice filling the Lada with AvtoRadio, broadcasting a disconcerting mix of Russian classics,

Western pop and dreary chat. There were few vehicles around at this hour and Foula hit the accelerator until there were no other lights, just the Lada walled in by the night on an open stretch of road making for home.

How far into the night, how far from Moscow, or how near to Latvia they had travelled, Nick could barely tell. For the last three kilometres the highway had cut its way through a forest and Nick swore that it felt as though they had driven to the border and back at least twice. In actual fact they had barely gone over two hundred kilometres, Foula humming some obscure tune under his breath, the little administrator asleep in a twisted heap. With the wipers struggling against the heavy snow, a skin of ice formed against the screen, the heater offering a frugal portion of warmth. Stubbornly refusing to play anything but a severe crackle as tuneless as Foula's humming, the radio had gone mute. Ahead of them the highway disappeared into a long curve. Scattered along its rough bare emergency shoulder, a trail of blown out tyre shreds poked through the snow. Then as they rounded the bend, the glow from the backed-up tail lights gave the snow an uncanny red hue.

'Not good,' predicted Nick as Foula slowed to a crawl. 'Big problem.'

'Accident?' Foula asked, half in hope.

'I think we're in for a spot of bother,' decided Nick.

Dropping through the gears Foula slowed, pulling up behind a Mercedes. A couple of hundred metres ahead, trucks, vans, cars and everything with an engine were being funnelled through a checkpoint. Nick ticked off the details: warning triangles, red and blue flashing strobe lanterns, marked and unmarked police cars and two BTR-80 armoured personnel carriers facing nose to nose, providing the final gap in a chicane the cleared vehicles had to pass through.

'We must turn around,' Lubov plaintively urged from the back.

In their customary disregard for lanes, Russian drivers were jockeying for position with cars and trucks on both sides blocking the Lada in. Foula was left with no choice but to crawl inexorably forward.

'We do what?' Foula desperately wanted to know, yanking on the handbrake, avoiding a trucker's mean stare.

'Climb out, move slowly around, stretch your legs and we'll change places,' said Nick. 'And give me a rough count of numbers manning the checkpoint.' Nick's guts twisted into a complicated knot as Foula stepped quickly into the snow. Nick slid over into the driving seat, his concentration firm, resolute.

Sliding down the windscreen, snow dissolved in sizzling patches on the warm bonnet. Nick sat hunched behind the wheel, an inscrutable Buddha watching as Foula nodded and grinned to other drivers in the queue. Gunning the engine Nick wound down his window but could only hear a woman's shrill laugh.

Passing around the Lada's bonnet, Foula took the precaution of making an exaggerated stretch as he surveyed the checkpoint.

'Maybe twenty, maybe more,' he said, getting in next to Nick.

Slowly the line moved forward, each vehicle and its occupants thoroughly questioned, searches made, papers checked and double-checked. There were four cars to go before it would be the Lada's turn. Nick's foot hovered over the accelerator his strategy played through twice in his head.

'Get down and stay down,' he advised Foula and Lubov.

Nick waited for the truck ahead to move, the car behind to set off and take its place. Timing was everything and Nick almost got it right. Slamming down hard on the gas he swung the Lada out of line, going for high revs as he went up through the gears, the back end swishing in a cloud of rubber as he ran at full speed for the checkpoint. The car waiting to go next never knew what hit it as Nick rammed it, careering it into one side of the checkpoint, using the momentum to force his way through. Long bursts of automatic fire lit up the tree line lifting Foula off his seat. Lobbed sideways he rolled into Nick, his arms flapping inanely around.

Yelled orders from running figures echoed inside the Lada through its shattered windows, followed by rapid flashes from automatic weapons that punctured the rear glass. Punching the accelerator for all it would give, Nick ducked down as bullets zipped in and out. He spun the wheel as the Lada's tyres screamed, burning for a grip on a reef of ice between the police cordon and personnel carriers. With a jolt, the tyres snatched and held, sending the Lada forward crushing a troop commander against his vehicle. Nick's jaw slammed shut, he bit his tongue and tasted blood. Banging into reverse, he stamped on the power and skidded clear, only for the other troop carrier to lurch forward ramming the Lada's boot, tipping it at a crazy angle. Hitting a rough strip between the highway's shoulder and trees, Nick swung out and on, not wanting to look behind, forcing his eyes ahead to where the highway flattened out and the darkness stretched enticingly all the way to Latvia.

The UAZ-469 Jeep came straight out of the forest and veered across

Nick's path, its wheels slapping on the highway like bare feet. Nick swung the Lada hard to one side clipping the flank of the UAZ; regaining control he pumped the accelerator again. The second UAZ hit him at speed. It caught the Lada square on, crumpling the passenger door, its headlights scorching Nick's eyes while the impact jarred his spine. A third UAZ broke from the forest and rammed him, buckling the windscreen into a cloud of glass.

Smoke and hot diesel fumes filled Nick's throat. Bounced, skewed side-on, the UAZ flipped the Lada onto its side, sliding it down the Baltic Highway in a shower of sparks. Nick gasped for breath but something sharp had jammed into his side. Creaking as it came to a rest by a drainage ditch, the Lada rocked gently and Nick scrunched into a ball, reached into the back shaking the little administrator, but he was already dead. Kicking open the rear door Nick tried to stand; in his mind he was already zigzagging low and hard for the forest, except his lungs wouldn't cooperate and he'd a million miles to cover. Far too easily for his liking, his legs buckled, and he hit the cold earth ditch in a heap. With all the strength he could muster he raised his head, vaguely taking in the fact that several pairs of military boots were pounding straight at him.

• • •

In London the fate of Nick, Foula and Lubov remained a matter of speculation and conjecture. Had they crossed the Latvian border? If not, how far had they to go to reach it? All random factors added to the permutations that Jill Portland, her head screaming with a colossal ache, had to consider as duty officer, though it wasn't Portland who'd take a final decision or make a final call.

Around a quarter to four that morning, Jane Stratton, Controller Central and Eastern Europe swept in, a large coffee cup in hand. Once engaged but never married, Jane had taken her thirties in a rush and her happiness somehow never survived. Lean, attractive, there was a sharpness about her as though inside she smouldered from a lasting hurt. Her auburn hair nestled on her shoulders framing a face blessed by natural beauty and strong green eyes. There was also a sense of aloofness that some men and women find appealing; that of a sports mistress perhaps, the type who can be both cruel and kind. Calm, her confident approach reassuring Portland, she listened as the duty officer explained that monitoring had picked up a burst of traffic they said pinpointed a position on the Baltic Highway and a precise location was being worked on.

Finally, at some point after five, Edward 'Teddy' Hawick, Deputy Chief of the Service put in an appearance. Not a natural early riser, Hawick grunted all through Portland's briefing, offering a discontented sigh through his nose when she informed him that monitoring estimated that a serious incident had unfolded eighty kilometres outside Velikiye Luki, and this had been confirmed by the Americans.

'If that is the respected wisdom from the Cousins, then I suggest we take appropriate action. You concur, Paul?' Hawick said, nodding his small head at Rossan.

'Yes, of course.'

'Then I'll leave that entirely in your capable hands,' Hawick announced, more or less dismissing Rossan. Thin, quite tall, his pepper-seed colour hair receding, Hawick had a silky gloss to his skin and prided himself on being something of a fastidious dresser. Only having hit his stride quite recently, his choice of hand-cut suits adorned with a watch-chain and fob gave him the appearance of a sixty-year-old second-tier diplomat; a man somewhat musty round the edges, though this was a deceptive foil to his very capable mind.

Twenty minutes later, Roland 'Roly' Blackmore, Director Global Production and Resources strolled in. Blackmore could have been conceived and born as Hawick's natural antithesis, his very own walking binary contradiction. Small, wiry, and compact, he moved as if he meant business. There was cunning in his ruddy weathered complexion; a fighter's face balanced by eyes bright and fresh, though for those unfortunate to cross him, of which there was a considerable number, they could only recount Roly's barbed wire stare. His hair had started to shrink at the temples, so he brushed the whole lot back and this, with its early streaks of grey, gave him a raffish, alluring air. A sharp, very elegant dresser, Blackmore signified his power through his wardrobe, which even at that early hour, had produced a dazzling white shirt and plain blue tie, all squared off inside a handsome grey suit. Bluff and to the point, Blackmore alerted departments and placed people on stand-by that Portland had never heard of, commandeering a secure briefing room for his base.

Taking time to make a furtive tour of what he termed Torr's tawdry empire, Hawick eventually called a full control and response summit, and declared that damage limitation must be the priority, the order of the day, he told them in a hundred different ways. At the same time, they dare not lose any advantage, so the Met Police's Special Branch teams – or as they had been relabelled, SO15 – were prepped for immediate strikes on soft Russian SVR targets flagged by the Security Service, better known as MI5.

As the regular day shift arrived, Portland still had not signed off and managed to corner Stratton and Rossan as they rushed from meeting to meeting. Go but don't go, they both said in agreement, then changed tack, until Portland came close to pulling her hair out. A yes or no, she demanded. But Rossan, erring on the side of caution, requested she remain to personally handle anything else coming out of Latvia or Moscow.

'Anything to confirm Nick and Foula's status or condition,' Rossan demanded. 'You stick to Palmer-Fenton from monitoring like a leech. Like a leech, you hear,' he shouted to her retreating back.

But when Portland went down the corridor, she found Palmer-Fenton's office empty, a coffee hardly touched, a jacket hanging lopsided from a chair, a flashing row of lights signalling incoming calls on four secure phones, all symbols of a crisis yet to hit. On her way back to Rossan and Stratton, Palmer-Fenton almost knocked her off her feet; his slack face red from the climb out of the basement lair where a direct feed from GCHQ was monitored round the clock. Cheltenham had snatched a live stream of traffic coming out of Velikiye Luki, Palmer-Fenton said, between catching his breath. What they had and it didn't constitute much, but apparently, it's a coded confirmation of five casualties, three of them dead.

Returning to Rossan and Stratton, Portland delivered what she just had gleaned from Monitoring. The details of which, Portland told them, were obviously vague, but they would continue to listen for more.

'If it isn't too much trouble,' snapped Stratton, turning briskly on her heels.

Rossan sniffed and blew his nose. 'Jane and Nick were really very close,' he disclosed. 'You've done quite enough,' he added.

'Get off home and take a rest.'

For Portland, it was more than enough.

• • •

Impatient, disregarding tired moans, the glances of frustration, Jane Stratton stalked the corridors as a woman possessed in the hours following Nick and Foula's unconfirmed status as missing. Urging, coaxing, demanding and bullying for more results, she left no one in peace in CO8's domain. Fatigued and utterly dejected, she had even tried to take a couple of hours of sleep as the shifts changed, as the briefings, updates and rumours wound inexorably on, but sleep, like Nick Torr and Alistair Foula was elusive. Bloody Nick Torr she thought, aiming for some distraction by sorting through FO demands for 'further clarification'.

On a secure cabinet in Nick's office, a spider plant was slowly dying. Laying claim to the office as her own this side of the river, Jane carefully fed the plant a dose of water. Each CO8 team had monitored its progress every time they passed, taking bets on how much more of Nick's tender loving care it could handle before finally wilting. Now it seemed past caring and leant drunkenly to the left.

Placed by the telephone she found a meeting request slip sent by RUS/OPS to Nick, the status box ticked urgent, the time and date set for two hours before Nick's departure for Latvia. But for some reason Nick had not acknowledged it, leaving the response boxes blank.

'You'd better bloody come home, Nick Torr,' she said aloud, fury churning away inside her. Suddenly she had an overwhelming desire to close her eyes, run and emerge into strong sunlight far, far away from this madness.

Restless, unable to settle, she set off in search of more updates and it was while she organised this, that Palmer-Fenton discovered her; on a meagre landing between floors delivering a severe upbraiding to a junior administration officer on the importance of following file search requests.

'Ah, Jane, you asked for the last position on Nick and Alistair,' Palmer-Fenton said, watching the officer scurry away. 'It's not the news we hoped for,' he said turning smartly, his brogues retorting off the polished stairs as he skipped down to his domain.

Following on behind, Jane passed floors where the night always made itself at home. She'd done enough late briefings over here to know how it felt as a shift dragged on for what felt a week, most floors dormant with only the odd voice carrying along soulless corridors; whispered secrets from a secret world huddling in corners. Picking up speed, she almost ran the final couple of metres down the long corridor, unable to stop herself overtaking Palmer-Fenton.

Palmer-Fenton took inordinate pride in his monitoring empire; a windowless vault jammed with plasma screens, computers and a team of intense men and women who rarely mixed with the infidels from other CO8 sections. On one wall, a set of screens providing satellite support above countries where CO8 teams were actively deployed. Alongside the screens transparent plotting panels held each team leader's call sign, scribed in blue marker to denote their very own operational patch.

'Here,' said Palmer-Fenton, pointing Jane to a panel allocated to Operation Salvage. 'We've created a timeline by calling up and assembling the most recent satellite images to provide a working scenario,' Palmer-Fenton explained. 'Though it cannot be classed as definitive by any means of the imagination, but we did have a tracker in the vehicle they took over the Russian border when they started out.'

Some of Nick's early movements including the drive in from Latvia were highlighted in yellow, others circled in red; none of them looked particularly good from where Jane stood.

'They must have known something was up after the collection from the way that damned car went round Moscow in circles. See how they were sat in that suburb of Golyanovo for more than twenty minutes. As far as I'm aware, there are no Burger Kings in that neck of the woods or if it's a halt for a pee, someone has a serious bladder problem.'

'And?' Jane wasn't in the mood for improvised laughs.

Palmer-Fenton scrunched up his nose and turned to one of his team.

'Bring up the full sequence, Lucy, if you will.'

Lucy hit a command on her keyboard and went back to monitoring a different screen.

'The tracker stopped there, right in the middle of the city, so I assume they bailed out and lost the car. Must have picked up a new vehicle, which was very little help to us,' Palmer-Fenton explained as the first image appeared.

'I can imagine,' snapped Jane.

'We do our best,' retorted Palmer-Fenton, grievously wounded. 'All we can confirm is from what we managed to pull down a few hours ago. We concentrated on the reports of a rumpus near Velikiye Luki, that is all we had to go on you know,' he reminded her crossly.

'And?'

'This was the last pass we could manage, and the satellite won't be over that position again for another fourteen hours,' he said, his earnest face assessing Jane.

'That's the best you've got?' She demanded of the blurred image filling the screen.

'It's not like using a digital camera,' Palmer-Fenton said in defence of a grainy image that had been magnified to its maximum limit. 'And,' he added, lowering his voice, looking around, 'it seems as if that reception committee on the highway were expecting them.'

'I'll pass on your comments,' said Jane, studying an enhanced satellite frame revealing a car on its side. Leaning forward she could just make out three body bags by the side of a military vehicle.

'Casualties, I'm afraid.'

'There's a chance that one of them could be alive,' said Jane.

'A possibility,' Palmer-Fenton said, not committing himself.

'If we get anything else...'

'I'll be across the river with Rossan,' said Jane.

'Super, got that,' he said, watching her hurry out.

Burning with an anger she couldn't quite quell, she set off over the river, the stiff October air clinging to her coat and hair after her walk over Vauxhall Bridge; the peevish glare of headlights stinging her eyes as she avoided Head Office's main entrance where marble clashed with gleaming chrome and smoked blast-proof glass. Jane pounded on; round to a discreet entrance reserved for senior staff and swiped herself in, entering one of the gates watched over by internal security.

Supervising Jane's entry, a square dumpy blonde called Lorna who controlled the gate from a blast proof pod. A thirty-year old with an incurable frown, Lorna was ticking off the days to her wedding that she was assiduously planning between controlling her sets of gates, remote cameras and a section of the basement car park's sliding mesh screen.

'Fifty-two to go,' sang Lorna, electronically admitting Jane after her card had been scanned once more.

'I hope he's worth it,' Jane called over her shoulder making for Lift 1. Stepping out on the eighth floor, the drawn faces and distinct chill that greeted her were intensified by the neutrally painted walls, done in a Farrow & Ball hue called Pale Hound. Nodding at Alison Moss, Executive Director from Personnel whose striking face was unusually tense, Jane cursed as she saw Tony Scorton. A diminutive Service lawyer, Director of Legal Affairs and an inveterate snob, he was seated in a Nicca armchair in a meeting bay part way along the floor.

Striding on, Jane was hailed by Scorton's shrill call.

'My dear Jane, what a calamity, am I correct, one hand lost and one missing?' Scorton sang, patting an armchair beside him.

Refusing the invitation to sit, Jane filled a cup from the water cooler as Scorton veered over to her, taking her to one side with a conspiratorial hand on her arm.

'Word travels fast,' said Jane without any warmth.

'Bad news faster than the rest,' he announced, letting go of Jane as he dispensed a coffee from a Flavia drinks station. 'More work for me and my boys and gals, that's the reason I've been summoned,' he said, blowing the heat from his coffee, his eyes pointing down the floor to C's lair. 'Do tell me more,' he urged. 'I hear the missing hand is none other than Nicholas Torr, our gallant swashbuckler. You know I am discretion personified.'

'You're a born gossip, Tony.'

Despite his olive skin, Scorton still managed a blush.

'Good Lord, that is a bit harsh my dear girl. I thought we had ironed out our differences after your glorious return from Washington last year, remember?'

How could she forget? An extended posting as she headed a joint cyber counter-terrorism working group with the Cousins, followed by a month of clearing legal hurdles with a leering Scorton.

'I can't confirm or deny,' Jane said, sighting-up a clear exit from the meeting bay. 'I'll tell Nick that you were asking after him.' Scorton smiled but Jane could tell she'd hit a nerve.

'Now, now, old thing, there's no point trying to hoodwink me. 'My sources are extremely reliable.'

'Goodness, Tony, you actually meet the living?'

She made a dash for freedom and heard Scorton's 'Impossible woman,' echo after her as Jane clenched her fists and rapped on Rossan's door.

'I'm in.'

Silenced by Rossan's raised hand, Jane was directed to a soft chair in front of his desk while he dealt with a call, handing out a severe berating to an unfortunate soul for some oversight.

'Of course I expect you to inform me immediately, you cretin,' snarled Rossan, slamming down the phone.

Sitting back, he studied her with a long gaze, one that gave him an unusual intense sobriety. Up out of his chair he was off, a man with something essential to do. 'How they holding up over there? What's the latest? Fancy a tea? No, of course not, you're a coffee person.' Rossan batted out the questions in a quick covering arc of fire as he crossed the room.

'No one's any wiser, nothing has been confirmed or denied by Moscow.'

'No, I've been liaising with the Cousins, and as much as they're sharing, it appears we've taken a major hit,' Rossan grumbled, not bothering to look up from his position; slouched by the long tablet window overlooking the Thames, pouring mineral water into a disposable cup, studying the contents. He brought a litre bottle with him each morning, rationing it frugally at hourly intervals.

'Downing Street and the FO are already prattling about deals, exchanges, discreet handovers if anyone has survived.'

Above a mahogany bookcase, a line of framed photos depicting Rossan's career meandered around the room. From a group of laughing students scrummed around Mercury fountain in Christ Church's Tom Quad, to grey faced men taking Rossan's hand on retiring. They all bore the foretaste of bitter memories; this is what I've done, my moment. Remember me this way.

'That's good news isn't it?' Jane asked.

'Bloody better be. We're between Scylla and Charybdis.' Screwing on the bottle top he glanced at the raw morning light swelling over the city, pushing down from the north. 'But that's not my decision.'

Behind Jane, Rossan's secretary sneaked open the door.

'Mr. Hawick and the Chief are running late but should be ready in fifteen minutes.'

'Anything to report?' Rossan asked, quizzically arching an eyebrow.

Shaking her head, Maureen closed the door with a neat click.

Leaving the cup on the windowsill, Rossan strode over to his desk, the metal tips on his heels a precise manoeuvre in sound.

When he sat down the scuffed leather chair squealed. Glancing down at a single sheet squared in the middle of his blotter, Rossan looked up before even reaching the last line; his sharp blue eyes snapped on Jane like a gun dog sighting its first downed grouse.

'The inquisition begins. RUS/OPS will be under the cosh, but that's expected,' he said loftily. Heading off Jane's attempted intervention with a raised hand, Rossan sat back. 'No alternative, so I take it we've no demarcation dispute?'

'I just want to get Nick or Alistair home,' Jane sighed, the hairs on the back of her neck tingling. Through the smoked grey window, the pallid morning grew stronger, forcing tines of light through a dark band of cloud.

'Who doesn't?' he said, his sophistry surfacing.

A ball of tension spun through her and whether it came from a lack of sleep or empty stomach, Jane couldn't decide. 'It's Moscow flexing its muscles,' she said.

'Is it?' He gave a vulpine smile, the eyebrow arched higher. 'Have that on good authority, do you?'

'Come on Paul, you know Moscow have been looking for a strong hand since Litvinenko.'

'Haven't they just,' said Rossan. Alexander Litvinenko, a perennial thorn in the Service's side, an ex-Russian FSB officer who, once granted asylum against Jane and Roly Blackmore's wise counsel, turned on his former Moscow masters in print, and for his endeavours he was painfully terminated with a dose of radiation. 'And we've given them one, that what you're implying?' He leant forward, elbows planted on his desk.

'You mean by someone here?' Jane flared.

'Someone somewhere, has to be. Axiomatic, I'd have thought.'

Angry at Rossan's flippancy a giddy twitch floated around her tummy along with an itch deep in her palms she couldn't ease.

'Something I don't know about, Paul?'

Again, he refused her. Keeping his distance which might only have constituted a desk length, yet it seemed an endless expanse to Jane after his supercilious shrug. 'The Vapour Trail Committee isn't going to be immune from scrutiny either. Hardly likely it's going to survive in its current formation.'

'Ruth already a scapegoat?' she demanded with feeling.

Surprised by Jane's passion, Rossan cast around the desk and hooked up a photograph of his wife Rebecca, wiping an imaginary smear off the glass. Even at home Rossan continually ran into female intolerance, indifference or anger. Rebecca, a debutante who'd sparkled quite considerably in her youth, had never forgiven him when she lost her figure after the births of their son and daughter.

'Without Viper there isn't much of a product line. You'd have to ask C or Teddy for a steer,' he said, seeming too pale under the light. 'But that's a secondary consideration. We have more pressing objectives we shouldn't lose sight of.'

Jane saw it clearly now, the reason for Rossan's obfuscation; it was her rise in C's estimation, her new standing in the order of battle. 'No one's been written off including Nick or Alistair,' Jane said. She waited for her anger to subside, to find its equilibrium.

'I'm glad to hear it.'

'You should be.'

'Good, I'm relieved we've reached a mutual understanding.'

Except she didn't think they'd reached anything mutual. 'I'd better go,' she said.

'Of course. Maybe you should drop by RUS/OPS, we don't want Mortland terrorising them without good reason.'

Closing Rossan's door she pondered on his scheming, all the way down to her own floor.

Four

Nick had been checked over by a surly Russian military medic en route to Moscow. Diagnosed with fractured ribs, severe lacerations, a flesh wound and a couple of loose teeth, he'd been given an injection to ease the pain, followed by a second the medic never fully explained. Pronounced reasonably fit, Nick was officially handed over on the city outskirts and rapidly transferred to a plain van.

Wasn't it simply marvellous how the world revolved thought Nick, moving slowly, his arms and legs reacting as though on time delay. Voices reached him from his left, heading out in a widening arc, low then high. Nick wiped his forehead with the back of his hand, unable to decide which was hot, which cold. In the distance a helicopter swept by, the engine faint and hoarse. Blinking hard he tried to focus, but something strange was going on with his eyes that seemed to insist he wasn't in the van but lying in a forest. Forcing himself up, he started along an ancient logger's track, weaving through thickening snow, dipping and bumping along the curving high banks protecting the track. This far into the forest the sun never came, and the air was frosty and sharp, tempered by pine. On through the underwood he avoided prone trunks of rotting timber, here and there a full trunk held a crooked branch up in distress. Listening, he heard the helicopter lose height, bank for another pass. Keeping low, he swung slowly into a small logger's camp of three cabins. Breaking cover he kept close to stacked logs and made for the first cabin.

Expecting to feel wood on his palm as he extended a hand to the cabin door, Nick recoiled from the cold metal skin of the van. Crouched in a corner he panted for breath, feeling really quite seasick as the van made three quick turns and slowed to a stop.

Outside, a dog let off a long train of barks and a flat practised voice yelled for it to be quiet. His perception totally muddled, Nick swam between reality and hallucination. Never accept an injection from a stranger he thought, always say 'No'.

Two pairs of capable hands half carried and dragged him out of the van. Trying to stand in a presentable fashion he tumbled to the floor. Like his life, he thought, things were never what he expected. Lifted and dragged, Nick was taken down endless corridors, the fixed fluorescent lights hurting his eyes. Someone gave a brusque order and he was set down in a room and a heavy door swung closed. He waited for his eyes to adjust to the gloom before crabbing over to a corner facing the door. It seemed hours until he heard boots approach in a quickstep as though following his scent. They hadn't forgotten about me after all he thought, deciding to do nothing but wait, his body pushed low. Any time now Nick reasoned, he would be beaten. They dragged him forwards, then back, yanked him right, then left, and Nick knew this to be his primary conditioning. This also involved having his hands cuffed painfully behind his back, while his eyes were roughly covered in a strip of coarse cloth. Curled into a protective ball he listened as the boots retreated, concluding the end of what seasoned interrogators class the 'happy hour'. As the boots became a faint echo, Nick forced his mind to follow a different route, to focus on a direction.

Lost in his own collective world of introspection, he missed their return down the corridor, aware too late of their arrival as a key found the lock. Swaying as they lifted him to his feet, Nick was guided and pulled up twenty-four rickety steps into a sterile office prepared in advance for his arrival. He heard voices low and heavy, one of them a woman, he felt the cold pinch through his eyes as they uncovered them. Then Nick made one defiant gesture, a futile headlong rush for the door. Tripped up, sprawled on a rough bare floor, the woman laughed quietly as they restrained him by his ankles to a metal chair bolted firmly down.

'Would you prefer me to speak Russian or English, Nick?' The woman asked from behind a desk, her face protected by the halo of light coming from a desk lamp she aimed directly at him.

'My name's Peter, not Nick. I'm a tourist and only speak English,' Nick volunteered, unwinding his initial cover story. 'Why am I being treated like this, I need to contact the British Embassy.'

'We're here to help you, Nick,' she offered, her English clear. 'My name is Anastasiya and my colleague is Alexei and we'd like to get you home as quickly as possible.'

Nick nodded, wondering if everyone he'd be meeting had picked their worknames out of a hat. 'I was hitching a ride and the car I was travelling in was involved in an accident. That's why I need to notify my Embassy.'

Ten minutes without a response, nothing from Anastasiya or Alexei except the gentle rustling of papers and the slow steady breathing from figures standing behind Nick. At least one of them also a woman he decided, catching a hint of a distinctive perfume. This one not part of the interrogation team, but one of the invited observers waiting to see what he'd deliver.

Clearing his throat Alexei broke the spell, his English containing an American ring. 'You're an important man Nick, you're the Director of CO8, so why lie to us?'

'I don't know what you're talking about,' objected Nick. 'I'm a tourist, take a look at my papers.'

'London don't care about you Nick,' Anastasiya said, the friendly smile in her voice gone. 'Your colleague Mr. Alistair Foula is dead, Nick,' she reminded him. 'You and he are British spies.'

'What did your contact want to sell?' Alexei demanded.

'You've got me mixed up with someone else. I just took a ride in the wrong car, that's all,' protested Nick knowing his cover was shot to pieces and they were merely warming up.

'Okay, Nick, we'll leave it there for today,' Anastasiya offered, her charm restored as though she were winding-up a sales seminar.

In an instant they'd bound Nick's hands and covered his eyes, then movement all around him as Alexei, Anastasiya and the VIPs solemnly trooped out before Nick descended back to his cell at double speed. That night they started with the electronic games; noise mostly, and even though his eyes were covered, Nick could see the strobe flashes. When they stopped the electronic show, Nick didn't know if it was night or day. Hunched into a corner he tried to regulate his breathing, reassert order on his senses. But they wouldn't give him the satisfaction of gaining any self-control.

Displaying remarkable diligence, they instituted a new regime. With his eyes bound tight, they pushed and tugged him on a slow shambling walk round the perimeter of a freezing high fenced courtyard, feet from snarling guard dogs. Fifteen steps to the first turn, ten to the next, nineteen to a spot where the cold really nipped his face, and eleven back to where he started. After his 'exercise' they provided water to drink, followed by a cigarette that he had trouble smoking through burst lips he guessed he must have received when the Lada went belly up.

The next day or maybe it was night, Nick really couldn't tell, nor by now did he care, a different phase of interrogation began. Led again by Anastasiya but this time she'd brought along some new friends who made him kneel, facing who or what he didn't know.

'What did the traitor Lubov wish to sell?' She asked, and Nick knew there was a sharper, intense edge to her question.

'My name is Peter May,' Nick said, 'I'm a visitor, a tourist. I don't know why you're asking me these questions.'

Strange how the first kick, hard to the middle of his back brought no pain. Nick smiled. Actually smiled as the foot laid into him again, fiercer, lower or higher, it made no difference. He was happy because they'd stripped him naked, taken his clothes, boots, and he knew they couldn't have found the SIM because they weren't sure what Lubov's treasure entailed.

'Nick, you're doing yourself only harm.' Anastasiya informed him. 'Think of your wife, how is she going to cope if you go home a cripple?'

'I'm not married, I live with my mum.'

Nick received another kick for his efforts; not to his back, but swung fiercely into his crotch, the pain made him vomit. No warning, no favours.

He fought back in his head, denying everything around him, even his own existence. His eyes weeping from the pressure of the rag were sticky at the corners, and he told himself it was all part of an established game, the rules accepted by both sides. They knew he had something to confess, Nick knew it too, it was just a matter of finding a compromise, a middle ground; they could record a victory, and he'd be left to heal and sent home without a mark on him. He vomited again.

'Clean him up,' Anastasiya commanded.

A bucket of cold water was tossed over him, ripping Nick's breath out of his lungs. Weak, his chest and legs wet, Nick felt two pairs of safe hands grip his arms and he was shuffled out. They took him down a passage of no considerable length to another room, this barely larger than the last, just as sparse; at its centre, a plain metal desk and chair. On one corner of the desk two typed confessions with a cheap fountain pen lying neatly alongside. From behind Nick a pair of hands ripped off the rag around his eyes, the sudden rush of light forcing him to squint and cringe. In the room, though he never saw them, he could sense a number of observers behind him, one of them the woman wearing her heady brand of perfume. Painfully he opened his eyes letting them adjust; the first thing he saw was the desk with someone dressed in an army officer's uniform staring up from his seat, calmly and quite detached assessing Nick's condition.

'I commend your resilience, Nick,' said the officer, 'But your stupidity to a lost cause is a quality I am unable to admire.'

'You have been abandoned by London,' Anastasiya said.

Cocking his head to one side Nick saw her for the first time, standing by the desk; mid-thirties, smartly dressed, neat blonde hair that seemed yellow in the light, large dark glasses and her arms folded across her chest, as though she could not get warm. She reminded Nick of an academic, someone who takes study seriously and he bet himself a fiver she was GRU and a trained shrink. Moving his head ever so slightly, Nick could just make out a large close-cropped thug in urban combats, either special forces or one of the permanent staff, a large ring on his middle finger.

'You are a criminal, a murderer, you killed two military personnel on the highway trying to escape,' the officer said, his opening sociability forgotten. 'In Russia we treat killers differently, you should realise that.'

'Is this a military court of law or a civilian one?' Nick asked, wondering why they'd omitted the one in the Puffa jacket outside Lubov's door. Maybe I didn't kill him after all?

A punch whipped into his mouth coming unseen from his right, popping out a loose tooth, opening up his lips once more. Further punches flowed freely, and a deep burning pain ran through his calves as someone enthusiastically set about them with a baton. Unable to hold his weight, his knees buckled, and he sprawled on his side. From this angle Nick decided his tormentor wielding the baton was also special forces, some of them had that look, young and keen, his bright eyes sunk under thick brows.

'You should sign the statement, Mr. Torr,' the officer advised Nick as he was dragged back on his feet, blood dribbling down his chin onto his naked chest. The statement in a final draft was pushed in front of his puffy swollen eyes, his crimes read out in a methodical voice. Nick wearily shaking his head suffered one last blow of frustration, delivered expertly to his damaged rib and he couldn't help a terrible scream that somehow got passed his bloated tongue before he passed out.

Dragged unceremoniously back to his cell, the guards left Nick in embarrassed silence. He came around propped against a freezing wall, a thin blanket that had once distantly belonged to the Red Cross draped around his waist and legs, while across his bruised chest they'd tucked a towel already stained by his vomit and blood. The statement he refused to sign, the record of his criminal actions as they called it, sat next to him and somehow, he found the energy to scrunch it and throw it into a corner. Above his head, a small window made of clear glass blocks. And while his mind closed down all the barriers through which they were trying to break into his past, he watched the night drip slowly into the corner of each thick glass square; distorted particles of streaky cloud racing across a swollen moon.

After his refusal to sign his confession, Nick's captivity entered a new dimension. Nudged awake by a boot at some point into a long dark night, three of them pinned Nick down taking an arm apiece and one to his legs as a strange hand felt for a vein, then the puncture as a needle entered his arm. As the drug flowed into his system, he watched them float out of his cell, grotesque figures who'd stepped straight out of fairground mirrors, before a heavy throbbing claimed his mind.

It was the light in Nick's head that troubled him the most. He didn't care about the deafness in one ear, the pain eating its way through his body, or the thought of death locked in his mind. He wondered if the light had come after another beating with a kick to his head but couldn't be sure. He even thought, though this was far too a strong description for the fragments that went through his mind, he imagined that he had died, and this was his personal hell. But he knew it wasn't because he had no sure belief in God or the Devil, knowing that the only two absolutes are birth and death, and having had one he was now most surely moving quickly towards the next.

If only the light would go from inside his eyes. Tomorrow he would demand to see a doctor. A stronger light seemed to flash around his skull, and he realised they were administering short doses of electric current. His name, he fought for a piece of it, nothing came. He dug deeper, but he saw only a face that he knew had once been his own. There came no name with it either.

Footsteps and sound. A disjointed voice periodically checking his condition, breaking off from questions he seemed to be answering. Nick craved sleep. The windows were boarded, painted white, preventing him from distinguishing day from night. This phase marking the end. Nick knew the signs from his training. Once you're denied the ability to appreciate light and dark there is nothing left for you, except the serious questions and serious pain before the confession you inevitably make. Everyone does finally, he recalled, some with relief others with hate; fighting every word that left their body, denying, struggling until the very last. Trying to turn his head to guard himself for a blow or punch, he realised he had lost all movement.

'Lubov had material for a senior ex-officer only,' mumbled Nick.

'What did he say?' demanded the army officer.

By a low table holding a digital recorder, Anastasiya and Alexei stared at him with the same impassivity they had shown since the first day of his capture.

Weakness, nothing but his own weakness, Nick told himself, cursing his body, its betrayal for tricking him into talking. He tried, really made an effort not to speak, but something was pulling answers over his swollen tongue, his inflamed gums that somehow dulled his words, threw them into the empty white space of the room without form, without shape; a peculiar language all his own.

'Why Nick? Why an ex-officer, Nick?' Anastasiya asked walking slowly, her steps sharp, acute, a perfect counterbalance to her unhurried voice as she came and stood at Nick's side.

'Tell us, Nick, then we don't have to put you on trial,' urged Alexei.

Trying to speak but denied by the shape and swelling of his mouth, Nick, with much effort shook his head. He giggled; couldn't help it, couldn't stop it. Slowly, with measured deliberation Nick slurred, in a feeble parched croak between his giggles, 'Lubov had evidence,' repeating it in a whisper that he refused to accept as his own, especially for Anastasiya bent close to his mouth.

A temporary lull followed his admission, a hiatus Nick vaguely registered from the ceasing of the blinding light behind his eyes. Defiantly, straining the individual muscles in his neck, Nick brought his head up a fraction, just high enough so he could register a blur of figures gathered around a low table as a murmured discussion bubbled on. Opening his cracked lips, forcing a sound past his thick tongue, Nick uttered a single fractured word. 'Mole.' There, Nick chided himself, you've gone and done it now, aware that this could be the only analysis of why Lubov wanted to deal only with an ex-senior officer. Then he sensed all the world had stopped to listen, everyone in the room had turned to hear what he had said.

'You're saying the traitor Lubov had evidence of a Moscow asset, Nick?' Alexei checked, returning to him, laying a proud hand on his shoulder. 'That what you're telling us?'

Nick wasn't sure what he was telling them anymore, knowing that he'd have less of the electrics, drugs and beating if he played along. 'Yes,' he mumbled.

'Where is the mole? Do you have the asset's name?' A voice from behind him asked, the woman VIP again, trailing her perfume as she moved closer, her mellow voice reminding Nick of a schoolteacher who had once attempted to teach him art.

From deep inside, Nick summoned up a last strand of resolve that he used to shake his head in denial. 'No one knows, only Lubov,' he muttered in his strange distorted language. 'Lubov... Lubov was the evidence.'

'That is why Lubov wanted to meet an ex-officer,' Anastasiya decided for them all, the problem solved.

Exhausted with his effort, Nick was breathing heavily and gave the feeblest of smiles as he nodded in agreement. Carried back to his stinking cell, Nick wanted to cry for help, but his ribs were too inflamed, his throat too dry and for the moment he couldn't prevent himself toppling on his side, slipping softly into a longed-for world of sleep and release.

Transferred during the night, Nick lapsed in and out of sleep, finally waking in a military hospital ward and a clean bed. A nurse on seeing him awake promptly marched over and ordered him to drink, holding a cup and feeding straw as he sipped a sweet milky watery mixture. Displaying the bedside manner and charm of a commissar, she said he would probably be in her charge for a week. With a disgusted wrinkle of her broad nose she asked Nick if the clear sack of clothes dumped by his bed were his? And if Nick's ribs hadn't felt as though they'd explode, he'd have hugged her; for the sack contained not only the clothes he'd been wearing when captured, but at the bottom, one pair of very muddy boots.

Five

Nick's stay in Moscow ran to five weeks and he was handed over in a simple ceremony on the Latvian border at Terehova. Met not by an all singing delegation from London, but a one-woman British Embassy, a senior member of the Foreign Office dispatched explicitly for his repatriation; Clare Lostock was his entire official reception committee. In her early fifties, she had neat straight grey hair, a full figure she covered in an elegant expensive jacket, tailored blouse, and knee length skirt. With a no-nonsense face that had made her desirable in her youth, Lostock had a surface elegance that wouldn't have been out of place on the front cover of a business magazine. Her eyes and mouth however, suggested a different side; a woman who, in the right company, knew how to have fun. Recoiling at Nick's appearance, resembling what her mother would have called a common tramp, Lostock formally received Nick on behalf of Her Majesty's Government. As a respected FO troubleshooter, Lostock was accustomed to bringing home damaged goods, which Nick on that day surely was.

'We are going straight to the airfield,' she briskly announced, not wishing to stare at her package slouched beside her in a totally dishevelled state.

'Great,' said Nick, shrugging off his lethargy.

As part of her strict mandate, Lostock never uttered another word during the drive to the Latvian Air Force base at Rēzekne where a Royal Air Force BAe 125 executive jet waited. She even scolded the flight attendant, a Leading Aircraftman from Cardiff who had the temerity to enquire if Nick would like a second glass of orange juice during the flight.

Touching down at RAF Northolt, a Ford Galaxy its windows tinted grey, swept out to park by the aircraft steps.

'Thanks for all the help,' said Nick as Lostock officially handed him over to two of the Service's Internal Security and Counter-intelligence Branch officers, the mutually despised Regulators from R5. As one of them opened the Galaxy's rear door, Nick impishly kissed Lostock's cheek before they could hustle him into the car.

'My pleasure,' said Lostock to the back of the speeding Galaxy.

Sandwiched between his two minders, Nick sat back as snatches of countryside slipped by; trees stripped of leaves the grass a dismal autumn green as the Galaxy headed for Hertfordshire.

'Do I get a clue where we're going?'

'Aspley.' One of the minder's answered, his scowl saying he didn't care to be troubled again.

Aspley Grange overlooked Berkhamsted with a proprietary air. A rambling Victorian Gothic house built for a brewing baron as a symbol of his social status, it became government property in the 1920s in lieu of unpaid taxes. The extensive walled estate was dominated by the large house with its added mansard roof, a wing with its own chapel, all set within secure grounds. Housing intelligence staff during the Second World War, it had been in Service hands since the 1950s, acquired in a surreptitious deal, or so the legend went. From three-quarters down its serpentine drive, Nick saw the chapel's spire rising above the trees, to its right the castellated turrets covering an older part of the house. Instead of stopping by Aspley's grand entrance, the Galaxy crunched round the wide drive, turning fast off the gravel onto a tarmac avenue by a complex of uninspired annexes added sometime in the Eighties.

Jerking to a stop outside a two-storey block, Nick's minders ushered him inside fast, a troublesome guest who had to be brought in by the servants' entrance. Inside, the bare breeze block walls had been tastefully rolled in cream emulsion, intensifying the strip lighting as it bounced back off floor tiles, buffed to a reflective gleam. Above the acoustic door to Suite 1, a pair of lights – one red, one green – set in the wall; as one of Nick's minders directed him inside with a stiff, straight arm, the red light blinked on. Sitting at a table Nick waited until the door gently closed, its lock rotated home. There were cameras tucked high into each corner and a two-way glass directly opposite the table in a far wall. Nick had been in the interrogation block on numerous occasions, during training, and when CO8 had brought in defectors who, according to Service euphemism, underwent 'active debriefing.'

The first interrogator to arrive was Bill McEntee, an avuncular figure who reminded Nick of a history master with his round, calm indefatigable face that carried a permanent lopsided grin.

'How are you Nicholas?' McEntee asked, crossing to the table, his brown brogues scuffed at the toes gliding along.

'I've been better Bill,' said Nick as McEntee sat himself down, unfastening his tweed jacket, dusting a speck of dust from his lapel. 'Thought you'd retired?'

'Kept me on for the specials,' McEntee said, taking out a small wireless receiver from his pocket, looping it over his ear. 'Technology,' he said, as though it was a disease, pressing it firmly into his ear. 'Moscow rough?'

'A touch on the cold side,' answered Nick, knowing his debriefing had just officially begun.

McEntee nodded slowly, as though requiring a good deal of time to digest this basic fact. During this moment of contemplation, the door slowly opened, and Vincent Soleby entered. McEntee's usual long-time partner, he was thin and tall and moved slowly, a studious man dressed in a shabby cardigan, brown trousers and a white shirt. He had a creased, lined face and a thick mane of white hair encircling a bald head. With his square metal glasses, he gave the appearance of a senior college fellow whose natural field might have been philosophy, which is in fact what he had once practised before entering the Service.

'Nick,' Soleby said, in a terse acknowledgement, slipping a bound dossier out from under his arm, throwing it onto the table with a slap.

'Vincent.' Nick felt a little bubble of concern rise. Soleby and McEntee, two of the Service's most revered thumbscrews were not here to shake his hand. 'I thought you were taking it easy, writing scholarly texts?'

'Mmm,' Soleby replied, undoing the green string holding the dossier together, spreading the Manila cover flat. 'I am, but they call me in from time to time, a complete bother,' he said, scanning a typed report.

'Shall we begin?' proposed McEntee, for the benefit of a technical officer taking care of the cameras and recording, plus today's unseen observers; and Nick couldn't begin to guess who might be tucked comfortably away behind the two-way glass.

'Very lax of you Nick,' Soleby stated, staring right into Nick's eyes, 'Not being able to keep a check on one of your troops, allowing her to moonlight like that.'

'What was Wynn working on?' McEntee wondered.

Nick, completely thrown, couldn't fathom where they were leading him.

'She wasn't working on anything,' said Nick, feeling his nerve return. 'She was on soft duties at the Mad House, she's only just transferred across to us.'

'Mmm,' said Soleby, licking his finger to get to a particular sheet in the dossier.

'What has she done? Not filled in her return to work papers? Not pulling her weight? Insulted someone from over the river?' Nick asked, digging for a clue.

McEntee, taking instruction through his earpiece receiver, shook his head solemnly. 'No, Nick, she's gone and got herself killed in Hamburg, that's what she's done.'

'How?' Nick slumped deep in the curved plastic chair, his arms laced across the table as the stinging mustard and grey walls seemed to move a foot closer. Why? he asked himself, the drone of McEntee's voice sounding a couple of miles away: *point blank... not a chance in hell...execution.*

'...do you know where her last posting was prior to having her babies and joining your dark side of the house?' McEntee continued.

'No. She came highly recommended by Rossan. She was going to be our Controller Targeting.'

'Moscow, that's where,' McEntee snapped.

'Then you have an almighty mess-up in Moscow,' Soleby added, pushing the dossier aside, closing its cover after apparently having seen enough.

'Operation Salvage. Run us through it, Nick,' suggested McEntee, his lopsided smile offering encouragement.

'Am I under investigation?' asked Nick, playing up for the microphones.

'Don't think so,' McEntee said, getting to his feet.

'Not as far as I know,' added Soleby.

'Moscow,' McEntee reminded Nick, standing away to the right. With his hands buried deep in his jacket pockets, tightening the tweed over his broad shoulders, he threw endless assumptions on sloppy procedures at Nick.

'They were waiting for us,' said Nick.

'Someone must have tipped them the wink then,' proposed McEntee sourly.

Soleby then took the initiative, his long arms clasped behind his head, asking Nick in a dozen different ways if he was working for Moscow and showed ill-concealed disbelief as Nick avoided every point through his controlled evasive replies.

'Come on Nick, we're only trying to get to the truth,' McEntee said after each blank answer, stroking his round chin.

'We're not dunderheads,' said Soleby, a muscle in his face ticked frantically up and down.

'Who did you discuss the operation with? Someone not of our parish or our calling perhaps?' McEntee speculated, doing a brisk circuit round the room. He was familiar with every inch of this suite; the chipped piece of blue floor tile that his heels regularly caught, the dimpled fluorescent strip light cover where dead flies collected.

'No one except Foula.'

'Consorting with the enemy, Nick, that what you were doing?' wondered Soleby, his muscle ticking away. 'What about with your wife? Break the rules in order to please her? Tell her because you're not seeing eye to eye? That what you did?'

'We barely talk.'

'Break your entry routine?' McEntee wondered, pushing off from his spot against the wall with his hands.

'No.'

'Suspect anything on the drive in?' McEntee continued, taking up the chase.

'Everything seemed fine.'

'And you changed the plates?'

'Yes.'

'Standard precaution?'

'Yes.'

'Then why'd you change them again?' Soleby broke in, shaking the blood back into his wrists, hands and fingers. 'Had an inkling, gut feeling, sixth sense? Because those on the car the Russians recovered from the Crimea Bridge didn't match the set you took in. That's a worry for us.'

They were good, very good conceded Nick. Astute, smart and persistent; in other circumstances or a different time in the past, Nick would have congratulated them on their exceptional performance, how they functioned as a team and bought them a drink in the Senior Officers' Bar in Aspley's main house. Now it was simply a question of how long he would survive.

'It's something I always do if I believe we're entering a particularly difficult theatre of operation.'

'So, you're saying your actions were justified?' Soleby asked.

'Weren't they?'

'That's what we'd like to hear, your version, your justification,' said McEntee.

He told them the events surrounding the collection without elaboration, including the little administrator's sudden decision to clear out there and then, his concern that his superiors were onto him But he never came close to detailing their detour to the little administrator's apartment or what he carried in the sole of his boot.

'Do you mind if we backtrack slightly?' wondered Soleby.

'Clearance for the operation came from RUS/OPS?' McEntee asked.

'Endorsed by the JIC and the Vapour Trail Group,' Nick replied.

'And what is the Vapour Trail Group?' McEntee pressed.

'Ask Parfrey, it's connected to Viper according to Foula.'

'You and Parfrey working for Moscow?' Soleby asked. 'A pair of traitors helping each other out? That why you took care of Wynn. Did she connect the dots during her tour? That why you had her transferred, to keep an eye on her? About to blow the whistle on you, was she?'

But this was one question too far, bringing Nick flying out of his seat.

Hitting the alarm circling the suite in a continuous wide strip, McEntee held himself against a section of wall, and Soleby made off for a neutral corner as two Regulators rushed in.

'Perhaps Mr. Torr could have a drink while we take a break,' McEntee said as Nick dropped back into his seat, arms folded, staring in fury at Soleby who made it out through the door first.

When they returned Nick had drunk a small bottle of warm mineral water and his mood had barely improved.

'Think Viper's bleating for a safe ride out justified an unauthorised extraction? Endangering not only your own life, but that of a fellow officer?' Soleby asked.

For a second, Nick thought they were going to bring a charge under health and safety as a means of ending his career. 'Thinking on my feet,' said Nick.

'Course you were,' McEntee smiled and shook his head. 'Who decided to crash the roadblock?' he demanded.

'I did and Foula went with it.' It seemed a hundred years ago instead of more than a month when they'd set off for home.

'But he's not here to verify that, is he?' Soleby chided Nick.

'They were waiting for us,' said Nick, rubbing the crooked bone in his nose, unable to forget Foula's limp arms flailing as the bullets tore into the Lada.

'Did Viper provide any insight into what his material might be?' Soleby asked.

Here it was thought Nick, the central question and he wondered which way he should take them. 'He didn't have time,' said Nick as a starter for ten. *A profitable exchange we will all benefit from*, Nick recalled. *Four for silver, five for gold, six for a secret never to be told.*

'So, why did Viper have the sudden urge to jump ship?' McEntee asked.

'Something had spooked him,' replied Nick, placing the sole of his boot as flat as it would go. 'He would reveal all when he was safely in London.'

'If Viper had, in your words, not mine, Nick, if Viper twigged he was "Ninety-seven per cent" certain he was blown, why on earth did you proceed to attempt to crash your way out?' Soleby wondered his long face puzzled.

'I didn't have time for him to apply for a visa,' said Nick sourly. 'And we weren't going for a crash crossing, we were going to lie low close to the border and wait for extraction.'

'Whether making a run for it was the right decision is a moot point,' McEntee said. 'Either way, there you are, gunning it for the border with what could be a hot asset in the back, Foula riding shotgun. I understand you were in a vulnerable position Nick. But what I can't square is Viper's sudden decision to up sticks and leave.'

'What made him jump ship, Nick? That is all we're trying to establish,' added Soleby.

'You know assets, they're unpredictable.'

Whatever McEntee knew about assets, he kept to himself. 'So, they catch you cold,' McEntee stated, 'trying to extract one of their flock. Was that their starting point for your discussion during your time in Moscow?'

'Discussion?' Nick scraped back his chair, the thumbscrews visibly tensing.

'Did they assume that Viper had handed over his material to you?' Soleby asked.

'It crossed their minds.'

'And did he?' Soleby demanded.

'No.'

'Don't lie, Nick,' McEntee warned him. 'If Viper was the means to end, why did they detain you for so long? Not checking the points on your licence, were they?'

'Come on, Nick,' Soleby cajoled him, 'What were they looking for?'

'A confession.'

'What to? An almighty cock-up?' McEntee said, his lopsided smile rising higher.

'Look,' began Nick, only to be cut-off by a flap from one of Soleby's enormous hands.

'You listen, Nick,' Soleby insisted and Nick complied as Soleby more or less accused him of deliberately misleading them and providing them with false information to cover his own guilty tracks.

'From our point of view the whole operation was ill-judged and poorly executed,' said McEntee. 'You're providing us with more questions than answers.'

'I made the right decisions given the circumstances at that time. I did happen to be up to my neck in a spot of bother,' Nick avowed, knowing full well that Operation Salvage should have been called Operation Shambles and he'd be having a word with Parfrey about it.

'Who was at the party in Moscow, Nick? Who was pulling the strings?' Soleby ventured, scratching his arm.

'FSB.'

'That it?' said McEntee, decidedly unimpressed.

'You implying that I've been turned?'

'Have you?' retorted Soleby, leaning forward.

'If you're going to pursue that line of questioning, I'm requesting legal representation.'

'Grow up, Nick and stop wasting our time,' proposed McEntee. 'You've signed the Official Secrets Act, remember.'

'So, you couldn't be sure if the SVR and GRU had joined their FSB buddies for this little soiree?' McEntee politely enquired.

'They didn't exactly wear name badges,' snapped Nick. 'That's the problem when you're blindfolded, you're not sure of what day it is. The friendly beatings don't help much either.'

'And Viper never passed anything over to you?' McEntee wondered, vexed that things were too messy.

Nick felt queasy, imagining the SIM cut into his sole was about to come to life and give him away. Double the pressure, double the chances of him slipping up, admitting to sins, confessing he'd squared the circle in an unorthodox style, and they were waiting to pounce. Sly smiles from the thumbscrews implying they had everything they needed to bring a charge, then suspension and goodnight Nick.

'Viper wanted out. Have neither of you been listening? He was spooked, had a bad case of the jitters because he thought he'd been tagged. He wasn't making much sense.'

'Just like you, Nick,' quipped Soleby.

'Go to hell.'

'You see Nick, we just can't seem to understand why Viper would be regarded as very important to his own lot or to us. According to his case officer, he'd turned off the tap, no product, just a load of tantrums. It's more fiction than fact,' sighed Soleby. 'I would be inclined to suggest that he was just playing us along, trying to sell us a cock and bull story for an increase in his monthly cash.'

'I think you're right,' said Nick, from behind gritted teeth, remembering the mess someone had made of the little administrator's wife and nephew, which was a lot of trouble for an asset with no product.

'Let's take it from the top again,' suggested McEntee, in an inquisitional hiss.

Which is exactly what they did. McEntee and Soleby smugly ignoring his explanations, going for disorientation by hurling names and facts in random order. Varying routines, alternating roles at each session, compounding the minutes into hours until he'd had enough as they entered the afternoon. At half-three, McEntee and Soleby sick of their own voices withdrew for a conference, locking him in with a watery cup of tea and a Penguin biscuit.

On their return, McEntee was flushed and Soleby seemed to have been forced to witness the burning of books. They've had to admit defeat thought Nick, and they've been hauled over the coals for their abject failure.

'For the moment,' McEntee said, the words burning his tongue, 'You're at liberty to leave.'

'That's very generous, Bill,' said Nick, up on his feet in seconds.

Collecting the dossier, Soleby stood to one side as McEntee led the retreat gliding towards the door. 'Catch you next time, Nick.'

'I'll save you the trouble, I'll have my false confession already typed up.'

'No need for sarcasm,' snapped Soleby following in the pocket of air left by his colleague.

Out in the corridor Nick was held in check by a pair of new Regulators. He was considering making a scene when Blackmore and Hawick turned the corner, displeasure oozing from Hawick's every pore. With a backward jab of his thumb Blackmore sent the Regulators retreating to a safe distance.

'Not the sort of home coming I'd like myself,' confessed Blackmore, a sly smile turning up the left corner of his mouth, 'but we need to be sure, Nick,' he explained, 'seems someone's telling us porkies and it's a priority we discover who.'

'Let me get back to work and I'll give you a name.'

'That's not an option,' said Hawick, the pronouncement curdling on his thin lips.

'What are my options?'

'If you've any inkling young Nicholas Torr what our dearly departed Viper had up his sleeve, I want to know,' said Blackmore, twisting a cygnet ring around his little finger. 'No one's denying you haven't had a rough ride, but Lubov's claim isn't stacking up.'

Trust me and be damned, thought Nick watching Blackmore ease away, operating as Hawick's whipper-in.

'I was just there to babysit...'

'That is immaterial for the present,' snapped Hawick cutting him off. 'C has decided, and I fully support his judicious decision,' he continued primly, 'that as a matter of urgency to safeguard the integrity of the Service, a full and frank Accountability Board will conduct a root and branch review of your actions. Until the Board sits, I have instructed Personnel that you are suspended. On full salary, naturally.'

'Naturally,' Nick answered, his fists clenched. 'What about Wynn, do I bear the responsibility for her as well?'

Hawick exchanged a glance with Blackmore. 'You will have to account for Wynn's unauthorised activities in Hamburg, have no doubt,' Hawick promised him, fizzing with authority.

And this second confirmation that Sally Wynn had died in Hamburg may not have made Nick any wiser as to why or what she was doing in the Hanseatic city, but he had the end of a trail to work from.

'If you're finished, am I cleared to leave now?'

'I most certainly am not,' Hawick erupted. 'First thing Monday morning

I want you back here for a formal debriefing. I want solid answers. I want to know exactly what transpired in Moscow and I want to know what Wynn was working on.'

So do I, Nick decided. 'Now can I leave?'

'Do not bother returning to Head Office, do not return to the Mad House, do not contact anyone currently or previously in the employ of the Service. You are in isolation until I or C say otherwise,' announced Hawick, raising himself on his toes.

'Naturally we have arranged transport for you.'

'What, back to Moscow?'

'Home, we'll be taking you home,' Hawick said finding somewhere for his eyes to assess.

'Fuck off while you've got the chance,' Blackmore said with a wink, arranging the point on a silk handkerchief in his breast pocket.

'We had these sent over from your office,' said Hawick, handing over a set of keys.

'Thanks.' Nick turned them over in his hand, the keys to his house, his marriage and maybe his future. He'd always left them in his office in the custody of a senior secretary to be collected on his return, up until what had now become his official excommunication.

'Nick,' called Blackmore as Nick started down the corridor. 'You need a shower and a change of clothes,' he advised with a broad smile.

• • •

Instead of the Ford Galaxy that delivered Nick to Aspley that morning, a black Toyota Prius waited for him at a side entrance to the interrogation block. A pasty woman officer from the interrogation staff with short straight hair sat needlessly over-revving the engine. On the quarter-light, two large pendants warned that it was against the law to smoke in this vehicle. Nick lit a cigarette and saw her top lip quivering, its fine line of dark hair unsettling him all through the drive back to London.

Dropped at the corner of Upper Firwood Road and Dunsop Avenue, he refused her offer of setting him down at his door on Palmer Road, preferring to settle into a loafing walk, taking a winding excursion home. He filed his way through Putney in what was left of a dull afternoon. Tomorrow I'll take Angie shopping, a trip to the Tate Modern if she's interested, give her some room to get her head together. Tonight, I'll book a table; Chinese,

Japanese, Thai, Indonesian, or whatever her whim dictated, just the two of us rekindling an old flame. In eleven years, they'd achieved what? An acrimonious existence as separate as if they were divorced Nick decided, and a dead son who'd only valued him for the presents he'd brought from his travels. After Thomas was killed by a hit and run driver when he was five, Angie blamed Nick for being away when she needed him the most. Everything, as always, laid at Nick's feet; he had become the blame guru.

The fickle light was evaporating and children home from school were playing out in groups, their sharp voices slicing through the damp air around the mellow walls of the Methodist church. Nothing else moved along the road and he felt the adrenalin tingle as he turned his key in the barrel of the night latch.

'Angie?'

The hallway floor was tiled in black and white mosaics, tiny diamonds stretching away into the large house built for a family not a broken marriage. An antique coat stand acted as a semaphore for who was in, and who was out. Angie was definitely in. He called her name again and wondered if she had another of her mysterious engagements, not bothering to use the mortise lock, her latest bête noire.

'Angie?'

She had a way with silence, her method of direct retribution, of punishing him for his absences, for not being a good husband, a good father. If Nick remained in the hallway, he was safe, he could stand here all night and not be drawn into an exchange in this mutually agreed no-man's-land. This afternoon he knew that confrontation was unavoidable, so he set off in search of the enemy. Opening a door to a sitting room there was no Angie but music coming from a midi system. He guessed Tchaikovsky but couldn't be sure; his heart sank, another salient retaken he thought.

Wandering down to the kitchen he poured a double measure of Laphroaig. He drank reluctantly, toasting the memory of Sally Wynn. He glanced in the oven where a casserole was simmering in solitude, and he wondered if it was to mark a family reunion or a new phase in Angie's routine minus a husband? He pulled a wicker hen off the upright freezer, its base a store for odds and ends. Flicking through disposable lighters, all of them empty, snapped necklace chains, broken buckles, strapless watches and drawing pins, Nick scattered the lot over a worktop until he found a paper clip. Slipping off his boot he pulled open cabinet drawers, found a paring knife and worked its thin blade over the sealed slot in its sole, carefully easing out the SIM. Unsheathing it from its plastic film, he inserted it into Angie's reserve cellphone, sitting perkily in its charging dock; her lifeline for the unforeseen emergencies, which evidently didn't include taking calls from her husband. One lone number glimmered for a Galina Myla, which, despite Nick's persistence, obstinately remained out of service; dead, unresponsive just like Lubov. Unlacing his other boot, he dumped them in the kitchen bin.

'Angie? I know you're in.' He was at the bottom of the stairs not wanting to inadvertently trespass; every room now had its own lexicon for the dissolution of their marriage.

A door somewhere upstairs clicked closed and Nick measured her light footfall, fifteen steps in all to make her appearance, remind him of her defiance.

'What happened?' Angie asked. 'You look dreadful.'

She stood at the head of the stairs long slender and attractive, a deceptive thirty-eight and he'd wondered if she lied about her age. She never used make-up and her plainness revealed no happiness, no despair. Her head was held to one side as though she needed this angle to get a better idea of him.

'It doesn't matter,' he said lightly, preferring no compassion.

'I hope you got a lift right to the front door.'

'Still got your sense of humour, then.'

'Was I supposed to expect you back today?' On so many different occasions, she'd expected a different figure standing there; fidgeting, avoiding her eyes as he, she or they explained how her husband was dead, critical, missing, but still a credit to the Firm.

'I tried calling to let you know, but you never answered.'

'It was charging.'

'It always is.'

'I mustn't have heard it.'

'You never do.'

She came four steps nearer, her head still cocked off centre. She'd dyed her hair blonde and parted it down the centre whilst he'd been away. A stark contrast to her clothes; comprising of everything black: polo neck, skirt, ribbed tights and pixie boots with broad buckles. She's in mourning Nick thought, we're divorced, and she hasn't bothered to let me know.

'I was at my mothers.'

She used her mother as a fortified outpost knowing he would never venture there. Angie's father, a retired merchant banker unconditionally dismissed Nick as a waste of effort and the last time Nick ran into her mother, she badgered him on his failings, his immunity to her daughter's needs.

'Any particular reason?'

'I've had a busy week. I've got a dealer interested in my work. Guy thinks next year is going to be my year,' she said, lowering the pointed toe of a boot towards the next step, testing the water. 'He's planning a retrospective before pushing my new work at his gallery in Hoxton.'

'Great.'

'Don't pretend that you care.'

'Fine. Listen, I want you to pack. Stay at your mothers or check into a hotel.' His head swam and the way he had to hold himself straight he wondered if his ribs had fully knitted together?

'No.'

'It's important.' He desperately wanted to smile, to laugh at the bizarre situation but he jammed his jaw together, flexing the bones in his cheeks.

'I'm bust Nick, Guy gave me a deadline to have everything finished.'

Perhaps I should have issued deadlines too, he thought. 'You can't stay here.'

There was a good nine feet and fifteen stairs between them. She folded her arms, her dark eyebrows accentuating her position of no surrender and no concessions, she'd made far too many in the past.

'I'm not being thrown out of my own house.'

'There's been an incident, I think it's best if you keep your distance from me and this place for a while.'

'No, Nick, don't say it, please don't lie to me, don't try and possess me through fear.'

'Any strangers called while I was away?' He wanted to hold her tight, remind himself how light and good her body felt.

'How bad is it?'

'An answer Angie, I need an answer. Yes or No?'

She slammed her hand on the banister. 'No,' she said, determined not to be treated as a child, not to be forever answering to Nick. Even though she hadn't allowed the woman claiming to represent a film location company into the house, she was damned if she'd tell him.

He broke a rule and moved up a stair. Instinctively Angie retreated, surrendering one for safety or insurance. She had a great thing about distance, physical and mental, she would never give, never actually come out of herself and reveal a weakness, an emotion. The glass was still in his hand, he wanted to take another pull, but that would give her another reason to despise him.

'Any callers you're not familiar with, you ring our emergency number, got that?'

When she laughed, Nick's pulse trebled.

'Do you understand?'

'Of course. Am I not permitted to make any decisions without the master of the house being present?'

Her righteousness annoyed him. 'Start packing.' He advanced and brushed past without looking at her. 'Now,' he called over his shoulder going into the bathroom, putting down the glass, running the shower.

'Not until you tell me what's going on?'

'Nothing's going on, it's just a precaution,' he shouted from inside the cubicle.

When he emerged draped in a towel Angie hadn't budged, waiting to resume, her fury yet to reach its peak.

'I've lost two officers and I haven't time to argue,' he warned her. He made for the bedroom and she followed cautiously behind.

'Lost how? At the airport? In the supermarket? Unaccounted for? Missing?' She asked outside the door.

'Lost as in dead,' said Nick, dressed in dark cords, blue shirt and sweater.

'Christ, what have you done?'

'Me?' Nick lifted his head from lacing his Oxford shoes to check if she was talking to him. 'I haven't done anything.'

The daylight had gone, and the upstairs corridor was all deep shadow. Down the walls, her unframed oils depicted abstract women with faces of purple and red. After she'd hung them, he'd asked for a clue, a preferred reading. She'd replied with a laugh that she was painting out her angst, her animus; and she'd done such a complete job that Tom would never pass them alone in the evening.

'Don't tell your folks there's a scare on, just say you need a break from me. That's always got you sympathy and a place to stay before. If you go to a hotel, pick one you know,' he explained, passing her on the way to the stairs.

'Don't be on your own if you can help it.'

'If I say no?'

'I can't guarantee your safety, I'm more or less suspended.'

'You're pathetic, know that?' she said, following him down the stairs.

'Course I am, that's what attracted you in the first place,' he called, deliberately banging about in the kitchen. Hung behind the dining table, receiving natural light from the French doors, the latest in a series of Angie's large-scale oils. This one he hadn't seen before, a colossal canvas of a naked, bleeding woman giving birth to a malformed infant. Must be denoting her latest layer of individuality decided Nick, collecting the keys to his car.

'Tell Guy you're going to have put back your exhibition,' Nick suggested, facing her.

'Guy has the exclusive rights to my work, and you're not in a position to tell me what to do.'

Maybe Guy had exclusive rights to her body too, he thought. 'I don't want anything to happen to you,' he said, in memory of something they once had, possibly shared.

She glanced at her watch then straightened her head, sighing. 'Really, that's very considerate of you Nick. Eleven years too late, but nice.'

She didn't even rate him enough to hate anymore; that special loathing and resentment they had so carefully nurtured the last few years had matured, acting as an invisible sibling that had managed to outlive Tom.

'If this place is so dangerous, are you going to stay?'

'I haven't decided,' he said, slipping the reserve cellphone into his pocket.

'Couldn't you have asked?'

'About what?'

'Taking the phone,' she said, scooping up the odds and ends, returning them to the base of the wicker hen.

'Do you mind?'

'You paid for it, a present to make up for one of your overdue trips if I remember. Have it.'

Accepting the offer, Nick thought it pointless trying to find anything else to say, nothing would justify his being there, his concern, so he left using his own phone to make two calls on his way out.

Six

The budget hotel was in Earls Court, a peeling scar in a Regency terrace of run-down bedsits around the corner from Philbeach Gardens. A hotel masquerading as an economy bed and breakfast, a sign in a window warned potential guests that it regrettably did not cater for families or pets. Drizzle soaked into its grey facade, spreading thin damp fingers over the grubby windows and large pools of rain gathered on its worn steps before running off onto the pavement.

The receptionist, a harsh woman with round sad eyes, dragged her gaze reluctantly from a magazine devoted to puzzles.

'What will it be dear?' she asked with an ironed smile as Nick entered.

Calling from a side office a heavy male voice intercepted her question, taking it upon himself the trouble of answering. 'Mr. Arrowsmith's expected, Glenda,' announced Freddy Easton.

Nick glimpsed him along with the hotel's archaic switchboard in a cluttered office behind Glenda. Easton wore a determined fixer's face and a blazer perpetually smeared by pipe ash. In his sixties, he limped from a shrapnel wound he boasted about when drunk. Nick could smell the tobacco on Easton's clothes from where he stood, as individual as a fingerprint; aromatic, a special blend of herbs mixed by a Bengali on Brick Lane.

'I'll walk you up, sir,' he offered gallantly.

'There's no need, Freddy, I'll find my own way.'

'He hasn't moved an inch. No one's been in either.'

Straightening his blazer as if to go on parade, Easton's watery eyes followed Nick as he turned the corner. Ireland? The Falklands? The first Gulf War? A trouble spot before that? Nick had forgotten where Easton had picked up his limp, pension and devotion to all matters of intelligence, allowing CO8 to use his hotel for meetings of an arm's-length nature.

The narrow stairway took Nick into a different world, its carpet as thin as paper, a fire extinguisher holding it in place at the landing's curve. Badly framed prints of Thames sailing barges were moored along the corridor and given half a chance they'd have upped anchor and never returned. Nick strode up four steps into an annex where fleur-de-lis wallpaper covered the bumps in a tight passage. The room was the sixth in a dull line of seven. Nick knocked once and walked right in.

'You Bensham?' asked Nick.

The little administrator's case officer, a young SIS officer nodded. Two chairs were pulled to attention before an electric fire, its one bar burning an inconsistent orange. Nick sidestepped the chairs, going instead to the window.

'Have a seat,' offered Nick, but Bensham refused to move, standing to attention in a square inflexible stance. For a terrible moment Nick feared Bensham was about to make a run for it, only for Bensham to sweep past him across the room to lay claim to a space of his own, the ends of his check scarf sucked outwards by the manoeuvre.

'I'm fine standing,' said Bensham. 'Really, I'm fine. I can't stay long.'

'I'll decide when you leave.'

With his solid fleshy build, his features had the appearance of a spoilt unhappy child. His fair hair had been cut fashionably short and his entire demeanour was set for self-defence. His square angular face carried a petulant assurance of his own ability; the arrogance never far from the surface in the suspicious eyes, the way his small mouth was twisted in a slight sneer.

'R5 interviewed you?' Nick asked.

'Tomorrow.'

'You going to tell them everything?'

'I don't understand?'

'The arrangements for the collection, the complete and utter disaster you organised.'

'Is this off the record?' Bensham demanded, his eyes narrowing in self-protection. 'I only agreed because Rossan said it would be.'

'No vision, no sound,' Nick told him. 'And it's Mr. Rossan to you.'

Completely unfazed, Bensham dug his hands deep into the pockets of his tailored overcoat. 'Viper was a complete nightmare,' he stated boldly, 'and there's no way I'm not taking the blame,' he concluded, his eyes waiting for agreement.

'You have no idea of the trouble I had, so behave,' Nick warned him, 'Sit. Tell me about Viper, and don't leave a thing out.'

Opting for a corner of the bed rather than a chair, Bensham pushed back his coat and let out an expansive sigh. 'After I'd got a Box 1 on completion of my training, I was assigned to Cent/East Europe,' he began as though rehearsing for an interview. 'I did ten months on various desks coordinating targets of primary interest requests, then I went on the floater list and got a Moscow slot with Viper attached.'

'Your big break.'

'Came sooner than I anticipated,' Bensham said, a stranger to modesty.

'How long were you his case officer?'

'Twelve months.'

'Viper your first asset?'

'Have to start somewhere.'

'And you were given a main product line.'

'That's what they said in RUS/OPS, but I guess I was just lucky. In the right place at the right time when the opening came up. Maternity cover, immediate start. Viper's handler was returning early, complications with the pregnancy.'

From quite a different meeting in quite different circumstances, Nick heard Rossan's recommendation of Sally Wynn: *...first rate experience, but she's had eighteen months maternity, so it might take a while to readjust...*

'You and Viper hit it off straight away?' he asked, furious at RUS/OPS' decision to pawn Lubov out to this twenty-something novice.

'Hardly,' he answered with a sarcastic smile. 'Viper was old school, one dog one master mentality. When I inherited him, he didn't like it, played up, sulked at me taking over the reins. But I'd been warned Viper was high maintenance.'

'Who supplied the advice?'

'Wynn at her pre-departure briefing, but I had my own game plan. New broom, new rules.'

'Any other challenges Viper presented?'

'Someone in RUS/OPS mentioned he didn't respond to pressure. I can't remember who.' Nor did he care, if his sneer was anything to go by.

When Nick failed to press him, Bensham took up his discourse once more. 'If Viper didn't get the attention he thought he deserved, he'd have a tantrum. Lecture me how lucky I was to have him, how he would be the making of my career. But he was a pretty easy read. Unstable, a volatile loner who hated his wife, his work, even himself, which meant it wouldn't take a lot to push him over the edge.'

'How close to the edge?'

'He'd stepped off but hadn't realised he was falling.'

'But he still delivered all the same?'

'RUS/OPS never pulled me up about the quality,' Bensham declared.

'If everything was running so smoothly,' Nick objected, 'at least from your side of the table, why arrange a collection?'

'He'd begun playing up,' Bensham revealed, unable to hide his hostility.

'How?'

'The product started to drop-off, then fell to a trickle.'

'When was this?'

'At the beginning of June. Delivered minor stuff, opinion summaries, nothing I couldn't have obtained from open sources,' he volunteered guardedly.

'As a diligent case officer,' Nick proposed, 'I'm sure you would have put it to Viper that if he could access *minor stuff*, why not his usual sought after take?'

'Presumed he was feeding the mill with scraps to justify his payments.'

'But you didn't verify?'

'Why should I, we weren't exactly getting along.'

'How long did this last?'

'Up until the collection,' Bensham admitted. 'I reduced contact and appraised RUS/OPS.'

'They were content with the arrangement?'

'Not a lot they could do,' he asserted. In Bensham's considered opinion, Viper was trying it on, playing the diva, demanding more attention. 'It didn't surprise me. He was unpredictable from day one, and if I'm honest, slightly unhinged as a bonus. I even went as far as proposing to RUS/OPS that it might be an idea to cut Viper loose for a while, let him realise he wasn't going to get his own way. After all, he'd virtually dried, wasn't supplying anything of any value, so I thought it might be expedient to let him have some tough love.'

'That was very astute of you. How did RUS/OPS respond?'

'Not very receptive. Viper hadn't fully adjusted, give him more time, the relationship would benefit from fine tuning, all the usual pandering for a five-star asset. But I made sure that it was going to be up to him who did the adapting, not me. I had to bring him on message first, so to speak.'

'With all your considerable experience, he must have been thankful you were looking after his interests.'

Rejecting any censure, he glared hard at Nick. 'He shouldn't have strung me along, should he,' Bensham whined, forever the victim.

'Strung along how?'

'Constantly giving me excuses,' Bensham declared petulantly. 'Expecting me to swallow his reason for the fall in product.'

'Which was?'

'A counter-intelligence sweep. He'd become jittery, on edge, surly. Wouldn't give any more insight. I thought he'd cut down on anything of merit to get himself a new case officer,' Bensham revealed with absolute conviction.

Only the little administrator must have sensed imminent danger, if not outright discovery and closed down the supply line as a precaution, as an attempt to save his life, Nick reasoned. 'You didn't believe him about a counter-intelligence operation?'

'Not really.'

'You took over when?'

Sensing an underhand motive behind Nick's question, Bensham took his time before replying: 'November.'

'And up until June he'd never hinted at a tightening of security?'

'No,' Bensham said with extreme caution.

'And this counter-intelligence sweep was general or specific?'

'General to start with,' admitted Bensham his conviction beginning to ebb. 'Then it became focused.'

'Explain?'

'He kept insisting the counter-intelligence hounds were closing in. They'd sniffed their way through two sections in his department, started on a third, and then it would be Viper's turn as boss man. It was just standard housekeeping, giving the hounds some exercise, I suggested. Wouldn't have it. He drove me crazy, pointed out over and over, the only sections to be given the treatment were those he had direct access to. At that point I'd had enough, seriously enough.'

'You passed on Viper's concerns to RUS/OPS?'

'Did I hell,' Bensham said, his decision justified with a generous smile. 'He had absolutely no chance I'd inform them my asset is such a delusional wreck, he's pointing the finger in your direction and screaming betrayal.'

'Is that what he did? He accused someone in RUS/OPS of betraying him?'

'Not in so many words.'

'Well what words *did* he use?'

Deflated, corralled into a dead-end, Bensham stared hopelessly up at Nick. He reflected for a moment before introducing the key evidence on his own behalf.

'Viper wanted out and guaranteed access to an ex-senior officer. No one except our most recent ex-Chief. He kept ranting about how I couldn't trust London. I'd have to open a new route, a clean channel to prepare for him bailing out and to handle all contact. He'd worked it all out. Wynn would be the cut-out and anyone she nominated could be relied on.'

'And how did you respond?' Nick pressed. 'You're caught in a dilemma, either you believe Viper, or you face the risk of condemning him, losing a primary asset.'

Switching his attention to his hands, Bensham created a lattice with his fingers, industriously examining each nail. 'I discreetly asked someone I could rely on in RUS/OPS to contact Wynn,' he admitted.

'Who?'

'Jo Lister. Spun it as a favour, no need to record it, but I really needed to get hold of Wynn for a steer on a prospect she'd kindly added to the basket but never taken to the checkout.'

'How did Wynn respond?'

'Stunned, wanted all the details, she was concerned how Viper was holding up,' he said, and for the first time appeared contrite. 'Assured me she'd see what she could do.'

'And you didn't have contact with her again?'

'Nothing. Either Viper had his clean channel, or we were back at square one.'

'Which was it?'

'As far as I was concerned, we hadn't made any progress.'

'In the weeks prior to the collection, the dynamic changed?' Nick asked, and not for the first time detected a sulky frown crease Bensham's brow.

Looking as though he would prefer anything but a clear conscience, Bensham looked up at Nick as if he didn't fully comprehend. 'Viper requested a crash meeting at the end of September,' he admitted. 'Presumed he'd seen the light. Seemed Wynn couldn't arrange the clean channel, and he'd woken up to the fact it was me or one way or another, he'd be shelved.'

'How did he seem? Better? Worse? All forgiven and back to normal?'

'Not exactly. His paranoia was still neatly wrapped and tied up in a conspiracy at our end,' Bensham flared in open revolt, his frustration getting the better of him. 'He complained that things were not moving fast enough. The counter-intelligence heavies were closing in, they were interrogating everybody in his department again.'

'Did you believe him?'

'Honestly, I didn't know what I believed,' Bensham confessed. 'He was in a state. He'd been due to audit a GRU outstation in Hamburg, but the trip was pulled at the last minute. Maybe it was a coincidence, maybe it was fantasy, I just couldn't decide. Viper told me everything had been planned for him to desert in Hamburg, but that was now a non-starter. Said it was my responsibility to make fresh arrangements, but I had to be discreet, I had to liaise through the ex-Chief. There was no way that was going to happen until he'd convinced me.'

'How did Viper react? Nick demanded.

'He wasn't best pleased,' Bensham sourly admitted. 'Blew a gasket, his top, blew nearly everything. Told me I didn't understand the danger he was in. If he didn't have immediate assistance, an exit arranged, it would be my fault and I was going to jeopardise and wreck years of work. We had a bit of a full-on row. I told him this was his last chance to impress me, he wasn't even close to getting a ticket anywhere. He'd better put up or shut up. I told him he needed to provide evidence, something to support his case.'

'That must have reassured him,' Nick cruelly observed. 'And Viper finally brought you proof, didn't he?'

From Bensham's reluctance to answer, Nick guessed he must have done a lot more than that.

'I didn't realise he was so serious.' Setting off down the room, Bensham needed someone or something to blame.

'Deadly serious,' Nick retorted, avoiding Bensham's difficulty. 'What did he bring?'

Bensham's bravado deserted him and Nick told him to take his time. By Nick's side, a lace curtain was strung across the window. Yellow with age it smelt of stale dust, a dead moth trapped in the tapestry had shed its wings like petals. A mobile advertising truck crawled by promoting a new brand of room freshener, a distorted Greensleeves belting from its speakers into the miserable day. Turning from the window Nick heard the tune still ringing on, hollow notes with nowhere to go.

'He told me he had uncovered the beginning of the deceit, but I was making him deliver too early, the risk was too great,' Bensham admitted at last. Expecting some form of reprieve, he turned sulkily away as Nick merely nodded as though the point wasn't that important after all.

'Did he explain what deceit?'

'He went on about it having a connection in London, and I thought he'd finally lost it, he's absolutely raving mad.'

'What did he mean by that?' asked Nick, his temper rising.

'I thought he was pumping up the value of his pitch, force my hand in arranging his exit,' said Bensham, tugging his scarf this way and that along his bullish neck, aiming for a point of equilibrium.

'He gave no other indication what he meant?' Nick's voice had become so low, so compressed, that to those who knew him they'd consider it dangerous.

'He said he could prove the deceit was operational,' Bensham said, jamming himself into a corner of the room. 'Look, none of it made any sense, it just sounded desperate. I panicked, made a stupid decision, okay.'

'Viper *was* desperate,' fumed Nick, 'and *okay* doesn't begin to cover what you did or didn't do,' he added, blocking Bensham's escape from the corner.

Perhaps resenting Nick's intensity, the youthful tucks around Bensham's mouth darkened, and his assurance deserted him once and for all, a dire spoiled face claiming its place. Finally, the novice intelligence officer reviewed his options with the sort of cold logic that they had drummed into him at Aspley during his initial training. 'I warned Viper that a hazy concept wasn't going to be enough. I needed additional material before I was going to stir up a ton of shit by approaching the ex-Chief,' he confessed, visibly relaxing as Nick stepped away. 'Viper wasn't for sharing, but he realised it really was time to put some goods on the stall,' he explained, his voice featureless. 'And that's when he gave me this crazy look, insisting I don't share with anyone but the senior officer. "Tell him the Oktober Projekt is active, it is the deceit, and it is more. Tell him I have discovered its purpose. Tell him it requires secrets and it protects secrets." He was manic, I really thought he was so unhinged he was going to turn me in.'

'Who did you tell?'

'Not directly, not officially. I spoke with Jo, watered it down, kept it vague, sold it as the Oktober Projekt is active and nothing more. Asked her to make some discreet checks if it actually meant anything.'

'What else?' Nick demanded, reading the vacillation register in Bensham's soft eyes.

'I was on the back foot' he protested, and receiving no quarter from Nick, glanced sharply away. 'I mentioned to Jo that Viper might be having a meltdown. He was suffering from a rabid dose of seeing monsters in his wardrobe, and it might be worth anticipating that we'd need a Get Out Of Jail card.'

'Monsters in his wardrobe being the trigger alert for Viper coming under the spotlight?'

Reluctantly nodding an affirmation, Bensham continued: 'Jo promised she wouldn't action anything until I decided there wasn't another option.'

The scale of Bensham's disclosure sent him pacing around the room once more. Catching his reflection in a cracked Tower of London souvenir mirror, Bensham scowled at the memory of being responsible for Viper's downfall.

'What happened?'

'The sky fell on me. Total and utter destructive fucking by the head of RUS/OPS,' Bensham admitted. 'I was told to back off, it would be handled. I had to coordinate the pickup of Oktober Projekt sample material for immediate analysis, my involvement over. Viper supplied the address, the date, the timing. RUS/OPS asked for a location report on possible risks, the good, bad and ugly. I managed one pass on foot in daylight. If they hadn't boxed us in, I'd have got another pass in at night.'

'Boxed in?'

'The Embassy. The Russians ramped up security, uniformed and plain clothes and they made sure we knew about it. Circle of steel, and once you got through that, they'd brought in extra surveillance teams, and they weren't shy. Forget dry cleaning your back by running a surveillance detection route, it would have taken a week. Viper couldn't even have got close to use a burst transmission device, even if he had one. But he wouldn't go near them, had no confidence in an electronic harvest. I fed it all back, including my detailed overview of the area, Viper's behaviour, proposed a medium to high-risk evaluation. Jo acknowledged, and that was followed by the advisory to stand down, a decision on extraction would follow. I guess that's why they sent you.'

'That's why they sent me,' Nick agreed, realising that Lubov was already a marked man before he and Foula even reached Moscow because Bensham had condemned the little administrator to death. Lubov must have suspected as much when his attempt to flee via Hamburg was blocked, so Lubov did what anybody would do; he tried to save himself, he made sure that his evidence went on ahead of him, sent in advance for his arrival in London.

'Viper really was my one chance at the big time,' Bensham decided forlornly. 'I'm still not sure which bit made sense and which bit was fantasy.'

At that precise moment Nick didn't know either. 'When R5 interview you, you'd save yourself a lot of trouble, if you give them the Oktober Projekt lite version,' he suggested.

Unconvinced by Nick's assurance, Bensham shook his head. 'I'm sorry,' he mumbled, fastening the buttons on his coat.

'You should be,' Nick answered as Bensham sloped off through the door.

Turning off the electric fire, Nick made his way down to reception, avoiding Easton's attempts at anything close to a conversation.

At the newsagents across the street a customer was accusing the assistant of short-changing him, their bitter feud hanging in the musty air. Nick bought a bar of chocolate between accusations; lingering in the doorway, spinning a wire rack of postcards crisp and brown from a forgotten sun, he watched a Service van drop off a team of two R5 Regulators. A check along both sides of the street from the hotel steps and the Regulators swept inside. Bensham has tried to cut a deal and save his own neck by giving them mine he thought; or Hawick has had me listed as wanted, a handsome bounty to be claimed, and even Freddy had to make ends meet. This is still their territory Nick reasoned. Their lies, their denials; these are the contours on the map. Striding smartly away from the newsagents Nick took a call on his phone.

• • •

Nick came out of the Tube at London Bridge station, and by Battle Bridge Lane he already had a scent of the river. The Thames was ebbing, and its mud reeked of salt and diesel. Around him he saw a river robbed of its soul, its warehouses gentrified, squeezed between utilitarian office blocks and apartments. The warehouses had been built to store exotic goods and had somehow survived the best intentions of the Luftwaffe during the Blitz, but they had succumbed to the developers and now stored people instead. Calling it Docklands was the supreme irony, he decided pressing on. And for once he played the good tourist, queuing to pay his entry fee to board H.M.S. *Belfast* on a grey freezing afternoon, complete with a small blue backpack on his shoulder, bought from a branch of Blacks in Kensington. Ambling round the upper deck, Nick selected a position on the starboard rail by the bow turrets. A handful of tourists strolled by venturing up to the bow. Towards the stern, a school party loud and boisterous intent on mutiny, and Nick prayed they weren't heading his way. Turning his back on the river, Nick watched Rossan pelt up the gangway as though the ship was about to sail without him.

'What on God's good earth are you playing at?' panted Rossan, pulling up at Nick's side, catching his breath.

'Getting some facts straightened out.'

'Bloody Bensham is threatening to scream blue murder, the cretin. You didn't strike him, Nick?' demanded Rossan, 'nothing physical occurred did it?'

'He provided me with background on Viper.'

'Have you forgotten you're suspended?' he raged.

'Just tying up a few loose ends in my own time.'

'Well make sure they're tied up pronto,' said Rossan, meshing his fingers together, forcing his leather gloves onto his fingers. Warily looking round, he inched closer. 'I'm risking a hell of a lot by being here. You're officially classed as dodgy currency, a contaminated entity.'

'Better make sure you've had all your jabs, Paul, don't know what you may catch off me.'

'Early retirement for a start,' Rossan said with feeling.

'What was Wynn doing freelancing?'

A party of Japanese in clear plastic rain capes scurried through the first wave of drizzle, clanking down below to the mess decks.

Rossan bided his time until they'd passed.

'It certainly wasn't for me. No one is admitting anything, and no one is telling, so forget it.'

'Someone sent her to Hamburg?'

'Let's walk,' suggested Rossan, touching Nick's arm, coaxing him away from the starboard rail. 'You're a friend and a valued senior officer, Nick,' he said, concern in his clear eyes. 'You and I both know that Moscow is now counted highly, a strategic partner in more ways than it used to be because of its perceived value in preventing terrorist attacks.'

'Sally Wynn had twin boys for Christ's sake, Paul. I'm not prepared to let this go.'

'I didn't say you should, but there are factions who wouldn't mind if you were thrown out on your ear, door slammed, thank you and bugger off.'

'Who knew about the collection apart from Parfrey?'

They'd stopped at the stern and Rossan gripped the rail looking towards Tower Bridge, his arms straight and locked tight.

'The usual suspects probably,' Rossan said slowly, 'any out of the box operations on Central and Eastern European soil are cleared by myself, Teddy, Roly and Jane. If it involves close friends or poses a high risk, C is approached for an overview.'

'No one else? No associates?' Nick asked, setting off without warning, Rossan having to hurry to catch up.

'Not to my knowledge,' Rossan said.

'Well someone uninvited came to the party,' said Nick. 'What about the Vapour Trail Group?'

'Damn it, Nick how do you know about that?' Rossan demanded. 'Your name never appeared on the induction list.'

'I know of its existence, Paul. What is it?'

'A preview and pre-circulation assessment group.'

'Primarily dealing with Viper's product?'

'Yes, damn it,' Rossan hissed. 'And one other product line. If you are thinking of asking me about the members, don't.'

'Who are they?'

'For God's sake, Nick,' Rossan protested, drawing up sharply.

'If it's blown, it's not going to make any difference,' Nick persisted.

Glancing off down river as if checking for a sight of land, Rossan shook his head. 'Parfrey as chair, Lister from RUS/OPS, Morgan fielding for the MoD, Holcombe the JIC's beadle and Dowling head FO sceptic. That is the substantive quorum. Other attendees if, and only when the product lines entered their latitude.'

'Roly?'

'Occasionally.'

'Jane?'

'Ditto.'

'You?'

'Yes, Nick, I attended on a few occasions.'

'Would its scope run to sanctioning the collection?'

'No. No, it damn well wouldn't,' Rossan fiercely corrected him. 'Facilitation of distribution, corroboration of product overlap, perhaps a received opinion on Viper's status, his safety... yes. The mandate to authorise the collection? No, never. That decision would have been arrived at following a risk evaluation undertaken by RUS/OPS. And, *no*, I wasn't included, the school had called, the eldest had come a cropper against the buttress playing Fives and gashed her head. Pretty nasty, pretty deep. The school advised that Rebecca and I attend. Satisfied?'

'Do I look satisfied?' Nick answered, setting the pace again, reflecting on where Foula gained his impression the Vapour Trail Group had consented to the operation.

'And Viper? How did we persuade him to cross the street? Did he volunteer? Did we apply heat?'

'Jamie Hayles brought him in, and that is your absolute limit. I am not disposed to go further than that.'

Braving the rain on a second slow tour of their own making, they passed under the barrels of the forecastle's six-inch guns.

'Look, Nick, you've spent so much time on the road recently that you're out of the loop as far as new allegiances on the eighth floor go,' Rossan disclosed with a bitter smile. 'Teddy is still nursing his ego after the appointment of our new Chief seriously derailed his ambitions. He didn't see it coming and makes no secret his role of Deputy Chief is compensation, a move sideways. Nick, for once listen. Teddy's always been an intriguer since he was thrust on us from King Charles Street. His fealty is to whoever he believes will strengthen his power base and that remains with the Foreign Office. Do not give him cause for excluding you permanently. I sincerely hope that you're going to stay out of town for the foreseeable future, or until you've had your review Board. Listen to me,' urged Rossan, gripping Nick's wrist. 'Teddy is a slick political act who finds darling Jane his new best friend and flavour of the month. He has willingly become C's doer of dirty deeds, and Roly and

I are simply tolerated and suffered in silence.'

'How far do we go back Paul?'

'A way and some more.'

Looking over to the boarding kiosk on the embankment, Nick noticed a lone figure patrolling forlornly backwards and forwards.

'That why you brought along a babysitter?' Nick nodded to Rossan's minder.

Rossan didn't immediately reply but seemed to be searching for the right answer to satisfy each of them. 'It's better for both of us this way,' said Rossan, his voice and his eyes unable to disguise his embarrassment.

'This pre-circulation assessment group,' Nick began. 'Paul hear me out,' he insisted when Rossan raised his hand in open revolt. 'How would it receive Viper's product line?'

'Exclusive preview format,' Rossan snapped back. 'If you're implying Viper's identity could be deducted from the actual source material, the answer is no, it couldn't. The raw take would be filtered, redacted and presented as a CX overview, topicality preserved, but as a guidance summary for principal areas of interest requested by our customers.'

'And the other thing?'

'I will suffer a lifetime of pain and torment if you disclose where you got this,' Rossan tetchily declared, his voice low and urgent, passing Nick a plain A4 buff envelope.

Nick tore back the gummed flap, glancing inside at a number of sheets; the incident report compiled by CO8's duty officer on the night of the collection. Nestling in the bottom, three worknames; three different identities never activated, three different lives, all of them accompanied by the relevant credentials bearing photographs of Nick with sullen expressions.

'If I am assisting you in carrying out unsanctioned activities, I don't want to know,' Rossan stressed, looking decidedly uncomfortable.

Slipping the package into his backpack Nick nodded his thanks. 'The timing of the collection was leaked. I don't know if it was deliberate, or just a stupid mistake, but they were waiting for us,' Nick disclosed, laying down his first marker on the trail.

'Damn it, Nick, if you go down that route you risk everything,' said Rossan in a temper. 'This is as far as I go.' Rossan added, 'from here on in, you walk by yourself. We haven't met, we haven't discussed a thing, we haven't even said hello.'

'I owe you.'

'You bloody do,' Rossan said, softly patting Nick's arm. 'Oh, by the way, Jane wants to see you, usual place, usual time.'

'Take care Paul.'

Halfway down the deck Rossan turned but didn't wave, seeming to Nick that his old friend was taking a last look at him, fixing this moment into his mind.

Seven

Nick arrived home after eleven that evening and the milk bottles were already out; four in a neat line that he almost kicked over. Angie had obviously ignored his warning and remained obstinately at home and Nick felt their separation was complete, two lives divided by their own needs and rituals. What could be more natural than a secret life here as well, he thought. We could arrange to avoid each other through the Dairy Crest milkman; skimmed, semi-skimmed, silver and organic, the Torr code for complete separation would never be broken. He'd eaten and waited for Jane at the Cittie of Yorke in Holborn, but she never turned up and after making a couple of pints last almost an hour, he'd written her off, not for the first time, and left.

The house was dark, an after-smell of casserole pressed into the warm air. In the kitchen he opened the fridge, finding a pack of Asahi Super Dry Beer taking up a shelf, the pack short by two bottles. Angie preferring not to dine alone but invite a mystery guest. And has this guest advised Angie to ignore my warning? he wondered pouring a very large whisky, feeling detached, an intruder.

Crossing the kitchen, he turned a lamp on in the alcove, light swimming out in a warm wave across the table. Two dirty plates, two pudding bowls, two spent bottles of wine – red and white – two Asahi bottles, also empty. So, what was the hurry Angie that stopped you clearing away? Amidst the remains of a dinner for two, a photographic timeline of Tom set out in uneven columns along the table. Nick tried to work out why Angie was reawakening the past?

Wanting an answer, Nick swung out into the dark hall. One stair, two climbed, drinking as he went, past Angie's barrier up to a smaller staircase and the second floor. Tom's room had become Angie's untouched shrine to their dead son; its door was slightly open, a spacecraft flight deck painted full size on the panels. Nick hadn't ventured in here for months and he pushed the door open, one hinge needed oiling he remembered too late. Everything untouched, a family memorial that reminded Nick how it had once been the centre of his life. The room still and sad, one vital ingredient would always be missing; pine bed and sleeping boy, a clown night light and serene breaths, unexpected joy.

He took a final glance and closed the door. He'd have given anything to hold Tom, apologise for ever raising his voice, showing his temper, his impatience, his annoyance. He felt every molecule of Tom flowing through him, a continuum between father and son; love, hope, joy, the promise of the future and Nick didn't want the responsibility for breaking the link.

His mind charged with burning memories, he raked back his head draining the whisky not noticing a large ceramic dish. Kicking it sideways it delivered its load of polished pebbles through the banister spindles, thumping on down the stairs. A dash of light hit the landing below and Nick sensed a figure waiting by his bedroom door. An explanation would be demanded, he'd apologise of course. Maybe he'd even get one of Angie's tearful polemics that he he'd never been able to find an answer for.

He abandoned his glass where the dish used to sit, rehearsing his excuse for trespassing into Tom's room, made his way down, and came face to face with Angie's lover. Standing in an oblong of light spilling from the main bedroom, Guy stood firm; naked except for boxer shorts and a hockey stick Angie kept by the bed for when Nick was away. The stick grasped firm, ready to take a strike.

'It's okay, Guy, he belongs to me,' Angie said standing in the doorway, dressed hurriedly in a baggy creased white T-shirt and black Agent Provocateur knickers.

'Thanks for the vote of confidence,' Nick responded. She feels no guilt, no remorse and no shame, he thought, but she never had, remembering the damage she inflicted when she stole him from her twin sister Alison. 'I think we need to talk. If you've got a spare minute.'

'Nick, not now, for God's sake,' sighed Angie.

'You'd better leave,' Guy decided, weighing the hockey stick in both hands with menace.

'Don't,' urged Angie coming to Guy's side.

But Angie's supplication was too little, and far too late. Seized by a rush of folly enjoyed by lovers, Guy pitched the hockey stick shoulder high in a two-handed grip. One moment he was standing, legs braced to swing, the next, Nick had disarmed him.

Though Nick swore he only went for the stick. he must have also had a piece of Guy; because after Angie screamed for him to stop, had slapped his face, Nick had Guy's arm bent in a nasty lock behind his back, ordering him to grab his clothes. Everything then moved at speed. With his shirt, jacket, trousers, shoes and socks in a bundle clasped to his chest, Nick ran Guy down the stairs taking the treads two at a time.

With Angie screaming 'bastard' all the way to the front door, Nick heaved her lover out onto the garden path kicking the door closed after him.

'We're finished,' yelled Angie as Nick came through the hall, adopting her usual defensive position on the stairs.

'I didn't know we'd even started,' shouted Nick going down to the kitchen, pouring a whisky, neat.

'You'd better leave,' she demanded from halfway up the stairs as Nick returned, placed a foot on the first tread as a sign of intent, though he wasn't ready to advance.

He drank greedily going for half the glass but couldn't swallow fast enough. To stop himself choking he closed his eyes. When he opened them, Angie was gone. So was the light. Drifting from the bathroom, he heard the shower's wet rays and the loud blast of a radio. A portable battery one she toted everywhere and used effectively to obliterate him from another of her senses. Up in the bedroom Nick turned on his bedside light, puncturing the darkness with a savage click. He viewed the room as though it bore the evidence from a scene of crime. The bed still held their imprint, fresh sheets ruffled and creased he noted, avoiding going near it, preferring a chair on his side of the bed. Though how many others could make that claim of avoiding Angie in that bed he couldn't decide. Silence from the radio marked Angie's return, walking straight in, naked. Too much wine Angie, too many dinners with Guy he decided, watching pouches of flab bounce at the top of her legs.

'I'm going to see a solicitor, on Monday,' she announced curtly, watching him with her sly eyes. Nakedness had never troubled her; she was as natural in any state and believed inhibitions were for the stupid and ugly. Another of her cannibalised beliefs she'd acquired at the Slade. What was the other?

Love is an unattainable state, sex is a base desire. He stared at her face deliberately avoiding her body.

'Great,' he said, realising that she actually wanted to make him feel inadequate, perhaps even crave what he couldn't have again. She shrugged and he couldn't help glimpsing the movement in her breasts.

Pulling on a clean T-shirt and knickers, she sat at her dressing table. She'd more pots of cream and lotions than an alchemist, he decided, watching her apply barriers to prevent wrinkles and lotions to dam the onset of middle age. Anger in one big icy hand slid over his intestines, squeezing, releasing, squeezing again; funnelling shock into the pit of his stomach. This, after all the years of trying, was finally the end. Blowing his hair off his hot forehead, Nick shook away the icy fingers. This then the end of a life not lived for cover, but his own life written off; discarded like a blown workname and this realisation sent his whole system plummeting on a continuous free-fall.

'I'll move out for a while,' he offered as she slipped between the sheets

No movement from Angie's side of the bed, her new total exclusion zone and Nick's eyes roved onto the curtains, picking out faces rising from the coloured swirls and blocks of print; demons, monsters and screaming mouths all sniggering, taunting him.

'Good, because it's over. You, me, this house, we've reached the end of the road,' Angie said dully. 'Just go, now, right now, we've nothing more to say.'

Instead he took a shower, the spray too hot, too cold; another tradesman Angie would have to hire to rectify the house's little misdemeanours. After re-strapping his ribs from the first-aid kit, and a change of clothes, he pulled down an overnight bag from the top of the wardrobe cramming in a few warm shirts, trousers, socks and underwear. If she wanted the house, she could have it. Downstairs he started throwing her symphonies and concertos to one side. A sudden rush of fury at her wilful rejection at reconciliation overloaded Nick's circuits, shorting his fuse. He rummaged through his CDs. Led Zeppelin, Pink Floyd, The Beatles, Hendrix, Roxy Music, Bowie, Brubeck were added to the bag; albums for the life lived, albums for the life ahead. By the telephone, a pad they used for passing on messages. Ripping out the numbers from a page she had titled *His Calls*, Nick skimmed the numbers and saw one of his missed calls attributed by Angie to 'The Bitch', his wife's shorthand for Jane Stratton.

Switching off the lights Nick grabbed his bag and banged the door behind him, the lion's head knocker rattling for all it was worth. On the street Nick made a visual sweep, left and right; his face tinted a pale orange from the street lamps before striding off for his car. Another of my funny habits Angie, the ones you always complained made us look ridiculous, though you wouldn't know how many times they might have saved your life. Same for the agents I had to run he recounted climbing into his Audi. Grubs out of the woodwork, that was what Angie used to call them. It's something she wouldn't understand, she'd never tried, never made the effort. This leaves us where exactly? he asked himself; two isolated lives that we'd tried to live as one, but it didn't take long for Angie to see through the charade, Nick decided and one day Angie, you're going to have to admit the truth, we hated ourselves and each other for not being able to love. He started the car and drove off at speed.

•••

Nick made the drive to Devon in just over four hours, reaching the remote detached cottage before four in the morning. Locking the Audi, hoisting his bag onto his shoulder a blast of sea air whipped his tiredness away, rising up over the cliff less than half a mile away. To stand in the darkness was a relief, as though an old friend had been anxiously waiting to greet him. This spot more than London was where he considered home, his nearest neighbours a row of ex-coastguard cottages used as holiday lets a quarter of mile further along the cliff, a small village for provisions lying a mile behind inland.

Both keys turned with effort and the swollen door, sticking in its frame as usual, required a brutal push from Nick's shoulder to swing it open. Cold damp air streamed around him and Nick began his usual ritual of acclimatisation. On a shelf inside the porch an oil lamp crackled and hissed as he lit it, his only means of illumination until he'd turned on the power. No gas and no telephone, no modern design fads and whims; this is how he wanted it, basic just like him. Inherited from his mother, the cottage was his hideaway; a jealously guarded retreat where he rarely invited anyone, much to Angie's disgust. She saw the place as a chance to impress, pleading with Nick to let her modernise it, redesign it, but he always refused. In summer he'd have all the sash windows open, the breeze carrying in the smell of sea, the fields, and a heady aroma of stock. In the evening, depending on the weather, the incense of wood smoke drifted in.

Opening the inner door to let the light follow him in, he felt the exhaustion rise through him like a fever. Dragging himself into the main room, Nick sat wearily down at a deal table set before the window, clutching a mug and bottle of Laphroaig. Outside, the dawn came with a rush, folding the light into the sea forming a damp November day starved by the cold. Between long pulls of Laphroaig, Nick rang Paul Rossan on his cellphone, the signal low, patchy, but sufficient. The call finished, he lit a cigarette and stared at the sea; dark and still, patches of soft morning light heaving and falling with the swell.

Having barely slept, the morning came as a relief and Nick had pulled on his jacket, setting off for a walk in a filthy mood, marching along the coastal path for about a mile before the weather finally broke. Ephemeral flecks of snow were flying in the air and the temperature must have been at least minus three with the wind chill, already his feet felt numb. He blew into his hands as the horizon darkened; either more snow or a storm was approaching, either one would be the only excuse he needed to turn around.

An icy gust whipped powdered snow against his face and Nick looked up with a frown when he heard his name being called. Jane stood at a curve in the path a hundred yards ahead of him, her hair mauled by the wind.

'They sent you to write me off?' he said, an uneasy edge to his voice.

'You know I'd never do that.' She held out her hand for him, taking his weight as he climbed over a wooden fence edging in a narrow steep path snaking down to a coastguard post perched on the tip of a cliff.

'How are things at the office?' he asked, jumping down.

'We're good,' she said. 'The damage assessment is underway, operational review, learn from our mistakes. If there's anything you can think of that will give us a steer, it would make a difference, obviously.'

'Obviously.'

'This a welfare check or part of the review? That *is* why you're here?'

'Not much patience for anyone right now, have you?' She linked his arm, letting him lead. And for the first time in this strange light, she could also see what a gruelling time he'd had in Moscow; as though part of the Nick she knew and once loved had never made it home.

'I'll recover.'

'Want to tell me about it?'

'Another time.'

'Sure.'

Below them the sea crashed into the rocks and gullies determined to go further inland. They must have walked three hundred yards before he turned to see if they were alone, Henchard keeping an appointment with his Lucetta. He lit a cigarette cupping his hands against the thickening snow.

'Teddy isn't going to back off?' Jane said, an infected edge to her voice.

'And what's required in return?' From her narrow frown he knew he was going too far, risking never finding what Lubov claimed to be so precious; unable to repay the deaths he'd been made responsible for.

'A little bit of faith,' she snapped, walking on, pulling up the collar of her thick coat as a screaming wind lifted a cloud of snow, whisking it over the headland in a fine spray.

'I'm right out of faith at the moment, can't say when the new supplies will be coming in.'

'I'll take a chance,' she said.

'Long wait, wouldn't recommend it.'

'I don't care.'

'How's Parfrey taking the fallout?'

'Surviving, and she sends her greetings.'

'Does she?' he replied, not sharing her mood.

Motoring in towards the coast a fishing boat ran for shelter, its shape lost against the dark sky, a small green starboard lamp fading and gleaming on its mast.

'So, what do you propose to do?' She couldn't bear to look at him, his face had the waxy tint of a victim, someone who'd given up, didn't care.

'Stay low, watch my back.'

'Good, you do that.'

'That your professional opinion?' His voice dipped, low and drained.

'You sure you can rely on me?' she huffed.

'I used to think I could, in the past.'

'You're not in a very forgiving mood, Nick.'

'I'm not the forgiving sort.'

Her face had a disquieting beauty to it as it fastened on him, half in tenderness, half in reproach; a disenchanted lover's glare probing the stubborn defences. In the turbulent stormy light, she looked younger, intense and annoyingly desirable.

'Maybe you should cooperate. Let me, Roly, Paul and Teddy handle it.'

Like a wounded animal he fought back. 'Is that what they asked you to offer?'

'No. And I haven't given up on you,' she said, rebuffing a stray thought of why she almost became his wife.

The coastguard hut loomed up at the end of the path, its whitewashed perimeter wall a cool grey in the damp light. They drifted in and sheltered from the wind and snow. Sitting close together on the same step they could have been survivors from a wreck. She raked her hair with her fingers; don't look at me, don't see how I've given away my concern, inside she wanted to scream. Tridents of lightening cut into the waves and the snow gave way to hailstones that peppered their legs.

'You think I'm here on C's orders?'

Looking deep into her eyes, Nick wondered how much he could trust anyone ever again? He grabbed a pebble and hurled it over the low wall. 'Are you?'

'I thought you knew me better than that,' she said, her head slightly turned as she gazed out into the heart of the bay, resting her chin on her arched knees as the hailstones stopped.

'I did, but now you're just a good friend.'

Shrugging her shoulders, Jane drew away from him. 'Don't push it, Nick.'

Sitting there with the sea grinding on the shale far below, he realised that Angie threatening to divorce him was another hole punched into the fabric of his life. When they told Nick his mother had died, committed suicide, he blamed his father, hated the sea with a bitterness that lasted months. He just didn't understand that empty hunger in his stomach, the unfairness of it all. It was as if someone had stolen the sun.

'Time we headed back,' Nick decided, hauling Jane to her feet.

When they reached the cottage, it was if they'd returned as strangers, not friends.

'How did you know where to find me?' he asked from inside his defences, his manner abrupt.

'Angie.'

'Did she tell you she'd thrown me out?'

'No.'

'This might actually be permanent.'

'Come stay with me,' Jane offered, tentatively approaching, then retreated, sensing the moment lost.

'It's not a problem,' insisted Nick.

'I wish you'd let me help,' she urged as he swept passed her. 'You're impossible,' she added.

In the kitchen he rested both hands on the worktop, his head sunk forward as he brought his raw nerves under control.

'The coffee's going to be a while,' he shouted through to her, clumsily spooning instant coffee into two mugs, his fingers swollen and tender from the cold.

'No problem,' Jane answered from the living room.

She stood by the window reliving the view. There were four sown arable fields running away to the cliff edge. Beneath the cliff, Horseley Cove, Sharpers Head, Sharpers Cove and Dutch End; the remainder of the view – the English Channel and a stormy half-formed horizon took the eye towards France. Jane knew the coastline and she knew the view; remembered from distant summers when the wispy fields of barley curved their heads a field at a time, bending on the warm drafts of feint breezes, days that she preferred not to dwell on. Pleasant tranquil times in the walled garden, lying on a blanket covering the grass stubble, the borders crowded with monkshood, buddleia, dog-rose and pellitory-of-the-wall. They'd spent hours here during their first summer together, Jane counting clouds, her head resting on Nick's stomach as he summoned up the ghosts of dead poets.

Picking up an embroidered scatter cushion she threw it on the sofa, one more of Angie's touches, a little bit of Putney transported down to make her feel more bohemian.

'You kept everything more or less the same,' she said, coming through into the kitchen, holding a chipped pirate figurine.

'It's how I like it.' He touched a big black kettle with the back of his hand, waiting for it to boil on a lazy AGA.

'Bought this in Kingsbridge, didn't we?' she said, turning the pirate round in her hands. 'We'd had too much to drink.'

'Probably.'

'We we're happy,' she said, catching a quick flash of pain on Nick's face.

'You had a thing about buying things as tokens of your life journey,' he said, pouring boiling water into the mugs. 'Each object makes the journey into the future secure, always knowing that there's something there to stop us becoming strangers with the past. That's how you explained it.'

Jane felt guilty that he remembered her philosophy so well. 'I still believe it.' Glancing at the whisky bottle and mug on the sink, she asked, 'Don't you?' She came and touched his hand.

For all the tenderness intended it might have been the tip of a knife, for Nick abruptly dragged his hand away covering his haste by adding milk to the coffee.

'I hadn't really thought about it,' he said stiffly.

Unable to comfort him as she had done in the past she stood back, consoling him with her strong eyes, deep and extremely green.

'You never had any faith in me,' she laughed. 'That was one of the reasons...' she caught herself and shrugged.

They moved through to the living room deliberately standing apart, the heat from the log stove trapped under the low ceiling, the warmth ferocious on their faces. The window had steamed up, so Nick dusted it with his lower arm, taking in the view; the long bead of golden light on the horizon, the dark wind stunned trees in the garden framed against the sea and bands of swirling sleet.

From the fields he heard a tractor churn through the sleet; coarse strong notes cutting through the molten air.

Behind him Jane was reminiscing to show how much she still cared, reminding Nick of this, of that; Nick not really paying attention letting her run on, as he knew she would. 'I'm sorry about you and Angie,' she finally admitted.

On how much she meant it, Nick wisely refused an urge to press her. Instead, he turned his attention to the window staring through the arms of sleet to the indistinct forms of ships slyly creeping by.

In one graceful curve she had risen from the sofa and gone to the kitchen. 'So, what's this about Wynn freelancing?' she called above the running water.

Listening while she washed her cup the pipes hammering under the pressure, he thought again of the little administrator's fear.

'I haven't a clue,' he told her. But someone had; the murder of Wynn in Hamburg and Lubov's failed extraction were intricately linked, of that he was now convinced.

'Well when you find out what she was working on, let me know, we really need an answer,' she said, returning from the kitchen.

'RUS/OPS had lost confidence in Viper's case officer, that a fair summary?'

She brushed a cobweb from the windowpane at a rush, using the back of her hand. 'From what I'm aware, the management of Viper had become untidy, far short of the standards expected. Ruth really has turned RUS/OPS around,' she said

'Good for her.'

'You haven't many friends left, Nick,' she reminded him angrily. 'Why not let me help you,' she urged facing him, her troubled face a mask with tiny hairline cracks starting to form. 'If you intended to terrorise Viper's handler, you should have cleared it with Ruth.'

'Thought she might be busy cleaning the stables.'

'For Christ's sake,' she snapped. 'Bensham reported you to R5. Mortland and Teddy are questioning your motive.'

'Just curious about how the operation unravelled.'

'Listen to me Nick. If Viper offered you an insight into his material. If he gave you anything, Nick, the actual product or the means to get to it, then for God's sake, share it.'

Withdrawn into his own dark world he refused to hear her petition, muttering something he could not catch she stormed off into the kitchen.

'I don't want any more death,' he said softly, as though it was a concept he had given much thought.

'You don't have the right to make those decisions,' she said, coming back, staring at him. 'Look, it's time I got going,' she announced, gathering up her bag and jacket.

'I appreciate the visit,' he said as he walked her to the door. 'No, seriously, I really do.'

'Anytime you need to talk, to share, you know I'll be waiting,' she smiled, kissing him gently on his cheek. Nick watched as she started the car, reversed it and set off up the track. He waved but Jane never waved back.

After Jane had gone, Nick poured a generous measure of Laphroaig into his mug, turned off all the lights, absently staring out at the sea. He fell asleep dreaming of reconciliation with Angie and awoke shivering and freezing as a car bumped down the track before dawn. He heard the engine's piercing notes before its headlights shattered the gloom, that mysterious murky light that always lingers on land bordering the sea, the car's bright beams forcing hard shadows against the living room wall.

Through the window he glimpsed the shape of a Service car coming to a halt. Opening the cottage door Nick waited for the driver to approach, a thin small man Nick knew as Ray who occasionally acted as a personal driver to Rossan.

'Sorry to bother you sir, but Mr. Blackmore asks if you could accompany me back to London.'

'What's happened?' demanded Nick, thinking of Angie.

'Afraid I'm not privy to that, sir, but I know I haven't to take no for an answer and we have to leave immediately. My colleague Peter,' he pointed to his passenger, 'will drive your vehicle back for you, sir.'

In the car Ray demonstrated all his skills as a professional courteous chauffeur, checking with Nick if the temperature was comfortable enough, if he minded Radio 2 played low, though Nick not really caring, only objected to the radio.

'You've no idea what's going on?' Nick tried again as Ray steered a true course through the village.

'Not a clue, sir, but it sounds like something major, because there's a call gone out for all the senior people.'

'Right.'

'Wouldn't happen to know where Miss Stratton might be contacted, would you sir? No one can find her.'

'I'm afraid I haven't seen her,' Nick told him, sitting back.

Eight

Bumping down the rutted disused railway track bed in the Service car, Nick grunted as each pothole delivered a decisive jab to his lower spine. Glancing ahead, he winced as the pain reached a crescendo before fading.

'This is as far I can go, sir,' said Ray, nudging the car up onto a dull grass mound, stopping a hundred yards short of a metal latticework bridge illuminated by the flashes from a crime scene photographer.

'It's fine, I'll walk.'

'Shall I wait for you, sir?'

'No, I'll manage, thanks,' said Nick, sliding out.

Drawn up at the head of the bridge he saw that the circus had really come to town. Area cars, traffic cars, unmarked Fords and Vauxhalls were parked at awkward angles surrounding the bridge like lifeboats around a listing ship. A far-away headache threatened more pain and Nick lit a cigarette before committing himself to another place of death, a moment of contemplation and assessment, enjoy. Had Hawick some perverse wish to pin something else on me? he wondered, marching forward. Coming up behind him the steady drone of a vehicle negotiating its way; moving to one side Nick made way for a private ambulance that had to wait at the perimeter police tape for admission. Three police constables in their absurd high visibility jackets wound back a length of tape, letting the ambulance through. As Nick was halted by one of the constables a series of camera flashes bounced out from under the bridge, and with his name and ID checked against an official list, Nick was logged as entering the crime scene.

Deviating from the old track bed he climbed a grass embankment. Steeper than Nick originally thought, he had to prevent himself slipping with his hands as he sought a vantage point on higher ground. When he stepped onto a concrete wall forming a buttress into the bridge, his palms were smeared with mud and his cords were grubby around the hems.

From up here he could make out a senior uniformed police officer, detectives, and from the manner they remained aloof, a couple of Security Service representatives shadowing the Firm's own dour band of Regulators hurrying backwards and forwards, holding snatched discussions in random groups then floating away. In their own small select huddle, Hawick, Rossan and Blackmore; their attention on what seemed to be a very slight figure suspended from the bridge, and Nick knew at once that Angie was safe.

Skidding back down the embankment Nick walked over and took Rossan to one side.

'Who is it?' Nick asked.

'Jo Lister, one of Parfrey's,' Rossan said, favouring Nick with a savage glare. 'I warned you Nick, I advised you to stay out of the way,' he added caustically.

Acknowledging Nick's arrival with a scowl, Blackmore looked skywards as he cracked out instruction into his phone: 'Before we *do* have the fucking media all over this would be helpful,' he added for good measure.

In the inky gloom the body moved gently in the cold air, forwards and back, a black pendulum keeping its own beat; swinging rhythmically under and out from the railway bridge.

'Is it being treated as suspicious?' Nick asked.

'We don't know.'

'Who found her?'

'A pair looking for a place to shag,' Blackmore pitched in, between calls.

'God help us,' said Rossan.

'What time did she die?'

'God knows.'

'So why she's still up there?'

'Treating it as a crime scene,' sighed Rossan with a dog weary sigh. 'They won't recover her until they've secured any evidence.'

Hawick in a complete lather, turned from the bridge and irritably ordered Rossan that they must have someone from Legal on scene immediately. 'We cover all angles, Paul. As fast as you can,' he said.

Giving Nick a weary shrug, Rossan moved off punching in a number on his phone.

'Where's Personnel in our hour of need?' yelled Blackmore and Rossan flung up his arms in a gesture of not knowing. 'Nicholas…,' called Blackmore, zeroing in on Nick.

'Why am I here?' Nick asked.

'This, Nicholas, is getting out of hand,' said Blackmore blithely, ignoring Nick's point.

'It's preventative measures,' said Nick quietly, his mood quickly souring.

'Can't somebody stop that thing rotating like that,' pleaded Hawick, distracted by Lister's body moving in the wind. 'You,' he said, swivelling to face Nick, 'need to provide an explanation for disregarding the conditions of your suspension,' he blazed, before being taken off to a discrete distance for an impromptu update by a Regulator.

'And you really have no idea what you're dealing with,' he pitched after Hawick.

'Parfrey's been informed,' snapped Rossan walking by, banging in a new set of numbers on his phone.

After being briefed by the tactical commander, Hawick returned. 'They haven't found a note. Here or at her address,' he explained, as though this was a crime in itself.

'This had better not blow up in our faces,' Blackmore fumed, as Hawick shouted at a Regulator to find Mortland, and make it quick.

'We must have total control, or we risk external meddling,' insisted Hawick.

'And we don't want Security trying to put *our* house in order,' complained Blackmore. 'That dunce Bensham has dropped you in it, Nicholas. Telling you all manner of tales apparently, one of them involving Jo Lister. Doesn't look rosy for you. The sages are in a huddle muttering about your loyalty. Anything to confess?'

'You're really irritating me, Roly, let's start with that.'

'Look at it from our perspective,' Blackmore demanded. 'You have a cosy heart-to-heart with Bensham, and here we are, awaiting a decision on whether it's suicide or foul play,' he added, pointing at the body,

'Foul play staged as suicide. It's neat, it's convenient,' Nick suggested.

'Too fucking convenient,' Blackmore agreed. 'What do we concur then? This slip of a girl screwed-up the pre-op planning and couldn't live with the shame? Bit hard on herself if it was.'

'She knew something about the operation,' proposed Nick, as another camera flash illuminated the rusty girders under the bridge.

'And what would that be?' Blackmore demanded incredulously.

'It's a bit late to ask her,' retorted Nick.

Hawick warned him not to be facetious and concentrate on what was going on.

'As far as I was aware, nothing is going on,' answered Nick. 'You've got everything under control.' So too had Moscow, he thought. In just a little over forty-eight hours since Bensham had identified Jo Lister, the response was immediate, deadly, suggesting a team was already in place to prevent disclosure.

'Good job you were in Devon, people might be getting the wrong impression about you, Nicholas,' Blackmore reminded him.

'Lucky me.'

'That is beside the point,' Hawick informed him. 'And at this precise moment, you hold a very precarious line. C is particularly determined that our past sins should not intrude into the present,' declared Hawick.

'Well he would, wouldn't he,' quipped Blackmore, 'One of the reasons that he was appointed wasn't it?'

Hawick on the back foot couldn't compete with Blackmore's candour, throwing up his arms up in despair.

Reappearing through a scrum of police, Rossan was grimmer than Nick could ever remember seeing him.

'We've just had confirmation that Lister,' he said nodding to the body, 'had requested an interview with R5.'

'Where *is* Mortland?' Hawick lamented.

'Probably torturing the star-crossed lovers who found the body,' snorted Blackmore.

'The media will amplify this out of all proportion. This could not have come at a more inopportune time,' lamented Hawick.

For your career? The Firm's reputation? thought Nick, disgusted.

'It'll blow over,' Blackmore proposed. 'It'll be boy trouble, or girl trouble, it usually is, and I've directed Mortland to make enquiries into her love life,' he added quite pleased with himself.

'Or Moscow trouble,' offered Nick.

'This a confirmed lead from your tête-à-tête with boy Bensham, is it?' Blackmore asked in a low aside, a sharp smile on his lips. 'He really *is* a moron.'

'We cannot and must not start making wild connections between the events in Moscow, Hamburg and here,' Hawick asserted.

'Why not?' said Nick, as the private ambulance passed through in preparation for carrying Jo Lister's body away.

'It isn't helpful at this critical time,' Hawick piped.

'Finally, now we might have clarity,' said Blackmore.

Heading towards them the head of Internal Security and Counter-intelligence, Andrew Mortland escorted by one of his Regulators, who had guided him on a private tour of the scene.

'I have spoken,' Mortland declared with the dour authority of a church elder dismissing his Regulator, 'to the Senior Investigating Officer.' He permitted himself a reflective pause, 'and the situation remains dynamic.'

Standing in front of Nick, Hawick and Blackmore, he took them all in, one at a time. An imposing figure, he employed his height as intimidation, along with his solid, hewn features. A scion of robust Highland stock, his father was a God-fearing man of the cloth, a bishop, no less; Mortland never strayed from the narrow path of righteously upholding the law of God and the Firm. According to the wits, he sprinkled brimstone on his cereal.

'Unconditionally, we could be witnessing the makings of a disaster,' he told them, his shoulders upright, his eyes steadfast. 'I anticipate...and the Chief anticipates...from here on in, this will be handled with discretion,' he declared.

'Wonderful,' Nick said under his breath, though it wasn't low enough because Mortland whipped round in his direction.

'As for *your* future,' Mortland declared, turning on Nick, 'as far as I have been informed, that remains undecided,' he stated curtly. 'And, gentlemen, we need to be formulating a damage control strategy,' he warned taking a few steps away from Nick, his sermon not over, 'because I anticipate we will have to deal with the full glare of intrusive media attention in the days ahead.' With his authority bestowed on them, he straightened his hair before stomping off.

'Hello... what the fuck's she doing here?' Blackmore roared as Jane appeared, 'who invited you?'

'Ruth contacted me,' she explained, not looking at Nick.

'Hasn't *she* been a busy bee,' Blackmore retorted, leading Jane away.

Tense and hostile at his temporary loss of power, Hawick attempted to rebuild his self-esteem and standing. 'You still have serious allegations to answer,' he insisted, turning on Nick.

'I've nothing to hide,' retorted Nick.

'We shall see,' Hawick said, fully wound up. 'No official contact with anyone, and I expect you to be at Aspley first thing in the morning.'

Not answering, Nick walked away thinking how it was such an awful and lonely place to die.

• • •

Vyacheslav Cheboksary avoided publicity. A billionaire who'd made his fortune from the Russian gas and oil industry, he assiduously refused interviews, appeared rarely at public functions and regarded London as the preferred home for his family. His Cadogan Place house covering five floors, peered imperiously over the square's private gardens, and seemed to Nick that morning to resemble more of an embassy than a family residence.

On his approach to the house, he revised what Mike Stanhill, a SO15 Detective Chief Inspector had told him over the telephone. 'Galina Myla entered a year ago as an INF 17. That's overseas domestic worker status to you and me, employed as a nanny. She entered when the family brought their entire Moscow household with them. She went walkabout six months ago. She's officially lost, and I mean lost. No trace, no arrests.'

Security cameras tracked him along the pavement, tilting to follow him up the steps to the front door. A door so highly glossed, Nick could see his reflection quite clearly, a door opened by a former butler to the royal family. One simmering glance at Nick's casual outfit, the butler loftily pointed out Nick's grievous sin. 'You require the lower entrance, *sir*,' and with measured disdain, he pointed him down the basement steps.

Before Nick had even given half of his details into an intercom labelled 'Domestic Office', a woman in her thirties snapped open a frosted glass panelled black door. Dressed in a smart business suit, she gathered her hair into a bunch and expertly applied a plain band to form a high ponytail in one movement.

'It is Sunday,' she began, her English good but not enough to mask her Moscow accent. 'And uninvited callers never, never use the main door of the house,' she continued, ripping into Nick.

'I'm trying to trace Galina Myla,' he replied, offering a measured smile from someone whose patience is routinely tested. 'I was hoping you would provide background on Galina.'

'You are?'

'It's not important who I am, Katya Malova,' Nick answered, his opening pitched with suitable weight to give it an unambiguous formality. 'I have returned from Moscow and it is essential that I locate Galina Myla.'

Hesitating, deciding how to respond she glanced quickly past Nick up to street level as if needing reassurance the caller had come alone.

'It is my day off,' she announced temperamentally, as if this provided a barrier in itself.

'I know,' Nick retorted, 'and your cooperation is appreciated.'

'You should have rung to make an appointment,' she countered, not prepared to admit Nick.

'Some visits have to be made without advance warning,' Nick said dryly, 'it is the way that we work.'

'Work? What work is this?' Malova snapped.

'What I do should not concern you,' Nick retorted, his manner severe. 'You, Katya Malova, as the household manager, have nothing to fear. Do you mind if we talk inside?'

Malova seemed to mind a great deal and Nick thought his visit was about to collapse, but Malova's sharp blue eyes scanned him, and in doing so, made sure they read the back of his hands. For as Katya knew, there was official Russia, and there was another Russia where visible tattoos were not worn for the sake of decoration. Sensing Nick perhaps existed somewhere between these two extreme worlds, and had so far offered no threat, she stepped aside, inviting Nick into her office.

Taking a seat behind her desk, she pointed Nick to a two-seat sofa in a corner between filing cabinets. Opening a jotter, uncapping a fountain pen, she signalled she was ready for business.

'What can you tell me about Galina Myla?' Nick wondered sitting back, his approach casual. 'Any small details may be important,' he stressed. 'Did she fit in? Was she reliable? Make friends easily?'

'Maybe if you tell me what you need, I can answer,' she said with an edge to her question. 'What has she done that she is hunted in this way?'

'She is involved in a delicate matter, and you, Katya, could make finding her much easier,' said Nick with severity. 'Please, it is important I have all the facts. Please make sure nothing is overlooked... or omitted... that would be appreciated. So, could you please tell me what you remember about Galina?'

Sitting back Katya Malova folded her arms across her chest and did just as Nick requested, recounting how Galina worked for the family in Moscow for seven months before business brought the household to London. Katya had interviewed Galina personally, and although she found no fault with her qualifications or work as a nanny, Katya sensed Galina would somehow be trouble.

'And this side of her character only revealed itself in London?' asked Nick.

'At first no,' Katya stated, adding for the record, that here in London Galina's work, if anything was exemplary. As a reward, her pay was increased, and she was given extra leisure hours. 'That is when the problems started. Galina would be late, too much drink in her little head from the night before, and,' Katya lowered her voice to a conspiratorial whisper, 'Galina was maybe starting to experiment with drugs.'

'You confronted her about this?' Nick asked, playing the role of confessor.

'I challenged her a few times and she laughed it off, but as her behaviour and attitude grew worse I,' and she paused for full effect, 'with the backing of the family who were now extremely concerned for Galina and their babies in her care, told Galina that she would have to undergo random drug tests. Fine, Galina shouts in my face, fine, you will find nothing and the next morning she doesn't report for work.'

'And when on duty, she gave no reason that she might have a different life?' Nick asked. 'A life you might know nothing about?'

Katya ran her gaze over Nick as though he'd confirmed he may not have tattoos, but in whatever profession he represented, she would swear, this visitor could be unforgiving when required. 'Of course. Naturally there is every chance that Galina had secrets. If she did, she may share them with her friends, but not me.'

'And they are also members of the household staff?'

Not quite knowing which way Nick was taking her, Katya nodded, hopelessly lost. Unfolding her arms, she rested her elbows on her desk, leaning forward. 'As far as I know, yes,' she divulged, as though it was essential she expressed her points clearly.

'Do you have the name of anyone Galina might have confided in?'

'Marfa, yes, she was Galina's best friend.'

'And Marfa is working today?'

Alas, it was her day off also, Katya regrettably confessed.

'Where do I find Marfa?'

'There is a separate house in Bow bought by the family as provision for the staff,' she announced proudly. 'They shared a room in the staff house.'

'What about visitors from home?'

'Her mother, perhaps, yes, her mother came over regularly,' Katya slowly remembered.

'And of course, Galina was also friends with Grigori Tesov, he is a chef.'

'Of course,' said Nick, as though he should have known.

'I will speak to Marfa and Grigori,' said Nick firmly.

Ripping off a sheet from a desk memorandum pad, Katya dashed off an address and handed it to Nick, a declaration if one were needed that there were people you did not cross, and Nick was, in this life and the next, surely one of them.

'Thank you, Katya Malova, I hope your help will be a great assistance,' Nick said, standing, preparing to leave. At the door, he turned as if he'd forgotten something. 'It would be appropriate if my visit isn't discussed, or that Galina's friends aren't told I will be calling to see them.'

'Of course,' she agreed.

Quite why she did it, Katya couldn't answer but as she followed Nick's departure up on the pavement, observed his powerful strides pounding past her window, she crossed herself, something she hadn't done since she was a child. Again, acting out of pure instinct and not her shrewd facility for reason, she pulled on her coat, and set out without a thought as to her destination. It was simply that she needed to be in the open and moving, as if Nick's visit had awoken something in her she couldn't or wouldn't face. In her reading of Nick, as brief as it may have been, Katya detected that primitive reaction inside her to danger; not necessarily evil, not wicked, but a stark realisation one has had a lucky escape.

Nine

An outdoor palm tree had been lovingly wrapped and taped to beat the winter frosts. Standing proud it dominated the front garden of the house in Priory Avenue, Crouch End. At some point in its past, the house had received a liberal coat of dark green paint to its exterior boards, guttering, frames and down pipes, but the recent addition of cream window blinds jarred with the colour scheme, something not quite balancing thought Nick. A small neat woman answered the door, almost apologising for being Steve's mum after Nick had explained he was a colleague of Jo's. She guided Nick down the hallway past a mountain bike parked under cornice shelves holding an ensemble of figurines. Steve Milneshaw was in the back room and a Met Family Liaison officer asked if she could help. Nick gave his name with no attempt at deceit, just God's own honest truth; who he was and who he represented, and she retreated along with Steve's mum, who faltered in the doorway.

'Would you like a cup of tea?' she asked Nick, 'because I was just about to make one.'

She's the sort who always would, decided Nick; whatever the triumph or tragedy, and he politely declined her offer.

'I'm sorry about Jo,' Nick offered, never any good at offering his condolences and Milneshaw nodded dumbly, the words not sinking in.

Milneshaw had become a prisoner in his mother's protective custody, surrounded by empty cups and newspapers scattered on the carpet around his feet.

'I'm trying to find out what happened to Jo,' Nick said, taking a seat in an armchair across from Milneshaw who could only smile at his girlfriend's name. 'If you don't wish to talk, or want me to leave, that's perfectly understandable. I'm not from Head office, Steve. I'm with CO8 and I was part of the operation Jo put together.'

'Jo,' said Milneshaw, his voice broken, flat. Then as though he'd been waiting for an excuse he was suddenly off, describing how they met in the basement gym, how their relationship developed, the times they spent in the staff bar, before he ended his narrative embarrassed. 'They said she...' Taking a long breath, he shook his head. 'They said they found a note at the office...she was unhappy...didn't think she had a future...nothing to live for...But that's not true...'

'Who found the note?'

Staring hard at Nick as though he needed to make a snap evaluation, the young desk officer took a considerable pause before replying.

'Head RUS/OPS... But Jo... She didn't....' Unable to continue Milneshaw sat back, rubbed his eyes and sniffed. 'She didn't kill herself,' he said, angry and hurt. A BALT/OPS desk officer, Milneshaw reached over six-foot; his light brown hair messy, a dark shadow of stubble cupping his jaw.

'That's what I want to establish,' Nick told him, deciding Milneshaw's face had never borne too much bad luck, his eyes were immature and soft; they were the eyes of a child who'd received its first taste of tragedy.

'She was here... the other night,' Milneshaw said, 'came around as usual and we'd watched a DVD, *Gladiator*, it was one of her favourites and she always cried at the end.' He patted the chair arm determined not to cry himself.

'The night she died,' Nick gently began, 'did you know if anyone had called her?'

'She never said she was meeting anyone, if that's what you mean,' Milneshaw replied.

'But if someone she trusted had arranged to meet her, she would have gone?'

Milneshaw nodded, reached over to a coffee table, lifted up a photograph of Lister and put it straight back down.

'Did she tell you why she planned to contact R5?'

'We're not allowed to discuss each other's duties.'

'That's the official policy,' said Nick, 'but the Firm is a hotbed of gossip, we all know that. And I am here to find out exactly what happened to Jo.'

Out of Nick's question, perhaps from its tone, Milneshaw grasped a measure of hope in place of despair. 'She was worked up about *that* shitty operation,' he said.

'Did she say why?'

'It should never have happened,' Milneshaw said, agitated, upset.

'Not taken place?' suggested Nick.

Nodding, Milneshaw gave a weary 'yes, probably', followed by what sounded like a choked sob. And with Nick promising not to reveal his sources, he went to the very limits of disclosure. 'If Jo was concerned about operational issues, she must have had genuine reasons for going to R5? Security Branch isn't exactly popular, or the first choice,' Nick volunteered with feeling.

Glaring at this accepted wisdom, Milneshaw shook his head. 'R5 was her final option,' he said, his voice rising, his patience, quite understandably, long gone.

'Had Jo attempted a different course of action?'

'She did everything according to protocols, said it was a pointless waste of time.' Milneshaw sat back and Nick, needing more, prompted him.

'I'm not sure I follow you?'

'She was angry that this operation had crashed and cost lives,' he admitted. 'Jo was really down, somehow feeling she shared some of the blame. I know she shouldn't have discussed it with me, but she wasn't sleeping. She just wasn't the Jo I knew. I tried everything to bring her out of it, but she was in a deep rut, so I...' Milneshaw closed his eyes, shook his head. 'So... I told her that if she felt so badly, she should voice her concerns.' He broke off to take a gulp from a cup commemorating a royal wedding or jubilee, Nick couldn't be sure which from where he sat. 'You see it's my fault.' He collapsed back into the chair.

'I know it's painful,' Nick assured him, 'but I need to know what Jo actually did next?'

'She spoke to her section head.'

'And?'

'Jo was accused of overreacting. Her comments would be noted.'

'That was it?'

Gripping the chair arms Milneshaw forced himself on, his face utterly pale and wan. 'Jo came around that evening and said she was resigning, she'd had enough. The head of RUS/OPS had called her in. She more or less accused Jo of malicious actions and it would be recorded on her personal file.'

'Did Jo explain what concerned her so deeply?' pressed Nick.

'She couldn't stop discussing it, every detail...' Milneshaw shook his head, not this time in sorrow or grief, but frustration.

'Concerning what exactly?'

Again, Milneshaw fumbled for an adequate response. 'The risk evaluation she'd compiled for this stupid operation. It was all rushed, fast moving, some sort of crisis. But you'll already know that.'

'It sounds about right,' Nick offered, plus there was good deal more that he wasn't willing to share. 'If you can give me any insight on what took place leading up to the operation, that would be useful.'

And Milneshaw with Nick promising not to reveal where he heard it, closed his swollen red eyes, reliving how Josephine Lister played a leading role in the hurried preparations for Operation Salvage.

'I don't know the exact timing of what happened,' he admitted, his young likeable face gripped by genuine regret, 'but Jo had presented her operational risk evaluation. There'd hardly been any time to prepare, so she was totally stressed. She didn't anticipate an all-star audience but that's what she got. Controller CENT/EAST EUROPE and Head RUS/OPS were already there. Sandford operational coordinator and Bibby from Legal showed up, Allendale the FO liaison put in an appearance, and a warlord from the top floor to came to slum it with the peasants.'

'The warlord,' Nick very carefully probed, 'did Jo happen to say who it was?'

'Maybe,' Milneshaw hesitatingly responded. 'They're making her a scapegoat, aren't they?' he asked wistfully, in defence of his dead girlfriend.

'Given the circumstances, yes,' Nick replied candidly. 'Jo's death could be used as an excuse to hide the failings of other officers,' he admitted, briefly catching the fuse of anger fizz in Milneshaw's eyes.

Barely moving or acknowledging Nick's presence, Milneshaw reflected on the responses open to him, his amiable face declaring his conflicting emotions. In the background, the forced staccato murmuring of his mother and the liaison officer bubbling from a different room. Placing his palms on his thighs, easing back to take a breath, Milneshaw revealed: 'It was Hawick.'

'Seems a little excessive?' suggested Nick. 'Stratton, Parfrey, Hawick, Sandford and Allendale, that's quite a gathering.'

'That's what she said,' Milneshaw disclosed protectively. 'Made her realise something was iffy,' he added.

'The risk evaluation, did Jo go into detail how it went?' Nick pressed. 'Anything you disclose will remain confidential.'

Accepting Nick's solemn pledge, Milneshaw nodded, moistened his lips. 'Jo didn't like anything about it. She was anxious, never slept the night before. Before she even did her piece, the mood was grim, and the FO liaison was ready to bite the head off anyone who glanced in her direction. Sandford was doing his best to keep the peace, but Jo said he succeeded in winding everybody up.'

'It's his forte, I'm afraid,' said Nick, appreciating the division and rancour already present before the operation was even sanctioned.

'They spent ages locked in a discussion concerning whether or not they needed ministerial clearance for deniability,' Milneshaw disclosed.

Then, for the briefest moment, he just stared hopelessly at Nick, as if he'd dried in the middle of a written examination. Equally as quickly he recovered his confidence, resuming his account of the meeting as if he'd been holding Jo's hand.

'Jo had a nasty case of the nerves, worrying she might have overlooked or underplayed any of the risks. But Sandford was great, Jo said. Flirty, but he did all he could to relax her. Asking how she was getting on, how he'd heard promising reports about her, warning the Head RUS/OPS better watch out because Jo was sharp and destined to go far. If it hadn't been for Sandford's encouragement, Jo would have clammed up, but he told her about his two tours in Moscow and how some areas used to scare him, gave him the shivers,' he recited methodically.

Me too, thought Nick, now perfectly still as Milneshaw smiled at a flash of memory, before his features darkened, and with an urgent rhythm to his languid voice, continued his testimony in Jo's memory.

'When Jo had given her evaluation, somebody asked her why the risk level was so pessimistic? She didn't back down or fold,' Milneshaw vowed proudly. 'Jo told them she could only go off the facts supplied by eyes on the ground. The package was scheduled for pickup from a neutral venue in southeast Moscow, location specified by the contact. Sandford wanted to abort, find an alternative, the exposure value was too high. The Controller CENT/EAST EUROPE knew it was time critical, but a delay could allow for a change of venue, reduce the risk for the collection team. Jo said Hawick was undecided, and he gave Head RUS/OPS the casting vote. She recommended proceed and downgraded the evaluation to medium.'

'How did Jo react?'

'It shocked her, made her angry. It got heated she said, everyone talking, and then Sandford really stirred things up.'

Milneshaw sat back and Nick, needing more, prompted him.

'What did he say?'

'Asked something about why the contact wasn't using his adapted smart phone for a burst transmission to offload the material.'

'Did Jo have an answer for him?'

Milneshaw nodded. 'Because local advice recommended it wasn't viable in the current situation.'

Which might have been the first sensible action Bensham had taken, thought Nick, and it occurred to him the Russians already knew; they were preparing for the collection, closing down all the options but one.

'Allendale lost it at that point, according to Jo. The Embassy was off-limits thanks to a security clampdown and the FO were raising hell with her, reporting how the Ambassador was furious at the disruption, the harassment, the brazen interference with communications and was putting the blame squarely in our court. Sandford joked it would have been a lot less effort if they were mounting a putsch. Jo reminded them the mode of delivery was covered in the asset's pre-evaluation summary. Local advice noted electronic harvest not an option. The contact doesn't trust it. And Sandford made a comment which Jo thought was really strange.'

'About what? Can you remember it?'

'Sandford had said "or us" ... I can't be sure.'

Because he doesn't trust it... *or us*, Nick repeated to himself, hearing the little administrator's warning to Bensham: *I don't share with anyone but the senior officer. Tell him the Oktober Projekt is active, it is the deceit, and it is more.*

'Did anyone else raise any other objections?'

'Head RUS/OPS insisted if they didn't green light the retrieval, they might not get another chance,' said Milneshaw, and the mobility had gone from his face; drained and impassive he stared hard at Nick.

'It wasn't Jo's fault,' Nick assured him.

'She didn't want to kick up a fuss, but knowing the collection was a disaster was eating away inside her. When I said she had to do something about it, that's when she spoke to her section head and it just snowballed. The head of RUS/OPS told Jo to drop it. But Jo wouldn't.'

That makes two of us, thought Nick.

'Did she confide in you what she was going to discuss with R5?'

'Jo mentioned a cover-up,' Milneshaw said, and for the first time, he gave Nick a questioning glance. 'She said the risk of retrieval had been ignored,' he added, pre-occupied, staring at Nick. 'Jo felt that she was trapped in a conspiracy.' Milneshaw inched himself forward and Nick saw how puffy his cheeks and eyes were as his face came into a pool of light from a table lamp. Rubbing his hands together, he took a deep sigh. 'And that's why she was going to R5. Do you believe Jo died because of that?' he appealed earnestly.

'I think it is tied in with it, Steve,' said Nick, sick and weary of having to carry another death on his shoulders. 'It's probably a wise precaution to forget we met,' proposed Nick, replaying Lubov's pledge: *It is proof of a great secret, and I am trusting you with it*. And what if I don't want the cursed thing? Nick was suddenly alert with a fresh sense of momentum.

'Will there be an investigation? You see, I can't let Jo down,' said Milneshaw with a sad smile, suddenly alert with a fresh sense of momentum.

Here it was, thought Nick, a chance to give a grieving boyfriend an excuse for not blaming himself, for not seeing his dead girlfriend as unstable, a woman on the edge who stepped away from life and committed suicide because she had nothing, and no one left.

'I don't know.'

For some reason he'd never understand, Nick stopped at the door, his hand half turning the handle.

'Steve, whatever people say about Jo, you're the one who knew her, and I think for that you're a lucky man.'

In the hallway Nick found Steve's mother, mumbled some inadequate platitudes, and hurried off for home. He needed solitude, a place to sit and reflect, find some familiar territory to escape from this madness.

•••

Nick had been on the road for five minutes when his cellphone rang. He heard Jane's breathless voice; terse, a register he thought he'd forgotten, giving precise information without any feeling. Where had he been? She'd been trying to reach him for ages. He'd had things to do, he told her. He didn't know she cared that much, he continued, until Jane's urgency cut him off mid flow. There'd been an incident with Angie. Yes, *Angela*. She'd been attacked. In hospital, the Royal London. Serious, it sounded bad, intensive care. Late this afternoon. No, she didn't know. Yes, she was at the hospital, and yes, she'd keep in touch.

He drove with the same recklessness as he did to be at his son's birth, though this had a different sense of urgency and fear. Thirty minutes to reach the hospital through slow Sunday traffic meandering aimlessly along. Seeping from the back of Nick's neck, a deep pain that spread up through his skull as he parked in a space reserved for consultants only, which he was in a way, except his speciality was secrets and the application of force. Going in through casualty he followed overhead signs down corridors with their lingering scent of warm food and fear. Porters wheeling their cargo, some of it human, passed him – squeak... squeak... squeak, fading, gone. Ward visitors and medical staff flowed along an endless corridor, their institutional pace bustling, infectious, as if the whole place was on the move. Stuck in his mind, Auden's *Miss Gee* waiting to be saved under pristine white sheets, though Angie's condition was real, not poetic. Why were hospitals so hot? Didn't germs flourish in heat? In intensive care a waiting area was set off to his right; a double-glazed capsule, but you could still hear the machines fighting against the odds. Serious professional faces streaming past; technology and quiet, the inconsistency of life and abrupt endings.

At a nurses' station Jane was already waiting, a coffee in her hand as staff passed silently into small wards, their voices conspiratorially low.

'Thank God you're here,' Jane said.

'Where is she?'

'Let's talk,' she nodded to a door leading to the family suites, spilt some of the coffee over her fingers and pulled a face.

'I need to see her.'

'Nick, I need to explain,' said Jane.

'Explain what?'

'Angie, she was beaten *and* shot, a really vicious attack,' Jane told him, her voice low, guiding him into one of the temporary family quarters.

Reserved for relatives who needed to stay close to intensive care, the suite was a series of interconnecting sterile boxes someone had tried to make as welcoming as home with green armchairs fighting against a floral pink paper. Sighted high on one wall, a flat screen TV could be viewed when taking meals or snacks at a round wooden grain laminate dining table. Under the window, a small waist high bookcase loaded with an eclectic mix of classics and paperbacks, a box of tissues placed discreetly on the second shelf. There was a bathroom and a double bedroom in the same depressing functional style, and to Nick everything seemed too empty; shells waiting for shadows to give them a taste of life.

'Shot?' he repeated.

'I'm sorry Nick. The police are withholding full disclosure.'

'How did it... what happened?'

'She was with someone. A friend called Guy?' Jane began not looking at Nick.

'An art dealer...gallery owner,' said Nick, numb. They came for me, he thought in a moment of stark realisation, wondering if the gallant Guy had put up a fight with the hockey stick? Wrong place, and definitely bad timing, Guy. You see, Angie should have mentioned I'm a spy and the real target.

'He was shot in the head and died at the scene.'

'And Angie?'

Jane lifted her head slowly, taking her time. 'She's in a bad way Nick, she put up a determined fight before she was shot.' Jane tried to hold him, but he broke away, took a step backwards.

'Show me....'

'Look, you can't blame yourself.'

Gesturing for Nick to follow her, Jane led him into a small unit and pointed to an end bed. Angie in a coma, a machine making all the effort as it did the breathing for her; tubes, wires, machines beeping, counting, measuring out her struggle. Flinching at her sallow face, Nick stepped forward to her side. Both Angie's eyes were closed and swollen; her lips bloated, misshaped, translucent and cracked. On one of her cheeks a deep bruise caused by a solid ring. Intravenous drips were running into the back of her hands and nose. Small scabs of eyeliner were dried around her lashes and he imagined her eyes packed with life before she was attacked. By the tape round her wrist, more swelling on her pale skin; bruises in a fingertip pattern where she'd been held down.

He spent ten minutes trying not to listen as a doctor gave Angie something close to a fifty-fifty chance; stressing how for someone her age the odds were seriously in her favour. He heard "... irreparable damage to the ventricular system... thalamus... trajectory along the coronal plane..." So, it came down to survival administered as roulette, all dependent on the path of the bullet, the important bits and pieces it destroyed. Well, wasn't life a lottery after all thought Nick, squeezing her hand, watching as Jane motioned that she'd be outside. Except Nick's eyes refused to provide a normal service, blurred, he saw only Jane's distorted face. A dimension had slipped allowing particles to scamper and dance into dozens of objects waiting to be invented. Nothing was normal any longer, and it never would be, he decided sitting back.

Angie didn't make it through the night. As her condition deteriorated, Nick and Angie's parents made the decision to take her off life support. Sharing his vigil with her mother and father, Nick had sat tight stroking her hand, a supplicant gesture that made him feel mute and inadequate. After he'd watched her fade away as her breathing changed pitch and finally ceased at three twenty-two a.m., Nick was gripped by an abject panic pushing him down the corridor, longing for air untouched by clotted institutional scent. Jane found him outside, her entreaties to come inside ignored, her attempts at comfort brutally repelled, stepping away from her arms each time she tried to hold him tight.

'Come back to my place, use the spare bed for as long as you like,' she offered, nothing else to give.

'No,' he responded, his voice surly, his refusal angry and sour.

'Where will you go?'

'Who cares.'

'I do.'

'I'm better left alone, that's the best thing you can do.'

Kissing his cheek, she walked off as Nick began a choked round of calls to friends and family, ringing from his cellphone in the hospital's cold foyer, repeating every word twice, his throat narrow and raw.

Most of the morning he spent with two investigating officers, receiving the distinct impression he was a suspect. Could he account for his movements? He could, but refused, and following a number of hasty calls, it was understood Nick's career with the Foreign Office was off-limits. Perhaps he could describe his relationship with Angela? A good marriage? Happy? Troubled? Did he know Guy? Who *was* Guy? Did Nick have access to a firearm? Nick's answers were dutifully received with polite impartiality, his cooperation noted; everything recorded, witnessed and dutifully signed the 11th November at twelve thirty-five. Nick, not for the first time in his life, was off the rails, out of control. Someone had gone and irrevocably tipped the scales towards destruction; Nick's or those responsible was hard to say right now. A hunger for finding Angie's killers consuming him, and he'd a sensation of walking on air as he went to the first pub he found open.

Drinking became Nick's direct route to grieving. Days of drunken hell when Nick disappeared off the radar, his only altercation came one afternoon in a small pub where they knew Nick quite well. On his way to the bar, Nick brushed the shoulder of a young City trader celebrating the close of play. 'Wanker,' he snapped at Nick level with his shoulder. Nick grabbed the trader by the throat, pushed him back against his leg and slammed him to the floor. He was only prevented from delivering a fatal punch by two bar staff pinning Nick's arms around his waist.

'Who's the wanker now?' he yelled.

A nervous silence absorbed the conversation and laughs. 'That's enough,' ordered a barman gripping Nick's arms tightly, brushing him through bewildered groups of drinkers. Nick laughed in their faces and their relief swelled to a noisy echo again as the barmen jostled him to the door. Walking in a daze, Nick's system buckled under the whisky, his legs soft and weak, his steps unsure and wooden as he bumped passers-by, muttering apologies or curses. Staggering until there was no one around, he slumped on a bench in a square on Victoria Embankment, heaving his coat around his knees, tears running down his cheeks.

After that, it was downhill all the way. Five feet-eleven tall and under twelve stones, Nick would never be big enough to face the memories of Angie. Another hard shadow he'd have to outrun, exposing his nerves and inadequacies. His wife was gone. He visualised Angie at the final second before she was attacked, wondering what she was thinking, what she'd been planning? For Nick, peace was a thing of the past, a corrupt state to be forgotten. The only tangible facts were the here and now, the events he created as a distraction, as a diversion, a narrative of his own to block out the memories.

That first night Nick found a room in a bed and breakfast hovel for those on a budget. Sitting by the window a cushion under his head on a straight-backed chair, he watched the street in case it had all been a dream, and Angie would be looking for him out there under the street lamp's fine glow. No lights in his room, just a plastic tumbler and a half-drunk bottle of Laphroaig by his side as he was tortured by the injustice of life; how he'd kissed Angie's forehead for the last time, her skin already very cold.

Terrified by his dark mood, he made a bolt for the waiting day. Catching a bus at random, Nick found his way to Kilburn realising he was shaking so badly he was drawing stares. Punishment? Revenge? Had he gone plain crazy? His head ached from trying to push missing segments together or was it from the whisky? Confused, scared, he alighted at the next stop, turning down streets he didn't know. Nausea hit him with the heat of a plague, doubling up he vomited bile and watery whisky into the gutter, his eyes wet with the effort. Across the street a nursing home promising residential care, and from its shabby state, it appeared nothing more, nothing less, than a farm trading on human weakness. In one of the front windows a wasted eighty-year old, her dressing gown grubby. She saw Nick straightening up and rapped on the window. It took a couple of moments before his stinging eyes could translate her lipped words behind the glass.

'Where's my husband? You seen my husband? Where's your father?' She mouthed, on and on until Nick turned and ran, another traitor too afraid to answer her questions.

Heading up the street a Salvation Army band floated towards him, a good three feet in the air. Out of each instrument came words not music, voices of people he'd known; colleagues, lovers, parents, the living and dead. Forming a circle round Nick one female Salvationist pushed through the band; Angie, her bonnet askew. Swimming up to Nick she touched his cheek.

'You're keeping the wrong company, Nick, booze isn't going to save you.'

'I need you Angie.'

'That was a bad one that came calling with his friends. You were a good husband, but now Tom is taking care of me.'

'I need you Angie.'

'Why not come to mass with the family, have a word with Father Antley.'

'Sure, book a bench for us all.'

'Repent, Nick, that's all you've got to do.'

Squeezing past Angie, Nick rolled and bumped his way down the street not daring to look back, his mind already denying him the prospect of repenting. A weird power had control of Nick's senses, his body drifted, its lever jammed on automatic. Thoughts were no longer becoming positive or succeeding concrete actions, a breakdown in the trillion of tiny wires in his brain. The tiredness suddenly crept through him in long heavy waves, his mind infected with grotesque faces, the day turning into a freak. Another drink would be required to shift him into a higher gear.

Ten

Nick went missing for two weeks; Mortland driving the search with manic fervour, insisting: 'He must be found, today, if you will, not tomorrow. Urgency and action will be our watchword. I want his movements, and I want him delivered to me.' Interpreting Mortland's commands in his own way, Paul Rossan had picked up Nick's wayward course late on a dismal afternoon as his friend and colleague wove an erratic trail across London. Each time Rossan had followed up a reliable sighting, Nick had vanished before he arrived. By the following midweek, Rossan wondered quite seriously if he wasn't chasing anything more substantial than a ghost. Even Nick's cottage had turned up a blank; Rossan taking an almighty risk, had somehow obtained a pool car along with a green probationer called Denshaw from Aspley, basing him at a village inn not far from Nick's cottage, instructing him to make regular checks.

Finally, when Rossan almost believed Nick to have walked straight off the edge of the world, he got a sheepish call from Denshaw to say Nick had surfaced. 'Well where, dammit, where?' Rossan blasted him, quietly fuming as Denshaw explained that the 'target' had spilled out of a taxi almost at his feet as he did one of his calls on the cottage. Denshaw went on to complain that the 'target' verbally and physically threatened him, before insisting that they share a drink. 'How long ago?' Rossan demanded, having to ask twice before the probationer volunteered that he thought it might have been yesterday evening. 'Do not move, do not pass go,' Rossan had ordered him, certain that Denshaw sounded hung-over and queasy. Enlisting the help of Danny Redman, a CO8 close-quarter combat instructor and long-standing partner of Nick, they set out for Devon.

After packing Denshaw back off to Aspley with a severe reprimand, including dark threats if he ever uttered a word, Rossan padded up the cottage's twisting staircase followed by Danny. 'Good God,' Rossan exclaimed, opening the spare bedroom door, genuinely shocked. Lying across a crumpled bed, duvet and sheets hanging down to the floor, his face staring blankly at them, a half-dressed Nick Torr was comatose, a red fire bucket placed strategically on the floor by his head. Stark, bare walled and furnished with a wardrobe, chests of drawers, dressing table and chairs – none of which matched – the room was scarred from years of seasonal living. There were scuffs, scratches and missing segments of plaster and in a pile pushed up in a corner, creased navigation charts showed Nick's life spent sailing. Every free surface had a covering of books all devoted to the sea, most of them second-hand. Rossan had trouble establishing if Nick had caused any damage, deciding eventually that nothing appeared freshly smashed.

'You are a filthy mess,' Rossan ungraciously observed, taking one of Nick's arms, Danny the other, both of them reeling from his stale whisky saturated breath. 'Time to get you cleaned up.'

Dragging Nick between them, his legs and feet trailing at obscure angles, Rossan and Danny got him along the landing, wedged his pliable body against the wall with Rossan's knee in his back as Danny opened the bathroom door. After bundling Nick into the bath, Danny stripped off his jacket and shirt, supporting Nick's head as Rossan turned on the shower. It took a good minute and a half until Nick gasped, jerked, gripped the rim of the bath and began a messy struggle, flailing at anything within his reach.

'Nick, it's Paul and Danny,' Rossan shouted above the shower's lukewarm spray.

'Piss off,' Nick managed in response, his words slurred, his voice weak and hoarse.

'You've no chance,' Danny said, preventing Nick from sliding down the bath and dozing off. Danny, who had shared enough perilous operations with Nick to know him well. Danny who was small and fluid, a springy walk to his step that could be mistaken for a jauntiness when it is nothing more than being prepared. Wiry, not muscular, all Danny's strength and endurance lay inside, while his face had a leanness derived from professional hardship; refined through the storms of many campaigns until the bone beneath the sallow skin revealed every single line like a battle scar, which some of the more recent ones were. His dark hair was not neatly cut but seemed to have been attacked with blunt scissors. One eyebrow, his right, was testimony to bouts in the boxing ring representing the army, where he had also mastered the fine art of close-quarters combat that CO8 determined his primary trade.

Ten minutes of holding the shower was enough to persuade Rossan that Nick also needed a good dose of hard love. 'If you want to find those who murdered Angela, you're not going to do it like this.'

How or where Nick got his energy from, Danny didn't know, but Nick flew at Rossan and it took Danny's expert holds to restrain him and sit him gently back down.

'We're here to help,' Rossan said, his jacket soaked.

Holding tight to the bath's side, Nick stared up at Rossan; a lost child suddenly found as the spray cascaded off his flattened hair, streaming down his face mixing with his tears.

Preparing Nick for the journey back took another hour. Leaving Nick in Danny's care, Rossan bought six bottles of mineral water, two litres in each, a plastic bucket, bin liners, air freshener and a packet of powerful aspirin from the village Spar. Unaided, Nick made it down the stairs, locked the cottage and slipped in beside Rossan in the back as Danny drove. To Nick, the drive felt as though he'd been returned from the dead. Neither Danny nor Rossan forced any conversation on him, which he was extremely grateful for, his mind only just having stopped freewheeling. Only once did they have to stop as Nick brought up nothing more toxic than water and coffee, but Rossan still had to give the car a blast of freshener. On the outskirts of London, Danny having monitored Nick's condition through his driving mirror, felt able to lighten the mood.

'Fancy going out for a few beers tonight, Nick?' Danny asked, half-turning, smiling.

'Only if you're buying.'

'Hawick is baying for your blood,' Rossan said on a more serious note.

'At the moment it's a hundred per cent distilled, so he can't have any.'

That short conversation marked Nick's return from a downward spiral taking him to breaking point Rossan observed, when later he was required to review events with a cold analytical eye. It was also the point if he was to be absolutely honest and objective, when Nick detached himself from friends, from old alliances. Not becoming introverted or maudlin but possessed by a burning determination that he could trust no one; nor could he, or would he, be deviated from what had now become a very personal battle.

'Take care,' said Danny as he stopped close to Nick's address.

'If you need anything, call me,' Rossan urged him as he climbed out.

Leaning into the car, one hand resting on the roof, Nick looked from Danny to Rossan. 'Thanks,' he said, slammed the door and walked off.

Flagrantly sitting on the single yellow line at the junction of Firwood Road and Palmer Road, a satellite television company's van was sited so its rear doors had a good field of vision covering Nick's house. One of Mortland's surveillance teams he decided, noting the prefix on its number plate. As he walked past its empty cab he wondered if there'd be two or three at work in the back? Monitoring, reporting to Mortland the very second Nick appeared. For good measure there was a Met section car parked opposite his house, and a uniform presence on his step. Welcome home Nick, he thought, welcome back to a world you've helped create. Swinging open the garden gate, he felt the energy in his legs suddenly drain as he established his identity with the uniform on his step. He noticed the locks had been changed and wondered if it was normal, part of police routine after a double murder? The door was already open, and he gave it a cursory shove.

He stepped into the dark hall, and the swell of an unwelcome voice met him, the strident tones of Angie's mother phrasing shrill orders to her husband on what room was next for cleaning.

'It's you', she said coming to check the latest arrival, her bitter contempt resurfacing, functioning at a hundred per cent.

'Now, Nicholas,' began her husband, his strategic speech prepared in advance, another of his polished boardroom presentations perfected during his career as a banker. 'We appreciate how difficult this must be, but,' and he sought approval from his wife, 'we thought it best if we made a start on sorting Angela's things. We're just boxing them up for now, make the place presentable. You can of course choose things for yourself. I also took the precautionary measure of having the locks changed as you weren't here.'

'Never was,' said Angie's mother as Nick accepted a set of shiny keys, 'that was always the problem. If he had been...,' she broke off with an anguished snort and went back to laying claim to her daughter again.

The last of the day's sun strayed through a long window, dull stalks falling across the detritus of his life. In every room Nick smelt dust and Angie's feint lingering scent, but what troubled him was the loss of Angie's voice, its disappearance too loud in itself. In the kitchen, even though its walls were scrubbed clean, as he rummaged through a cupboard for his case of Laphroaig, he found blood smattered along the top of a cabinet door. Is this where they cornered her, beat her, executed her? All the cupboards had been emptied, the contents stored in sturdy packing boxes. Finding the remains of his Laphroaig, Nick took out two bottles, and grabbing a large mineral water, prepared to control his withdrawal.

Armed with his liquid solace, Nick made straight for Angie's studio; a terrible silence unbroken from the bottom step to the landing and her door when the stairs used to be her territory, Angie's pulpit for lecturing him. Everything around him wasn't as he wanted to remember it, the familiar things he now dreaded to touch. Beside the window, Angie's easel and stool kicked over, her plan chest ransacked, her last sketch screwed in a ball lying with pencils and a smashed glass in the fireplace. Hanging out of the plan chest a plain hardback book Angie used as a diary; illustrated outpourings, her intimate feelings that Nick began to read and immediately wanted to put down, forget he'd ever seen it. Angie had lied to Nick when he'd asked months ago if there'd been someone else. There always had been a string of lovers; Guy merely being the latest.

A world underground she'd made her own, formed from secret conventions and moments to savour. Reading between the lines on several entries, he found that Angie believed the actual sex was secondary to the excitement she gained from cheating on him. Having Tom was a mistake; a tortuous period she wanted erased and never repeated, she'd written in an assertive hand. Turning one page, Nick came across a pressed flower and a small black and white photograph showing a pretty girl aged six or seven who he guessed was Angie, posing in a forest. This before you became a victim in love and marriage? he wondered, a couple of petals coming away on his fingers. Well at least I know, he thought, ripping out pages, screwing them up and burning them one by one in the fireplace. For a good while afterwards, the air smelt of sooty smoke and specks of ash smeared the tiled hearth.

Dialling through the stations on a radio Angie used for background noise when painting, he caught a snatch of Roxy Music and thought he should perhaps adopt *In Every Dream Home A Heartache* as his personal anthem. With the lyrics buzzing through his head, Nick turned the radio off, knowing that Mr. Ferry may not have been writing about this sort of heartache, but he was correct in assuming that heaven was out of reach. Sitting back on a leather armchair, closing his eyes he began to doze, coming around when the doorbell went. Listening hard he heard clipped introductions followed by one other voice as they were admitted. They ascended in single file, Nick measuring the progress by each loose stair tread they hit.

Then Mortland marched smartly in followed by a thin woman in her thirties. Introducing herself as an R5 officer, she advised Nick he could call her Denise. Nick promised he would.

'I bear the Service's condolences,' Mortland declared, 'from the Chief himself, all the way down.'

'Everybody,' Denise added needlessly, looking Nick up and down.

'Thanks.'

'Yes, well, you've made the right decision by returning,' Mortland began after a rude interlude, struggling for an approach. 'The Deputy Chief would have come himself, but you know how it is.'

'Not really.'

'This is awkward for us all you know. But we have procedures to observe,' he said, casting a glance to Denise halted midway across the room as she stared out of the window.

'Mustn't forget the procedures,' said Nick, wondering if Denise was Mortland's secret weapon?

Denise had chosen her best investigative outfit for the visit; a charcoal grey business suit, dark tights and patent shoes with minimum heels, though none of it seemed to be cut to deal with personal tragedy. Her hair, not a natural colour, was a mix of highlights tailored in a bob.

'I have been appointed to handle your case,' Denise said, taking up residence in a far corner half hidden in shadow.

Without effort or resistance Nick submitted, reaching a lazy arm over the side of the chair he dragged up the bottle of Laphroaig, poured a small measure and drowned it with water. His granite features not registering a flutter of emotion, Mortland observed without a word as still the sorting and packing continued below. It took Nick two attempts to clear his throat before he spoke.

'I didn't know I was a case?'

With no intention of surrendering R5's claim on Nick, Mortland assumed responsibility for providing an answer. 'The police have ruled your wife's death and her... friend as murder by person or persons unknown. It is paramount to stress here and now, that after exhaustive consideration by wise heads, the agreed consensus rules out any connection between the events in Moscow. An unhappy coincidence. The police have a number of leads to pursue. One of them being this was a break-in that went tragically wrong.'

'Break-in?' The severity in Nick's voice took them by surprise. 'A break-in? When Angie and her boyfriend were executed?'

In her corner Denise gave an involuntary sigh, sensing her moment at last. 'Perhaps it is better to make Mr. Torr fully aware of his position,' she proposed, her velveteen voice correct and exact, a response to the hopelessness, to the chaos inflicted on the living by the dead.

Without the benefit of shadow, Mortland stranded in full view of Nick, glared in disbelief. 'And I was on course to do just that,' he tartly objected. 'The police, aware of your personal and professional circumstances, have agreed that we handle this end of the investigation. A few questions for you. Tidy up the loose ends, smooth out the wrinkles, that sort of thing.'

'How long have you known your wife had a lover?' Denise demanded, from her shadowy corner, earning Mortland's reproach with a sharp warning glance. 'That could be taken as a motive,' she blithely added.

'What?' said Nick and Mortland in wonderful stereo, though for completely different reasons.

Pouring himself another whisky Nick hardly bothered with the water, taking a long pull, his outrage growing. For too many years he'd struggled under the bureaucratic hammer attempting to tame his individual way of working; blow after blow forging him on the Firm's mighty anvil – praise and punishment, praise and punishment, praise and punishment – conform.

'Very well,' Mortland proposed with a haughty glance at Nick. 'I am aware, and sympathetic to the reasons why you may not feel inclined to discuss this at the present time, but that doesn't mean the issues will go away.'

'Your mental health must be taken into consideration after Moscow,' Denise added, sailing merrily along. 'Was your wife's affair the last straw?' Her voice offered no hope.

They were conspiring against him. Nick sensed and felt it, saw their ritual deceit brightening their eyes, the unspoken agreement and their chosen pattern of closing him in, smothering him with bureaucracy.

'You know what all this is related to,' Nick retorted, directing his response to Mortland and Mortland alone.

'Are we expected to believe that Moscow had involvement?' Denise countered, the main assault under way.

Over Mortland's shoulder Nick stared at low shreds of cloud sweeping by the window, bringing rain or dusk he couldn't tell.

'Believe what you want, isn't that R5's standard practice?' Nick flared. His mood ruthless, he refilled his tumbler. 'Are you implying I murdered my wife and her lover?'

'Did you?' Denise snapped back.

'The house was ransacked, ripped apart. I suppose I did that to conceal my involvement?'

'It would make sense.'

'Get out,' demanded Nick. 'Leave.'

Clearly unsure on how to proceed, Denise emerged from her corner, glanced at Mortland for approval, received it and shook the weight from one foot to another.

'This isn't over,' she decreed.

'No, it's not,' agreed Nick.

In the street children played through the last of the day. Nick closed his mind to their voices, their laughs and shouts. Down the hall, someone ran water in the kitchen. He remembered the buckets and detergents at the bottom of the stairs. 'Blood everywhere,' he'd heard Angie's mother complaining. Mortland circled the room, a hell-fire preacher in search of sinners.

'Go.' Nick's tone an ultimatum.

'Do you not think you've not had enough of that?' Mortland jabbed a finger towards the whisky. 'You're strained Torr, we understand. But let's not forget we can only arrive at a conclusion on the facts you provide.'

Too tired to argue, too weary to move from the chair, Nick's energy was reserved for lifting, pouring and drinking. He stared at Mortland. Why do I hate you? Why do you pretend to care?

'Try to see some sense,' Mortland insisted, looming over him; an absolution prepared if only Nick would confess.

Nick wanted to strike him hard, one punch, a blow designed for maximum damage. Then the hate passed, leaving him weak.

'You are doing yourself no credit,' Mortland added, bent over Nick, his sickly breath warm and close. 'This is all for your own good. I know how you feel, but I strongly advise you to cooperate and bring closure.'

'Accept a cover-up?' Nick was on his feet, fired up, angry. 'Pretend it didn't happen to protect our reputation? Is Hawick afraid of losing influence and allies?'

Already Denise recognised the futility of her mission, crossed to the door, pulled on her gloves, putting each finger determinedly in; a woman much used to paying great attention to small details.

'I must firmly remind you, that you are still required to make yourself available for a formal review regarding your actions in Moscow. Non-attendance will not be overlooked in any circumstances. You are required to be at Aspley by eleven in the morning,' Mortland announced, heading for the door. 'Sober,' he snapped and was gone, followed by Denise who made a comment on psychological assessment on her way down the stairs.

Grabbing the bottle of Laphroaig Nick hurled it after them, though his aim was a touch off; a little too high, and the bottle exploded against the wall above the door. Crunching through glass shards Nick went out onto the landing, gripping the banister he yelled: 'Out, everyone out. This is still my house.' All the way down the stairs he repeated his command at the top of his voice, even obligingly holding open his front door as Angie's mother strutted out.

Unsteady on his feet, he rested his head on the door frame, its coolness sinking into his temple, his mind pawing for something to say. Angie's father touched Nick's shoulder on the way past but neither of them spoke. Armed with his second watered down bottle of whisky, Nick took refuge in the room facing the street, dragging a slashed chair to the window, giving him a view of his path and front door. They came for Lubov's piece of treasure, but Angie and her lover just happened to be in the way, he decided almost beyond caring. Having forgotten to bring a glass, he drank out of the bottle, and at some point, he'd fallen asleep; for Nick woke suddenly with a jerk when he heard his name being called, sweat covering his face, a thin film, cold and sticky.

'I'd heard you were back in town. I was just passing and thought I'd drop in.'

Helpless and hating himself, Nick stared at Jane crouched by his side. From the street a heavy infectious laugh streaked into the room, reaching his brain like a sharp pain. His mind would not settle, and a steady cramp pulled at his belly. He wanted to be alone, he wanted peace, he wanted noise and he wanted company.

It is forgiveness and absolution what I need more than anything, he thought. And his good friend Laphroaig of course, who could always be relied upon to dull his appetite, to push another aspect of normality far, far away.

'Help yourself,' Nick said, offering the bottle; a stiffening inside his head, a weakness in his arms shaking the muscles in his hand. Careful he thought, seeing Jane flinch.

'What you need is a tea or a coffee,' Jane said, taking the whisky from him.

But Nick shook the suggestion away, bitter and weary.

'Have one yourself, have it on the house,' he said faking a smile. 'In fact, you can have the house.'

'Come and stay with me. It's not going to do you any good here all by yourself.'

'I'm all right,' he answered, feeling for the bottle unable to comprehend where it had gone. 'I've some things to sort out.'

Jane shook her head, pouring the whisky into a potted fig tree reposing firm and tall in the corner.

'You'll kill it,' he warned her, 'But one more death in this house isn't going to matter.'

'Is this how you're going to make things right?' Jane asked, pitching the drained bottle onto a sofa, its back cushions slashed open. Coming to his side, she perched on the chair arm.

'Nice perfume,' said Nick, 'noticed it in Devon, what is it?'

Pushing herself away, Jane twisted between boxes piled by the sofa. 'Nothing special, thought it was time for a change,' she said with a sad smile.

'So do I,' said Nick with an approving wave. 'Change is good, change is better than a rest. Look at me, I used to have a family, wife and son, now I've got nothing, amazing what change can do for you.'

'Nick, you're going to have to get some professional help,' she decided, collecting her bag from a coffee table. 'If you need somewhere to stay or just want to talk, let me know.'

Stay, he thought, stay tonight and tomorrow will be better. Was it contempt or pity that he saw in her eyes at that very moment; he never really knew, but it was enough.

'Scouts honour,' promised Nick, though he'd only ever been a Cub.

A final smile that bore no warmth, a peck on his unshaven cheek and Jane had gone, nothing more than a dull shadow lost on the street. He called her name, but she never turned.

Roused by Jane's coldness, Nick decided on action. After a cold shower and two black coffees, he made his way down to the utility room. Here a similar scene of wanton destruction as in the rest of house; the tumble dryer and washing machine hauled out from the wall when Angie's killers checked the floor for concealed hiding places; the panels from the suspended ceiling flicked out, laying bare its aluminium carcass, ducting and cable. Warm, but not hot, Nick thought, going to a large industrial switch disconnector box he'd fitted. Above its chrome handle he'd placed high-voltage and danger of death warning stickers. Inside there were no fuses, but two passports and credit cards taped to the back panel, both bearing different worknames, a necessity for the sudden need to escape. Back in the kitchen Nick added a bottle of mineral water to a carrier bag and a box of ibuprofen.

Leaving through the French doors, Nick stayed on the grass to deaden his steps. At the bottom of the garden he dropped the carrier bag over the fence and climbed after it. Down Ravenna Road, out onto St. John's Avenue he started to run. At a quarter-past ten on a bitter London evening, Nick had started to organise himself, thinking ahead, refining his strategy, organising his plan of attack.

Adopting tradecraft as if he were in hostile territory, Nick became a nomad, never staying in once place more than he needed, choosing a big corner pub in Greenwich that advertised economical rates, 'Contractors Welcome.' Paying in advance in the bar, its horseshoe counter decked in fake Victoriana, Nick took the backstairs to his room with a sunken heart. With every step upwards the carpet grew dirtier and there was a smell of damp tea cloths drying and stale dog. On the first landing, a receptionist greeted him with a dusty smile, a scab of a man with bronze teeth and strands of sickly red hair combed flat across a pale skull, his white shirt stained down the front.

Nick signed the book with yet another false name and for his trouble received a room with a shower that produced nothing more tempting than a slow cold trickle; its tray littered with toenail clippings. A gas fire levelled on one end by a wedge of damp timber, spat viciously when lit. Next to the window a kettle clogged with grime from countless contractor's hands, it stood with tea bags and pots of dated milk on a tray engraved with kittens. Down the hall the communal toilet jabbered and sang, conspiring with the traffic on the fly-over to give him no rest. Breakfast served from seven till nine could be smelt under his door, but Nick stole out without eating, as tired as on entering and a few pounds poorer.

Eleven

An hour in the cold air promising rain and Nick's head was clear. He wanted time to think and found it walking to Battersea in that strange unnatural hour before dawn when an eerie calm stalked the streets, and with it came a pale unequal light and fresh unleaded air flavoured by all of London's parks. The sky had started to divide, and a flux of cloud rolled up the Thames along with the morning grind into work. Nick's route was chosen at random, a palliative that did nothing to lessen the Ford Galaxy's grip on his heels. They had static and mobile units covering all exits from Palmer Road he realised, and they'd radioed for support.

Coming close to the river he felt its strong pull, though he could barely see it. A man tired and grey shuffled along as he exercised a troubled dog, bidding Nick a crisp good morning before dodging into the dips and hollows of Battersea Park to be stolen by the gloom. The first dabs of rain hit the pavement; a taxi sailed by, its light out, as Nick tired, turned the way he'd come, facing into the wet breeze by the river, shivering as it met his skin.

He took a train from Battersea to Victoria and the watchers were sharp, one of them keeping with him at the far end of the carriage. A different team picked Nick up when he went underground to Euston, a third team taking over during the journey to Berkhamsted. This last pair also warned of his coming, with a car despatched to collect Nick outside the station; nothing said on the drive, a silent twenty minutes only broken by clearance to proceed at Aspley's gate lodge. At the main house they were also ready for him, Strowther a staff instructor and Motte, Director of Training, forming a hasty duo beside a burly receptionist, a lone ex-RSM in drab plain clothes who knew the best pubs within a mile radius. They both immediately fell forward with offerings of sympathy. Strowther shook him warmly by the hand.

'We appreciate this is a bad time, but it's C's orders, his law you see,' Strowther explained, pained and slightly embarrassed. Gently he patted Nick's shoulder before beating a hasty retreat.

Closer now, Motte laid a silky hand on Nick's elbow, steering him to the back stairs, charming as ever, a perfect host escorting a tradesman through his house.

'We're all simply devastated, Nick. I mean your wife... that took the wind out of all our sails. It must be quite a terrible shock. Well, obviously it is, but you know what I mean?'

'Yes, thanks Motte, I know.' You mean I have encountered the murder of someone I loved and changed, he thought. Then who wouldn't? Another gate of wisdom that I've been unlucky enough to open.

They climbed barely uttering another word, emerging on the top floor Motte dictating the speed, walking quickly down a passage long and high, school lampshades pricking out their path. In place of the expected left turn to a corridor housing the staff offices and meeting rooms, Motte wheeled sharp right and headed up a cramped flight of linoleum stairs into the mansard roof.

'Here we go,' he grinned, all silly and childish, the type worn on first dates, rapping twice at a commonplace mustard door.

'Appreciated,' said Nick, only for Motte to smile sheepishly and push open the door.

'So, you managed to make it. Brilliant under the circumstances,' said Hawick inviting Nick in. 'Gave us all a bit of a worry skipping over the fence like that. Should have let us know what you were up to, we'd have sent a car. Right Terry?'

'Gone myself,' said Motte grinning inanely, backing out, closing the door with a gentle click.

Looking round Nick saw the attic room hardly altered; as airless as ever it was when it served as a junior common room, and over the fireplace he could still make out the holed plaster where the dartboard used to sit. They never throw anything out, he thought pulling a plastic chair from a dusty stack, its seat splashed with green paint. Squeezing it between crates of cardboard binders, he sat heavily down.

'There are inconsistencies we need to discuss, agreed?' Pausing here,

Hawick expected a response of some kind, but Nick sat amidst the memorabilia, unmoved, tightening inside as his anger mounted, an electric charge steadily increasing.

'Moscow were tipped-off about the collection,' said Nick. 'How about discussing that?'

'I can only deal with facts,' conceded Hawick. 'Wynn was terminated in Hamburg, fact.' Emphasising 'terminated' with a severe whisper, Hawick smiled weakly. 'You were the only one to emerge out of Moscow, fact. Shall we deal with those facts?'

'That fact is, Teddy, that I don't know why Wynn was *terminated*,' said Nick, pitching his weight to the edge of the chair. 'The fact is, I was lucky to survive in Moscow. The fact is, something else came along, remember? Nothing too serious, just the murder of Angie.'

'Had dealings with your old Lat sources recently?' Hawick said slowly, finding an empty file carousal that he spun slowly, then with increasing force. His gaze however remained constantly on Nick; level, precise, carefully measured, a marksman sighting up his prey. 'Anything I should know about? A link to Moscow, perhaps? Maybe Hamburg?' Hawick's mawkish eyes settled on Nick.

'I don't know what you're talking about?' Nick protested.

Resenting Hawick's overbearing condescending approach, Nick said nothing more, but watched Hawick through the debris of so many operations used as training props, boxed like previous lives waiting for a second chance.

'Is that a denial?' Hawick said, his fingers now prowling amongst faded stencils on top of a Gestetner copier.

'There's nothing to deny. Can I leave now? Thanks for the lack of support and inconvenience, by the way,' he said, suddenly on his feet.

'Sit down,' Hawick sternly countered, his gaze soft and dewy.

'Is that an order?'

'I'm afraid it is, yes, it is,' he responded after an age. Drifting to the mantelpiece Hawick accepted the logic at his leisure.

Uncomfortable, restless, Nick had no stomach for Hawick's trite concern. Getting to his feet he went to a tiny casement window long rotten, yet somehow managed to inch it apart for some air.

'Perhaps you could give this some attention,' Hawick said. 'It is rather serious all said and done.'

'What is it you would like to know?' he asked, his resentment simmering.

'Your movements in the hours prior to the murder of your wife? Precisely, exactly, what were they?' wondered Hawick casually; taking his time, pulling out his fob watch, releasing the cover and allowing the details to sink in.

Despite the chill playing down his back and arms, Nick still suffered from the oppressive heat in the room, leaving him no air to breathe.

'Why?'

Slowly Hawick advanced towards the door, light and free on his feet, a moth choosing its spot. 'Latvians, Nicholas. The solid, dependable Lats that provided Gav Rafford with an excellent product line. The Lats Rafford sent over the border as his soldier ants. Drivers, cleaners, secretaries, all in gainful employment inside Mother Russia. The Lats you inherited when they resettled here. A couple of them, according to their case files, you retained as talent spotters in our fair and glorious city. Those Lats, Nicholas. The haze clearing?'

'I haven't had any contact in ages.'

'Can we try a touch harder, if it's not too much trouble,' Hawick insisted, his face reddening, his entire flimsy body arching.

The anger welled up inside Nick, too many hours wasted, the deaths, the needless questions. 'Where is this leading?

Undaunted Hawick strode off again, searching with his slender fingers in boxes and trays clogged with dust. 'This, Nicholas, is leading to you having an adequate explanation why R5 have just recovered a cellphone belonging to one of those Lat's from your home. He's disappeared, care to elaborate on that, Mmm?' Hawick decreed, his gaze flicking to the door, the time consulted yet again, twisting his watch chain with long slim fingers.

What Latvian would that be? wondered Nick, his mind scrabbling for a foothold, attempting to retrace his movements though all he could recover amounted to whisky clouded fragments without knowing which were real, which the product of his imagination.

'It's been planted,' said Nick, his voice dancing through the rude light. 'It's Moscow,' he said, realising that his explanation even sounded lame to him.

'I see. Your answer is noted.'

Who by? wondered Nick, speculating if was just special guests Hawick had invited to listen in, or a whole team with a different agenda?

'Did R5 receive an anonymous tip to search my place? Or were they just passing and chanced their luck?' he asked, thinking of Lister's claim to her boyfriend: *Jo said it was like being trapped in a conspiracy.*

'I appreciate your concern.'

No, you don't appreciate a thing, Nick thought, the only recent concern you've experienced is when a gate barrier jams on the Tube. Back at the window the cold calmed him. He glanced into the grounds and thought how far away the trees looked, the distant section of perimeter wall; beyond that there would be traffic, the everyday normality he'd shut out for too long.

Hawick came full circle, stopping in front of the fireplace his arms folded neatly. 'You're telling me that you've no knowledge of this Latvian, Juris Valgos?' he purred condescendingly, his wizened head locked on Nick.

'No comment.' Nick reached him in three strides, felling Hawick with one rapier punch.

Snatching open the door, he saw Mortland and his good friend Denise waiting for him at the bottom of the stairs. Nick floored Mortland with a rising fast blow, Denise with a powerful elbow to her nose, followed by a single tight punch to the nape of her neck. Off and running, he avoided the main stairs. Behind him he could hear Hawick screaming the house down, but Nick never turned, kicking faster. On a landing, an administrative officer had the misfortune to get in Nick's way and he was sent crashing from a shoulder charge that cracked his collarbone, his files cascading to the floor.

Out into the grounds Nick ran, walked, ran and walked, zigzagging to a corner of the perimeter wall. Scrambling, digging in his toes he hauled himself over and landed in a crouch, absorbing the shock to his ankles. Straightening up, patting his passports and credit cards in his pocket, he hurried off in the opposite direction to the station; a fugitive in what had become a strange and hostile land.

Outside a pub two miles up the road Nick rang for a taxi using the name of Deacon, making the final call on his phone before dumping it. In Hemel Hempstead, Nick used both credit cards at different cash machines withdrawing three hundred pounds from each. Choosing busy stores where the assistants would be less likely to remember him, Nick bought a pair of swimming trunks, towel, leather holdall, and a full change of clothes complete with a stripped knitted hat.

At the sports centre, Nick paid for a swim, spent five minutes in the pool and left in his new outfit, stuffing two carrier bags full of his old clothes into a bin. Off two different market stalls specialising in electronics, Nick bought three second-hand cellphones, then bought eight SIM cards from a shop boasting it could unlock any handset. From the bus station he caught the service to Watford through Kings Langley, took a train between Watford Junction and Heathrow, then a coach into central London. During each leg of his journey from Aspley, Nick began to reassemble details of his days spent drinking; small snatches of memory he slotted together, a jigsaw he'd never complete, but it would provide part of the picture. Slowly, some of his movements in those wasted hours began to make perfect sense.

Slipping in and out of shops and department stores along Oxford Street, always exiting onto the street through a side door, Nick headed off into the afternoon laced with rain colder than snow. Running off his jacket it soaked his legs, finding its way into his shoes, until Nick was damp from waist to toes. He was hot, he was cold. Dizzy from hunger or a fever chasing him, the pavement felt soft, his knees uncertain, unsure. He crossed the river by Southwark Bridge and the Thames was as dirty as the sky. A tug nursed a string of barges downstream, their containers packed with rubbish. Brazen gulls shrieked, diving around the barges, lifting and falling, as weightless as scraps of paper. Somewhere above him an aircraft thundered low towards the airport, leaving nothing but a whine and a sparkle of light in the dark clouds. Shivering, his shirt a damp stain round his back, Nick pressed on.

Inside the Imperial War Museum Nick wandered through its bric-a-brac of death, amongst noisy school parties and old soldiers in search of their youth, roaming its galleries seeking out a final resolution. 'Feeling all right, sir?' An attendant enquired, with just enough sneer to discourage modern lunatics from lingering like ghosts of Bedlam's past. Perfectly, Nick assured him, slipping away.

He found his quarry in the domed reading room that had once been a chapel; Jamie Hayles, former Head of Moscow Station, former Head RUS/OPS, his neat manicured hands clasped behind a head of immaculate grey hair. Jamie Hayles wore the grace of a country gentleman and the brooding slouch of an academic of which he had lately become.

'Hello Jamie,' Nick said, coming to the side of Jamie's desk.

'Good God!' His tight supple body whipped forward, his arms coming down like scimitars, trying to cover the documents laid before him all in the same movement. 'Nick, my dear boy, wonderful, what a surprise,' he began, the words tumbling out, 'I... thought you were...'

'Thought what, Jamie?'

'Nothing....' His florid face opened into a robust smile. 'Take a pew.'

Nick did as he was bid. 'But try to keep it low,' insisted Jamie, tilting his body to Nick, 'the nannies here don't hold with rowdies and expect total devotion to their blessed works.'

'We need to talk, Jamie?'

Accepting this forthright admission with a graceful smile, as though Jamie wouldn't have expected anything less from Nicholas Torr. 'Perhaps we should have this discussion elsewhere,' he offered.

'I think we should,' Nick assured him. 'Got somewhere in mind?'

'My place,' he proposed.

Twelve

They arrived by cab wisely choosing not to walk after all, a thick shower hammered on the roof and the street had a greyness that belonged to dusk. Arriving at a picture framer's off the Old Kent Road caged in by developer's boards and supported on the opposite side by a tattered mini market sagging on its bricks. Crisp bags and chocolate bar wrappers had blown in the mesh screens around the windows and fluttered manically; weird butterflies with no hope of survival.

Slow moving traffic snaked grudgingly round a Transit van hauled onto the kerb, its dented bonnet propped open. A genuine breakdown? wondered Nick, allowing one final glance for good measure before stepping inside. Across a workshop cold and dank, Jamie pushed a way through workbenches stained by glue and frames that had gone out of fashion suspended from the ceiling.

'It's all seen its prime like me,' he said climbing four stairs to a platform with a band saw and a curtained off corner for an office. 'I should get someone in to make it work or clear the hell out,' he added, throwing trade journals on the floor so Nick could sit down at a dining chair opposite a large counterweighted drawing board.

'Faking maps, Jamie?' Nick asked, glimpsing a half-completed hand drawn First World War trench system on the board.

'Faithful, accurate copies which I frame and flog,' Jamie explained without much enthusiasm. 'Plus, the historical account to go with them.'

'As long as you're busy.'

'Well this is a surprise,' he gushed, ignoring Nick's point.

'I thought it might be.'

'Wasn't sure when or if you'd call,' Jamie said, stowing away his plastic shopping bag. Pulling back a length of red and white gingham fabric, its edges badly frayed, it was threaded on a plastic wire he used it to curtain off a small grey safe under a workbench. Stooping low, grunting as he searched, Jamie brought out a large Jiffy Bag, handing it to Nick. 'This what you came for?' he asked, closing up the safe, sliding back the gingham.

Ripping open the bag Nick reminded himself of its contents; two more passports bearing different worknames, with credit cards to match and Angie's reserve cellphone. Part of the jigsaw of when he was missing Nick remembered, involving three drunken attempts to write Jamie's name and address; making a complete arse of himself into the bargain when he despatched them at a post office somewhere during his travels.

'Had contact from anyone in the Firm recently?'

Jamie folded his arms, studying Nick. 'Personally, or professionally?'

'Professionally.'

'Thumping the condescending Deputy Chief and assaulting two of R5's skull crushers in one morning is going some. Nice work, by the way. But according to *my* source, you've topped that by making a Lat vanish into thin air. There's a reward for whoever claps eyes on you and turns you in. R5 has branded you a menace, a danger to anyone who so much as blinks in your direction.'

'Thinking of claiming the reward?'

'And have to look over my shoulder for the rest of my natural? Not a chance,' he admitted at last, roosting on an old high bar stool. 'None of the old hands I spoke to had you down as a cold-blooded savage, though a few did think that your temper would be up after your wife's death. But that wouldn't have you involved in despatching a Lat for no apparent reason,' he said, folding an elastic band around his fingers. 'You didn't er... have dealings with the Lat, did you?' he asked, a timely afterthought.

'No Jamie, I didn't. It's linked to a collection in Moscow, you heard about that too?'

'My source may have mentioned it.'

'I need background Jamie.'

'You need help, Nick. The voices from the top of the mountain have already pronounced you guilty. I may have been off the books for three years, but I still keep my ear to the ground. And I don't hold out much hope now that Hawick and saint Jane are really running the show. Hawick's set his eyes on the glittering prize, and views you as a threat. For that reason, he's dangerous.'

'You're well informed, Jamie, you *must* have a source with considerable influence?'

Whether he had or not, Jamie wasn't prepared to disclose his methods of collecting his raw material.

'Forget all about Moscow, get yourself off somewhere quiet and grieve for Angela.'

'Later. Right now, Jamie, I need some answers, starting with the recruitment of Viper in Moscow.'

Scratching his neck, Jamie picked up a pencil and started wrapping the rubber band around it. 'You're asking the wrong chap, Nick. Sally Wynn was the one who pulled Lubov in, all I did was bait the line.'

'We all know it's the baiting that's the tricky bit,' said Nick, with a smile. 'Unfortunately, I can't ask Sally.'

'I heard.'

In a flurry of action, Jamie rolled up sheets of tracing paper, sliding them into a cardboard tube, then fastidiously tidied away his pencils; and if Nick didn't know better, this sudden impulse might be mistaken for stage fright.

'And I still want to hear about Viper?' Nick insisted.

Accepting he had no alternative; Jamie recounted the recruitment of Viper, or to those enjoying privileged clearance – Vasily Aramovich Lubov. As Jamie told it, he hadn't long returned to London from Moscow and had pitched camp in RUS/OPS, run by the formidable Wallace before she hung up her coat on the peg for the last time. He had odd jobs, but mostly he was making a damn nuisance of himself, more or less easing himself into the hot seat as Wallace's replacement. The watchers had reported a new arrival at the Embassy, not previously known, no trace on the accredited list, seemed he just popped up out of thin air which caused a bit of a stir. Wallace passed it up the chain for a decision because it crossed the border onto the turf of their relatives in Security, but Jamie had already decided the new face was worth having a closer look at. It was the dog-end of Aubrey-Spencer's time as Chief, the political vultures were circling, his days were numbered, so he'd agreed with Jamie they might as well have a speculative flutter, and he pointed Jamie at Vasily.

'On your first look, how did you read him? Novice? Veteran?'

'Hopeless,' Jamie admitted. 'For two days running, the watchers clung to Vasily as he spent his late afternoons window shopping. Never gave any serious effort to glancing over his shoulder, left the Embassy on foot, meandered through Hyde Park taking different routes, and that was his counter-surveillance, thank you very much. No minders, not a soul trailing after him.'

'That must have been a relief,' suggested Nick.

'A gift. Every Christmas and every birthday all rolled up in one,' Jamie admitted. 'With that level of tradecraft, Vasily didn't strike me as a regular fixture in the Embassy's dark side of the house, or it was a very cunning attempt at planting a double on us. Vasily did all the big stores, but he always ended up at the Burlington Arcade, nosed pressed against the glass of a shop flogging objet d'art. The object of his desires, a very exquisite chess set, and he'd as much a chance acquiring it as he had securing a trip to the moon.

'I sidled up to him, struck up a conversation on the merits of chess and Vasily acts all coy. He eventually admitted he's here for another three days, he's a civil servant, running his sharp eye over the Embassy's housekeeping budget. As cover goes, it's paper thin, but if you haven't got a made-to-measure legend, keep it simple, and keep it friends with the truth. With the clock on Vasily's stay running, I had one pitch, and I gambled the lot, inviting Vasily for a game and the opportunity to enjoy a decent pint of English cask ale. For a moment Vasily is undecided, but with a furtive glance at the chess set, he agrees, and we set a date for the following afternoon.'

'Do you play?'

'Nothing more advanced than a wood pusher,' confessed Jamie.

Fulfilling the role of a genial host, Jamie maintained the finest tradition of providing his guest with a good time, allowing Vasily to literally wipe the board with him, and after Jamie had stumped up for several pints to celebrate Vasily's command of the game, not to mention the odd vodka to cement diplomatic relations, Jamie closed in. 'Mentioned the boutique owner was a chum, and I could get the set he admired at cost price or less.' The offer teased Vasily out of his shell, but in the end, he demurred, regretting his salary would not even run to that, not after he had suffered a demotion. Wisely Jamie didn't jump in but proceeded very slowly to play out more line. 'Always allow wriggle room,' he judiciously recommended.

'Very wise,' Nick agreed, relapsing into silence.

'Call it gut instinct, a sixth sense, but Vasily had something, not just a hint of potential, he had talent written all over him. Important thing was to maintain the connection, open up a channel for future exploitation. We talked a bit of history, bit of politics, nothing too strenuous. Bit by bit we did a full three-sixty, back to where we started, discussing the chess set in the arcade, our own mutual appreciation society for quality artistry. In the end, we both decided the thing was grossly overpriced, which was a real shame because it was a beauty. Hand carved, an absolute stunner, it would be a joy to own. Gave him a good ten minutes to reflect on not being able to afford it, then proposed all was not lost. I'd have a word with my chum in the shop, do some serious haggling to get the price down. Big question was, what did Vasily think it was worth? He came up with a ridiculously low figure, somewhere in the region of three hundred, might even have been less, but he was an accountant and it was his own money. If I managed to get it for that price, did he want me to have it forwarded to him through the Embassy? You'd think I'd turned the heat up already. "No...no...no... it would have to be private arrangement," he insisted and promptly ripped out a page of his little notebook and dashed off his address. We had footage of the arcade, inside the pub, and one of the team had the perfect angle to catch Vasily committing pen to paper. Told him not to worry if he couldn't pay there and then, we'd arrange for payment at a later date. It was the least anyone could do for a new friend. Assured him that I'd do my best, and he just beamed as if he'd struck the deal of a lifetime.'

He just hadn't read the small print, thought Nick. And having pulled off the difficult phase of walking Lubov across the street, Jamie had to keep him there.

'What about the chess set, did he receive it?'

'Blew RUS/OPS emergency float for that month, it cost two-thousand and sixty quid, excluding delivery, and I hadn't cleared it with Wallace. Well, it was last minute, on the hoof,' he admitted with a wry grin.

'The follow-up, you ran that too?'

'We had his home address and brought in a team via Estonia to keep a score of his movements and stack up a profile,' Jamie declared with pride. 'Married, and she never let him forget it. Before his demotion everything was on the up and up. Enough salary to reduce marital strife, a move to a larger apartment, a nice Volkswagen, and his chess, played weekends in Sokolniki Park. Then after his fall from grace, they relocated to Golyanovo District, flogged the car but he didn't abandon his chess, even if it was an hour's commute. We worked out the best approach, and Sokolniki came out top every time. Realised during my contact with Vasily in London he'd require mollycoddling, so I asked for Wynn, she was in the slot for Moscow anyway, and I'd be able to butter him up until she was able to take over in six months' time.'

'But you were responsible for re-establishing contact?'

Which turned out to be a long walk in the park, Jamie revealed. He browsed all the tables in Sokolniki until he caught the familiar face of Vasily; melancholy, a lost soul until he began to play, then he came alive. Jamie watched him from afar for another three weeks, timing his approach to get alongside Vasily as he headed for the Metro.

'Never thought the penny would drop after I'd latched onto him,' Jamie disclosed, the heavy lines on his brow creasing as he frowned. 'Asked him if the chess set had arrived safely? By some miracle it had, but it took him three attempts to admit it. From the panic in his eyes, anyone would have thought he was being robbed. It took another circuit around the park before he began to string a coherent sentence together. We strolled and hit the small talk, nothing damaging, a genial catching up. How was he doing? Family well? Work treating him any better? All the usual crap. Left it at that and toddled off.'

'And he turned up the following weekend for his game?'

'That was the test, wasn't it? Would it be a no-show, or would he bring along the FSB for company? As a precaution I kept a good amount of clear water between me and the chess area, and he turned up alone. Like clockwork, thought he'd been manufactured in Switzerland,' said Jamie reliving the moment with a gentle smile. 'Waited for him to exercise his mind, and for a change of scenery, bought him a coffee at one of the kiosks. Very gently, I increased the heat, a mild reminder he owed me for the chess set. He shunted out a handful of excuses, and promised to settle, but could it be in a month's time? His reduction in salary was a problem. He could have as long as he desired, in fact, he could forget the debt, I proposed. As a matter of fact, he could earn some money on the side. We were on this avenue leading off from the rotunda, it was that awful moment when you commit and there's not a soul who can help. Stopped dead in his tracks didn't he, and Vasily gave me such a melancholy look of disillusionment before nodding acceptance of my terms. Obvious from day one Vasily could be bought, it was the money or nothing, and that's what I gave him. Kept my sales patter running, the benefits of having a monthly lump sum untaxed, preferably accumulating overseas ready for the day he wanted to collect. The alternative wasn't really worth considering. I had evidence of our meeting in London that would find its way to his government employers, with the downside of having to confess to his wife.'

'And he didn't disappoint, did he Jamie?' said Nick. 'He even had a circle of admirers in London, didn't he? I heard his product was assessed exclusively by the Vapour Trail Group?'

Granting Nick a stern look of reproach, Jamie eased off the stool, stretched and settled again.

'Who got to take a look at it wasn't my concern. Vasily was star material, and in the beginning all that mattered was drilling the well. For a couple of months I thought it might even be dry. It was just like breaking in a new pair of shoes, nothing too demanding. First we had to weigh and examine Vasily's excess baggage.'

And Jamie disclosed he did that over several Sundays after Vasily's chess sessions.

'Told him he had to be straight, I needed the good and the bad. And he just gave that docile nod of his and coughed the lot.'

As Jamie recounted it, a studious air of intensity settled across his features. 'Vasily Aramovich Lubov was a meticulous forensic accountant, who for good or ill, entered the Defence Ministry as a dedicated career professional, brimming with the misplaced hubris of youth that his qualifications were ancillary to his talents. He strove, he excelled, he flourished. At thirty he had risen to the not so inconsiderable height of assistant director in the financial auditing inspectorate. Life was good for Vasily. He anticipated a stellar rise into senior management, but he ignored that nagging inner voice urging moderation, that know-all voice whispering: "caution." Vasily is determined to gain his promotion by supervising a rigorous pruning exercise. He becomes a zealot, a one-man mission, determined the Ministry will not have its pockets picked by unscrupulous departments. What Vasily requires is a cause célèbre to draw the attention of his superiors. With a quite spectacular aptitude for wanting to put a brilliant career behind him, our hero singles out a section in the property directorate. He labours at his task, scrutinising capital expenditure assets, and when he's gone over every last rouble, Vasily's keen nose for irregular accounting practices is positively twitching. His blood's up and discretion doesn't get a look in. He made the fatal mistake of allowing his aspirations to govern his good sense and creates an unholy song and dance about the anomalies. He refuses to sign-off on a certification of compliance for the department's accounts, requesting a formal interview with the directorate's finance officer....'

Pausing to marshal his facts into sequence, Jamie used his finger in the style of a conductor's baton to compose them, and once satisfied, proceeded.

'A couple of hours after Vasily kicked up a storm, he's ordered to the Minister's office where there's a reception committee of three. The Minister and two visitors who were rounding off a sombre discussion and it wasn't about the weather. Was this Vasily's moment of glory? His reward, his recognition, the confirmation of his promotion? Was it hell. It was the drop, Nicholas. The Minister looked him up and down as if Vasily was a degenerate, never uttered a syllable and pounded out. The visitors comprised a General in his finest, the other, according to Vasily, seemed as if he'd risen from the grave, a famished thing dressed so solemnly and humbly Vasily's muddled brain cast him as an exile, a wanderer, and he named him *Leshy* after the forest creature of legend. The General did all the talking, congratulating Vasily for his diligence, his astute skills, his mastery of accounting principles, but Vasily observed how the General would glance at Leshy as if needing approval. And that's when Vasily belatedly woke up to the fact it was *Leshy* who held the power. His eyes, his face belonged to a predator, and he never once took his gaze off Vasily, a stare so penetrating Vasily swore it reached into his soul. And Vasily's reward for his heroic act of forensic accountancy? Immediate transfer to a newly formed department whose sole responsibility will be the financial security of sensitive operations.'

'GRU.'

'The genuine thing, tooth and claw.'

'What had he uncovered?'

'Sleight of hand in a funding stream directed to Veterans Rehabilitation Clinic No.2 in the Metrogorodok District, northeast of Moscow. We got RUS/OPS to check, nothing returned on it, a blank. But the finances suggested otherwise, the money pointed to it being some kind of GRU establishment. In a stroke, Vasily found himself a gamekeeper turned poacher, consigned to the GRU's dark financial labyrinth. In his department, Vasily would be the king. But this is more curse than blessing. Vasily's department will have the unfortunate privilege of falling under the watchful remit of Leshy, and our meticulous auditor answers to no one else, not even the Minister. On the one hand, he must ensure the GRU's accounts become undetectable by using his talents to hoodwink the Ministry, on the other, he must keep the *sensitive operations* lubricated with sufficient funds. And that was the fate of Vasily. His professional dreams stalled, and for good measure, he's permanently shackled to Leshy. Part of his duties included audits of residencies and outstations. London was his first trip. Vasily, though he didn't know it, was everything we looked for in an asset who has the potential to strike gold.'

'What about the Oktober Projekt, did Lubov mention it?' Nick asked, taking an unexpected direction, this time without a smile.

Blowing out his cheeks, Jamie shook his head in the sort of declaration that the wise reserve for foolish questions. 'Not to me, and anyway that's ancient history, nothing more,' he declared as though Nick really should have known better.

'Ancient history didn't kill Lubov, Foula, Angie or Sally Wynn,' said Nick his temper rising. 'I've had it from the horse's mouth, Jamie, from Lubov's last inadequate handler. The Oktober Projekt was Lubov's treasure, ours if we gave him sanctuary.'

'What else was he peddling? Unicorn rides? Personal introductions to Santa? Lifetime visits from the tooth fairy? It's a myth, Nicholas. Disinformation to have us chasing our tails, and it looks as if we still are. But if it's the Oktober Projekt according to Jamie you desire, that's what you shall have,' he declared, tossing the pencil and band aside. 'The myth started in the Seventies, way before your time. This place supposedly went by the name of OKT/NC/673 Projekt, a strategic facility 250 miles east of Moscow.'

'GRU, KGB?'

'Allegedly a military language facility. Right, we've heard that one before,' said Jamie. 'The myth started to get some clothes in the Nineties when Aubrey-Spencer was head of station in Moscow running his own stable of thoroughbred assets. Giles Monroe was his number two. I was head of station in Czecho, due to take over from Aubrey-Spencer, which is when he briefed me about something the Cousins had paid top dollar for. Word was, they'd caught a whiff of a new operational strategy being bolted together at this place outside Nizhny Novgorod, which back then was called Gorky. Place was a big secret, apparently real hush hush even by Moscow's standards. What made the Cousins sit up, was a tip suggesting the training was for a selected cadre of recruits. No group interaction, the prospective recruits were formed into cells, three to each cell. And that's how they received their training. Remote and isolated, slap in the middle of a forest, the area was closed to foreigners. No one could get close to confirm its existence, and even when we had the benefit of satellite coverage, they identified nothing conclusive. Buildings, barracks, workshops, could have been any military facility, and probably was. Monroe checked it out, pressed his sources, worked his agents to the bone and even they came up empty handed. Given the way Monroe's assets always provided a decent cut of meat for the top table, that just seemed to prove that the Cousins had paid through the nose for a myth.'

'But the myth wouldn't die, would it, Jamie?' queried Nick, noting not for the first time how Jamie, the experienced fieldman that he was, had begun closing down the hatches, sealing himself in.

'During Gavin's turn as our Lat illegal he raised a head of steam, claiming he had a positive sounding on Nizhny Novgorod. I was fighting off a fresh outbreak of FSB counter-intelligence operations with Roly's assistance. So, it was pretty much Gavin's show, shuttling back and forth between Riga and saint Jane who was earning her Moscow stripes. Gavin announced he'd finally nailed the myth, hit the genuine seam.'

'Confirmation of what Jamie?'

'Confirmation it *was* a GRU facility,' Jamie grudgingly admitted. 'Uncorroborated, but enough to suggest the place was flourishing.'

'What happened, Jamie?' Nick sensed Jamie was playing for time, attempting to take him down an unconnected side road.

'Operation Windfall is what happened. Finished Gavin, and almost a few others, including me.' Unwilling to continue, Jamie had reached the final watertight hatch, which he wasn't prepared to open for anyone, including Nicholas Torr.

'Myth or not regarding its true purpose, at least you had proof that the place existed,' put in Nick, wisely electing not to dwell on Operation Windfall.

'Yes,' admitted Jamie, his voice distant as though he was reviewing doomed events first-hand, before slowly returning to the disquieting awkward present. 'Then it became myth again, nothing, sank once more gracefully out of sight.'

Altering course, Nick delivered a direct question; and from the way Jamie all too quickly yawned and stretched, he'd hoped would not be forthcoming.

'Has Aubrey-Spencer approached you recently? You and Gavin been put back on the beat, unofficially? Come on, Jamie, you can tell me?'

'Why would he do that?'

'That's what you need to tell me, Jamie, get it off your chest, help me out.'

'If you don't go looking for trouble, it won't find you, Nicholas,' Jamie said his mood darkening. 'Not when it involves the top floor.'

For a moment or two, Jamie made no commitment, weighing up his options, then with a shake of his head, he began. 'You never heard this from me.'

'Heard what?'

'He was the best Chief I can remember serving,' Jamie admitted with considerable pride. 'Thought it was disgraceful how he was levered out, forced to take the JIC or slink off into the wilderness.'

'What did he want, Jamie? Your advice? Your wisdom?'

Unable to derail Nick, Jamie threw up his hands in submission.

'A favour for old time's sake.'

'That it?'

Suddenly finding an urgent desire to rearrange his drawing pens, Jamie muttered 'Oh hell,' before returning his focus to Nick.

'He wanted me to run an errand for him,' Jamie admitted, 'wanted me to drop off something in Hamburg.' He shrugged, reliving the trip, his slack face the brunt of an inner anxiety, pulled one way then another.

'Now who would that have been to see?' Nick challenged him. 'Bump into Jack while you were there, did you Jamie?'

'I had to keep Jack out of it,' he said in a low forlorn voice, 'Aubrey-Spencer had something for Harry.'

'Harry Bransk? The last time I worked with Harry he tried to rip me off,' said Nick, 'Harry's a snake. Anything else Jamie, while we're on the subject of making Nick happy.'

'Aubrey-Spencer wanted something picking up from Benny's.'

'Did he?' replied Nick, getting to his feet. 'And that would be what, exactly?'

'A spot of pen and ink work,' Jamie tetchily revealed. 'Full set of papers to be deposited with Harry. Satisfied?'

'I don't know, am I? But thanks for the background, Jamie. Better for all concerned if we keep my visit to ourselves.'

Relieved his interrogation was over, Jamie sprang off the stool, shook

Nick by the hand. 'My lips are sealed, you know me.'

And Nick did, all too well. Within half an hour if Nick was unlucky, Jamie would be telegraphing the details of their meeting to Aubrey-Spencer. Outside the Transit had gone, but Nick once more had the impression that he wasn't alone.

Thirteen

Already the frost had eaten into the day by the time Nick left Jamie's; crisp and mean it rode on the wind that met Nick around every corner, blew into his face, got into his skin. Taking three buses when one would have done, getting off each time before his stop, Nick practised the endless ritual of evasion, the perpetual myth of security, the old deceit.

In Knightsbridge he fell in with the flow of shoppers, breaking suddenly away to his left or right to amble, to spread out his steps, to enter by one door and leave by another. All the time waiting for a similar move, the dropped glance, a rapid change of direction. In Wandsworth, he found another remote bolt-hole for the night, in a B&B reeking of fried sauerkraut and garlic; after paying cash up front, he jammed his bag under the single bed and resumed his quest. For the remainder of the journey he risked a cab, knowing watchers of any persuasion prefer the pavement to the road, cabs to buses. He spent an hour in a café on Roman Road drinking coffee, playing on the pinball by the window, lazily firing the flippers, more interested on what moved outside. Then as the afternoon light finally lapsed, he tipped the machine to tilt and left.

There was little to compare between the Russian billionaire's residence in Kensington and the quarters provided for his staff in Bow. A square concrete stub made up of six flats, it marked where a wartime bomb had fallen on a parade of shops backing onto the rail lines twisting out of Liverpool Street Station. What more could his staff ask for? decided Nick, passing a convenience store offering more alcohol than groceries, a Cantonese take-away and 24-hour chemist. Nick provided no name into the entryphone, but holding his finger on the intercom, set off a continuous buzzing.

Natasha smiled, her round plump face bronzed from artificial tan, her

English poor, but she had enough to understand Nick's unannounced arrival concerned Galina, nodding discreetly as she led him up into a communal lounge. Four other staff members sat around, none of them smiling, and when Natasha explained the reason for his visit in Russian, they all discovered they had more pressing matters requiring their attention. Yes, Natasha nodded, Marfa and Grigori were in, she'd seen them earlier, yes, she'd go and get them and beamed a broad smile at this chance to leave.

Assorted armchairs were arranged between second-hand furniture; the scratches, knocks and oddly paired handles the toll of serving temporary accommodation. A television had been left playing, its sound almost mute, Russian stations beamed in by satellite. Posters advertising Russian films and bands Nick had never heard of brightened dull magnolia walls. In the kitchen Nick could see three microwaves and three upright industrial freezers. Marfa Dobrya, Galina's fellow nanny arrived first, followed by Grigori Tesov who complained in a surly voice to Marfa that he had only just returned from work. Marfa slight and petite, her blonde hair gathered in a high, strict ponytail, opted for a wing back chair looking lost between its arms. Dark, broad and tall, Grigori dropped into an armchair draping one of his legs over its side, his hooded eyes locked onto the television.

'You are friends with Galina Myla?' Nick began.

'Who wants to know?' Grigori demanded, not taking his eyes from the screen.

'I do,' said Nick, 'is that a problem?'

Grigori merely snorted, stretching for the remote, surfing through the channels. Not taking her eyes off Nick, Marfa had a narrow smile locked on her lips, too scared to complain even if she resented losing her leisure time.

'If she's in some sort of trouble, I can help her,' Nick advised them. 'It is important I find her quickly.'

'This a complete waste of time,' Grigori told Marfa over his shoulder in Russian, 'so get rid of the moron.'

Giving the impression that he had no understanding of this little exchange, Nick stared blankly from Grigori to Marfa. 'Who knew Galina well?' he asked slowly.

'I was very good friend to Galina,' Marfa volunteered.

'Silly bitch,' Grigori muttered in Russian, then with Nick's sharp eyes turned on him he said, 'Sure, I made friends with her.'

'Did she give any reason for leaving?'

Glancing quickly at Grigori, but not without Nick noticing, Marfa said, 'Galina made other friends also, some not so good.'

'Where did she meet these other people?'

Crossing her legs, Marfa simply smiled, leaving an empty space that Grigori was eventually forced to fill.

'Okay, I took her out a few times,' he admitted, and Marfa muttered an incredulous 'a few' in Russian.

'You were her boyfriend?'

Deciding that he wasn't sure what this encompassed, Grigori feigned bafflement until Nick enlightened him, 'her lover?'

Going into immediate denial, Grigori switched off the TV and sat up. 'Friends, okay, I just wanted a good time, Galina also wanted good time.'

'A good time where?'

'Bars and clubs okay,' said Grigori, getting a little animated.

'And this is why she left, disappeared?' Nick considered his own question as though it somehow lacked the immediacy required by the situation. 'What made her leave?' he added for good measure.

Shrugging, Grigori wasn't prepared to fully commit. 'Sure, she wanted good time all the time,' he admitted, waiting for the next question.

Instead, Nick turned his attention to Marfa. 'Was Galina in trouble of any kind? Did Galina mention any problems? Did she er...become pregnant perhaps?'

'It was not that making of problem,' she answered, shaking her head vehemently, looking at Grigori. 'She did not want to return home.'

Launching a verbal attack in Russian on Marfa, Grigori told her to keep her stupid mouth shut. Refusing, shaking her head, Marfa snapped back that she was sick of lying. Nick, giving the appearance of docile incomprehension, calmly sat through the crossfire appearing totally bemused.

'And do you know the reason, by any chance?' Nick asked Grigori when a lull had formed.

Examining his hands as though he might find an excuse or a lie there, Grigori held them out as though he needed Nick to verify them too. 'All she wanted to do was party, became one crazy chick, missing work, staying out all night.'

'Where did she go when she stayed out?'

Shrugging away Nick's question, Grigori folded his muscular arms across his chest, refusing to be drawn.

'It's Galina's safety I am worried about,' Nick stressed.

'She met a guy,' Grigori sullenly volunteered. I warned her, okay, I warned her she was crazy. Who is this guy? Tell me? She wouldn't listen okay, wanted to live her life twenty-four-seven.'

'Where was this?'

'In bar.' And Grigori once more sought refuge in a defiant silence.

Realising he could endanger everything with his next step, Nick handled it as loosely as he dared.

'This new friend, did you meet him?'

But neither of them would admit they had, which left Nick with the impression Galina had committed more than a minor infraction.

'You wouldn't know his name by any chance?'

Concentrating for no more than a couple of seconds, Grigori sullenly shook his head.

'Sebastian,' admitted Marfa. 'This is when she began taking the coke,' she disclosed, a tiny flush giving her rosebud cheeks.

'And this caused other problems?'

'Plenty, okay,' Grigori aggressively stepped in.

'In which way did this cause trouble?'

'She needed money, always more money to pay for coke,' Marfa revealed.

'Begged from us all here, asked for loans and then stole from us,' Grigori told Nick.

'Just from here?'

'No,' Marfa said, her eyes sad, recounting the breakdown of a friendship. 'She took from the family too. She no listen to me, Grigori, anyone. Family warn her they fire her and send her home.'

'Where did she get the money from to buy her drugs?' Nick persisted, not releasing the thread.

Sitting back into the chair, Marfa looked even smaller. Folding her legs over each other, she tried to smile but it lasted a second. 'She tell me Sebastian got her job at a club, helping, bar work you say....'

'But you don't think that was true?' Nick pushed, and Marfa shared a sorry glance with Grigori.

'No, I think she was dancing, men pay for her body. She use, what you say, alias.'

'I see,' said Nick, as though this was the most natural thing Galina Myla could have done and he came across it every day. 'Can you remember what name she used for her work?'

'Angel,' Martha disclosed, quietly embarrassed.

'Which club would this be?'

'A private club, okay,' said Grigori, taking over from a distressed Marfa. 'I went once to talk to her, okay, ask her to come back, we going to help her, but she not interested.'

'The name of the club?'

'Temptation,' offered Grigori and Nick dutifully nodded.

'Now,' proposed Nick, wrapping things up, 'I would like to see the possessions that Galina left behind.'

'I fetch them,' Grigori gallantly offered.

Alone with Marfa, Nick laid out his final question, one that he had been saving for the very end. 'What about Galina's family? Anyone ever visit?'

Leaning forward, propping her elbows on her knees, Marfa took her time, taking a deep breath. 'For sure, I think yes, her mother visited Galina.'

'Did she,' said Nick matter-of-factly, 'and that would be from Moscow?'

'Moscow, yes,' Marfa said, a keenness in her voice from someone who wishes she was also back at home. 'Galina had home in Golyanovo district, I never go there, but she tell me all about it. She laugh at people on her floor, her landing, that is right?'

'Landing, yes, landing is right,' Nick assured her, as Grigori brought in a bright purple suitcase with only one wheel. Golyanovo is spot on he thought, Golyanovo is where Lubov resided and hoarded his very special treasure.

In the few possessions Galina had left behind Nick found nothing that might have come from Lubov; just a depressing collection of clothes, shampoos, family photographs, snapshots of London, including a printed selfie of Galina, Tower Bridge in the background, and a diary half completed; artefacts from a different life. A life where the little administrator went about his everyday business spying for the British. *It is proof of a great secret, and I am trusting you with it*, and Galina, thought Nick, don't forget Galina. As Nick tucked the selfie of Galina safely into his pocket, he thanked Marfa and Grigori for their cooperation. Behind him, their sniping and accusations in Russian flowed freely as Nick made good on his offer to let himself out.

•••

The club occupied a back lane hugging the underbelly of Waterloo Station. Its brickwork was an adult shade of black, above its entrance an orange neon sign promised 'Temptation for Gentlemen'. Caught in unflattering daylight, the club appeared stranded, exposed, miserable, an orphan of the night. The hour not yet close to three on a crisp Saturday afternoon, the air chilled, numbing Nick as he pressed an intercom marked 'Service'. A woman's polished voice answered, prompting him to enter his membership key code. If he wasn't a member, she listed a choice of options, repeating them in Russian, German and French. Electing for the VIP package, Nick keyed in the appropriate digits as instructed, waited for the sound of the door release and entered. The discrete theme continued in the foyer; a square holding pen, its décor a mix of informal elegance, the predominant colour a hellfire red. Crimson doors concealed the main route to temptation guarded by a bulky member of the security team, who scrutinised Nick with the professional's instinct for trouble.

Waiting for Nick on a red leather button-back sofa, a willowy attractive woman in her late twenties. 'Hi, welcome, I'm Jenny,' she revealed, her confidence absolute, and Nick rated her accent as a by-product of a privileged education. She could be coy or flirtatious he decided, and she owned a versatile range of expressions depending on how she read the potential of the clients. In her striking red evening dress, it was difficult to decide where Jenny ended and the sofa began, but there were subtle clues: the revealing slash showing off a pale leg tantalisingly draped over the other denoted one boundary, the prominent deep cleavage another. Her hair, a natural honey blonde, cascaded forward over one shoulder to rest over her left breast.

'Please,' she said, patting a place next to her on the sofa, her tranquil smile suggesting she'd devoted her life to the sole purpose of reserving the space exclusively for Nick. 'The Temptation VIP package...'

She fronts the house, a touch of high-class, and she's not on the menu decided Nick, listening as Jenny decanted the VIP membership privileges, her energy making her desirable. '...one bottle of champagne...private dances...exclusive bar area...Intimate contact...'

'This *is* legal?' Nick naïvely intervened, breaking her spell. 'I mean if I pay for sex...?'

'Don't be silly,' Jenny laughed. 'Your membership includes an introduction fee that guarantees social interaction between dancers and clients on the premises. And that is it,' she stressed in her school debating voice. 'If any of our girls agree to go on dates with clients, that is their decision and their own business as consenting adults.'

'You think of everything.'

'We do…'

'That include Sebastian?'

'Sebastian?'

Her smile didn't falter, but Nick caught the flicker of hesitation in her grey eyes, the sharp recalibration of her performance.

'Let me make some checks,' she proposed, recovering her momentum. 'If you need anything, speak to Trev,' she added, and in one graceful move was off the sofa.

'Great,' agreed Nick as she glided elegantly away.

But something must have passed between Jenny and Trev, because Nick felt the sudden drop in goodwill as Trev switched gears; moving up from passive to reactive. Mixed martial arts? Trev possessed at least one combat sport Nick reasoned.

When Jenny returned, she'd brought reinforcements, and this pair were strictly muscle, the attack dogs for supporting Trev decided Nick. Dressed as twins in matching black T-shirts, and trousers, their hair cropped close to their skulls, they hauled Nick to his feet.

'Ricky would like a word,' Jenny said, resuming her pose on the sofa.

'Not Sebastian?'

'Not today,' said Jenny, permitting him an elegant farewell smile.

The club was split on different levels, realised Nick as they escorted him through a bar area and small restaurant; its blackboard menu overpriced, the wines and champagne list extortionate. Discreetly placed in an alcove, a door marked STAFF. Beyond it, a long corridor once more painted in adult black, its bulkhead lights stark, the shadows unforgiving. Nick heard the dispute before they reached it; a one-sided verbal battering somewhere ahead.

'But, Ricky, that's twice…'

'…I don't care if he's a fucking biter…' a slim figure was roaring into the face of a dancer. '…he's a regular, VIP…' He had her head pinned against the brickwork in a one-handed hold, his fingers splayed around her jaw. Taking a moment's respite, he swung around to Nick.

'Office,' he said, and Nick was forcibly propelled along.

He counted down seven black doors, none of them bearing handles, just mortice locks and silver escutcheons. The final door contained a chrome handle, and he read it as evidence that this was Ricky's centre of operations.

'And just who the fuck is Sebastian to *you*?' Ricky wanted to know, arriving briskly to unlock the door.

'A name.'

'Really,' Ricky said, stepping nimbly inside. 'And?' he asked.

'A means to an end,' Nick offered, a firm pair of strong hands placed between his shoulders driving him forwards.

The same strong hands came from behind and began to frisk him, removing his wallet.

'An aperitif for our visitor, Leon, if you wouldn't mind,' decided Ricky, accepting Nick's wallet.

The punch was delivered at full power to Nick's flank, between ribcage and hip. It denied Nick air, it ripped the strength out of his legs, sinking him to his knees gasping, his eyes watery, blurred.

'Now we have established that honesty *will be* your best policy,' Ricky explained reasonably, 'we won't need to trouble Leon again. He is a stickler for procedure.'

He's a right-hander too, Nick had noted, his vision clearing, and he uses a wide stance to swing.

'And you are who?' Ricky wondered, as Leon dragged Nick upright.

In a neat black Savile Row suit, white collarless shirt and hand-stitched loafers, Ricky was considered a diamond by his friends, of which he had many. Light and wafer thin there wasn't an ounce of fat on him. His flat iron face showed the deep roots of a sunbed tan, his hair forever short by habit was crew cut, dyed black. At his antique pedestal desk, he emptied Nick's wallet, dealing the contents in a precise line on his desk. Selecting the driving licence, he held it between thumb and forefinger, comparing the image with the real thing.

'Well, Mr. Cowling, I'm not sure if I'm ready to forgive you for rocking up to my door and putting Jenny on the spot,' he admitted, tossing the licence onto his desk.

Without troubling Nick for a response, Ricky poured himself a coffee from a filter machine. He raised his matte black mug in a toast, its side captioned: BOSS.

'Assuming that you're fucking witless as to how I operate,' he said, setting the mug on his desk where a telephone, laptop, two-way radio and sealed envelope were arranged on its red inlaid leather pad. 'I will enlighten you.'

'That's appreciated.'

'Don't mention it,' said Ricky, 'doesn't cost anything for manners. Now, where was I?'

'You were going to tell me if you knew Sebastian,' offered Nick.

'No, son, I wasn't. I am a service provider and I do not fucking tolerate disruption to the running of this wonderful establishment. I deliver peace, goodwill and a memorable show for my guests. Unlike you, son, they do pay top dollar for the experience. You mentioned something about this Sebastian being a means to an end? Want to clarify?'

Seating himself behind his desk, Ricky stretched back in his expansively cushioned chair, sampled his coffee.

'I'd like to talk to him,' said Nick.

'You're out of luck, son. Sebastian's not known at this address, so you can't. End of message. That a fair summary, Leon?'

'Spot on, Boss,' Leon agreed from behind Nick.

'I really do need to have a chat with him,' Nick insisted.

'For fuck's sake,' Ricky sighed, 'Leon, I don't think he understands. Can you reinforce the message?'

In the two seconds Leon required to adjust his stance, Nick struck fast, and he struck hard. A right fist, fingertips folded into the palm forming a wedge, were driven into Leon's windpipe. Clutching at his throat, he rocked forward for air. And that's when his down-turned face made contact with Nick's rising knee, a fierce punishing impact exploding Leon's nose, his lips. Two more tactical strikes by Nick; the first dislocating Leon's right shoulder, the follow-up inflicting a fracture to Leon's right wrist.

'You're a fucking animal,' Ricky yelled, lunging for the radio.

And he yelled again, though this was more of a wounded howl, as Nick already at his side, had a tight hold on the back of Ricky's neck, slamming his face into the desk.

'You've fucking killed him,' Ricky muttered, a handkerchief staunching the blood from his nose as he peered over the desk at Leon.

Suffering, but far from deceased, Leon very slowly picked himself up, grunting at each painful stage of recovery and remained on his feet, his shaking legs notwithstanding.

'Go and get seen to,' Ricky ordered.

'Sebastian,' Nick reminded Ricky after Leon's lumbering departure.

Viewing Nick with a hostile stare, Ricky swabbed the remaining blood from around his mouth; his top lip already beginning to swell.

'A posh little fucker, a spotter for some of the clubs. Gets paid a commission if he finds potential talent,' Ricky admitted.

'And he supplies coke?'

'Yeah, he provides. White, snow, blow, lines, rails, bumps, whatever you want to fucking call it. Don't touch the shit myself, but there you are, everyone to their own little habits, keeps the world ticking over.'

Raising both arms above his head as a show of no unfriendly intentions, Ricky moved away from his desk, walking slowly to a trolley stocked with whisky, vodka and white rum.

'And?'

'You want his life story?' Ricky poured himself a healthy whisky, splashed in a touch of chilled soda water he took from a mini fridge.

'A short biographical note will be sufficient,' Nick decided.

'Mum's a QC, God bless our lawyers, and his old man's a top player at the World Bank. Our Sebastian's a spoilt brat, a proper handful,' Ricky resumed safely behind his desk. 'Played up at three very expensive schools and walked away from uni, bored. Fancied himself an entrepreneur, and who doesn't? Organised a few raves, but fuck that shit, it's all hard graft. Then up pops an idea, his magic moment. Raves, gigs and festivals. What do the punters crave along with bands, booze and sex?'

'Drugs,' said Nick.

'Ten points to the man in the red corner,' Ricky announced, wincing as the Scotch made contact with his lips. 'Sebastian is bright, that education hasn't been flushed down the fucking pan after all. He starts supplying weed and very good he was too. He uses his profits to upscale – excuse the pun – to coke and other naughty mind-bending shit.'

'The talent he brings in, they owe Sebastian?' wondered Nick.

'Plays the boyfriend, providing the shit at a price a fucking zombie could pay. Builds up the dependence, starts jacking up the price and they've a debt to pay off.'

'Galina Myla,' said Nick. 'She's Russian.' He passed over the selfie.

Pulling his face as though encountering a significant test, Ricky nodded. 'Angel,' he said, 'Yeah, he introduced her,' he admitted, his small head lolled to one side as he sluiced the Scotch around his gums and swallowed.

A house line buzzed on the desk phone and Ricky snatched it up. 'I fucking know... he's in my office,' he bawled down the line. 'No... no Old Bill... well get him to fucking casualty. No... no need to come up.' Slamming down the handset, he used a remote to flick through CCTV windows on three plasma screens.

It beats the hell out of daytime television Nick decided, sharing the bird's-eye view from behind the bars and back of house. On one of the club's stages, two naked women smeared each other with body paint and lotion. The main stage featured a dancer pouting and grinding through her routine around a pole in a sinuous, tantalising rhythm. Unable to locate a sign of the wounded Leon, Ricky ended the feed, transferring all his attention to Nick.

'You've got balls, son, coming in here like this. Leon is one of my best boys. Maybe you ought to work for me? I admire initiative,' he added, tapping his temple. 'My old man started this business in the Sixties. Two strippers and cases of dodgy champers in a crappy basement in Soho.' Happy to have put Nick in the picture, Ricky sat proudly back and beat his chest, a sign of contrition, confession or pride.

'Galina Myla, stage name Angel,' said Nick, 'what happened to her?'

'You are persistent, I will give you that,' he said, pushing the selfie back across the desk. 'We've got a Star, Venus, Paradise and Divine on our line-up, but Angel, she was different,' he vowed, and rotated the envelope on his desk full circle with the tip of his index finger. 'She was class, okay, Angel was top drawer material, in mint condition physically. She had the potential to be my highest earner. But mentally, she was on a fucking collision course with reality, a head case.'

'Because of her habit?'

'And that was all fucking Sebastian, not me,' Ricky flashed, his tone a warning, 'Look son,' he continued, inching his drained tumbler along the desk, 'I've seen what you're capable of. I'm not about to lie,' he vowed, sitting forward, pivoting both elbows on his desk, his hands clasped as if in prayer. 'In this business, son, you wouldn't believe the turnover in girls. It's a fucking merry-go-round, and they change their stage names as often as they wax. And that, I assure you, is frequent,' he confided and seemed to mean it. 'She was talent, a hit with the guests, gave 'em what they wanted, got a name for herself, plenty of the City boys started requesting her for private dances. Decided she was a fucking celebrity. Played the diva, had serious mood swings and she started to self-destruct. Offstage, onstage, it was a fucking sight to behold... for all the wrong reasons.'

'You fired her?'

'I had no choice,' he protested. 'Come on son, don't be fucking soft. Do the girls always provide legitimate details? No, they fucking don't. Some of my girls are pro-trained dancers, some are students, some are single mums, some do it for the buzz. I don't discriminate on the grounds of race, colour or class. If they can turn it on and entertain the punters, they're in. If they can keep 'em coming back for more, they get a bonus. If a punter invites them back to his hotel room, they know it's not for afternoon tea. End of. Did that apply to Angel? Yes, it fucking did.' He pushed away from his desk, glancing all the while over his shoulder as he refilled his tumbler.

And while Nick thought this might have a ring of truth, he ventured no encouragement and gave him no lead.

'What is your interest in her? She jilted you? Robbed you? Where's the fire?' Ricky finally asked, propped casually on the edge of his desk.

'Some very influential people in Moscow want her found.'

'You're not representing *those* fucking nutters by any chance?' Guarded, Ricky tried for a smile, but it never quite came off. Perhaps as a distraction from the dilemma he faced, he opened his laptop scanned his screen, before promptly closing it.

'Where is she?'

Whether buying time or genuinely uncertain, Ricky simply remained silent as Nick very slowly returned everything to his wallet.

'Me and you,' he said at last, 'admittedly we got off at the wrong stop initially, let's put it down to a genuine misunderstanding.'

'Misunderstanding,' said Nick, he liked that. 'As far as the people in Moscow are concerned, I'm the soft option,' Nick said, feeding Ricky's imagination. 'Where is she?'

'Out of fucking control wasn't she,' he confessed, staring into his tumbler. 'She still owed Sebastian, so he moved her. Owns a twenty-four-hour massage, the talent lives above. Punters pay over the odds for a topless session. If they want more, they're entertained in the girls' rooms as boyfriends. And that's where you'll find Angel.'

'The address,' Nick demanded. 'Now.'

On a pad he took from his desk drawer, Ricky wrote fast, as though providing a statement and he was supremely confident of his alibi.

Passing over the note Ricky held out his hand for Nick to shake, but his offer wasn't accepted.

'You've got to trust me on this,' he pledged. 'Without trust we have nothing,' he added, enjoying a philosophical moment, flopping back in his cushioned chair. 'Call back another time, VIP tickets, on the house,' he promised raising his hand as a pledge of honour. 'This life, son, it's all about timing, and yours, unfortunately, is off on this occasion. You've missed her by a month. See yourself out,' he said, making the necessary call on the house line.

Taking the same route back through the club, Nick waited for Leon's friends to come and pay their respects, but no one did. Sebastian, supplier and pimp Nick reasoned, the world survives on threats; threat, counter threat. *Here comes the candle to light you to bed, here comes the chopper to chop off your head.* He didn't bother with the main entrance, his mood not quite ready for facing Jenny, electing instead for a fire door opening into a passageway. Returning to the street, he made a call on his phone and bounded off in need of a coffee or something stronger in Waterloo Station. Lighting a cigarette, he started to walk. 'Timing, Ricky,' he said under his breath, the best results always come from timing, trust has nothing to do with it. Weary, considering the problems ahead, he walked briskly, his head filled by the prospect of never securing rest.

Fourteen

From his side of the drive Rossan traced the dark stone angles solid against the pale night sky; stiff, confident, his reassuring bulwark against the devious secret world he inhabited. Spying was in the blood, a family tradition. A senior Private Secretary to Churchill during the war, Rossan's grandfather had spent his days steeped in clandestine operations, counting Stewart Menzies, the wartime Chief of the Service as a close friend.

For a moment Rossan stood in jealous admiration of his grandfather having known exactly whose side he was on. His father also a veteran of the Firm, rounding off his career as Head of Station in Buenos Aires, where he remains with wife number two, ten years his junior, a partner in a very lucrative bookstore. Could Rossan claim that same assurance felt by his grandfather, that he was fighting a noble cause, coming home to Wiltshire at weekends, back to his pillared doorway with its added quaint porch for a warm welcome. Rossan could even pick out a single course of stone marking his renovations and the addition of an extra wing to accommodate his expanding family. Away from the house the gracious sweep of lawn ran to his right, where a single cedar rose out from the middle of rhododendrons and holly like a candle in a Christmas table display.

'Good God, Paul, I thought you'd got lost,' his wife called.

Rebecca, four years younger still possessed the deportment expected from a daughter of a hereditary peer, a viscount at that, dressing not according to fashion or style, but what came first to hand. Standing inside the dark porch, she'd slipped the catch silently and stepped out. From a pocket she took a box of matches and lit the wicks on the oil lamps either side of the door. In this shallow yellow light, her face had a resonant power, the kind never accentuated by cosmetics. She saw him look at her left eye slightly closed and puffy, the first darkening of a bruise shading her skin, the result of a fall from Nero her thoroughbred hunter.

'I'm sure they won't think that you beat me,' she said as Rossan drew nearer.

'Believe what they like,' he said, making one last check. In the deep beds by the porch high arched bands of rosemary had died back, in the air the sweet scent of burning logs swam gently on the chilly evening breeze.

A car started down the drive and they both stepped instinctively back, their shadows temporarily trapped and defined by headlights, two cutaway paper figures suspended.

'Lovers looking for somewhere to shag,' she said casually, and Rebecca's words had no coarseness; a matter of fact that didn't shock. Reversing, the car seemed to take the brightness of the evening with it, leaving a velvet darkness behind. 'Come on, we'd better change before they start to arrive,' she proposed, linking arms with her husband.

Of course, C arrived late, his customary apology and bottle of 1985 Red Bordeaux from Château Rauzan-Segla proffered to smooth over anything burnt or ruined, though Rebecca still glared and fumed right through dinner. As a Service wife, Rebecca graciously made small talk with the others gathered around the table; Roly Blackmore whom she thought a tad too louche, Jane Stratton she decided was on the rise, Teddy Hawick a sycophantic creep and C, the severe Martin Bailrigg, holding court as if the house were his own. Really, she wouldn't have minded if Paul had invited them, but it had been the odious Hawick who graciously invited himself and his colleagues, suggesting Paul could host what he termed a 'council of war.' This, after coffee and a lengthy pause, was the next item on the menu, so Rebecca effortlessly excused herself and left them to it.

'Give him an amnesty, allow him to come in under certain terms and conditions,' Blackmore magnanimously proposed playing his favourite role as devil's advocate.

'Torr simply has to be found,' Hawick chimed his favourite mantra, his cheeks a little too red.

'Sinner or sinned against?' Bailrigg mused over the rim of his glass held high, rotating it slowly, its cut surface producing shell bursts of diamond light flashing out an SOS.

'He's assaulted three officers,' Hawick primly announced, 'we have a missing Latvian…'

'You boxed him in, Teddy, what do you expect,' Bailrigg shot across the table. 'The Lat... his wife's murder... Moscow... he's onto something, and he's running us ragged and making us appear like damn fools. He's terrorised Lubov's case officer for background, and all considered, it's not amounting to the behaviour of a guilty man I'd have thought. Yeah or nay?' Placing his glass gently down, he studied each of them in turn, his intimidating stare remaining on Hawick. 'Finding him pronto might save us a lot of work, might even get him off the hook and save me another curtsy at Downing Street.'

'I have Mortland working on it,' Hawick said, his cheeks once more colouring. 'Torr is a rogue element, he is unpredictable, but he will be brought to heel, he will be accountable,' he added, desperately.

'Want to put that in writing, Teddy?' Bailrigg proposed mischievously.

Holding his fire during the malicious mauling of Nick's character and reputation, Rossan decided Hawick had gone quite mad; but unwilling to sit idly back a moment longer, he intervened.

'Far from being a rogue, Nick is an outstanding officer who has consistently delivered. On occasion, risking his life,' he said with a good deal of passion. 'Damn it all, his wife has been murdered...'

'And her lover,' Hawick interceded.

'Below the belt, Teddy,' Bailrigg flared.

'Kick in the balls,' drawled Roly.

'And I for one,' Rossan continued, 'can understand how such a loss is highly traumatic.'

'He's never behaved in this way before,' said Jane in qualification, 'perhaps for the moment we should give him the benefit of the doubt.'

'Depends what terms and conditions we offer him,' Blackmore said freely, 'doesn't need a lot for him to cause irreparable damage,' he added, another twist of the knife.

'I thought he'd already accomplished that,' Hawick mewed.

'His house contained, Teddy?'

'Around the clock, full teams,' Hawick answered with relish.

'And thanks to Jane, we've got all his known hideaways,' Bailrigg disclosed with a smile, toasting her.

Dear God, thought Rossan, he's been fawning over her the entire evening, and shot Jane a questioning look, as to why she'd dump Nick further into the mire.

'Funeral must be coming up soon,' Blackmore said laconically. 'We have plans for that, do we?'

Whether he intended asking if the Service would be sending formal representation, or had a different intention, Hawick found another opportunity to assassinate Nick.

'I had heard a divorce was imminent. It's not a secret *that* union has hardly been a success. If he does have the nerve to show his face, I've had Mortland arrange for a snatch team to be ready,' he said, quite the zealot.

'Better call off the dogs on that number, Teddy,' Bailrigg announced, 'not going to happen.'

'So, Roly,' Hawick piped up deflecting the censure, noting Blackmore's abstention, 'how should we proceed?'

As each head pivoted slowly round on him, Blackmore smiled. 'Haven't a clue, Teddy. You're our resident Bad Angel,' he grinned, returning to his leisurely admiration of a rather nice oil of a bay hunter which he thought just might be an original.

'Well, Teddy?' Bailrigg pressed, sharing a glance with Jane.

'Cut off his options, flush him out,' Hawick proposed.'

Undecided just how to deal with Nick, they talked round the whole issue again coming from a different angle, until Rossan could bear it no longer, and as a genial host suggested they sleep on it and pick up the threads over breakfast. So, with a final nightcap dispensed, his guests delivered safely to their rooms, the fire checked, doors locked, Rossan finally retired at a quarter past one only to find Rebecca propped up in bed still reading the Marquis of Lorne's biography of Palmerston.

'Thought you would be weary of politics by now,' he said, rather ungraciously, getting undressed.

'And I thought you would have managed to get that cabal to bed much sooner,' she retorted, slipping a page over. 'Why you all can't just let Nick alone is beyond me,' she said, removing her glasses which Rossan took to be an omen for one of Rebecca's polemical points of order. 'The poor man is probably working out which one of your guests is hand in glove with the Russians.'

Sitting on the corner of the bed he stared at his wife, one Lobb Oxford full brogue on his knee its cedar shoetree half inserted, he marvelled at how Rebecca did it, sometimes he thought she knew more of Service intrigue than he did.

• • •

After Danny collected Nick in a very ordinary CO8 pool car, they drove east towards Peckham, Jefferson Airplane's *Somebody to Love* on the radio. Through rifts in dark cloud snatches of a high brilliant moon made the streets appear immaculate, strangely clean. Nick, his eyes closed, was on the drive out of Moscow with the little accountant and Foula, hearing rapid fire and seeing the roadblock again; rough images pasted together to form a graphic close-up, the provenance of nightmares, knowledge as bitter as bile.

'How are things at the Mad House?'

'Appalling, we're all under suspicion. Stratton has been given temporary command and Hawick's holding her hand. Mortland's running around like he's been stung by wasps,' Danny explained. 'Only essential operations are being sanctioned.'

'Sounds like its punishment,' Nick commiserated, and sank back into a bout of detached contemplation.

On through Deptford the traffic thinning, specks of rain peppering the windscreen, a shoal of clouds the colour of sulphur pressing in as they came upriver with the tide. Glimpsed through his window the streets flicking rapidly by, Nick mutely observing them with the intensity of a stranger new to the city. The escaping light from shops forming brilliant silver puddles on the wet pavements. The lonely figures moving slowly, heads bowed against the cold night rain. The fast walkers absorbed with an inner purpose. The young men and women uncaring, living the moment.

'This it? It's a complete dump,' announced Danny, nudging Nick.

In front of them a Victorian shop sat with its back huddled against the southern approach for the Blackwall Tunnel. In a different life it had housed a tobacconist, and on its worn gable wall Nick glimpsed the ghost lettering for CAPSTAN CIGARETTES. The shop's front windows were clad in a grey privacy wrap that had wrinkled and blistered in the sun. A decal fixed at eye level yelled: SENSUAL MASSAGE. In the side glass next to the doorway, a life size vinyl Nordic goddess in white bikini smiled ecstatically.

'How do you want to play this?' asked Danny, parking behind a builder's skip buckled by fire. 'Do I really need to ask?' he added.

'Not really.'

'Hard it is,' proposed Danny.

'Hard,' agreed Nick, taking in the front of the building, noting the rooms showing a light upstairs. 'Definitely hard,' he announced.

The entrance opened into a grubby waiting area where a row of plastic chairs sat in a kindergarten pattern of alternating yellow and blue. Tuned to a shopping channel, a wall mounted television featured a radiant female presenter busily endorsing a range of beauty and haircare products. Each time a heavy truck thundered over the fly-over, the screen gave a seismic tremble. Two of the chairs were filled. In one, a twenty-year old in jeans T-shirt and a faded leather jacket rapidly tapped the toes of his trainers on the heavily soiled black and white floor tiles. In the other, a fifty-year old, his thinning hair greasy, his beard ragged, his tracksuit flecked with the remains of breakfast, lunch and dinner. Both of them scrutinised Nick and Danny's arrival with a mixture of wariness and latent aggression.

'Thirty minutes, eighty quid. Sixty minutes, one-hundred and ten. And that's excluding drinks. Girlfriend experience starts at two-hundred,' recited a pale woman in her twenties from behind a fake teak reception counter, her hair tawny, her skin glossy from foundation.

'Angel working tonight?' Nick asked.

'Who wants to know?' she demanded.

'Her twin brothers,' Nick replied. 'Ground floor, first floor, second floor…where is she?'

With a furtive glance at her shopping channel, the receptionist cocked her head sideways and bawled: 'Ray.'

He came promptly at a swagger from the dark regions of the shop through a side door, his pride in his physique and toned muscles justifiable. A combination, which in normal circumstances proved quite sufficient to deal with the unruly, inebriated and plain obnoxious clientele. But on this occasion Ray was at a disadvantage. Not only were Danny and Nick trained, they were unforgiving. So, when Ray made the elemental mistake of selecting Danny as the obvious target on the deceptive logic that he stood a full head shorter than Nick, the minder was irrevocably committed.

'Those two jokers,' the receptionist informed him, gesturing to Danny and Nick.

'Right, fuck off. Out, both of you,' he bellowed, his Newcastle accent rich, heavy.

'I believe this is your cue to leave, boys,' Danny politely suggested to the two wary clients.

In a totally mistimed charge, Ray launched a wild swing at Danny. Nimble, fast on his feet, Danny ducked, but instead of backing-off, he used the motive force in his legs to add not only momentum, but a considerable burst of power to the headbutt he delivered with perfect timing. Parrying a flailing punch, Danny landed one rapid blow then another, until Ray stuck one hand above his head in submission.

'Where is she?' Nick demanded once again of the receptionist.

'2a. She's working.'

'Not anymore,' said Danny. 'No police either.'

The stairs were gained down a stifling corridor, the air tainted by cheap scented lotion and hot bodies. Nick led, taking the treads two a time, the bannister shaking as he powered up. At a plywood-faced door Danny gripped the handle, tried it slowly, shaking his head. Counting down to three on his fingers, he promptly kicked the door open. The air inside stank, the flat a tip, not cared for in years. And there on a double bed, Galina Myla rising and falling as she straddled a fat client. Never missing a stroke, she seemed surreally untroubled, as though having her door taken off its hinges was an everyday event. Only when Nick took hold of her arm, dragging her off the punter did she react, locking eyes with Nick as she slithered under a dirty sheet for protection.

'What the fuck, I haven't fucking finished,' protested the punter, struggling to sit up, groping for his pants. 'I paid this bitch for half an hour.'

Using both hands locked together in a backhanded punch to the punter's gut, Danny doubled him up. Spilling him off the bed, he sent him crashing into a bedside cabinet. Scared, Galina began a scream that Nick reduced to a low keening wail by ordering her in Russian to be quiet. Pushing and kicking, Danny herded her client to the door warning him that if he ever came back, Danny would surely make him hurt some more.

'You have a choice, Galina Myla,' Nick severely informed her in Russian, 'tell me the truth or face serious consequences.'

Red eyed and craving for a fix, she started yelling insults and oaths at Nick in Russian with the sheet yanked up at her neck. Taking hold of her wrists, Nick shook her hard until Galina Myla was calm.

'Someone gave you a cellphone as a present? Who gave you the phone?' Nick continued in Russian.

Looking bemused, her eyes darting to the door expecting Ray to appear, Nick had to shout the question in his best official voice. Jumping, pulling the sheet tighter, she shook and trembled.

'My mother, on a visit, but I can't remember when. Is my mother in trouble?' She began crying.

'Your mother could be in very grave trouble Galina Myla,' Nick said, 'It all depends if you tell me the truth.' 'I will do my best,' she vowed.

'Do you remember a neighbour from your Moscow block, Vasily Lubov?' To which Galina nodded. 'Did Lubov send anything with your mother for you to look after?' Galina nodded again. 'Tell me, Galina Myla, tell me all about it,' insisted Nick.

And Galina in a slight hesitant and fumbling voice did as the stranger directed her. Her mother is so proud of her only daughter working in London that she visits whenever she can, the last time must have been in October. Only Galina doesn't let her see her daughter this way; she makes an effort, dresses up, meets in the hotel where her mother stays. Her mother asked if she remembered Lubov from across the landing and Galina did. Imagine, her mother told her; imagine the strangest thing my little Galina. As she was leaving for London her mother bumped into Lubov on the stairs. Lubov was excited, shaking, asking her if she could do him a big favour, take this present to London for him, he was meant to send it to his wife's niece studying in London, but he simply forgot. If she leaves it with her daughter Galina, he'll make arrangements for it to be collected. He even has a cellphone her daughter can have; free, a gift for her assistance, and someone will call the daughter on the new phone to arrange for the collection.

But her mother was not sure if she should inconvenience Galina with unnecessary tasks. Galina has a very good job, a busy one, she explained; her daughter is responsible for the infants of a very wealthy man. Lubov said he understood, told her mother not to worry, he'd still keep a watch over her place while she's away. 'My mother felt bad, so she accepted the cellphone and present.'

'Where is the present Galina?'

How many times she'd rehearsed her words Nick couldn't tell, but she delivered them with plain conviction.

'No one called immediately, no one came,' she cried, 'I thought no one wanted it, so I opened the gift, it was an iPhone and I liked it better than the other cellphone Lubov gave my mother for me to keep. But not the music or the other things on it.'

'What things, Galina Myla, what besides music was on the iPhone?'

'Files, many files. I didn't know if they were important, so I copied them onto a laptop, put them into an old folder.'

'And where is the laptop? What folder did you copy them to?'

'It is my laptop. The file was for old nursery rosters from the house of Cheboksary.'

'Where is the laptop?'

'It is gone,' she wept. 'Someone rang on the cellphone asking about the present.'

'Who rang?'

'He spoke Russian, but I think he was not from my country,' she admitted, crying. 'He knew who I was, where I lived in Moscow and said he was a friend of Lubov, and he was coming to collect the present. I was scared, I had opened the present, so I had to pretend that the laptop was the gift.'

'And did he come and collect it?'

'The next day, he made me meet him on a bridge, there were two of them. One, a very tall man, the other man, the one I spoke to, he was small, smiled like a fox and he had a scar above his top lip. The tall man was very sad, he did not smile, and he walked with a limp. They took my laptop and said I had done a great service for them.'

'Did you look at these files?' Nick wondered.

'No, they did not interest me,' she said and burst into tears again, 'Will you send my mother to prison for what I have done? Were they important government files?' Galina sobbed.

'Yes, Galina Myla, they were very important government files,' Nick told her. 'Where is the iPhone?'

'I needed money. I sold it.'

For a good few minutes Nick studied her, glanced round at the pit where she was forced to work and sleep.

'Get dressed, Galina Myla, put on your best clothes, you are going home to your mother.' And Nick didn't care how Rossan arranged it; he'd pay for the flight himself if he had to, even for a stay in a Moscow clinic, because he was determined that someone would come out of this mess with a chance.

Fifteen

There were no other cars ahead and no headlights behind. What remained of the dawn retreated along the road in front of Nick, dragging the remainder of the night with it. A conifer plantation sat on either side of the road, high and dark; a tunnel that he never broke out of. Except for the firebreaks and the natural woodland left to rot, its branches torn flat in defeat. Every now and then, he glimpsed a piece of the same lake, grey as slate with boats tethered until spring. Esthwaite Water he remembered. He had watched his mirror all the way from the motorway and nothing rolled onto the ferry after him but a haggard Land Rover with a trailer full of sheep. Yet he still drove with caution, feeling the car buck in the wind.

The road was narrow, single track, dropping out of sight as rapidly as it climbed. On distant peaks there was snow and it might have been Switzerland or Germany, only the fells were too English, too rugged, not awesome enough; just high slopes weeping scree and forest into the valley and lake below. Then there were the farms, tucked low with gritty names and twin power cables on creosote poles feeding them the modern world. He recalled a sign too. Only it was nothing more than a decrepit plank shedding its paint, and Nick saw it far too late. Reversing, he followed a flaking arrow up a rough track; it is where spies come to die, he thought, and I am one of them.

He crossed a sheep grid and the car shook beneath him, spilling his map onto the floor. Out of the trees the wind tore through the branches in a wild shrieking symphony. Then the track shrank into wheel ruts with a grass hump strewn with rocks that smacked against the sump. He glimpsed a holed canoe abandoned in the ditch, and further along, orange fragments from a life jacket snarled on barbed wire as if the lake had risen and washed them there. A board tied to smashed gates had 'Broom Hall Adventure Centre' printed as big as a warning. Nick hit the firm drive and saw it all over again as he remembered it; house, school and sanctuary all at the same time, with somewhere in its history a seminary for priests who never smiled.

An impressive hall of granite with two stiff wings and a whiff of Victorian eaves, there was a sense of grandeur long since departed. Over lawns worn bare and never reseeded, dirty ropes and car tyres were draped like rotten streamers and balloons from mature branches waiting for the saw. It could be Aspley all over again, and the only thing missing he thought, was the mock-up walls and fences to scale. Only you're trying to sell a different type of adventure here; one not involving death thought Nick. He parked in a gravel sweep next to a Ford minibus dumped on bricks, the centre's name faint down its side. The hall faced the lake and the wind swept off it cold and bitter, straight into his face. A notice board sat in a glass case dangling by wire from a trellis panel in a lychgate porch. Empty of papers, rusty drawing pins made brown islands in a sea of mouldy green baize. Next to a bell chain a cryptic notice read: 'Twice'. Nick gave it two long tugs and heard nothing.

'I'm afraid it's like everything else round here and given up the ghost. Can I help?'

She had come out of the woods, a red setter at her heels.

'I was hoping to have a word with Gav,' explained Nick. Her advantage was height matched by a natural beauty and Nick thought she would always use them to get her way. Her ash blonde hair was combed forward from the crown out to the sides, the rest splayed in an angle. She sent the dog in advance sniffing his legs, friend or foe. Slowly she closed the distance.

'Gavin's down at the moorings,' she said, making a point of using his name in full: in capitals, in thanks, woman and girl in the same smile. She waved a decadent arm towards the lake. 'Some problem with a staging or pontoon, or whatever the silly things are called.' Her eyes were bright blue and given an energy by her pale translucent skin. Tall and beautiful she moved in on him, holding him in a firm greeting with her eyes and point-to-point smile. Her defensive eyes wouldn't let go of Nick, estimating, worrying, unsure and remotely concerned. 'Does Gavin know that you are coming, Mr....?'

'Call me Nick. No, I was just passing.'

'I hope you won't take this as a rude question,' she said with disarming energy, 'but exactly why do you want to see Gavin?' she asked, challenging him.

'Old times.'

'Jazz, stop that,' she commanded, but the dog took no notice pushing its nose inquiringly into his crotch. She apologised with a weak 'Silly thing,' the woman in her dampening the smile. 'Suppose you'd better come in and wait then,' she offered with lukewarm charm. 'We'll take the back, we'll never get in this way, the lock appears to be jammed. Only Gavin has the secret of getting it to open.'

'Sure,' said Nick, stepping around the dog.

Walking round the house she did all the talking; throwing comments over her shoulder as sharp as a fin, all her plans for transforming the place into a country hotel. Nick smiled, refusing the bait. Unlocking a door that needed oil, she kicked off her boots in what used to be the games store, the reek of damp cricket nets still in the air; mouldy, full of the seasons gone. For the hall had once been a prep school run by Gavin's father after he left the Service, until the mounting cost of repairs or the pupils had driven him to suicide. Nick remembered the stories of a priest hole and a bishop's grave in the grounds that no one had ever found. Still playing her part, she guided him through a refectory with its trestle tables and rush matting between the aisles and a great fireplace that could spit roast a boar; through a kitchen big enough to serve a hundred boys, into a scullery modernised and equipped for two. She ran her fingers through her hair lifting, flicking it this way and that, making an effort to be noted.

'I'm Tessa by the way, Gavin's second chance at marriage. Fancy a drink?'

'Coffee if it's no trouble,' said Nick, recalling Gav's first wife, Grace. She was a brunette, dark eyed, sultry, given to much spending and fits of pique when Gav refused to dote on her. Grace preserved in a photograph carried by Gav because it inspired him into a state of pure hate. Nick saw the first wife's eyes now, staring up out of Gav's wallet, round, inconsolable and devastating.

'Don't be silly,' she scolded, grinding the beans with a no-nonsense routine that Nick guessed must have served her well with Gav. A fire had been lit in a small grate and she made a fuss of adding logs while the coffee filtered.

'He shouldn't be long now,' she said, keeping her back away from Nick. 'Gavin's problem is that he does get so absorbed in whatever he's doing.'

'I know,' Nick agreed, and Tessa glared at him as though he had spoken out of turn.

'Oh, known him long?' She was standing by the fireplace arms folded fully, on guard. 'Except I don't think he's mentioned you?'

'He wouldn't.'

How much Tessa shared Nick's reading of her husband was hard to say. She gave a little trite smile not quite prepared to engage him any further. Drinking his coffee in silence; a full ten minutes passed before Nick heard a heavy door slam, signalling the arrival of Gavin Rafford, long-time friend and once, a distinguished member of the Firm.

'How did you and Gavin meet?' Tessa felt able to ask now, certain that her husband was coming to the rescue.

'We worked together,' Gav answered, entering the kitchen. 'In the bad old days.'

Short of six foot and muscular he carried his weight forward as though he'd need it in a hurry. His dark hair tussled by the wind knocked a couple of years off his age, and he dressed with no intention of maturing; clad in jeans, boots and a heavy leather jacket. He hadn't shaved for two days and the dark growth deepened his heavy jaw, a roadie home from a gruelling tour. Only the sluggishness in his right leg was never going to get better and he dragged it after him as though it didn't belong, giving him a rolling gait. Nodding at Nick he helped himself to coffee, pouring without finesse, his heavy hands too clumsy for Tessa's precious cups.

'Hello Gav.'

'Can't say I'm pleased to see you,' said Gav, sipping his coffee, the steam rising into his face. 'I don't know what you want but say your piece and leave.'

'Angie's dead, she was murdered.'

Tessa's fingers plucked consolingly at a chain round her neck, unsure who or where to look at. An 'Oh God' mouthed, an empty comic strip bubble that floated up and away over her head.

'Let's talk,' he said to Nick, then turning to Tessa, 'Won't be long.'

'Fine,' she said, watching them go.

With Gav pounding ahead at a fast hobble, Nick followed him into hallowed corridors stripped of their treasure; a chandelier by the great staircase, a tapestry from the panelled hall, and a suite of armour from outside his father's study. They are selling the place piece by piece thought Nick, the possessions of one generation becoming the salvation for the next, he decided as Gav directed him sharply into the study. His fingers to his lips, Gav locked the door, stood a radio on the floor the volume turned three quarters up; a throwback to the days when they improvised against the stealers of sound.

'Angie... that's hard.'

'I thought you might have heard, Gav, a team from Moscow looking for me, but they found Angie instead.'

'No... Christ.'

A deep scowl clouding his face, Gav threw himself into a broker's chair, its cushions knotted by tape to its spindles. Now Gav's office, the room carried mementos of the school like lingering debts. A robust chair for visitors, a bookcase gathering unopened letters and in one long group photograph after another, the tiered ranks of boarders, their faces bleached by passing summers joined by cobwebs into a forgotten strand of scattered generations.

'Whisky's in the old man's cabinet, use the malt, the other stuff I save for prospective clients, the few that I get. If I'd have known, I'd have sent flowers, a wreath,' he said, his eyes watching Nick locate the whisky.

'I haven't arranged the funeral yet.'

'Right, sure, just let me know.'

On top of the cabinet Nick came face to face with Gav's father, Josh Rafford in a Bakelite frame. A new man, one of C. P. Snow's troubled breed, a very civil servant. He poured for them both, nothing extra, just neat and long.

'No one been in touch then?' Nick asked, handing Gav a glass.

'No...wouldn't expect it after all these years, bit remote, not on the District Line, are we. Cheers,' he said toasting Nick.

'Cheers. Suppose you are a bit cut-off,' said Nick, taking a seat in front of a solid wooden desk the whisky warming his throat. 'How's business?' Nick started off gently, not wanting Gav to bolt.

'Terrible, health and safety, risk assessments and injury lawyers almost wiped out adventure training,' said Gav, the old fieldman in him avoiding playing straight into Nick's hands.

'Tessa seems nice.'

'Tessa is good.' Gav had drained his glass and was up and refilling. 'Want another?'

'I'll pass.'

He poured a second glass for himself, neat again, nothing allowed to impede the numbing effect. 'A toast. Here's to the bastards of this world and the next.'

'Sod them all.'

His glass seriously recharged for the third time, Gav took cover behind his desk. 'Want to tell me the real reason for dragging yourself all the way up here?'

'A collection in Moscow was fouled up. I was a guest of the GRU. Don't suppose you heard about that either?'

'Not a whisper,' said Gav, drinking too quickly.

'I was tasked to make a collection from an asset, code-name Viper, real name Vasily Aramovich Lubov. Ring any bells?'

'Nope,' said Gav, tapping his temple, 'the old memory bank is pretty low.'

'They were waiting for us, Lubov and Foula were killed,' said Nick, pursuing the thread, 'but Lubov had sent his material on ahead and the tricky thing is that I need to locate it.'

'Come on Nick, this is Gav you're talking to, don't insult me with all this bullshit. You were never any good at waffle.'

Accepting Gav's invitation Nick went straight to the point. 'A laptop,' Nick began, 'you wouldn't know where I could find it?'

Gav shrugged not committing himself one way or another.

'You've run product lines, Gav. Made arrangements for secure delivery, know how the system operates.'

'Bloody lifetime ago,' added Gav.

Pressing on with his opening thrust, Nick continued: 'Lubov couldn't have contacted you to arrange for a collection, so who did?'

Refusing to be drawn Gav stared into space making his mind up which way he'd jump. Finally, draining his glass, he asked, 'Is this official?'

'Unofficial all the way,' Nick admitted. 'I'm in a spot of bother actually. Suspended, under suspicion of blowing the operation.'

With a deep sigh, Gav signalled his decision to talk.

'I heard. Jamie gave me a call,' Gav confessed.

'And the laptop?' asked Nick, wondering what else Gav had been told.

'Well, I'll keep it simple,' promised Gav. 'A favour for old times...' he confessed, before suddenly breaking off. 'Tessa... what do you think of her, really, different to Grace eh?'

'Totally,' said Nick, 'she knows about Moscow?'

'Just that I got a lame leg working for Her Majesty a long time ago.'

Moscow, the beginning of Gav's nightmare Nick recalled; Gav boxed in and cornered, shattering his knee against the steering wheel of his escape vehicle as he attempted to ram his way out of a cordon in a fit of blind fury.

'The laptop,' Nick prompted him.

'Jamie called up, out of the blue, said our Chief wanted help. What Chief, I asked. I'm off the payroll, or hadn't he heard. Aubrey-Spencer, Jamie tells me, he's got Jamie back in harness and wants me buckled up beside him.'

'How did Jamie sell it?'

With a hollow laugh, Gav disclosed: 'If I accepted, it might offer some closure to Operation Windfall.' He winced at the name. 'Jamie said it would be nothing strenuous, a brush contact because we couldn't use a dead drop as this contact was flaky, couldn't be relied on.'

'But you accepted?' asked Nick, sensing Gav's unease, but he pushed him along by adding, 'and everything went to plan?'

'She was scared totally out of her boots,' Gav disclosed. 'But she held her nerve and I made the collection.'

'Where's the laptop now, Gav?'

'Aubrey-Spencer has it,' he sighed. 'There, you've got the lot,' he smiled wanly.

But Nick had only just begun. 'Operation Windfall, Gav, what did you think Jamie meant by closure?'

'My six months board and lodging care of the GRU. Chris Parlick, my support, got out by the skin of his teeth and Jane got to watch it all go down the pan from Washington didn't she, lucky sod. How is she, by the way, still delicious?'

'Much the same,' answered Nick.

'I could never understand why she and...'

'We weren't really suited,' said Nick, 'I was an episode and she moved on, different tastes. You were telling me about Latvia?'

'Was I?' said Gav, thinking he'd poured water on Nick's fire.

'Yes, Gav, you were,' Nick reminded him. 'Jamie suggested you'd nailed the myth, hit the truth.'

'Hell, it's all water under the bridge,' Gav warned. 'I'd latched onto a very pretty translator, probably for no other reason than pure devilment. I just got a tingle she was a GRU thoroughbred,' he admitted, with an extensive sigh. 'One hazy evening, Katrina has a cry on my generous shoulder. Katrina loves her work, but she must have committed a grave, but undisclosed sin.

Haven't we all, I told her.'

'She was showing you a lot of leg, Gav. Sounds like a lure.'

'And she got executed for it,' he blazed, his mood quite ugly.

'I'm sorry, Gav.'

'Makes no difference now,' Gav declared, sailing into calmer waters. 'The thorn in Katrina's paw concerned her missing out on London's bright lights. After Nizhny Novgorod, she'd set her heart and soul for London, but she was fast forwarded to Riga.'

Gav, who admitted to being very sozzled at the time, smiled, nodded, gave her all his loving sympathy. 'To my utter amazement, she neither called the local hoods nor reported it to the big boys in Moscow.'

'What did she have, Gav?' Nick sensed that Gav was playing for time, attempting to take Nick down an unconnected side road.

'What do you think?' Gav retorted with a hint of venom. 'Katrina *was* the speck of gold dust in the seam.'

Subdued, brooding, his countenance thoroughly morose, Gav turned back the tarnished pages, living the nightmare again. She told Gav she'd been selected for an eighteen-month stint at Nizhny Novgorod. She'd secured a place on the training and appraisal programme prior to residency postings, known to staff and instructors as the *Academy*. Physical tests, psychometric tests, character profiling, aptitude, enhanced vetting. If they had it, she did it, jumping through all the hoops. Gav had played it low-key, teasing her, betting she'd had plenty of admirers in her class. But Katrina sharply put Gav right. The instructors were strict, any personal fraternising would be dealt with harshly, resulting in immediate expulsion. They were issued with worknames on arrival, but that was standard protocol, it denoted the beginning of the journey towards graduating as GRU residency operatives.

'Did she describe the facility?' Nick wondered when Gav had broken cover to refill his glass.

'Sprawling place, lot of it underground,' Gav disclosed, wandering back to his chair. 'She reckoned the place had been there for years, maybe even used for rocket development. Now it was the GRU's main training facility. They'd got rid of the dachas scattered around Moscow, contained it all in a centre of excellence with secure compounds.'

'What made her so sure she would be going to London?'

At Nick's question, a real storm of conflicting emotions raged inside Gav, his eyes narrowed, and his features hardened.

'Had her final pre-launch briefings, advanced language courses, the familiarisation routine on English culture and traditions,' he flared, not for a minute softening his tone. 'A member of her group was removed, no reason given, and that was it. Within an hour the group was scratched from the programme. Katrina was reassigned, Riga next stop with dire warnings of the perils for disclosure.'

'In London, she'd have been what, Gav? Official status, residency role... duties... how was it packaged?'

'Embassy, Trade Section,' Gav snapped. 'Rank undisclosed, residency communication supervisor.'

'And why Riga?'

'Residency posting, communication administrator,' Gav sullenly admitted. 'A grade higher than the Embassy cat. Ordered to keep her head down, but she was getting restless, careless. Didn't get on with her boss, thought they'd post her to another backwater. If we wanted Katrina, we had to move fast.'

Seeming to accept Gav's account on face value, Nick's mind appeared to be somewhere else entirely. A minute, two, then three lapsed, before Nick emerged from his period of introspection. He ventured, as if a matter of conjecture: 'It really is quite brilliant how they almost pulled it off, Gav, isn't it?' he proposed, his manner low-key.

'The hell you talking about?'

'The Oktober Projekt, the Nizhny Novgorod facility. It's the *Emperor's New Clothes* in reverse. Let's say, for the sake of argument, let's say Riga had always been intended to be *the* penultimate stage in her intermediate legalisation as an illegal, the last soft stop, the final polish for her new legend as... oh, I don't know, but for the sake of argument, let's make her a translator shall we. I suppose any of the Balt states would have served the same purpose...'

Rising fast, Gav made a lunge for Nick. 'She didn't play me,' he declared angrily, sinking back into his chair.

'But *she* just happened to run into you,' Nick continued, his patience and calm determination endless. 'And coincidently, she happens to be a graduate of Nizhny Novgorod. She's had first-hand experience of its facilities, and quite willingly paints over all those troublesome rumours concerning the Oktober Projekt, giving it a new lick of gloss as a standard training programme. It exists, she confirms it, but as the GRU facility for preparing residency operatives. Until the Seventies Nizhny Novgorod was invisible as far as we were concerned, we had rumours that became a myth. The facility couldn't be hidden forever, not with improved satellite capability, so why not turn the myth on its head, give it a new, quite ordinary, set of clothes, conceal its true purpose with disinformation. You see, Gav, I think Katrina was *meant* to defect all along, it was just a matter of creating a plausible cover story. It's one of the first things they teach at Aspley, tell a small lie to conceal the bigger truth. What could be more natural, a GRU defector, a prize catch, she would have an assigned case officer to debrief her, and those meetings would have legitimacy, perfectly acceptable interaction.'

To Nick's offer of a refill, Gav simply nodded, slouched deep in his chair, his wide shoulders slumped. And when Nick returned his glass, he cupped it in both hands in front of his chest, his face expressionless, the colour drained.

'But she didn't make it over the line, did she?' Gav eventually asserted, downing his whisky in one, the glass hitting the desk with a purposeful crack.

'It would look a little odd if Katrina suddenly changed her mind overnight, Gav. Something went wrong, her defection was cancelled, postponed by Moscow,' reasoned Nick. Reasoning also, this time for his own consideration, that he possessed the awful realisation that Gav had unknowingly fatally comprised his soldier ants. And more recently, for a reason yet undisclosed, sealed the fate of Juris Valgos; whom, as far as Nick remembered, was definitely on the side of the angels.

'You almost have Katrina in the bag,' Nick resumed after an unbearable silence,' it's down to making the necessary arrangements, finalising the details. Jamie cleared the way with London, I presume? And I'm sure Jane will have done her bit from Moscow. She was still in Moscow at that point, was she?'

'Why?' Gav asked defensively.

'Just getting some background facts in order,' Nick replied.

'Jane was on the up and up, even then,' Gav admitted. 'She was coming to the end of her tour, which was a blow because, she is a good deal softer on the eyes than Roly.'

'She is,' Nick agreed.

Throwing up his large hands in a gesture of hopeless confusion, Gav shook his head. 'Bit of chaos at that time if I remember. Aycliffe broke his hip skiing, so Jane was put on the next plane to Washington. Rossan was in and out of Berlin like a yo-yo and Roly was giving Jamie hell in Moscow.'

'And Katrina's defection,' Nick tentatively advanced, 'well, that was forcibly curtailed at short notice.'

And there was one question that he couldn't avoid putting to Gav. 'When they picked you up on the wrong side of the border, Gav, how did that seem?'

Gav stared at Nick for a long time as though he'd never considered the question before. 'They used me and my network as cover to call off Katrina's extraction, didn't they?'

'I'm sorry, but that's how it looks.'

'Makes sense how fast they collared me,' Gav disclosed, 'Bang, I was busted,' he recalled, his eyes narrowing. 'All too damn easy for them, wasn't it?' Gav ground to a full stop, unwilling to linger over the details.

But Nick couldn't have the luxury of ignorance nor denial. 'How did they lure you in? I need it all, Gav, I really do.'

'They must have had one of my boys, Pāvils under the screw for a while,' Gav reflected. 'Usual arrangements for a contact meeting in Ostrov. Ten minutes in, and they threw the net over us. I was the last in the barrel and got star treatment. Didn't worry that much, keep my cool, play it long, sit it out for a week, and I'd be home. Fat chance. Moved me out almost immediately, and I thought this isn't good. Hadn't a clue where I was heading, but it was a long slog, and I wasn't going in the direction of home or Moscow.' Closing his eyes, Gav had to dig deep before continuing.

Prepared to let him have as long as he needed to open the final door, Nick barely moved, unwilling to offer distraction or an excuse for Gav to run for cover.

'Knew it was the coast by the smell. Sea and diesel fuel. And then inside the gates they took off the blindfold and bundled me out. I knew, Christ, I knew then I was in a spot of trouble. It could only be one place.'

'Kronstadt,' said Nick.

'Used to scare the pants of new entrants with it, didn't they? "Forget the FSB's Lefortovo prison, that's a walk in the park compared to the island. And you won't be enjoying the delights of St. Petersburg during your stay." Know the first thing they showed me?'

'Haven't a clue.'

'Three wooden upright posts for the poor sods they executed by firing squad and they let me know they'd be using them pretty soon. The place had a red brick exterior but everything in it was covered in thick black paint. Walls, ceilings, the hearts and minds of the guards, the lot, all daubed in black. Officially, it was Naval Detention Institution No.5, but it's exclusive to the GRU and it was a laugh a minute.'

'Was there any mention of the others they had in the bag? Any reference to Katrina?' Nick asked.

'They made sure I saw a couple of boys and girls from the network when they walked me upright from my cell and believe me, that made a change from being pulled and pushed around doubled over. Passed them on the corridor, but they were ghosts, nothing left. They'd been squeezed dry in Moscow, then shipped up to the island for a final shakedown. You never forget the screams,' he snapped; the loathing, horror and contempt at his treatment another trauma, but unlike his shattered knee, this would never heal.

Backing off, Nick offered Gav a less painful route to follow. 'How did they play you, Gav? Low-key? Priority? Or were you the bonus?'

'Prime target, Nick, never seen anything like it, number one guest wasn't I. They had a file all ready and waiting for me. Not local goons either, special detachment had come in just for us.'

'You certain?' Nick asked, realising that his own interrogation had followed the very same pattern.

'Of course I'm certain,' countered Gav, 'they were GRU, and they were the pros. After I'd done my fairy tale for the day they'd get straight onto the questioning, well, that was something else. Had a neat old dentist's chair they strapped you in, big lights overhead... and...,' but Gav shied away from completing his sentence

'What did they want to know?'

'What didn't they,' snorted Gav. 'Tell us what you know about Nizhny Novgorod? Tell us what you know about Katrina?'

'Did you give them anything?'

Gav shrugged. 'Bullshit to begin with, least I could, getting names and places mixed up. But they just laughed, told me to stop being silly, I was only making things worse for myself. Then they started on the beatings, two a day, regular as clockwork.' Breaking off, Gav, rotated his glass on the desk as his thoughts realigned themselves. 'If you're right, and I'm not saying you are, it was all a sham.'

'I'm afraid so, Gav.'

'Shit.' And after a moment's pause, he continued, his voice drained. 'Then I got my trial, all for show, lasted a good five minutes before they packed me off to the camp.'

'And the camp was…'

'Hard fucking labour, Nick, but boy, was I glad to get away from that place and those screams.'

'And they questioned you after the move from the prison?'

'Once a week, snow, rain or shine. Who did I report to, did I know this name, that name, who ran this, are you sure this was the courier, the cut-out, the handler? Then they'd always come back to Nizhny Novgorod, how much did Katrina actually tell, did she provide details of her training for London?'

'They knew their stuff,' said Nick, speculating, though it is never a guaranteed formula, just why Moscow were so concerned that anything relating to the Oktober Projekt had to convince London it was a standard training programme for residency operatives.

'Too bloody much of it,' retorted Gav, looking at Nick as though he'd just made his own connection, a long-lost discovery. A shotgun retorted in the woods and Gav flinched. Through the window Nick saw starlings dotted on a telephone wire like beads on a rosary lift off together in a swirl as the shotgun blasted away again.

'I was finished after that and then when the old man….'

'You know what happened to Katrina?'

'They shot her… or so they claimed.'

And Nick could see Gav in five or ten years' time, the hair a little greyer pulled farther back off his brow, sitting at the headmaster's desk much as he did now, a faraway glint in his eye, the glass pressed to his lips and the same coils of mildewed rope and fell boots drying in the corners.

'Sometimes I miss the Firm, sometimes I hate it with a vengeance.'

'But you did the right thing for Aubrey-Spencer,' Nick assured him, watching the old fervour rise in Gav's eyes.

'Sure.' And perhaps reflecting on his days with Nick, Gav went silent.

'You haven't mentioned the laptop to anyone else?'

'No, I bloody haven't,' snapped Gav, his mood darkening.

'I had to ask.'

Gav had receded into another world; laughing though not as a result of humour but from something couched in pain. 'Sure, I would have been disappointed if you hadn't.' Gav closed his eyes, leant back and sighed.

'One other thing,' Nick proposed as if it was of no great importance. 'What made you take Juris along when you collected the laptop? You did have him with you, didn't you?'

Staring at Nick with a downright hostile countenance, Gav shrugged. 'If things went fluid and the contact made a break for it or had brought company, I'm not the quickest out of the blocks.'

'That's fine, Gav, perfectly reasonable,' Nick soothed him. 'Bump into any old faces while you down there?'

This time the question seemed to catch Gav completely unprepared. 'Had a pint with Roly, Paul and Jane,' he admitted cautiously. 'Not against the law, is it?'

'No, Gav, it certainly isn't,' Nick smiled. 'I suppose the reason for your trip came up?' he added.

With more than a shrewd awareness of where he was being steered, Gav nodded. 'Didn't blab, if that's what you mean. Kept it vague, said I was doing a favour for an old friend. I may have mentioned I was riding tandem with Juris on the back saddle. Why?'

'Juris is missing.'

'Shit.'

They sat in silence for a while, each of them contemplating what they both knew to be an unspoken truth about Juris' disappearance and Gav's sudden arrest in Russia. Examining his glass, Gav the first to find his voice also found an excuse for Nick leaving.

'Let's go and find Tessa, she'll want to say bye before you set off, she's sorting out colour schemes for when we refurbish the dorms.'

With Gav setting a brisk pace they made a silent ascent up through the hall into a dormer garret pushed into the eaves, its partitioned cubicles stopping short of the ceiling. Under a glaring row of lights Gav called for Tessa, swinging his bad leg after good, a mechanical hobble controlled from his waist. On through a common room into a storeroom stacked with wire framed beds and beaten wooden cabinets, Gav marched forlornly searching for his wife. But they never found her. Only the lingering fear from generations of boys worked into the corridors; and over it, a distant trail of perfume like the foretaste of another failed marriage. Back in the utility kitchen, Gav made the coffee with ponderous care, fighting against the whisky in his fingers.

'We must keep in touch,' Gav proposed, breaking the silence.

'That would be good,' said Nick, knowing they never would.

Then Gav walked Nick to his car, talking the same dreams that Tessa knew off by heart. Standing under the porch he waved Nick off, just as his father must have done for pupils at the end of each term; the same tired smile, the awkward clumsy stance, and the same inevitable tragedy in his eyes.

Sixteen

Nick made it back to London just before seven that evening, recklessly accelerating through curtains of spray as he overtook one articulated lorry after another on the M6. Exhausted more than he wanted to admit, Nick coaxed himself up the flights of stairs to his seventh-floor room in an economy hotel a couple of minutes' walk from Baker Street. It was a double room complete with plastic flowers, a panoramic rooftop view and a series of framed prints of Sherlock Holmes and Dr. Watson covering the stains on the flowery sateen wallpaper. There was a wardrobe in knotted pine straight from Taiwan and an electroplated brass effect bed, though the cobwebs strung in festoons around the corners were thankfully real.

Uncapping his bottle of Laphroaig, Nick picked out a dark hair inside the tooth mug and settled himself on the bed. Sometime before nine his phone rang. Not Hawick, Jane or Roly calling to make amends or pledge a fresh start, but Paul Rossan cutting off a yawn, asking for his location, no he couldn't tell him why, just that Nick should be outside in ten minutes.

The driver was young, fierce; a natural blond, his lips making a scar in his pale face as he nodded his welcome to Nick in the passenger seat. Confidently, assured, relaxed, the blond drove without a word; briskly, business like, as though born for a life behind the wheel, an air of showmanship in every move, perfected to demonstrate his ability, his skill. The persistent rain that dogged the entire journey had lessened as they reached Greenwich; reduced to a few weak drops that hit the car with no real effort as they turned onto Shooters Hill Road.

'This is as far as we go,' the blond informed him, stopping with a jolt. 'The shelter on the mound. Would seem that you're expected there, sir,' he said with anything but respect. 'In the park, Mr. Torr, it's been cleared,' he added rudely, Nick wondering if Rossan had them specially bred.

Left on the pavement under a clear sky with too many stars to count, Nick began to walk. A brisk wind had dried the road and it might never have rained he thought, entering the park, except for the grass still wet, sodden and slippery as though from a heavy dew. Behind him he heard the occasional car as he climbed into the night, through chestnut trees coiled against the sky like barbed wire. His eyes adjusted gradually to the light, to the dim outlines, brittle silhouettes and fuzzy shapes formed by the street lamps below. He pressed on, a bonfire haze in the air, stopping twice to look back, and once he thought he saw movement, standing his ground, his eyes straining until they hurt. He saw nothing more.

The shelter covered the centre of a well-trodden mound; the grass worn into mud by the many feet of a varied army who for one reason or another made it the target of their assaults. Not tonight though, for Nick glimpsed the vague outlines of three teams he guessed Rossan had dispatched discreetly ringing the shelter. Inside he smelt urine, stale bread and alcohol leaking from an assortment of beer cans scattered like spent shells. He lit a cigarette and held his lighter up to the walls. He read that 'Micki loves Debbi' a thousand times and was thankful they weren't there to prove it. He listened to a drunken song in the distance; a distorted youthful chant, guttural notes resonant and menacing. Out of an avenue of chestnuts he picked up a figure working steadily up the hill, stopping at intervals as if taking bearings. Nick stepped away from the edge; the tranquillity of the night disturbing, almost too satisfying, hypnotic in its splendour. He listened to the footfall on the boards then a torch beam clicked full in his face.

'You got my invitation,' growled Sir Charles Aubrey-Spencer, who until six months previously had run the Service, and on retiring, some speculated on political grounds, grudgingly became Chair of the Joint Intelligence Committee.

'Cut it out,' Nick protested, shielding his eyes; swimming and stinging his night vision gone, mischievously ruined.

'I am honoured to witness the return of the prodigal son, one Nicholas Torr, no less.' Aubrey-Spencer lowered his torch, drew a line across the stained boards and crossed it; his own bright Rubicon that instantly disappeared. 'I feel rather neglected and offended that you haven't bothered to include me on your list of people you needed to see.'

'Don't worry, you were there, close to the top,' retorted Nick, blinded still.

'Was I indeed?' Aubrey-Spencer had a habit of speaking in a low tremor. Crisp, resilient, pitched low so the other person had to make the effort of paying attention. 'Damn tragedy about Angela, damn tragedy. You'll be wanting to know about the laptop I suppose?'

'If it saves another life, yes, I'd like to know about the laptop,' Nick said, his voice rising.

'Then calm down and hear me out,' Aubrey-Spencer insisted, his voice placatory yet grave, as if addressing a committee of his own choosing.

Unbridled, fearing the moment lost, Nick would have none of it. 'You listen,' he said lurching forward. 'Angela was murdered because Moscow assumed I had Lubov's material when it was safe and sound all the time,' Nick seethed.

'I suppose you have good reason to be righteous.'

'I hope it was worth it?'

'I've always known it's been worth it.'

Nick remained against the far wall, silent, watching Aubrey-Spencer fidget with the torch.

'Despite decades of protecting ourselves from Moscow's advances, the threat hasn't decreased, it's multiplied, it has become a dynamic confrontation. They have us on the back foot. It's our own fault for looking the other way. Our intelligence infrastructure was too damn slow to adapt to the Soviet Bloc's implosion. It never came in the way we anticipated or adequately planned for. We were dazzled by the apparent flowering of democracy, the welcome demise of communism in exchange for capitalism. Equality for the masses, empowerment for the few. It hasn't decreased Moscow's appetite for what we hold dear, has it. Energy, finance, defence, industry, political freedom... they want the lot, and they've increased their resources accordingly. Latest count is we have two hundred of Moscow's dedicated operators hell-bent on thieving our secrets. Fivefold the number who plied their trade here during the Cold War. And let's not overlook how they are permitted free movement. I suppose that's the price we pay for holding hands with the Kremlin to formalise counter-terrorism cooperation.'

'And the price I've paid?'

'Your anger is understandable,' Aubrey-Spencer conceded.

'You have no idea how angry I am.'

'The parameters may have changed, Nicholas, but the core mode of attack remains valid. Penetration of opinion, systems, institutions. Whether it is intimate and personal or remotely as a cyber incursion, the damage destabilises our domestic governance and international relationships. Our political masters are fickle, they always follow the course of least resistance. They talk tough and deliver the minimum for fear of retaliation.'

'The Oktober Projekt is part of this penetration strategy?'

'I believe it is.'

'And Lubov had proof? What *did* he possess that cost him his life?'

'Everything and nothing,' Aubrey-Spencer declared, rocking sadly to and fro, his bulk one massive boulder against a velvet sky. 'A lead of sorts, he spotted the dim speck of gold and continued digging, seeking the mother lode.'

'And he hit it?'

'Part of it. But time, betrayal and the ridiculously inept case officer they inflicted on him thwarted his plans. In the period he served us, Lubov's product opened a rear window into the actions of several GRU directorates through the financing of operations and residencies. His tracking of the money revealed covert bases established in Syria, Libya, Yemen, the funding allocated to political manipulation. Vasily provided us with an unprecedented overview.'

'But not everything.'

'An incomplete panorama in some respects, but we have landmarks to work from. He put the Veterans Rehabilitation Clinic No.2 and a centre at Nikolina Gora on the map for us. Both suggest autonomy from GRU Centre, both are conveniently located in Moscow's suburbs and enjoy restricted access, both under the control of an unidentified directorate.'

'Does that include the academy at Nizhny Novgorod.'

'The so-called Military-Foreign Affairs Academy, or the centre for Advanced Linguistics Academy. It hides in clear sight under a number of spurious aliases, but that is where the myth of a clandestine training facility began. So too did the first whisper of the Oktober Projekt which Lubov had diligently begun to tease towards the light until he was prevented from proceeding.'

'Permanently,' offered Nick sounding inexplicably withdrawn. 'How did he discover it?'

'Through a totally innocuous glitch delaying the release of a funding tranche for the Nizhny Novgorod facility. One of the facility's director's calls Lubov, roars at him for being an imbecile, for being the son of imbeciles, for being the grandson of imbeciles. An unpleasant haranguing and berating are delivered to our star asset for the non-arrival of said capital. The cock-up means a certain procedure must now be undertaken by Lubov. He is ordered to personally supervise the specified deposit into a Panama account. He is ordered that the transfer must be completed within the hour. The sum and account number would be securely forwarded to him. As Lubov told it to Wynn, if he hadn't received such a very thorough and nasty bollocking, he would have complied without a second thought. But he was piqued, his curiosity was aroused, and he started digging.'

On the prowl again, Aubrey-Spencer flung the beam of light in front of him, trekking after it to a distant corner of the shelter.

'What's on the laptop?'

'The results of his labours. Financial records compiled from his back bearings covering the movement of funds over several years. A trail leading him from the Nizhny Novgorod facility via Panama to Hamburg, the axis of a money laundering operation. Very dirty laundry, as it happens, Nicholas.'

'Funding for the Oktober Projekt?'

'Absolutely. Controlled from Nizhny Novgorod where it was split and employed on the GRU's dirty work. I suspect it is for the upkeep of high value assets. A financial web, and who knows where it ends.'

'Lubov, if he hadn't been sold out. The counter-intelligence sweep in his Ministry was triggered because a high value asset worked out an approximate source corollary from Lubov's product,' proposed Nick. 'Once they had the provenance, it was only a matter of time before they'd identify the supplier.'

'Lubov is neither stupid nor a dullard and realises that he's running out of time. His case officer refuses to buy into Lubov's warning of a witch-hunt operation. He is forced to take matters into his own hands and that is when Wynn stepped in and contacted me. She met with Lubov in Moscow three times, verified his fears, calmed him. We'd made arrangements for Lubov's extraction during his scheduled audit of an outstation in Hamburg. The trip was curtailed, the opportunity lost. The fool of a case officer compounded his inadequacy by demanding Lubov justifies his extraction with evidence RUS/OPS would buy into,' Aubrey-Spencer seethed. The torch wavered in a glaring circle leaving a solid trail before dipping once more. The reflected light hardly flattering, deepening the fat on his several chins.

'Somebody bought it,' said Nick, and it occurred to him the damage control operation driven by Moscow wasn't only triggered by Bensham's release of the Oktober Projekt's code-name to London, but his declaration that *it is active*, which prompted such a ruthless response. 'How did you know about the laptop?'

'He failed to show for a last meeting with Wynn before Hamburg. They had a fallback, a dead-letter box where Wynn found a garbled note about a phone and a girl. By the time Rafford tracked her down she had somehow corrupted the files. Once Lubov declared his hand, he and all those that sailed alongside him were a liability.'

'The financial records on the laptop?' Nick wondered.

'The files were encrypted and are now corrupted, but we had Hamburg as journey's end for the funds.'

'Sally Wynn wouldn't let it go, would she?' Nick demanded, his mood rancorous.

'No, Nicholas she wouldn't. We had the flow of money from Nizhny Novgorod to a bank in Panama, then onwards through a number of front companies to Hamburg. After that, we don't know. That is where the trail ended, and Wynn had begun to work on the connections.'

'You sent Wynn without support?'

'No, I did not, that would have been reckless,' Aubrey-Spencer shot angrily back. 'There was an intermediary in Hamburg handling the arrangements for Lubov's extraction. When that fizzled out, he provided back-up for Wynn.'

'Harry Bransk?'

'Yes, Harry Bransk. He and Wynn had the distinct advantage of not being directly connected to Head Office's sphere of operations,' he added.

With a grudging sigh Aubrey-Spencer dragged his feet over the boards, appraising them through the waxy path of torchlight.

'She wasn't contaminated, that what you mean?'

'Act your age, Nicholas, you know damn well the direction the Oktober Projekt is taking us.'

'A highly placed asset inside the Firm, or closely connected to it.'

'That was the explicit warning Lubov gave Wynn for me, and it left me holding Occam's razor. The simplest thing was to believe him, the hardest would be finding ways to disprove him. After considering the options, the obvious solution was to accept Lubov's forewarning as legitimate. And I did. Couldn't very well pitch up at Head Office for a grace and favour coffee with my successor, chat about the weather and ambush him with: "By the way, I think you've a nasty traitor looking over your shoulder." Martin is an exceptionally talented officer, he served me well as Head Counter-intelligence, and given time, he'll prove to be a gifted Chief. He'd have responded in the same way that I would have done and demanded proof. Anyway, Lubov never provided insight which would have narrowed down the hunt for a traitor, so the best policy was to play it remotely.

'Consider everyone a suspect.'

'Had a suspicion something was afoot after Rafford's ill-fated Operation Windfall, but suspicion isn't the nailing of a traitor to the cross. Something about that operation, Nicholas just didn't sit well. The circumstances of his encounter with the lovely Katrina was blessed with too much good fortune. Had a quiet word with the Minister at the time, made her aware of my concerns that we were dealing with the high probability of at least one sleeper, possibly more, all agents of influence quite capable of wreaking the same catastrophic damage achieved by Philby. I was assured the matter would receive suitable consideration. Suitable consideration, Nicholas, fancy that. Someone got to her, or she was so minded of the fallout if the Cousins got wind of it, she buried it. Did I have proof? Did I hell. So, here we are.'

'Here we are.' *Tell him the Oktober Projekt is active, it is the deceit, and it is more. Tell him I have discovered its purpose. Tell him it requires secrets and it protects secrets*, Lubov had insisted. 'Katrina wasn't shot, was she?'

'I very much doubt it. She was disappeared, allowed to remain dormant, to be reactivated after a suitable period,' confessed Aubrey-Spencer, his mood dark. 'Find Katrina and we find our traitor or traitors.

'By following the money?'

'It would be a colossal affront to the lives already lost if we didn't finish what Lubov began.'

'Independent of Head Office, run as a black bag operation? That what you had in mind?' suggested Nick.

'Don't be so damn facetious,' Aubrey-Spencer warned. 'There is some exceptionally clever scheming taking place, and it makes my skin crawl.' He felt in his pocket, took out a packet of mints and fumbled to get one in his mouth. 'All bets are off concerning whom or what we face, Nicholas. There will be fallout, there will be casualties, that is inevitable. However, you have my undivided support and can call upon the meagre resources at my disposal.'

'Thanks for sharing. A touch late, but thanks.'

'As you appear receptive, I think you ought to know Juris Valgos' body has been recovered from the Thames.'

'How did he die?'

'The post-mortem is inconclusive. The police *will* be requiring a word at some point. Rossan is holding them off, but I'm afraid it is inevitable.'

'I suppose it is.'

'You take the fight to Moscow, Nicholas, play hard and play dirty. Everyone's so obsessed with the war on terror that they've taken their eyes off Moscow. If I was at the helm, I wouldn't have blinked, but I'm not and that's that. Seek and you shall always find. Hamburg, that is the guiding point on the compass. If you require further assistance, contact me through Rossan,' Aubrey-Spencer declared, prowling along a side wall. 'You can rely on him.'

'Will do,' promised Nick.

'Watch your back, young Nicholas. This is friendly advice to stay wise understand,' advised Aubrey-Spencer, clambering out of the shelter. 'Fare you well.'

Nick went after him, all the way to the top of the mound, watching the beam from Aubrey-Spencer's torch weave a jaunty path into the tree line before being snuffed out. Around him the park started to settle once more for the night and Nick lit a cigarette as the darkness reclaimed the mound. In the air he caught the smell of fallen damp leaves. His dogged resolve to have answers undiminished, his commitment to expose the traitor established on a cold London night, the pain of Angie's death kept at bay by the alchemy of the night; a clear sky crowned by a vivid healthy moon and shimmering stars. Returning into the depths of the shelter, its planks reeking of urine, he listened to the night traffic below him, a reminder of the normality he was turning his back on.

Seventeen

No one could ignore Andrejs Valgos. Standing behind a row of cellar railings with an assortment of plastic cups and an odd beer can marked extra strength punched through the rusty points, a faded sign was more or less hanging over his head; TWILLER FOR QUALITY MEAT. The 'F' and 'M' had slipped down, but Andrejs didn't seem bothered by the rearranged message. He had blood on his hands and smears of it on his white butcher's coat. Pushing solemnly at pieces of discarded market litter with his feet, he struck his final wholesale deal of the afternoon, his bloated face a patchwork of colour and glimpses of past emotions, and Nick held back until Andrejs' customer moved off.

Approaching in full view to provide ample warning, Nick nodded a greeting to Andrejs. 'I want to talk to you about Juris,' Nick said, watching Andrejs' face rise and stiffen, the muscles in each cheek brace. Breaking off writing in a notebook, his reddened hands locked into each other for protection. Stepping forward his weight on his left foot, Andrejs hit Nick with a fierce right hook splitting his lip, rocking Nick back on his heels.

That's okay, Nick thought, wiping the blood away with the back of his hand. I can understand he's angry, he thinks I'm mixed up with the death of his brother.

'Whatever you've been told, I had no involvement,' Nick vowed.

'I don't do no more talk. You want talk, you go find my sister, she talk about Juris all day. I got business to run, got that.'

'If Juris *was* murdered, it *was* on Moscow's orders,' said Nick bluntly, not prepared to move, letting the information sink in.

'Who say?'

'I do.'

'Me, I don't have no more involvement with Russians, got that,' he cried, as if he needed to start by refuting allegations.

'That's fine.'

'If you sure, come into office and we talk.' Andrejs tossed back his dark head and walked off, a plodding shuffle in both feet.

The office was a cabin nailed up out of plywood sheets, proclaiming Twiller & Sons painted unevenly above a door neither of Andrejs' sons would ever walk through. After Nick followed him inside, Andrejs hammered a rubber wedge under the door with the heel of a boot. He dropped his notebook and pencil into separate coat pockets clotted a deeper brown. When he frowned, folds of skin deepened around his nose and to the side of his mouth.

'Did Juris mention anything about being contacted recently by anyone from the Firm, or anyone from the old days?' Nick asked, propped against a tatty trucker's map of major trunk routes, his lip throbbing as it swelled. There were no windows and the other walls were crowded with invoices and bills stamped Final Demand.

Taken off guard, Andrejs shook his head, every day he prepared himself for another crushing blow despite Irka, his second wife, going to church each morning to pray nothing more would happen. With Andrejs' first wife losing two sons, and Irka herself never able to become a mother, she saw everything as a punishment for an unknown family sin, and at any moment, God would send another disaster. Andrejs accepted her pious reliance on fate, providing enough space for religion to take over. What did he mind? Running like a dog in the night, changing addresses, moving to a different country, he lived with the reality in order to accept this world's candid price as opposed to the mystical promises of the next.

'Juris never been same since his friends betrayed and murdered,' said Andrejs, reclaiming his composure. 'I tell you now, for all time. I say the family not interested no more in spying for English.' He whipped a wad of invoices from a hook and his movement shook the cabin's wall.

'Maybe Juris had something to prove, make something right from the past.'

Flinging the sheaf of papers Andrejs went for Nick. His chapped hands splayed wide on Nick's chest, he swore, he cursed, he used all his brute power, but barely moved Nick a fraction towards the door.

'Get out,' he raged, his hands dropped at his sides. This tough spy could go rot in hell before he would strike him again, stain his pride once more. 'My family fought the Russians in Latvia, we made sacrifices. You hear that?' he said bitterly, in a trance. 'Juris no get involved with them.'

From the file Nick had compiled on Juris he remembered the Valgos family history. One uncle executed by the Russians in 1953, his body put on public display in the marketplace, another uncle had undertaken courier work for the Service. And Andrejs' first wife, one of Gav's soldier ants living and working in Moscow; four months pregnant with twin boys when the network was blown, she was tortured and never recovered after her release from prison, committing suicide. Andrejs and Juris abandoned everything they possessed, moving to Britain to begin their lives again.

'What I do know, Andrejs, is that Juris *did* some work for the Firm recently. Nothing major, a straightforward collection, and this placed him in great danger. I'm pretty sure someone else must have contacted him,' suggested Nick. 'You talked to him every day, he must have said something,' he added, his hand outstretched in an appeal.

'Go, get out,' Andrejs said, knocking Nick's hand sideways.

'Juris made an easy target, and you want to ignore it, pretend it didn't happen?' Nick countered.

He saw the mention of fidelity sting Andrejs who looked blankly for somewhere to sit; a stool or chair, both were outside the arc of his hands. His knees gave and his body sagged. Sinking his elbows onto the lid of a freezer cabinet, he sent a stack of telephone directories skidding onto the bed of a set of scales. Irka you should pray more he thought, your prayers are not getting through. He'd ask her to pick a different saint. Their life destroyed and wasted for no gains.

'Help me Andrejs, make them hurt for a change, make them know what it is to feel fear.'

'A chance to make good old wounds? That's what you think I should do? Against shadows, against people who have no names? You understand nothing, nothing of them and their methods.' The words came without any control, his face flushed.

'A chance to prove your brother was betrayed, set-up.'

'No one wants to listen.'

'Who contacted him, Andrejs, who contacted Juris?'

'Since he had big win on lotto two year ago, he forgot who he was, where he come from,' answered Andrejs, an empty chaff of a man blown dry by the winds of battles he never stayed to fight. 'He invests in these start-up companies, behaving crazy like he's a damn tycoon on *Dragon's Den*. I ask him why he wasting his money on dreams that not going to make a penny? He tells me, they are all our people, our community, he is giving them a chance.'

'Who was it Andrejs?'

Shaking his head, swallowing hard, Andrejs recounted the event for Nick. 'He a damn fool, a headstrong kid, never listen, okay.'

'Okay,' said Nick.

'Two days before he go missing, we celebrate our sister Elita's name day, a family meal, big party. You met Elita?'

'Yes, I met her once,' said Nick, and it was unforgettable. A hotel room in Paddington, a welfare check on Juris, and Elita padded in at his side uninvited; tempestuous from the second she entered, she gave a performance of such hostile intensity as she petitioned on Juris' behalf, the meeting ended in chaos.

'You met her husband Georgs?'

'No, I haven't had the pleasure.' And if he was anything like Elita, that would just be fine by Nick.

'After meal Juris gets a call on his cellphone, goes outside in garden. When Juris come back, he is grinning, bigger grin than damn circus clown. "You won lotto again? Not more people begging for money? Please Juris, I look after you this time." He just look at me like I'm a stranger. "It is business. It is private. You don't worry, it is good, it is Sergei." I don't know more details, he were not specific. Sergei Gorshov is crook. Elita and me, we tell Juris, you don't even take a damn toffee off him, nothing. Because he born in Riga, that don't make him one of us. Because he hangs round Lats don't make him one of us. He is Russian Lat, and he is trouble. We always telling Juris this, but he don't listen, he thinks he smarter. Juris gets big ideas, loses his way, thinks he can fool these crooks.'

'Did they arrange a meeting?'

'Gorshov is swine, he deserve to rot in hell. I said enough, now leave,' he protested, going to a ledge and stretching for a flask with a grunt. 'You make me nervous staying here.' He poured himself a stream of coffee into a mug.

'Someone betrayed Juris, someone lured him to his death, Andrejs.'

Blowing his coffee, Valgos gave a curt laugh.

'Sure. Me and my sister warned him not to go. We tell him, tell Ingrid that you walking into trouble for sure. Go on crazy holiday, go visit places you not seen, but don't go to any damn meeting. Go police, tell them Gorshov is a crook, and he always up to no good. Juris laugh, he say he can take care of himself. Sure, like a five-year old kid, I tell him,' he said, an appeal to a dozen missing jurors.

Ingrid. How could Nick have forgotten Ingrid? Not a Russian or a Lat, but a survivor of life;s cruel twists and turns. 'Ingrid went with him, she went to the meeting with Juris?' he asked, not knowing if this was a question too many.

Not seeming to care how many more questions Nick had lined up, Valgos nodded. 'He take her damn everywhere,' said Valgos, crossing himself in protection from the foolishness of his brother. 'She guard him like damn dog since he won money.' He drank off the coffee and slew the dregs across the floor. 'He take her everywhere, show her good time, buying her presents, car, even that damn business. I told him she no good, but Juris don't listen, he say to me he will provide enough for me to retire. He says he will buy me a car, any damn car I like. Top of the range. "Andrejs, you are my brother, let me provide better life for you. Why you so stubborn?" I tell him I work for a living, I earn my money and damn pride, I don't want damn charity. He took her to meeting, I sure of it. I told him, you stupid twice over. He say no risk, and I no see him again.'

The tension had all fizzled out and Andrejs recognised the omens; the tremble in your arms, a weakness climbing through your legs as the past and present merged. Screwing the cup on the flask he jerked his head in approving nods.

'Sergei Gorshov is too smart for Juris to handle, pretends he is one of us, believes we accept him. He could talk blossom out on the trees in the middle of winter. It's because of people like him my first wife and sons gone, phantoms.' He held up his hands in pain, in acknowledgement.

'Juris was a good man, a true Latvian and he died because he believed in freedom.'

'You want Andrejs' trust too? Go, I've nothing left to give. Don't come again, I have nothing more to say. You stay away.'

'I promise.' As he turned to leave, Nick saw Andrejs' eyes flinch and thought you understand, you know too, we all have to visit the dead once in a while before we can get on with living.

Eighteen

Downstream from Greenwich between abandoned wharves, a thriving car dismantler's yard jutted out into the Thames. From across a potholed road Nick weary from a night without sleep, watched the skeleton of a Ford clamped in the powerful hydraulic grabs of a crane lift from a stack of gutted cars then swing towards a crusher. Ringed by a high razor wire topped fence, steel sheets were welded to the yard's gates. Someone had dribbled CHEAP PARTS AND CAR SALVAGE across the rusting steel in yellow paint. In a neater hand, an additional edict: ALL CALLERS MUST REPORT TO THE GENERAL OFFICE.

The general office was a shell of naked concrete blocks crowned by a flat roof. It stood in an outer compound flanked on either side by shipping containers, its windows curtained with security grills. Grey daubs of primer ran in rashes down their dented and scratched doors and panels, each container labelled according to its salvaged contents, beginning with GEAR BOXES. A full-length counter too high for anyone to lean on was unattended, a doorbell screwed off-centre to its battered surface. Nick pressed it once and a klaxon peeled out across the yard louder than a ship's siren, bringing a woman in red overalls, the tight fit accentuating her figure, her raven hair perfectly curled, rolling in luxurious waves to her petite shoulders. She looked Nick over from behind her counter, surrounded by laminated parts catalogues, car manuals, a computer, and cash register. All of them liberally consulted, all of them grubby. A scenic calendar of Britain hung from a loop of wire; November was devoted to a pretty view of a harbour at night.

'Hello, Ingrid.'

'You heard then?' Her voice see-sawed in estuary Essex. 'Couldn't swim, so he wouldn't go playing by the river, would he?' she continued as though she'd been programmed.

'I really am sorry.' said Nick.

'You and me.' She sucked the tip of a biro, kicked up a smile that was anything but sweet and drifted to a desk telephone. 'Charlie... the automatic gearbox for the Merc... Yeah... I know... Make sure it's on the pallet for the courier,' she said, her sharp voice offering no compromise, her biro poised over the keypad. 'I'm in a conference... got company... Well tell Gary to get it sorted pronto,' she said appraising Nick as if assessing his value. 'In *my* office... Do not disturb.'

Jabbing the keypad to end the call as though it required disciplining, she stared hard at Nick, her hazel eyes intense. 'Hearts of gold...But they'll walk all over you if give 'em a chance,' she rattled on, holding up the handset as evidence.

'If it's any consolation, I don't think it was an accident,' Nick said.

'Not going to bring him back, is it?' she hissed, and pitched the biro on the counter. 'This way,' she added, composed, reasonable, gesturing with her head to a door designated PRIVATE and STAFF ONLY.

'Andrejs spoken to you?' he asked, going for the door.

'Andrejs is a bum, sister's a head case,' she yelled as Nick followed her out to an inner compound, a wall of noise from the crushing plant closing in around them.

Striding ahead there was a fluid grace to Ingrid's movement as she wove a course down narrow clinker tracks between vehicles stacked in columns, a heavy veil of stale oil in the air, picking her way into a section of the yard where commercial vehicles were stripped and gutted. 'Motors have always been a passion,' she declared, halting at a stack of recent arrivals that hadn't been drained of fuel, oil and other noxious substances. 'Suppose it's in the family, with dad and my brothers time-served mechanics.'

'Must be,' Nick agreed, watching Ingrid inspect an assorted collection of tippers, JCBs, trucks, vans and other wrecks with their window glass intact. The evidence would be there in Ingrid's file, a registry appendix cross-referenced to Juris, the details faithfully corroborated. Her life reduced to cold hard specifics, including her employment history; some of it legitimate, some of it borderline, and some downright risqué, including her time as a model.

'With a bit of luck, I should clear a couple of grand on each of 'em,' she speculated.

Proof, Nick supposed, how Juris' faith in her hadn't been misplaced.

Up ahead, tucked carefully beside a road sweeper and a Hapag Lloyd container that no one had bothered to label, a Portakabin isolated on an island of granite hardcore. Attached to one corner of the office, a small mast carrying a power line. Wrapped around it, a tattered kite mauled by the wind flapped with the urgency of a semaphore flag. A hard breeze dipped and swirled off the river, snatching at Ingrid's voice as she unlocked the door.

'... but as his resettlement officer, you wouldn't know...'

'Wouldn't know what?' he asked, having missed part of Ingrid's statement as he followed her inside.

'The shit he had to put up with off Andrejs,' she repeated, kicking the door closed, the oil smeared tread on her boot leaving a vivid glistening print.

Sliding into an office chair, its blue upholstery threadbare revealing the foam filling like yellowing bone, she used both hands to compose her curls, and fully restored, Ingrid resumed her candid evaluation of Andrejs.

'He's never been the same since Juris had his win. Envy, pure jealousy,' she said, lighting a cigarette. 'Have a seat.'

Or pride, thought Nick, Andrejs is big on pride he remembered, pulling up a wooden chair.

Around the walls a compilation of blue racking jammed with a range of salvaged parts – headlights, interior trim, pumps, motors, dashboard instrument clusters. To the right, an electric wall clock silently beat the time, counting another hour Ingrid would have to survive without Juris.

'Wait 'til he finds out I've got the lot, he'll be round with *the* sister,' she predicted, head back, coolly streaming the smoke towards the ceiling. 'They'll try to fight it, but they've no chance. It's all legal, done through a proper law firm. "Ingrid is my princess, best woman for me," Juris says to the solicitor. "I want to do right thing, make sure she is looked after like she look after me." Told him not be soft, but I'd never seen him so damn sure of himself. Couldn't shut him up. "No, it is true, Ingrid is best ever thing that happen to me. She is going to be my wife." And I was going to be...' Angrily stubbing out the cigarette in an ashtray, complete with a replica tyre around its rim, she braced the front edge of her desk with both hands, her small knuckles whitening. 'Not going to happen now, is it,' she declared, her eyes challenging Nick.

'No,' agreed Nick.

'But you're not here to pass the tissues, or hold my hand, are you darlin'? Who knows, I might be lucky in love again. Still got my looks.'

And she had. Despite her resilient, tough outer core, there was another side to Ingrid, and there always had been, recalled Nick. Attractive even without the make-up she'd worn at most of their meetings when she'd accompanied Juris, there was an inner appeal that manifested itself in her eyes; bright and alive, intense with desire.

'Andrejs mentioned that Juris had a meeting just before he died. A business or investment opportunity?' Nick said, teasing out his opening.

'Wasn't *that* a waste of time,' she disclosed with a good deal of feeling. 'But Juris was Juris. When he was in one of his moods, he could be a proper little bastard. Right up to us turning up for this shitty meeting, he kept on and on how this deal could turn into a nice little earner. Annoyed the fuck out of me, he did. We had to dress smart, we had to look professional. I tell you, he was a real pain in the rear.'

'Why all the effort? What was so special about this deal?'

Rolling her slim lighter over and over in the palm of her hand, Ingrid took a considerable time before answering. From behind her desk – a big old sturdy wooden thing laden with parts catalogues, a couple of spanners, a nest of plastic in trays, each one overflowing – she displayed a sense of cool determination. She had an inner confidence, a resilience that matched her considerable intelligence.

'This investment was going to be a real winner for a change,' she disclosed, letting the lighter slip from her palm onto the desk. 'You remember how Juris liked a flutter on the horses, even considered setting himself up as an owner, but I talked him out of it.'

Admitting he knew Juris' partiality for gambling, Nick appeared quite content to wait, sitting out each stage of Ingrid's unfolding story as the office gently quivered each time a condemned vehicle noisily entered the crusher.

'This fella we met, Sergei something or other. Big brother Andrejs tried to scare Juris off like he always does. I know his game, it's just so there'd be more money in the pot for himself when he inherited. Got that wrong, didn't he?'

'Seems so,' said Nick, but Andrejs might also have saved his brother's life if Juris had only listened. 'What was he like?'

'He was a creep, undressed me with his eyes the second we walked in.'

'The meeting wasn't at Juris' house?'

Her lips pursed as if she was about to make a life changing decision, Ingrid shook her head, her curls swishing against her shoulders.

'Listening to Juris I thought this fella was some sort of international entrepreneur. Yeah, right. It's Juris with his head in the clouds as usual, talking everything up. Way he went on and on, you'd think this bloke owned Harrods. All cobblers. Knew, knew as soon as Juris tells me where we're going. And where's this high-powered meeting being held? At a grotty three-star hotel in Victoria. Sergei's in business all right, he owns a dozen mini markets catering to his expat pals, Juris finally lets me know in the lift. Some international outfit this is turning out to be, I thought. He's a rogue, and didn't I know it. Handing round cartons of fags, told us they were imported by a friend. *Imported...* smuggled he meant, and not a penny of tax paid.' And as evidence, she held up her packet, the health warning in Cyrillic. 'You going to answer that?' she wondered, as Nick's phone rang for the third time in rapid succession. 'Someone else needed resettling?'

'Probably,' answered Nick, silencing his phone, but not before noting it was Rossan calling.

'There's resettlement and then there's resettlement, isn't there darlin'?'

'The office likes to keep me busy.'

'Bet they do.'

'You didn't think much of Sergei?'

Concentrating her gaze on Nick, she gave a dismissive frown. 'Smarmy, not blessed with looks either. Big, sweaty, kept pawing me every chance he got. A proper smooth talker, he spouted on about how he had a contact looking for a smart investor. At least he got one bit right,' she laughed, her intelligent eyes locked on Nick, daring him to contradict her. 'When Juris heard the investment would be in a club and casino, he was almost drooling. The place was in Hamburg. Small, upmarket, it just needed taking to the next level, and with the right investor, a chain of them was possible. Juris, God help me, said it sounded like a winning combination. Sergei wanted Juris to go and see the place for himself, get a feel of how it operated. Place called the Brazil, Brazilian or something.'

'But he didn't go.'

'No, he bloody didn't. He wasn't going without me, not to a bleedin' casino. I gave Juris the eye and he got the message. Danced and squirmed for a good ten minutes until he got up enough bottle to tell Sergei he'd think about it, and we left it at that. Juris sulked something rotten all the next day, but that was him, sometimes he needed saving from himself.'

'Then he disappeared.'

'Yeah, into thin air,' she sighed, smoking a second cigarette. 'Got a call on his phone. Told me it was the sister and he was popping around. Never saw him again.'

'You've told the police all this?'

'Why? I done something wrong?' she demanded on the defensive.

'They'll probably want to talk to you again,' said Nick at the door.

'And do I mention the visit from his resettlement officer?' she asked, following him to the door.

'Probably better if we don't complicate things.'

Back into the noise of the compound he looked back once, briefly, and he glimpsed Ingrid in the doorway; Ingrid a millionaire with her passion for cars, propped against the frame, arms folded, one leg crossed over the other supported by the toes of her down-turned boot. Another victim he thought, one more life ruined to preserve the secrets of the Oktober Projekt. Out of the gates, his phone once more demanding his immediate attention.

'Where the hell have you been?' Rossan wanted to know, his tone astringent.

'Clearing my name...'

Abruptly cutting Nick off, Rossan urgent, his declaration blunt: 'We've made a breakthrough ...'

So have I, thought Nick, but it's probably not what you'll want to hear.

'...Valgos' phone records...we have an address...give me your location,' he demanded, 'and for God's sake, don't move. I will send a car.'

•••

Now at a quarter to six on a bitter evening, Rossan was, in his own words, giving the dog a sight of the hare as Nick was driven across London at speed in a Range Rover, its rear windows tinted. There was a high moon brilliant and full, its silver wash running down damp buildings, their windows dappled by sleet. From the west, drifts of dark angry cloud sped along as if they had somewhere better to go, the traffic sparse and the driver took a couple of junctions in Holborn and the City at red. In Bethnal Green a team of emergency glaziers hammered up sheets of plywood at a grocer's, while the lights from other shops squinted through screens as the alarms peeled on like church bells. On Eastway they passed sodden football pitches on Hackney Marsh glistening as if quicksilver. Nick saw floodlights on tapering stems sprouting from Temple Mills rail depot, and with his window down for the air, could hear the grumbling of freight wagons as they were shunted into formation.

As Rossan called again demanding their position, the driver took a bridge far too fast and the exhaust ripped into the road. A sticky icy breeze filled the air coating everything it brushed against with a cold film. The area had no heart, and its soul was resting for the night, girding strength for another daytime attack of inner-city living. An estate office was clothed in mesh grilles as if preparing for a siege. Whilst next door, a grocery store had windows of plywood sheets fly-posted with offers of self-help, pub gigs, the latest albums; everything but the promise of work. Drake Road ran straight and long, a black scar barely lit, its high blocks and maisonettes butted together in architectural whimsy. The concrete towers were stacked like rotting hulks at anchor. Maybe Lubov's treasure is cursed like pirate gold, Nick thought as the driver attempted to find somewhere to park amongst a crowd of police and Service vehicles. 'This is you, sir,' he said, abandoning Nick at the mouth of a cul-de-sac. 'Mr. Mortland is already on scene, sir,' he added. Suitably primed, Nick strode off at a healthy pace.

Half a dozen radios echoed into the night; ghostly voices lost in the shadows as Nick approached. Held at an outer cordon, there seemed an inordinately long delay before Nick received clearance to proceed towards a neat semi-detached property on Brunmear Road, Leyton. The door, a plain white composite affair, lay in pieces in the tidy ornate front garden. Waiting imperiously on the step, Mortland framed in the hallway light stood ready to receive Nick, to formally endorse his invitation as a guest.

'The man himself, the all action hero,' Mortland said by way of a greeting, his pulpit voice carried off into the evening on a bitter wind. 'There have been developments,' he added, blocking Nick's access.

'Sergei Gorshov one of them?'

'Maybe he is. But this does not exclude you from further investigation,' Mortland unambiguously decided, his unyielding clever face braced for dissent. 'We have traced several calls made on Valgos' phone to this address,' he revealed, his breath pluming away in the cold air.

'And you discreetly paid a visit,' Nick caustically observed.

'Better come in, we can't have a scene on the step, can we?'

'No,' agreed Nick reasonably.

There were traces of blood behind the door and a pile of broken glass. In amongst it all, a child's pushchair with a crushed rattle that Mortland shunted aside with his foot as he gave one of his rummaging team fresh instructions before returning his attention to Nick.

'I have operational control, that understood?'

'If it makes you feel better. Casualties?' Nick wondered stepping over the blood.

'One of the entry team. Received a nasty cut,' Mortland grudgingly disclosed, drawing Nick after him down the hall. 'He's had a plaster on it, he'll live.'

Banging and shouts came from every part of the house. Carpet lay in heaps, and in the front room Nick saw the same destruction; at its centre a woman crying silently as she rocked her baby.

'The wife,' Mortland said as if pointing out an exhibit. Gripping Nick's arm Mortland attempted to steer him along, but Nick could only stare at a girl about four as she stroked her mother's hair, guarded by one of Mortland's Regulators. Around their feet a pile of birthday presents prematurely ripped from their paper.

The small girl tried to reach a doll in a box, but the Regulator held her back. Breaking from Mortland, Nick went over, took the doll and pressed it into the child's hands.

'Let her keep it,' he said, knowing he had broken a dozen different protocols.

'How touching,' said Mortland, only to be silenced by Nick's glare.

'You didn't find Gorshov, did you?'

Pained to admit it, Mortland scowled at Nick. 'Flown the nest, in the wind, half-way back to Russia. We are checking.'

'He knew you were coming,' Nick said flatly, without a note of triumph.

'Called you up, disclosed his plans, did he?' Mortland mocked, continuing the tour ushering Nick into a rear sitting room.

'Must have missed his call.'

In here the R5 rummagers had been at work too, clear evidence sacks lay tagged waiting for removal, even the bookcases had been cannibalised noted Nick. And now they were dismantling anything that offered the opportunity for concealment. Give them until morning he thought, pushing by two of them, and the house will be uninhabitable. Out in the hall, Nick heard Martin Bailrigg's languorous voice rise and fall as he issued instruction on his way into the kitchen with a number of others trailing in his footsteps. Putting Mortland behind him, Nick walked straight in without bothering to knock. Gathered loyally around Bailrigg were his two acolytes, Jane and Hawick.

'Bit late to take an interest,' Nick said loudly to the back of Bailrigg's head. Three faces turned to him. 'Well, isn't it?' he added, knocking Mortland's hand from his shoulder. Unable to keep his passion and indignation down, Nick slammed his fist against the door. 'Well?'

'Need I remind you that you have no authority here,' Hawick decreed. 'Need I also remind you that you are guilty of assaulting a senior officer, namely myself.' And misreading Nick's mood entirely, spurred by a desire to humiliate, he launched a stinging rebuke. 'Perhaps if you had devoted so much energy to your marriage, your wife would not have sought affection elsewhere,' he ventured with undisguised relish; an unremitting loathing gathered in his eyes, raising a fresh rush of colour to his cheeks.

Whipping forward, Nick had Hawick by his jacket collar, ramming him backwards into a freezer, spilling fridge magnets across the linoleum floor. Pinning him there, Nick pressed forward. 'You have no idea what I'm capable of.'

'Nick...Nick....' Prising Nick's hands loose, Jane walked him away as Hawick worked his head one way then another as he adjusted his collar.

A long silence drew round the kitchen pressing and sharp, with no one inclined to step into its space. Everyone had turned to Bailrigg, expectantly awaiting his response. A tall thin figure, his hair combed back but tugged out of place by the wind, Bailrigg wore a waxed Barbour jacket, his hands jammed into the pockets and he gave the impression of a head gamekeeper about to brief his beaters. In the other rooms, the banging too had ceased, and the only sound came from a kitchen clock beating steadily on, one thunderous tick after another.

'If you'll excuse me gentlemen... and Jane,' Bailrigg said graciously, and gripping Nick's arm walked him briskly out of the kitchen. 'Upstairs,' he insisted. Hawick on their heels came to an abrupt halt as Bailrigg swung round on him. 'You remain down here and keep out of the damn way,' he snapped, closing the door softly.

There were three bedrooms, and the first they came to belonged to the children. The rummagers must have turned the heating off thought Nick, the room cold, the trapped odour of clothes airing, though Nick never glimpsed any. The cot lay dismantled in a corner its mattress separated from the vinyl cover. Over the floor the contents of cupboards were jumbled in unequal piles of toys and clothes and Bailrigg assigned himself the base of a child's divan, under his feet the torn sections of an animal freeze and a clown night light pulled apart.

'Don't you ever do that again,' he said with conviction. 'Hear me Torr? I don't give a damn if you deserve a thousand and one explanations. You do not attack a senior officer. Not for a second time, and not within sight of me.'

Nick heard him out, sliding back a thumb catch he put all his effort into forcing up a sash window, the night air hitting him in a freezing rush, bringing with it the sound of traffic far away.

'Do I get to finish this now?'

Picking up a glass bubble, Bailrigg shook it hard bringing a flurry of artificial snow to the tiny figures outside a plastic stable.

'I'm not offering any apologies, Torr, because I have nothing to apologise for. I was reacting to the facts, and they were not in your favour. Now is a different matter, you have given us a sight of Moscow's dynamic presence,' he said, shaking the snow scene once more, this time quite viciously. 'And, as embarrassing as it is, Gorshov playing us for fools. Not that he didn't enjoy significant help from us.'

'In what way?'

'You'll enjoy this ...' He rolled back his cuff, glanced at his watch. 'Approximately three hours ago there was, so I'm told, a communication malfunction.'

'How did we help?'

'Complete balls-up on timing. Teddy, Mortland and the police may have shown their hand too early.'

'Nothing major, then.'

'We're hardly likely to get an accurate bearing on what Gorshov's actual role was, its scope, his operational status, anytime soon.'

'What *do* I get?'

'You get an understanding, an agreement, call it damn well what you like. You employ your CO8 resources wisely, and report to no other damn soul but me from now on. You are quite competent to work out the most appropriate means of achieving that. What you've got so far may have whet my appetite, but if you expect me to turn this Service inside out to prove Lubov was betrayed by one of us or someone close to us, I need a damn sight more before I officially commit. I'm not in the habit of offering a panacea for the comfort they bring either,' he said, disheartened by the snow scene. 'If it's official sanction you want, then you've got it, but you'd better start to listen up, because that's all I'm giving and it's bitter pill and it probably won't make the slightest difference to your usual mode of operating.'

In the ochre glow seeping in from a street lamp, Bailrigg had become a vague shadow; his face robbed of its clarity, its definition, all that remained was a featureless expression, a realisation that he had taken a decision that could destroy his career.

'If Moscow have sacrificed the Gorshovs, they are protecting something far more valuable. Why else would they commit to such a vigorous response?' said Nick, watching as more sacks went into the back of a van.

'Then bring proof,' Bailrigg said rising with an effort to his feet. 'You don't deliver, and the sharks are going to tear you apart. And you'll have Teddy on their tails nibbling vindictively away. You remember that, hear me? I said remember that?'

'I will,' Nick assured him, and they stared at each other for no more than a couple of seconds.

'You keep your investigation low-key. I do not want to see you or hear you on my side of the river.'

'There'll be no compromises.'

'I know,' said Bailrigg with a hearty sigh. 'This isn't your personal El Dorado or Golden Fleece, you've got to share.' Bailrigg frowned and his whole sad face appeared ready to collapse. Below them the girl continued to whimper.

'Oh, I will.'

'You're back on semi-official status now, Torr, bear that well. You've a brief, a point of contact, which if absolutely necessary is Rossan, and Rossan alone.'

'You think we're dealing with an agent of influence, don't you?'

'I don't have to answer that, Torr,' said Bailrigg.

'Politics again.'

'Damn right it's politics, and that is my province, which doesn't concern you. And that's why you're only going to share with me. Got that?'

'I'll bear that in mind.'

'No. You'll bloody obey it. I don't enjoy my officers talking to outsiders, even if they're old friends and distinguished company. You prove anything and it has to be writ in triplicate. You make a case that is thrown out, and both of us take a long time to walk to the pavilion. No previous scores, no previous success to be included. Fail and we're out. For good,' said Bailrigg weakly, utterly consumed by the night's events.

Nick pulled down the window and the whole frame rattled as he brought it home. They each remained in their different quarter of the room, the heavy presence of Moscow separating them.

'As long as I know the rules,' said Nick and very quietly walked out.

Downstairs the rummagers were preparing to start on the floorboards, the beams of their head torches slicing through the darkness and dust. A supervisor in overalls tacked up a necklace of bulbs, while a companion started a portable generator in the back garden. They were determined to pick the house clean thought Nick, a thorough and professional display to reclaim some pride. By morning there would only be a carcass left. In the front room the woman and children were gone, Jane and Mortland locked in a serious conference under temporary lamps. Seeing Nick at the door, Jane touched Mortland's arm and came over.

'You've been avoiding me,' she said.

'Have I?'

'I thought I was a good friend? Isn't that what we agreed in Devon?'

'We are,' Nick assured her. 'Any leads?'

Stepping out onto the front step, pulling Nick along, Jane stared at him, trying to work out his reticence, this sudden retreat into a defensive shell. 'Brigitta and Sergei, an average couple on nodding terms with the neighbours, kept themselves to themselves. Between looking after the kids, she ran a stall at one of the antique markets held in St. James' Piccadilly.'

'What's her background?'

'Russian Lat like her husband,' Jane disclosed with a heave of her shoulders. 'She's pretty scared, refusing to admit she's involved, but we've already uncovered a small haul of evidence that proves otherwise. Cellphones, could be used for burst transmission, Canadian, US and Irish passports, all blanks. Over eighty thousand in euros, the equivalent in sterling and dollars. If she's going to give up any assets, she hasn't shown any interest yet. She's content to sit it out,' Jane continued, fixing Nick with a grievous stare.

But Sergei, on the other hand, had reacted quite differently when presented with the opportunity to save himself, Nick reasoned, displaying very nimble footwork to ensure he evaded the net.

'And we screwed-up with the entry?' he demanded, his tone scathing.

'Utter fuck-up,' said Blackmore striding up the path, his overcoat unbuttoned, flapping magnificently at his sides; the messenger who has missed the battle. 'Better tell him,' he suggested to Jane.

'The wife spotted a couple of the entry teams' vans when she brought the eldest girl home from school. They should have been a couple of streets away holding off, but miscommunication...'

'She gave him the stay away routine and he didn't come home, clever boy,' Roly added. 'Not that we missed much. My bet? He's a minnow, nothing higher than an enabler offering B&B to the serious players passing through.'

'And we accept her version?' Nick asked, already knowing the answer. 'We don't question if she might have been warned in advance?' he demanded, his patience utterly sapped.

Neither Jane nor Blackmore felt inclined to confirm and Nick sadly shook his head, setting off down the path.

'You'll have your pound of flesh,' promised Blackmore as he reached the gate.

'I'll have more than that,' Nick retorted. 'Just don't get in my way.'

When Blackmore reviewed this oblique statement of Nick's much later, he only then appreciated that Nick's words were uttered more as a warning, rather than a general observation.

Completely drained of energy Nick tramped miserably back to the Range Rover, its driver passing his time with a crossword. Drizzle floated in front of Nick and the rattle of the generator in the garden mocked his going. Tomorrow there would be another victim, he decided, but for tonight he would settle quite happily for a couple of hours of undisturbed sleep.

Nineteen

Nick arrived at the cemetery a good half-hour after everyone else. Paying off the taxi at the gates, he bought a handful of carnations from a wooden shack, its striped awning bleached pale by the different seasons. He stole through the tall gates, a November mist heavier than sea fog smothering the high slopes too steep for graves. His nerves no longer relaxed, they were somebody else's, on loan and out of tune with his body. He was in a constant state of readiness, alert and tense, everything became suspect; cars and vans were a threat, Moscow's shadow inside every one of them.

Narrow paths surrounded him, stretching out between the crematorium and a railway cutting going nowhere except the unknown. A crumpled figure hobbled past on a path of gravel and rotting leaves, disappearing quickly as if he'd never existed. Nick halted and tried to remember his way amongst forlorn carved angels standing as glum as sentries, their faces mauled by age and sepulchral ruins hacked at by vandals. Twice he stumbled in the gloom over wiry roots erupting on the path.

Somewhere a dog was barking and a harsh voice, girl's or woman's, called it to heel. Disturbed by the noise, rooks cried in flight, coming down to hunch sullenly in the high branches. A council estate peered at him from his right, a front line of lace curtains and satellite dishes separated by a concrete wall with holes beaten in it. Then he recalled how the path divided; to the left broad and uphill all the way to the crematorium, the other, the one he was on, ran twisting and dipping towards the railway cutting. For this last part Nick took to the grass walking between graves, and sometimes over them, glancing at the chiselled names on the headstones. On one plot a bright marble slab declared eternal hope with a confident assertion: 'Resting Where No Shadow Falls.' Only Moscow's Nick thought, gaining his bearings.

Ahead a hearse and its dark cousins pulled up beside a low island of clay, a clot of mourners gathered around. Family and friends consoling Angie's parents, her mother taking centre stage; respects paid, promises made to be broken. Nick knew there was no point approaching; Angie's mother would only make a scene, accuse him of even being late for her daughter's funeral, another example if one were needed, of his despicable, errant behaviour. Hanging back until they'd all driven off, Nick walked slowly to the grave where Angie was joining their son. He cast his carnations on a pile of wreaths with their smudged accolades and depressing clichés the dead always receive, colour from the flowers proud against a bed of freshly turned clay. He tilted a couple of damp cards and they left a smear of white paste on his fingers, biodegradable just like Angie. One wreath outdoing the rest, an impressive display forming a huge cross of white and yellow chrysanthemums, its card written in Latin, which Nick roughly translated as 'No life is wasted when lost securing the future'. There wasn't a name to go with the noble declaration, and Nick tore off the card, folded it into his pocket.

The mist had begun to thin, wisps of smoky air hovering a foot above the earth, a surreal impression of a curtain partly raised. Behind him he heard the reality of the traffic sluggishly pushing up the main road. Heard too the real fall of feet on gravel, pausing, starting up again. Magwitch come to demand a file? Or Lubov risen like Banquo for revenge?

'You'll make them pay,' said Rossan, his thin shoulders hunched towards the grave.

'Will I?'

'Isn't that the plan?'

Staring down at Angie's final home, Nick wondered if Lubov's treasure was worth pursuing? Its price too high?

'Come on, let's walk.'

So they set off in a slow procession, Nick a pace ahead walking towards the cutting where the mist hung in tatters, the ground steaming as a weak sun stole into the gloom. Once more he had a vague uncertainty about him; introspective, a man with the answer but no question. A train sped past leaving the hum of electric current in the air.

'Any sightings of Gorshov?' Nick asked.

'If there has been, we haven't been informed. Of course, Teddy and

Mortland could spring him on us, earn themselves a piece of redemption for the entry fiasco. But I rather doubt it,' said Rossan, his warm breath streaming after them in the cold air. 'There's no trace of him leaving the country.' Rossan looked Nick square in the eye, started to speak then hesitated.

'What is it?'

Moistening his lips, brushing his nose with his thumb, Rossan delved into his pocket removing a small clear evidence bag. 'The police returned it,' he said, having to clear his throat, handing the bag across.

Nick felt a rush of blood heat his cheeks, turn his hand cold as he stared at the bag. Forcing his fingers to move he opened the bag, shaking out a Hirsh ring; inside its band a simple engraving bearing Angie and Nick's names with the date of their marriage.

'Thanks,' he said, closing his hand gripping the ring tight.

A footbridge with smashed lights suddenly reared up in front of them. Nick took the rungs two at a time stopping three from the top and turning. 'Moscow have used Angie to tie us in knots,' he suggested, pocketing the ring.

With Nick leading the way they crossed the bridge. On their right a crescent of shops curving away, their lights streaking the mist with golden strands as smudged outlines passed their windows. A hairdresser's offered cheap rates for pensioners, but none had been tempted as three stylists lounged by the door drinking coffee.

'We do have a means of undoing the knot,' said Rossan.

'Enough for me to work on?'

'They've been sweating Brigitta, or whatever her damn name is. She fed us the usual first round chaff, but it appears she is warming to the prospect of sharing in return for a very swift flight home for herself and the children. Downing Street and the FO are extremely keen to buy into it, they have her down for discreet repatriation. Minimum embarrassment, minimum retaliation,' said Rossan. 'A deal of sorts has been struck with Security by Teddy. We have first strike, and they scoop up the rest. If indeed there are any targets of primary interest.'

'But there's going to be nothing of real value to strike, or scoop up, is there?'

'Not from what the thumbscrews have so far reported,' Rossan disclosed with a sigh.

'She'll never give us anything of merit, it's not in the GRU DNA,' Nick suggested, 'she probably isn't even aware of the Oktober Projekt.'

'I'm afraid you'll have to follow this up on your own, remember C's orders. You're back, but you're out. You're official, but you're not. You are his weapon of choice, but you're deniable. You report to him, but you report to me.'

'He's covering all the angles, and that includes listening to Hawick urging caution.'

'I don't think some people appreciate you not being top of the wanted tree,' Rossan confessed as they stopped outside a betting shop. 'Hawick, Jane and Roly are continually locked in conference, the atmosphere utterly toxic.'

'They're providing mutual protection,' suggested Nick, 'they have no intention of being brought down in the crossfire.'

'With regard to the other business, she's taken sick leave. And you most certainly didn't get that from me,' he said, passing Nick a folded square of paper. 'Take care,' advised Rossan, patting Nick's shoulder before walking off.

'Oh, I will,' said Nick, lost in thought, glancing at the address written in Rossan's precise hand. Lighting a cigarette, he stood there, watching the footbridge trying to determine if he'd actually seen a figure loitering on the other side or was it just the mist playing tricks.

He wrapped his fingers around the folded paper in his pocket; another trail to Moscow waiting to be uncovered he decided, trooping off to the station. I'll rest soon he promised himself, turning abruptly to see the figure do exactly the same; no attempt to disguise his role as an appointed surveillance officer – or in CO8 jargon, a footpad. Reporting to Mortland? Hawick? To C? Or Moscow's asset? Nick wondered, pressing on, his steps quickening.

On the train back to London Nick gazed distractedly from the window counting off the minutes, thinking of Lubov and all those who had died because of his secret. Of how death stalked him continually, how it always managed to be there at his side; as though he were tied inexorably to it, haunted, threatened, never allowed peace. Leaving Victoria station, Nick huddled up his body and walked carelessly into a mean day. But for the moment, Nick concentrated on getting to Aldwych by bus from Millbank and from there on by foot; variations to a theme as he collected a very tidy family saloon from the car park on Upper St. Martins Lane, a Peugeot unconnected to the Firm, the key palmed to Nick by Danny in a classic brush pass.

Thin arms of late afternoon river mist started to stretch out over the city, a wet haze forming on the windscreen. For an hour he drove without a destination in mind, his route fluid as he adopted a surveillance detection routine. Which eventually paid off when he noted the same black Vectra behind him on far too many occasions to be a coincidence; another unashamed reminder he was not trusted. On every precious mile the Vectra doggedly made itself known; sticking so close Nick thought he was towing an old friend. Up to now his life seemed to be moving in tandem with phases of the earth – light and dark, sun and stars, people living, people dead. Driving into Greenwich he parked close to the river. Behind him the masts and spars of the Cutty Sark visible as spectral traces in the thickening mist, as if she was sitting out the weather before getting underway. As he walked away from the Peugeot, he heard the Vectra slow, the click of a car door behind him; so, you fancy a run for your money, do you? Nick set his eyes firmly ahead as the river mist thickened, dousing his face.

Glancing back every few yards, Nick moved deeper onto the peninsula, a footpad faithfully trailing behind, his very own shadow of treachery. Crossing towards Maynard's Wharf, he slowed to throw another glance behind. There was at least one on foot with the Vectra maintaining its distance Nick reasoned, travelling parallel with the river, the streets subdued and silent, the still air chilled. He turned without warning into a doorway of a rag merchants, its filthy windows filled by multicoloured piles of old clothes like prehistoric strata. When the footpad drew level, Nick came out faster than he went in. He struck three times. The last combination of his knee and hand dropped the footpad in a groaning pile.

Impassively watching from the Vectra, the driver kicked the accelerator in applause. Game on, thought Nick, walking off, the car clinging to his heels as he drifted through hanging bands of mist; his journey determined, his purpose equally resolute. All the while, another footpad loped dutifully along behind him. Footsteps that we can never call our own, Nick repeated in a mindless canto, the headlights melting the sticky mist as he pushed on, turning in a wide arc. For this side of the river still held him, here he had business to complete. Maybe the footpads weren't interested in his destination; maybe their orders were to prevent him from getting there?

considered Nick lengthening his stride, upping his pace.

The mist thicker now creeping up walls spreading itself out, reducing everything before him to dim and shapeless outlines. So that when he came to The Speedwell Inn, the mist lay dense in its mock Tudor galleries giving the impression of the stern of a galleon run aground. And Nick, a doughty pilgrim of a different age, snubbed the marmalade light and laughter of the tourist bar and headed instead into the back room and a much smaller snug where, thankfully, no attempt at a theme had been made. With a whisky in his hand Nick settled at a table by the window. There was a full five-minute lull before the footpad crept into the bar, uncomfortable, edging through the solemn drinkers to buy himself a half, positioning himself by a fruit machine as though absorbed by the whirling skein of coloured lights.

His glass empty, Nick made his way to the lavatories down a flight of steps, noting the emergency exit set back to his right. Instead of a stall, he chose a cubicle and waited. The footpad with only himself to blame, followed. Nick heard the outer door close, the footpad's shoes on the tiles, counting each one as each cubicle door was tried in turn. Standing on the toilet bowl, his hands on the greasy top edge of the unlocked door, Nick waited for the pressure. Swinging the door inwards at the same time as the footpad pushed, and with the full weight of his knee, he caught the footpad just under the jaw.

Nick propelled forward by his own momentum, hit him twice more in rapid succession. 'Bloody drunks,' said Nick stepping over the footpad's floored body, as someone came in and headed for the stalls. He heard a quip on tourists before the toilet door sprang shut, but by then he was through the emergency exit. Out into the yard he climbed up a stack of beer kegs, balanced on the rib of wall before dropping into the street. Cutting back away from the river then changing direction again, his back clean, Nick made his way to Marshside Dock.

• • •

He glimpsed a shadow dart away from a window in the main saloon the moment he drew level with the houseboat; a converted Dutch barge, the *Boudica*, tethered listlessly to a pontoon. He knocked on the wheelhouse door but received no answer. He tried the handle, but it was locked. Then she appeared in the wheelhouse, Ruth Parfrey reluctant to answer or grant him entry, one arm folded across her chest, the other raised vertically, the fist bunched and held in front of her lips.

'A couple of minutes, Ruth, that's all I want,' Nick explained, his voice lifted to carry through the door. Still she didn't respond, and he read the panic in her eyes, and a hint of alarm too. 'A quick chat and I'm gone,' he pledged, his persistence finally persuading her to open the door.

'You'd better come in,' she said belligerently, though the fight had already gone out of her.

From the wheelhouse, modified into a sun deck with wicker armchairs, potted palms and cane furniture grouped in a circle, she led Nick down to the main saloon. Two long sofas hugged the hull's walls, a far bulkhead held bookcases, and in a corner a wood burning stove filled the air with its thick warmth. As far as Nick remembered Parfrey lived alone, but down here there was a sense of things being shared, of two people, not one.

'What is it?' she asked, dumping herself onto a sofa folding up newspapers, putting a plate filled with crumbs by her feet. 'I'm not feeling particularly well, that's why I've taken a couple of days leave, must be coming down with something.'

'It won't take long,' Nick assured her. 'RUS/OPS is usually sitting on top of everything pretty tight, I just need some background on the Gorshovs? Were they known to us?'

Laughing as though Nick had told a filthy joke, she shook her head.

'You know I can't discuss that for a number of reasons,' she said, grabbing for a box of tissues.

'What about Lubov?'

'What about him?'

'I'm not asking for you for a complete damage assessment, just your thoughts on his credibility. He must have been targeted for a reason. What was Jo's concern about the operation?'

'That's simply another area that I can't possibly comment on,' she warned him, dabbing her nose. 'Jo's death has been difficult to deal with.'

'It must be, but I'm sure we'll get the facts eventually.'

'Look, I'm sorry about your loss... about your wife, about what happened to you in Moscow, but there's nothing that I can do to make a difference.'

'It's too late to make a difference, at least for Jo... and Angie. Why *did* Jo come to see you?'

'You'll have to leave.'

'Jo spoke with her section head, then she came to you. Then she made an appointment with R5. Something must have been troubling her?' Nick reminded her.

Scratching her neck Parfrey was suddenly on her feet; finding more things to tidy, making a regular run between the galley and saloon as she collected cups and glasses. 'Without a letter of authority, I can't help you,' she said, the tidying exhausted; this her last word her fixed stare declared, after she'd continually rebutted Nick's questions during her chores.

'Why was the risk assessment status downgraded?'

'Please go or I'll call Mortland,' she yelled, close to tears.

'Okay, that's fine,' said Nick, turning to leave, Parfrey quick to walk him out.

'Nice perfume,' he said over his shoulder.

'I'm not wearing any,' she told him, strangely flustered.

But someone had, and the fragrance for Nick, was worryingly familiar.

Out on the deck Nick nodded. 'Jane hasn't called to see you by any chance?' he asked and Parfrey tensed, standing in the doorway she simply shook her head, refusing to move until she was sure Nick was on his way before slamming the wheelhouse door with feeling.

• • •

The next morning, Nick suitably wired for sound wove in and out of the stalls in St. James's churchyard, Piccadilly. A market set up three times a week, this morning's pitches were selling handcrafted jewellery, paintings, organic soap, perfumes and what a couple of traders classed 'Modern Antiques'. At one of them, browsing through Russian dolls and Soviet military memorabilia in the form of caps, badges and flags, Mathew Buscott appeared unimpressed at the authenticity or quality. But you would, wouldn't you decided Nick, giving his team gathered in loose formation the nod to move in; you're an aficionado aren't you Mathew, an avid collector who runs a website devoted to artefacts connected to the old Soviet military machine. But that's in your free time, Mathew, when you're not chauffeuring executives in your very nice Mercedes.

Behind the stall, Hannah, a CO8 operative cupped her hands together and blew into them to ward off the chill.

'Where's Brigitta? She asked me to call,' Buscott challenged Hannah, his nasally voice acerbic, overbearing.

'I'm afraid Brigitta is unavailable today.' Nick announced tucking himself in by Buscott.

Holding up a Soviet issue army officer's cap, Buscott stared at Nick then noted Danny behind him. Turning the cap round as though searching for flaws, he said, 'Cops?' He threw the cap back onto a pile. 'If you're not, you've no right to detain me,' he added.

'Well, we're not here for the antiques,' Nick said, gesturing towards other members of his team, 'And neither are they.'

Taking Buscott by the arm Nick manoeuvred him away from the stall. With Danny on Buscott's right and Nick at his left, the remainder of the team converged in a blocking formation, and in this coordinated pattern, they walked him to an unmarked grey minibus parked in the alley off Jermyn Street, its rear compartment obscured by privacy tints. There to receive them, two more of Nick's operators, whom with very little effort, loaded Buscott into the passenger compartment. Entering the minibus Buscott shook his head and Nick wondered if this was an act of contempt or acceptance of his fate? With the door promptly glided closed, the pavement covered by CO8 operators, Nick wedged Buscott between himself and Danny.

'This is illegal detention,' he objected staring at Nick.

'We're having a chat, what's illegal about that? countered Nick.

To Nick, sitting on Buscott's right, the chauffeur's face seemed considerably older than his photograph used on his company and memorabilia websites. Broad and squat, his firm face was slightly rounded, the cheeks just beginning to sag a touch, his wavy hair and beard neatly groomed, the robust black frames of his glasses added to the air of a confident self-employed professional.

'Who are you lot?'

'The people who know what you've been up to,' Danny fired back.

'This about the jobs for Sergei?' Buscott wondered, his response cautious.

'That's right, it's about Sergei. What can you tell us about him?' Nick asked, sitting back, as if he was about to undertake a long journey.

'Haven't seen him in months,' Buscott stated, staring ahead. 'I haven't a clue what this is about,' he warned, his mood souring.

'What type of service did you provide for Sergei? Cooperate and the court may take your assistance into account,' Nick suggested.

'Hang on a fucking minute...' Levering himself forward, Buscott swung a fist at Danny, and half out of his seat scrambling for the door promptly sat back down once more, both hands clutching his groin where Danny's elbow had connected. 'Jesus Christ,' he moaned, head forward rocking with the pain.

An interval of almost ten minutes followed this minor altercation, during which time Nick despatched one of his team for bottled water.

'Better?' Nick asked.

'What do you think?' Buscott whined, sipping his water.

'I think you really need to explain how you've been helping Sergei,' Nick proposed.

'What's in it for me?'

'A criminal conviction if you don't cooperate. and that's guaranteed,' Danny obliquely informed him.

'Driving, nothing major,' Buscott declared, emphasising his defence with rapid hand gestures, the bottle of water clamped between his knees.

'How did you meet?' Nick asked as a heavy hail shower drummed on the minibus' roof. 'Was it Brigitta?'

'No, it was Sergei. Collected him from Heathrow. He'd been on a business trip... Moscow, I think he said. Booked me a few times after that, seemed okay, a bit flash, bit of a bragger. but he paid, and that's all that matters at the end of the day.'

'I'm sure it does,' Nick agreed.

'Asked me if I wanted some lucrative work. Bit of driving, under the radar, cash up front and a bonus for safe delivery. Bit naughty, but what the fuck, it was only booze and smokes for regulars at his stores.'

'You agreed?' asked Nick.

'Why not?' he sniffed, head back, pinching the bridge of his nose with forefinger and thumb. 'Sinus trouble,' he said as way of explanation. In his own good time, he resumed: 'Decent runs to Hamburg to pick up the goods,' he explained, staring straight ahead through the windscreen as if he was on the road again. 'Piece of cake, the cash came in handy, bought the wife a nice spot of pampering each month.'

'And then?' Nick prompted, his tone bristling with irritation.

Suddenly reticent, Buscott took an absolute age over a drink of water. 'Changed the collection routine,' he eventually divulged, screwing the cap back on the bottle. 'Made arrangements with this bloke who had a boat, a yacht down in Suffolk. Plan was to use the yacht to bring in the goods and I'd collect them, bring them up here. Went down and met the bloke, discussed the loads he could carry. Did a run and everything was peachy, we unloaded the boat on the river at night and I was back home before breakfast. Earned more moving Sergei's goods than I do in a month of regular driving.'

'Anything else Sergei wanted moving?'

Glancing rapidly at Nick, Buscott curled his top lip and shrugged. 'Only once.'

'Which was?'

'Different,' Buscott admitted vaguely.

Through the windscreen, its lower edge and wipers covered in a ribbon of hail, Nick watched a woman marching towards them down the alley dragging a tartan shopping trolley, halting every few yards to peer into the commercial bins. Stopping in front of the minibus, she squinted through the windscreen, yelling they were perverts and demanding gin until one of the team moved her on.

'Different how?' Nick resumed.

'Four blokes, friends of Sergei's,' Buscott said, staring down at his shoes.

'Good friends? New friends? What type of friends?'

Requiring a nudge from Danny, Buscott sullenly described them. 'Workers, contractors, people he'd hired to refit some of his stores.

'And you collected them at the airport?'

'Suffolk, came across on the boat.'

'Did Sergei explain this unusual arrangement?'

Sergei might have recited the entire works of Shakespeare for all Buscott cared to reveal, but only after another sharp prompt from Danny, did he feel able to remember the details.

'He knew them from way back,' Buscott said, twisting the half-empty bottle around in his hands. 'They were blokes he trusted, didn't charge an arm and leg for a bit of rewiring, painting, that sort of thing.'

'That sort of thing...' Nick repeated ominously. 'Did you give them a hand?'

Reacting to the immediate shift in Nick's temperament, Buscott issued an ultimatum: 'What's this all about?'

'What kind of help did you give them?' Nick blunt, full force, slamming his palm into the headrest of the seat in front.

'Okay...okay...' said Buscott, one arm raised as a gesture of cooperation. 'Sergei asked me to arrange the transport, so I did. Hired a van for them.'

'Where did they stay?'

'Flat above one of Sergei's stores. Listen,' Buscott appealed, 'if they were involved in anything naughty, that has nothing to do with me.'

'Accessory after the fact,' Nick said calmly.

'Accessory to *what*?' This time it was Buscott who became agitated.

'Murder,' Danny answered.

'Possibly three,' Nick added, recalling Angie's last moments in hospital, Jo Lister suspended under a bridge and the disappearance of Juris.

'Jesus Christ...'

'I think you'll need a solicitor,' proposed Danny, sliding back the door, calling their driver over.

After the minibus drove off with Buscott under Danny's hawkish supervision, Nick walked, needed the space to release the tension that had slowly consumed him. The flat above Gorshov's store would be searched, though he didn't hold out much prospect of Mortland's rummagers finding anything meaningful. On the Embankment the cold numbing his back, Nick made a series of calls. The first to Mike Stanhill lasted a little over two minutes, and for several reasons of his own Nick had no concern as to whom might be listening. The second and third calls ran a good deal longer as Nick rang a number in Helsinki and then one in Hamburg. Heading towards Westminster Bridge he rested against the parapet, the river was falling fast leaving the lights of Westminster embedded in the mud, a siren started somewhere behind him and lasted in his ears until he'd crossed to the opposite bank.

Twenty

Nick arrived in Sussex the next afternoon just as it began to snow. Stretching away to his left the town lay folded open in front of him, a panoramic map of a classic English seaside resort; civilised order on ordnance grid squares, symmetrical living by the sea. Parked on a quiet stretch of coast road, Nick, quite close to exhaustion and unshaven, required a period of reflection to align his thoughts; his mood filthy, the sun playing hide and seek behind stiff blotches of cloud all the way to Hastings in the distance; thin shafts of sunlight lifting out the contours of retirement retreats built to one wondrous haphazard plan. He replayed Rossan's call that brought him on this strange odyssey.

'Her mother found her and rang for an ambulance, but she refused to go to hospital, demanding to speak to you, only you, and gave them our emergency number. The duty officer called me, and I promised he'd be posted to Mars if he breathed a word, assured him that she's unwell,' Rossan had explained, his manner not approaching tolerant. 'When I spoke to her over the phone, she sounded as mad as a hatter, so I sent reinforcements and a friendly doctor. And I am on my way.'

'Who's with her?'

'Redman, Lumb and Hill.'

'No one else has been informed?'

'Not a soul,' Rossan had vowed. 'Her parents are pretty shook up,' he'd added. 'Retired missionaries and if anyone discovers I've broken every protocol under the sun I'm finished.'

The bungalow was post-war built from smooth red brick, standing solid and firm with stone mullioned bay windows. It was one of those places that would never change over the years, an architectural time machine, decided Nick as he parked on a private road behind a line of Service cars. Overgrown fields flowed from the bungalow on three sides, tended until illness or age let them revert back to weeds and high grass that stretched away to a sharp peak of headland. A small market garden business left to rot with a cluster of wooden sheds, glasshouses and garages gently falling apart. One of them, a brick coal store, its door owed a coat of paint, held one end of a blue clothesline. Pegged along the line washing fluttering as neatly as pennons in the needle cold wind; clothes for a couple surviving on slim pensions, all of them tumbled of colour and designed for comfort rather than fashion. The bungalow's salt smeared windows faced straight out to sea, its smooth render showed its age, and its roof had a couple of tiles missing. The front door was rubbed raw by winter gales and faded to a pale lilac by summer sun. When Nick pressed the door-bell, he heard discordant chimes play *What a Friend We Have in Jesus*. On the step, an empty milk holder, 'None Today', arrowed with a sad little plastic arm. Moving briskly on a gravel path circling the property, Rossan clearly irritated, arriving from the back garden, his plunging strides giving him an added air of urgency.

'How is she?' asked Nick.

'Under control,' snapped Rossan. 'We can't hear a damn thing because of the television,' he added, opening the door with a key looped on a piece of string.

'Back room with Lumb,' said Danny, standing aside for Nick to enter. 'Parents are in the front with Hill.'

Nick heard the television before opening the door. Inside, he nodded a greeting to Hill, one of Rossan's diligent analysts sitting across from the couple, separated by a generation and a continent.

'I've tried my hardest sir,' Hill whispered, coming over to Rossan. 'But I can't really get through to them.'

On the television a game show host exhorted a contestant to have another go; if only we could thought Nick, glancing around, taking in the statuettes, spears, clubs and shields vying with tribal masks for a piece of space. In no apparent order they summarised the couple's lifetime as missionaries, members of some zealous tribe that must have saved souls in exchange for primitive goods. This is their horde for retirement he thought; a cluttered bungalow in an unfashionable resort with views of the sea and orderly avenues to comfort you right up to death. Now we've gone and broken the spell.

'Your daughter is suffering from stress,' Rossan said very loud, standing over the husband, hands snuggled into his pockets. 'That's why we're here.'

'A dreadful mess,' the old man said, shaking his head. 'Shirley,' he pointed to his wife. 'Angina. Lucky it didn't finish her.'

'I'll go and have a word,' suggested Nick as Rossan crouching, tried once more to explain their presence to a very frail woman.

A long-case clock marched Nick down the hall, gracefully keeping pace with his steps. In a back room facing the garden, Ruth Parfrey sat upright on a spindle back Windsor chair at a writing desk of light oak polished until it shone. She had that sort of English transient beauty that would leave her a little plainer after each child, though for Parfrey that had never been a consideration; she also had both wrists heavily bandaged, gauze dressings covering self-inflicted wounds made with one of her father's razor blades. Above her head, a large photograph glued to card, its rough edges finished with dark strips of tape. Surrounded by laughing children her parents posed sternly for the camera, their arms round a child apiece, but there was no warmth in the embrace. In the background a tin mission with a huge wooden cross dominating a blistering African sky. From where Nick stood the cross appeared to have been rammed right through the mission's roof, as though angrily staking a claim on behalf of God.

'Hello Ruth,' said Nick as Lumb, a small gentle woman with serious eyes took herself out of the room. 'How are you feeling?'

'Oh... Nick, thanks for coming,' Parfrey answered not bothering to lift her face, and Nick wondered if she'd been prescribed tranquillisers or painkillers and how much blood she might have lost?

The sound from the television dipped, the channel changed. From the kitchen Nick heard the rattle of cups and clank of a tray as Danny set about the refreshments.

'What can I do for you?' Nick asked, sitting across from her.

'I wanted to tell you about working for Moscow,' Parfrey said, staring at her wrists. 'It's only now when I've had time to reflect, that I recognise how much damage I've caused.'

'That's very generous of you Ruth. Do you feel up to sharing it?'

But before she could begin, Danny knocked once, bringing in a metal tray leaving two cups of tea on a beaten copper table too low to be of any practical use. Out of an immense canvas bag Parfrey pulled out her cigarettes and a box of matches; defiantly, in childish sweeps of her hand she lit one, holding it at the very tip of her fingers to keep them clear of the smoke that slunk away to the ceiling.

'It began when I was a student, I suppose. I'd an increasing disillusionment with the UK's subservience to American policy. And I suppose the illegal Iraq war compounded the moral vacuity of our political class.'

'That's very noble of you,' observed Nick, his tone acerbic, querulous.

'I knew you wouldn't understand,' she flung back.

'I've outgrown sixth form ideology.'

Smiling away his rebuke, Parfrey shook her head. 'If you want to destroy the system, I suppose the most appropriate place to begin is from within it. I wanted to become an active participant, not a spectator. And that's it, no blinding light, just a realisation,' she said slowly, 'I'm not going to provide dates and names now,' she added.

'*Suppose*, Ruth? A Participant? You've participated in quite a lot and there are seven people dead. That's down to you Ruth.' In a determined, calm voice, Nick named each one in a valedictory roll of honour, including Lubov's wife and nephew.

'It must be hard for you to accept.'

'I'm trying, believe me, I'm working on it,' Nick promised. 'So how did you know that Lubov was on to you?'

Stubbing out her cigarette she turned her head away, in profile its classic lines more beautiful than ever, but when she faced him again there was a grimace on her pale lips that just stopped short of being a scowl. 'Just a feeling that he'd got very close.'

'And that was it?'

'I suppose.'

She reached for her cup drinking her tea automatically, her gaze set on a missionary chart depicting colonial Africa, its border spotted with tufts of mould. Around its edges, small photographs of 1950s missionaries with neat ink ruled lines joining them to their destinations; their churches all probably forgotten, a good few of the young faces probably dead. Over Ruth's voice asking if he really understood, he heard the sea in the distance, and somewhere inside his head, a voice of his own urging restraint.

'What more did I need?' she said with no particular emotion, a plain everyday statement, and slipped back into a protracted silence as though determining if she could actually go ahead with her story.

Nick let the silence develop, a temporary break to increase the pain.

Looking at Parfrey then away, he sensed she was trying to shut him out completely. Along the hall, the clock chased away another hour, and the bungalow settled back on its dusty haunches in preparation for another dull evening. A cold wind came up off the sea and gusted inland, strumming telephone wires and playing down the roof, only the screeching lament of gulls penetrated the stillness.

'It really wasn't until I became head RUS/OPS and chair of the Vapour Trail Group that Viper's high-grade product began ringing alarm bells. I suppose it could be only a matter of time before he hit on something incriminating,' she said abruptly. 'I was correct I guess.' And she trailed off again dumping her cup on the table with a bang.

A waist-high bookcase sat in a corner set aside for reading. Close to them, a solid fuel boiler, an unsightly cream box with a wired glass door to let you see the flames. In a dainty hearth, little tools hanging from a metal tree. Under a green Anglepoise dipping its head; Dickens, Austen, Eliot, Trollope and Goethe fought for room with atlases, encyclopaedias and dictionaries.

'Take your time,' Nick suggested, though he knew that commodity was what they lacked the most.

'Then Bensham confirmed it didn't he. Bensham sent the priority cable disclosing Viper had run into evidence of the Oktober Projekt. I realised that if Viper had made such progress, he'd probably already have unearthed a financial genealogy for it. If he had that, he had me, so to speak. Simple, that's all I needed, that's all I'd been waiting for. Don't you see, it was a stark choice of him or me, and I elected for self-preservation.'

If only everything about Lubov and his treasure was so simple and neat, thought Nick as Parfrey slumped back, her energy exhausted. He stared blankly through French doors to a strip of lawn running at a curious angle; next to it a greenhouse still thawing from the night's frost, a compost heap rising wildly by its side. At the top end of the garden a cluster of apple trees, the fruit ripened deep red, some already rotting on the branches, others pecked at by birds. Turning his attention back into the room, Nick noticed prints of bible classes hung in sad groups forever waiting to be converted, all their eyes fixed accusingly on him from the facing wall. And by the door on a rosewood table, an engraved panorama of Hong Kong taken at night had slipped and gouged into the veneer.

'That's why I messed up the preparation for the collection, downgraded the risk assessment,' she said drawing on an inner reserve, her expression animated, her eyes alight with a strange passion. 'Viper had to be prevented from passing on his sample. It was Viper or me.'

'No one else suggested downgrading the risk assessment, did they, Ruth? Did someone persuade you the collection *had* to proceed?'

'Why would they do that?'

Just for a fraction of a second, a flicker of contempt passed across Parfrey's face.

'And you just passed on all your concerns to your handler?' Nick proposed.

In an adjoining garden a fire clouded the air with spirals of damp wood smoke.

'Viper had to be stopped, he had to be found, and the counter-intelligence operation was part of the strategy. Track and terminate my handler called it,' she said, rhythmically rocking in her chair.

And some more, thought Nick. 'So, you had no concern that Foula and I were walking into a trap?' Nick wanted to know. 'Jo Lister's murder meant nothing to you either?' Nick pushed her as close to the facts that he dared to go; not prepared to reveal how much he knew about Lubov's treasure. 'My wife?'

'There are always casualties.'

A sense of urgency had become apparent in both of them. It brought Nick to the edge of his chair, and as a paradox, drove Parfrey deeper into hers; as if the weight of questions had become physically too much for her.

'Jo, your wife, Alistair, the others, I never wanted any of that.'

'But none of them deserved to die, did they?' Nick curtly reminded her.

'No,' Parfrey agreed, 'Jo probably suspected that I'd sabotaged the collection, she was killed because she would eventually link me to blowing Operation Salvage.'

'Did you get a bonus?'

Nick's accusation had awoken something deep in her and she stared at Nick with a real hatred. 'I just did what I believed was necessary to protect myself. You posed a valid threat. You could have possessed a sample of Viper's evidence. I never thought they'd hurt your wife.'

'But they did,' Nick said, calling for Lumb.

In the hall Nick leant wearily against an Anaglypta papered wall, massaging his neck as Rossan strode along to join him.

'Do you believe her?'

'Possibly,' said Nick. 'She does seem to have a genuine hatred for our political incompetence, but whether she acted on it is a different thing entirely.'

'So why is she doing it?' Rossan asked.

'I don't know.'

'And we do what?'

'Move her to a safe house, get her some medical attention, sweat her and see if she changes her story.'

'I'll call ahead,' Rossan promised. 'Better let her parents know that's she's coming with us.'

Finally, after a long hour of inertia they were preparing to leave when Lumb popped her head around the door.

'She's asking for a favour,' she said, glancing between Nick and Rossan. 'Could she have ten minutes in the garden?'

'Your decision,' Nick said to Rossan.

Checking his watch, Rossan nodded. 'Ten minutes and no more, she doesn't even deserve that. And you stay with her.'

Nick nodded Parfrey out with Lumb, and he even walked them down the hall, escorting them through kitchen to the door and watched them stroll away on the path.

'When we've finally put this business behind us, come and stay with us for a few days. Rebecca will spoil you and...'

Replaying the sequence numerous times much later, Nick's sequence always began at the moment Hill appeared and yelled 'Garden.' He ran, followed by Rossan and Danny, but they were already too late. Towards the top end of the garden behind a trellis, they found Lumb out cold, sprawled in a line of berberis hedging. Twenty feet away a wooden workshop well ablaze, the flames hungrily clawing their way out of the apex roof, a column of soiled white smoke surging after them. Attempting to get close enough to force the door, Nick and Danny were driven back when a pair of the thin panes glazing the windows shattered, the fire emitting a growl as it consumed the inrush of air. In his most severe officer's voice, Rossan commanding Hill to call the emergency services. After hauling Lumb to safety, they'd retreated part way down the garden as a precaution; Rossan deeming the risk too high should the workshop contain propane cylinders. After leading the stunned and groggy Lumb back into the bungalow, by the time Nick had calmed her, the sirens no longer came from the television, but were very close and very real. Rossan organising and authoritative, had control of the scene, a role he took extremely seriously as he rehearsed his words before going into see Parfrey's parents. As the front room door closed behind Rossan, a gale of hysterical laughter rushed out, followed by studio cheers and a ripple of glitzy music. A retired afternoon on the coast Nick thought; time to unwind, forget the week gone and the one to come; forget who we are and how many lives we selfishly ruin.

• • •

By half past eight that evening a heavy pink sky promised snow and Parfrey's parents had been escorted to temporary accommodation. The fire had been extinguished, though the charred wooden planks that had collapsed in on themselves half-heartedly smouldered, dribbles of smoke trailing up out of the garden. Years of creosoting had made the workshop burn with ferocity, the fire service incident commander revealed to Rossan, confirming too, a body had been located. The bungalow reeked of smoke as Nick mooched between rooms waiting for answers. He'd spoken briefly to Lumb with Rossan fussing in the background. Her account, volunteered after refusing medical attention, assisted no doubt by a slug of brandy after Danny found a bottle in a kitchen cupboard, produced a simple account of the walk in the garden with its tragic consequences. Nearing the trellis, Parfrey had pointed out the apple trees, reminiscing how her father used to press them for midsummer cider. Falling for the distraction, Lumb never saw the blow, but reckoned it was one of the feral types taught at Aspley to incapacitate. Exchanging a doubtful glance with Nick, forbidding Lumb from touching another drop of brandy, Rossan resumed his crisis management, presiding over the arrangements to have the relevant authorities notified.

Uncertainty beat away inside Nick, his temples throbbed, and his face burnt. On this jigsaw piece of isthmus, that horror of how Parfrey took her own life seemed too wrong to contemplate, too surreal. Time moved in abstract lurches all around him. As the night slowly wound on losing its grip, the house became a scene of ceaseless activity. Detached, his role nothing more than a *flâneur*, Nick took everything in as he moved from room to room as different teams went about their work. As Mortland's rummagers arrived, a trim, athletically built female CID officer who'd identified herself to Nick as 'Jameson, your liaison', reported what she had so far.

'The fire investigation officer found evidence of an accelerant. Petrol, fuel for a lawnmower is the most probable cause. Doused the workshop, herself...'

They stood stiffly together, two strangers discussing death, her eyes warm and friendly.

'The body reveals an incision to the throat, appears self-inflicted. Until the forensic pathologist has taken a look, we can't know for sure,' she disclosed. 'Miss Parfrey was a colleague?'

Yes, admitted Nick, though he didn't actually work directly with her. At the reference to work, she nodded, her firm tight face made it perfectly clear her liaison duties had a defined boundary she was forbidden to cross. She hadn't been told what Nick did, only that he asks, and he is given full access and answers.

'From the indicators we have, everything implies suicide,' she admitted. 'Ruth made an attempt earlier, I believe?'

'Apparently,' answered Nick, 'I wasn't here.'

'But you did speak to her?'

'She asked to see me, we chatted. As far as I'm aware, she had no issues with her mental health until today,' said Nick. 'A little subdued perhaps, mildly stressed, but she didn't reveal anything close to desperation when I spoke with her.'

'Sometimes it is difficult to tell until it's too late.'

'I suppose it is.'

With a good deal of expert intuition, Jameson drew out of Nick the mandatory background to compile her assessment, mapping the final hours of Parfrey's life. When the forbidden territory of Parfrey's career intervened, she discreetly stepped away. By the end of her delicate interrogation, they'd covered all the safe ground and a little bit of wasteland too, wandering off into the other suicides she'd attended.

'There's the stigma that it's an act of cowardice,' she confessed. 'It's not. You need courage to go through with it. My first one was suicide by train. He didn't jump, he laid with his neck across the rail. Severed his head, and it wasn't neat or clean. I just couldn't imagine lying there waiting for that moment, deciding you have nothing to live for. Which I guess is how Ruth must have felt. It's odd, but the manner in which she did it seems so spur of the moment.'

'She encountered an unexpected difficulty in her career.'

'Right, well, time I checked on progress again,' she said, walking off. But she fared little better wherever she strode on her mission to understand Parfrey's motivation. Mortland's hurriedly assembled teams, men and women roused from their beds, treated Jameson as an intrusion, responding warily to her questions with non-committal shakes of the head and vague answers that eventually forced her to retreat to her own corner of the bungalow.

A stocky pathologist spent thirty minutes in a forensic tent pitched mid-way down the garden where Parfrey's severely burned remains awaited removal. It reminded Nick of a mini marque erected for a family celebration. Gradually, room by room, Mortland's serious men and women eased the bungalow apart; the rummagers bagging anything they believed connected to Parfrey, photographing each find, all the details logged and annotated meticulously, their white hooded suits giving them a spectral presence. Each and every one of these scenes fixed like deep splinters under a membrane in Nick's memory.

'Atypical suicide,' the pathologist confirmed on his return from the garden. 'Self-inflicted. The wound is visible over the anterior aspect of the neck and I'd say it was done with a curved blade. Given the location of where she was found, possibly a pruning knife. Hard to tell if there's any hesitation marks, but the incision was purposeful, oblique, starting on the left. External carotid artery and internal jugular vein were incised. She would have fainted immediately,' he announced. Cheerful and reflective, he mumbled his farewell; traces of Parfrey's charred flesh on his gloves, a few smears of ash on the white cuffs of his forensic suit.

When Rossan found Nick in the hallway, the search had been completed. 'Nothing of significance,' he reported. 'We could not have foreseen such extreme action. No one should feel they bear any responsibility for what took place.'

'No? I pushed her pretty hard, Paul. I didn't believe her, and she read it.'

'You do not know that,' said Rossan, his cheeks rosy from the demands of crisis management.

'And I don't know that she didn't,' said Nick remotely. 'Something triggered her.'

'This is not the time to speculate,' hissed Rossan. He glanced over his shoulder, peered ahead before leaning in close to Nick. 'We do not know why she had a complete and utter meltdown. It isn't the actions of someone being rational.'

'That's the problem, it's too irrational,' snapped Nick. 'When did she come down here?'

'According to her father, it was Tuesday evening, she arrived after six. She brought one small bag, and she hadn't let them know in advance she intended to visit which she normally did.'

'That's the same day I went to see her.'

'Meaning what exactly?' Rossan demanded, fighting to keep his voice low and moderate.

'She told someone about my visit. Maybe she didn't get the reaction she expected.'

'Her handler?'

'But if she was such a crucial asset, why wasn't there a plan for extraction? As a rule, the GRU don't abandon prestigious agents, do they Paul? They spirit them away, grant them residency, and they make sure everybody knows X, Y or Z prefers sanctuary in Moscow compared to what they've left behind,' Nick said forcefully.

'You mean the damage and embarrassment they have caused,' Rossan curtly observed.

'Did she call anyone from down here?'

'Mortland is requesting her phone records and those for the landline.'

'Visitors?'

'Her father seemed to think not, but she went out for long walks.'

'Why here and why now? She met someone, Paul, and I don't believe it was her handler.'

'Damn it, Nick,' sighed Rossan. 'If you are wrong, we proceed with a needless witch-hunt.'

'If I'm right?'

'If you need me, I'll be persuading Jameson that we really don't hate her.'

So, Nick lingered. Cross-legged in an adjoining room a female rummager diligently wrote up her report, her knees pulled in to let the steady procession past, Nick storing the details; this was genuine Pinter, real theatre of the absurd. Away from the bungalow the snow rolled down into a waiting greedy sea.

A bustle in the hall, a dark hurrying shape scooting past the dusky wallpaper and Bailrigg moved towards Nick with an angry roll of his shoulders. His eyes, dark and intense, read the scene with a fieldman's quick understanding. Attending him a senior uniformed officer who took a full assessment with one glance, said something in a respectful growl and abruptly left. Someone switched on a lamp and a sleepy bulb lit the hall.

'A walk if you will,' declared Bailrigg, clutching Nick's arm to guide him out into the snow. 'An appraisal, right now.'

Below Nick in the semi-darkness a wild sea hammered pebbles up the shore, a pale light fluttered on the horizon like dirty washing on a line; and dawn had forced the sky and sea apart as weak light flooded into the crack. They walked without feeling the cold, nipping brandy from Bailrigg's silver hip flask every couple of yards. Out to sea Nick saw the lights of a passing ship wink at nothingness and fade out of sight; along the road gulls curled round the tops of street lamps for warmth. In the town a church clock hit a quarter as a milk float jingled somewhere out of sight. Ahead on an obelisk carved to the dead of two wars, a R5 Regulator stamped his boots on the bottom step to keep warm; the sporadic chatter from his radio drifted towards them adding to the unreality. Completely absorbed by his own troubled thoughts, Bailrigg stared into the distance, unconcerned that the snow coated grass was soaking his trousers and shoes.

'Well?' Bailrigg demanded at last.

'Parfrey confessed and she committed suicide.'

'I am aware of the baseline facts. Humour me, give me your interpretation. There appears to be an evolving consensus that I have lost control, that granting me stewardship of the Service was a monumental error of judgement. It is judiciously hinted that I have to make amends. The PM and Foreign Secretary are climbing the walls, our Minister requires this to be tidied up fast. He is insisting on minimising damage to our reputation, meaning his. I've had my quota of bollockings thank you very much. Between us, I anticipated we would have this contained, but after this, I'm not sure. Your interpretation, and there's need to spare my blushes.'

'The whole confession just didn't add up,' Nick disclosed, the cold seeping through his shoes, numbing his toes.

'Your reasoning?'

'This way, Parfrey made sure that she'd take the fall,' said Nick remotely. 'This way, she made it convenient for me to stop pursuing the Oktober Projekt.'

'Which leaves us what? Lubov's cry from the wilderness claiming one of our own or someone close to us has sold their soul to the GRU?' he said. 'That is whole aim of the Oktober Projekt is it not? Oh, don't look so surprised, Nicholas. I have bumped into the rumour that Nizhny Novgorod is a wolf in sheep's clothing at various junctures in my career. Some people forget that I've worked my way up from a naïve probationer. Trod the RUS/OPS boards for a number of seasons, did the Middle East, watering down Moscow's influence, and occasionally, there'd be a contact hawking stories about Nizhny Novgorod. Cropped up from time to time when I'd been made head boy of counter-intelligence. Aubrey-Spencer gave me a free run to shake down the shadows, but nothing of substance fell out. Problem was, we never had anything tangible until Lubov pulled the rabbit out the hat.'

'I'm not chasing rabbits,' said Nick.

'No, you're chasing something far more dangerous,' Bailrigg admitted. 'As soon as Teddy heard about this latest catastrophe, he ran to the Minister. But that's Teddy. Cut him in half, and I'm not suggesting you do, but you'll find diplomat written in bold like the lettering on a stick of rock. Teddy is stoking the Whitehall fires of doom, priming the assassins, waiting for his chance to mount a coup against me. He's already got the Minister onside. In his infinite wisdom and with his usual brilliant clueless grasp of the situation, our Minister has made it expressly clear HMG views this incident as a line drawn in the sand. He opens his mouth and we listen.'

'Well he's wrong,' countered Nick savagely. 'If we turn our backs and walk away, we admit defeat. Is that what we do?'

'Why do we discount Parfrey?' Bailrigg demanded, upping the pace.

'What if Parfrey really chose to die because of remorse and guilt after realising *she* had been betrayed? An admission she placed her faith in someone who manipulated her. Viper told Bensham he had "uncovered the beginning of the deceit." And if we accept Parfrey as Moscow's asset, we accept the deceit.'

The sky was filling with colour; an unseen hand had slashed the black canvas and a glorious deep orange seeped into the wounds. Nick took more brandy and the alcohol cleansed his head, seeing for the first time the shabbiness of the resort. Guest houses in lurid pinks and blues; arcades for rainy days, rock stalls in flaking white and a theme bar, this one a Western Saloon with ranch doors painted by unconvinced English hands. A foul weather shelter with an overturned bench and sand streaked glass sat hunched in front of them. It came at a point where the promenade broadened out; next to it a telescope had been ripped off its pedestal and the mounting held up a torn rusted knuckle.

'She did it out of misplaced loyalty? To protect someone she cares for, someone she never suspected of being Moscow's servant? That the gist of it or am I being thick?' Bailrigg declared in a rare show of contrition.

'I don't know.'

'What do you know? And no waffle,' Bailrigg commanded.

'The Nizhny Novgorod facility may be connected to the Veterans Rehabilitation Clinic No.2 and a centre at Nikolina Gora.'

'Of course they are, stop being modest. Three GRU establishments positively identified by Lubov, our crafty accountant, which earned him rave reviews, so I gather. I'll overlook how you came to be in possession of Vapour Trail Group material. But I won't have Aubrey-Spencer using my officers for his private enterprises. Arranging a secret date in the park with you is a minor sin, using Wynn a mortal offence, and he's been told. Aubrey-Spencer give you a glimpse of his treatise during your evening trek in the wilderness?'

'Not in detail.'

'I'll spare you the pain of the full thing and give you the juicy bits. Three establishments, Nicholas, and Lubov stuck a pin in them for us. What links them, binds together? It might, or might not be, the Oktober Projekt, we don't have any corroborated evidence. We do have Lubov's encounter with the furtive Leshy, and according to him, Leshy was the one calling the shots. If we dot our i's and cross our t's, we might have first sight of who's pulling the strings. You getting this at the back?'

A slipway ran into the sea opposite them, and waves washed shingle noisily against its concrete braces; an entire army slogging up the beach. Nick didn't feel inclined to answer and faced into the wind.

'He doesn't answer to GRU Centre,' Nick volunteered after a pause.

'Merit point for you, Nicholas, gold star, well done. Aubrey-Spencer has also concluded how other wispy references to a Ghost, a Hermit, a Pilgrim, equals the one and same Leshy, or as my contact assures me, a graduate of Nizhny Novgorod who lives under the workname of Tazi, rank classified, background undetermined. But he has very influential backers within the Kremlin's grey cardinals.'

'Allowing him to run a penetration operation,' Nick ventured.

'Against yours truly, and I want the devious bastard stopped,' declared Bailrigg with venom.

'If we're not his only target?' queried Nick, gaining a foul glare in response.

'If they're out there, you find them.'

Bailrigg climbed over an ankle high brick wall into a car park partly claimed by the sea, gulls and paper cups bobbing on its choppy waves. A police traffic car blocked the entrance, a second unmarked Volvo sat by an official Service car parked in a far corner overlooking the sea. By its door, Mortland in the middle of a phone call.

'Resources?'

'Beg, steal or borrow, but do not come to me. None of this need to have happened if it hadn't been for that damn clown Bensham. Where do we recruit these people from?'

Four anglers in chest waders and weekend waterproofs had piled out of a Jeep with a small boat in tow. Gathered round the traffic car blocking the entrance, they were in the middle of a heated debate over access, pointing to the sea. But Nick ignored their plight as his mind started to retrace the route he had followed since Moscow; a solution to finding Lubov's traitor had long been gathering in Nick along the way. Drawn together in Moscow during the restless days and nights of his captivity, pushed into a direction by Angie's death, dragged in another by Jo Lister; he had formed it clearly without pedantry with no affinity to emotions or previous relationships. Now in the perfect calmness of an English morning, it seemed inadequate. Silent, he stared at everything and nothing. Gulls floated on the cold air too light to be real, lifting and dropping freely. The anglers, having reached a compromise were attempting to reverse their flimsy craft between a boulder wall.

'Have you identified any potential suspects?' he asked.

'I may have, and it's on a need to know basis. At moment, you don't need to know,' Bailrigg decided.

As they drew near to Mortland, snippets of his conference carried on the wind to Nick. '... the tragic loss of a valued officer... under extreme pressure... was being treated for depression and had our full support. You know the score.'

Evidently someone did, for Mortland snapped a gracious nod in Bailrigg's direction and returned to the warmth of his Volvo.

'Jo Lister can be cleared of any involvement,' proposed Nick firmly.

'For some people in our parish that truth will be unpalatable,' Bailrigg observed. 'Remember the Eleventh Commandment, Nicholas. Thou shall not get caught,' he added, nodding in a farewell.

'I wasn't intending to do,' said Nick, slamming the door, banging twice on the roof as he stood back.

With a curt wave Bailrigg sat back, appraising Nick as if he had only at this very moment come to see him for who he really was. Although the car was an automatic, Bailrigg's driver still made driving a chore as they headed along the prom with a police car none too discreetly behind. No friends, no prisoners, decided Nick as the Service car had a nasty brush with a cyclist at the bottom of the road. And every step forward would not be on the road to heaven he thought, splashing his way across the car park. Around him the morning wore a freshness unlike any other hour of the day; washed, unused, it smelt starched and untouched by any previous labours and for Nick it seemed to be heralding a new beginning.

Twenty-One

Nick flew out of Heathrow using a passport in the workname of Ingol on a late afternoon flight. Before checking in, he dawdled with the well-timed patience of a seasoned fieldman, lingering in concourse shops with no intention of buying a thing, paying more attention to his back than making a purchase. From Stockholm he flew to Germany using a different name, aware how far the stakes had been raised.

At Kiel-Holtenau airport he entered a Germany of a different age; a former military base, a home to flying schools, clubs, small planes and executive jets. Nick headed into its Balkan restaurant the furniture laden with wax and middle-aged waitresses buttoned up in black. He sat at a table overlooking the runway ordering beer and schnapps, settling back, unhurried, as though awaiting a friend. He had a perfect view of the door but let his attention drift to a panoramic window. Out on the runway, the Cessna Citation on its return to Stockholm, taxied along the tarmac belt ringed by conifers, disappearing in a dull roar into the charcoal sky. In defiant bits the last of the day fled through the trees without a fight, the runway lights glittering like gold bars. He remained for another thirty minutes, his gaze not far from the door. I'm getting soft Nick told himself, you've proved you're unmarked so move.

Which he did.

Onto a train to Hamburg and into a taxi smelling of stale leather that let him down on ABC-Straße the temperature low, the freezing air leaving a salty smear on his skin. He traversed through a late crowd of drinkers their breaths billowing behind them in white trails, the cold gripping his bones cutting right through the glow of the schnapps, and he shook at its bite.

Petra's antiques shop was on Speckstraße and charged New York prices for common junk. Its window display held liberated tat like lacquered tables and poor canvases covered by heavy second coats of oil, alongside ships in dusty bottles, pitchers and basins pilfered from Baltic wrecks. The door had a night bell set on the lintel and it brought Petra Speyer to answer its call, taking him in like an orphan, making a fuss of him, determined to appear elated.

'Nick this is good, but my God, look at you. When was the last time you slept? I got your message, and of course, I haven't mentioned your arrival to anyone. Fantastic.'

She kissed him; left cheek, right cheek, one for good luck. 'Hello Petra.'

'Come through, come on, let's get you warm,' she said, taking him by the hand into a corner of the shop. 'Sit, sit, tell me all the news. Coffee? Of course, you must drink.' When she smiled her whole face burned with the effort, and her auburn hair layered short and cut in from underneath gave Petra a youthful charm.

She made coffee adding whisky to it and when the coffee ran out, they set about drinking the whisky neat under the coral globe of a desk lamp giving them both a rosy glow. In her youth Speyer had trained as an artist, once quite seriously tempted towards following it as a career. Carrying her beauty into middle age it had become something of a talisman against the onslaught of age, and only recently had it begun showing the fragile signs of wear. Now Nick could see the scars from laughter run into her gentle face, the deeper creases in the corner of each eye, a chilling blue that endlessly quizzed him.

'How long since you were here last with me?' she teased after they had exhausted the small talk.

'Too long.'

'Jack's fishing, up to no good,' she decided. Petra, an irregular in CO8's menagerie for a good few seasons; a night owl who watched and listened and when the opportunity arose, struck up lucrative conversations, mostly with commercial captains using the port. When she inherited Jack Balgrey, the Service resident as her lifeline with the Mad House, Petra somehow lost her enthusiasm. Jack, her support, working out of the office of Druyer GmbH, a one-man company wholly owned by the Service as its Hamburg base, purportedly dealing with imports and exports as well as property management, though its core business was spying.

'It's better Jack doesn't know I'm in Hamburg,' said Nick, pouring them both another generous glass.

'What do I need to know?'

So, Nick laid out his story, beginning with Moscow; Speyer dipped forward her elbows on her knees barely moving, dissolving everything with long blinks and brief nods. Afterwards she sat back lighting a cigarette, expelling the smoke in a sharp plume up at the ceiling where it fanned slowly out winding through cheap parrot cages and ships' lamps held aloft by wire. A clock rounded the hour, its delicate strokes of brass cymbals floating into the dusty vaporous light. 'You need to be kept in the clear, Harry Bransk will do all the legwork,' he concluded.

She considered him through the smoke; a lengthy sideways glance, shrewd and uneven. 'Bransk is trouble, he's not somebody that I would trust,' she said, not even able to look at Nick.

'I need him,' he said, his hands clamped tight round his glass.

Her two-piece business suit showed off her legs and she consciously smoothed down the hem over dark blue tights. She stubbed out the cigarette in an ashtray belonging to a shipping line, its colours hauled round the edge in limp pennants.

'You better watch your back.'

'He's made all the connections once before.'

'He's slime.' She spread out her pretty hands, their smooth palms to Nick in an appeal.

'I need somewhere to stay,' he said, wandering through overpriced vases and brass plant holders that would always stain green. 'Until I find a local base.'

'Why not a month, a year, forever? Then you help me sell all this trash?' she laughed, straining at the effort.

Resigned, persuaded, numbed by his silent eyes, Petra led him through to the back of the shop, to a stockroom piled high with tea chests full of Dresden porcelain packed in bubble wrap for shipment, and a fake Baroque writing table with cabriole legs already sold to a Japanese dealer. The last clear space taken by a folding bed with a sleeping bag, pillow and blanket arranged neatly. Ready, she told him, for the nights she didn't go home because there was a story to be bought, or if someone needed shelter, or for the nights she quarrelled with Hans, her sometimes husband. She showed him the toilet, the knack of flushing it on the third go, also the temperamental kettle, store of coffee, tea and dried milk on a stockroom shelf. Then she handed him the keys and set off for a meeting with another bored agent, an elderly captain from Rostock, who never had anything to offer but a promise of marriage that Petra always politely declined.

•••

Harry Bransk impatiently silenced the car radio, his progress along Altsädter Straße on this bitter December night frustrated by a lane light dangling off a wire like a Christmas lantern. He mouthed a long silent curse at the chaos around him, at the salt air carrying the fresh scent of approaching snow, at being rudely summoned by Nick Torr. The green light gave the all clear across Mohlenhofstraße and leaving his disgust in the rising clouds of fumes, he eased back the clutch sending the Audi forward. He had memories of countless drives such as this, dying a hundred times during them, waiting for the move that would never be your own, the one mistake that you could never predict. Now, once again, he became lost in his old habits, routines that made sleep a sanctuary.

He took in the city from the window, his heavy rutted face worn down by disappointment counted off the turnings. For Harry Bransk's life consisted of several wrong turnings, all of them singularly painful and in one form or another removing him further from the crumbling shell of a Slovenian village outside Maribor, where all those lives ago he had begun his apprenticeship to the secret world. An inauspicious start as it was, running messages across the Austrian border during the Ten-Day War, it nevertheless prepared him for a life of deceit and treachery, of not having a shadow to call your own.

Through his mirror he watched for any signs of being followed, but so many thoughts clouded his mind that he had trouble concentrating. A car broken down in front had brought the traffic to a slow line creeping by the old Elbe tunnel, the urgency made him burn. His hands slipped on the steering wheel, he wanted to break from the queue to make up lost time, but he did nothing to attract attention. On the move again and the St. Pauli landing stages slipped past, bold against the river, stark like scaffolds, then the orange flashes of the breakdown truck were behind him.

Slowly it began to snow, as if the weather like his concern had made the same tortuous journey from Helsinki that served as a second home to Harry. He drove on, slowing down for the side roads, into a night drained of colour, washed down the gutters along with the swimming headlights. He swung into a street shuttered and deserted, kept going until he was under the tanks of a petrol dock blotting out the sky. And beside the swollen quays, just as he knew he'd find it, a marine bunkering yard stained with the rotten fingers of decline. He steered close to bitumen jacketed pipes running the length of a concrete pier. At its end, a line of sheds, their timber walls buckled and cracked, window frames lying over squares of shattered glass. Turning off the engine he let down the window.

He heard the whine of generators and pumps feeding a ship down river, he heard the rapid tattoo of dripping snow on oil drums as it swept off the corrugated roofs and burst gutters. He heard the voice that trampled across the years, following him as it always did from a café down an uneven cobbled court in Bratislava, sometime home to curious travellers, artists, pimps and whores. Where one fine summer evening Harry Bransk had first worked with Nick Torr.

'You're late, Harry,' observed Nick from the darkness of a doorway.

With the car at his back Harry moved cautiously forward, the old world his again and with it came the unknown; the promises made to be broken, the lies to keep you alive.

'Hey, Nick, just like old times,' said Harry, watching Nick step into the fuzzy light hanging in place of a door.

'Is it?' Nick answered, his voice sharp. Harry Bransk a fixer, a dealer, the purveyor of dreams, and as some claimed, an associate of the Devil himself. Bransk had a sturdy body, its muscles toned by a rigid fitness regime, and it was topped by a street fighter's face marred in many skirmishes, while his eyes having grown too wise told of many victories. A face that served as a commodity for whoever paid the highest dollar it said, and Nick knew that Bransk always came with an unseen price. Harry also had an elegance about him that manifested itself in his taste for expensive clothes, but he wore them like rags.

'So, what brings you to my neck of the woods?' Harry asked.

Nick held up his hand, his palm flat to Bransk in a warning to step no closer, keeping Harry out in the open.

'I've heard it told from a mutual friend that you've been fixing things for an acquaintance in London?'

'I've let this person down in some way? The service I provided is not what they wanted? Tell me Nick? We have no secrets you and me. Or you finally come to collect what I owe, that it? Come to tell me the good days are over?' Harry's smile was a thin sharp slit worn carefully, an experienced street merchant who rarely squandered anything.

'A mutual friend came to see you Harry,' said Nick as Bransk listened patiently. 'You made arrangements for a guest to travel with us, but the trip was called off. The same friend returned to work a lead, though unfortunately she met with an accident and could not continue.'

'That's a pity,' Harry replied. 'Not many people recover from having their face blown off. Real mess so I heard,' Harry added with a measure of caution, aware that old friends have a habit of becoming deadly.

'Thing is, Harry, I think that someone sold my friend out, struck a different deal. I'm not saying it was you, but you're sort of connected to it all, Harry. This makes me nervous, gets me thinking maybe Harry's made one deal he shouldn't?'

'It's regrettable, Nick, too bad, if that's your opinion,' said Harry, a man used to dealing with disappointment. 'You here to pull the trigger, Nick? Because I have to tell you, okay, you got this all wrong.'

'How wrong Harry?'

'Some people do not have our understanding, okay. Making arrangements, okay, let's start there. The people I deal with, they're not always pleasant okay, they behave erratically. They make demands but never see the cost. I am in business, okay, I have to think of costs all the time. This is going to affect me badly, Nick.' He tried a smile, but it perished on his lips. 'I'm taking a rough ride on all sides, Nick. Now this. It doesn't make me happy that you're expecting me to take all the blame.'

'It's a bad world, Harry and we've all got to take care.'

'True, very true,' he said, deeply pained, 'Our mutual friend from London, okay, the one who made the travel arrangements for your guest, sure she returned. I remember now, she was interested in a certain business.'

'I like you more when you cooperate, Harry.'

'So, we got the makings of an agreement?'

'We've made a start, Harry.'

'Okay, so now we need to discuss terms and conditions, Nick, you know how these things work,' Harry announced.

'I want what you provided previously, Harry, in good faith before I put any money on the drum.'

'Come on Nick, I am caught in the middle here. Times are lean, it's rough trying to please everyone. Why let misunderstandings divide warriors like us when the enemy never could? Tell me, Nick, why are you still involved with all this craziness?'

'It's in the blood, Harry, you know that.'

'Okay, okay, you get your good faith,' announced Harry. 'Our mutual friend wanted me to prepare the ground. She was going to follow the trail I'd open up.' He tried another smile without success.

'Did the trail start at the Brazillia Casino by any chance Harry?'

'You're one hundred per cent ahead of me, here Nick. Someone offering better terms than me?'

'This is personal, Harry, my wife's dead and it wasn't natural causes.'

As with all deals especially when agreeing terms, there comes a moment of extreme danger, and an inner sense told Harry that this was what he faced right now. 'You think this is all connected, Nick?'

'No doubt about it Harry.'

Harry whistled, nodding thoughtfully, he took in Nick's news, which actually caused him to shiver. 'Sure, it all begins at the casino, but I only gave our friend the facts, lit up the trail. I got no involvement in what happened to her,' said Harry, making absolutely sure Nick knew whose side he was on. 'What terms you offering, Nick because if this is personal then things get tricky, know what I mean?'

'Full payment on completion Harry, expenses and a retainer as of now.'

'That's a dumb deal, Nick, know that,' offered Harry. 'You don't mind me saying that Nick?'

'I don't mind Harry, but it's all I've got,' said Nick. 'I want an answer by tonight or I'm going to expect you to disappear.'

The snow ran into Bransk's eyes, but he didn't wipe them, keeping his hands low by his side, visible and still. Above them a helicopter hammered through the low cloud, and Nick withdrew into the shadow.

'You're going to tie up all the loose ends for me, Harry. I'm short on time, you want me to spread the word that you're off the books, unreliable, a risk?'

'Hamburg's good to me, okay. I do plenty of business here with my regular clients. I have a lot to lose. I think perhaps you should know that,' said Harry, sounding deeply offended. 'Okay, okay, I accept your kind offer,' Harry said, for once not absolutely sure of his ground or safety.

'So, what did you provide for our friend?' Nick asked.

'An introduction from someone who had a connection.'

'Do I get to meet them?'

'That's not possible, Nick, he's keeping out of sight, okay, tucked himself away the day after our friend ran into that spot of trouble.'

'The information?'

Harry's face tightened into a grimace at having to provide information for free. 'A name, okay. Franziska, she was the key to unlock the money box. That's it, Nick, I only recovered the basics to complete negotiations.'

'What else do I need to know?'

'The casino is sort of exclusive, invitation or recommendation only,' Harry said. 'Blackjack, roulette, dice, whores and dancing girls go right across the scale; high-class, low-class, no-class.'

'A single owner?'

'One-man show, Nick, know what I mean. The place is owned by a shrewd operator called Günter Blümhof, but if that's his real name is anyone's guess.'

'Background?'

'Blümhof came from the rough side of the tracks, okay, and through some risky deals with persons unknown, he managed to get enough finance to buy the casino. This gives him the muscle to progress, not much, but enough. The Brazillia and his sideline of strip bars keeps his head above water pretty damn good. One regular guest, a Russian, he got so many names it's like pinning a damn tail on donkey, but eventually I got a fix. Sergei Gorshov... also signs his IOUs as Pytor Kotelnkov, GRU hood, and he makes frequent trips to Switzerland, place near the German border, Winterthur. Blümhof runs a very tight operation and protects his privacy, okay. You don't want to get caught asking any wrong questions, not here in Hamburg or you end up with no face.'

'I need a way in, Harry, a recommendation to get me through the door.'

'This is risky, okay. I warned our friend not to approach and look what happened.'

'It's not a request, Harry.'

There are types of men in this world that Harry Bransk knew you could walk away from, forget them, ignore them and take on life with the same hunger. This he knew did not remotely apply to Nick Torr. In Bratislava during a clandestine meeting with a sulky Slovakian arms smuggler, Harry playing the buyer in a sting operation to intercept the weapons; young and too fierce, pushing for a move up the scales, he broke all the rules in the book and a good few more. Demanding sight of the AK-47s Harry was lucky to walk away with cuts and bruises. If it hadn't been for Nick having no qualms in breaking the neck of Harry's attacker, there was every chance Harry would have been bundled into a van and disappeared for good.

'This is not favourable, Nick, you're asking a lot, okay.'

Listening intently, Nick had folded his arms and wore the same impassive look across his face as he had done that night in Bratislava.

'Is there something that you want to add, Harry? Something that I need to know?'

'These people, Nick, well, they're nervous, suspect everyone. This goes wrong and they going to hit us hard. You, me, maybe Petra, Jack, all of London's representatives in Hamburg.'

'You got options on this, Harry? You taking more than sides this time? Got something to settle perhaps?' asked Nick, unfolding his arms, an act that somehow heightened the feeling of misgiving for Bransk.

The snow had soaked through Harry's overcoat. He could feel it on his shoulders, cold damp patches slowly spreading down his back and arms, but he closed his mind to the discomfort.

'Not this one. Strictly business all the way.'

'The rules of engagement have changed now, Harry. You earn your fee and a bonus by making the arrangements, starting with getting me through the door tonight.'

'Sure, whatever you want, Nick. Harry's officially working for you, nothing's impossible. I'll see what I can do, where do I reach you?'

'That doesn't work like that this time either, Harry. You give me a number I can reach you twenty-four-seven.'

'Sure,' agreed Harry, taking out his phone.

After Nick had stored the number on his mobile he turned, having nothing more to say. Walking to his car Harry opened up the collar on a heavy overcoat bought in Stockholm and thought of how this deal could be his last, if he played it right, he might even have enough to retire.

Twenty-Two

Sometimes you needed to establish the facts and decide how much of you was evil, how much was good for no other reason than to prove a point; to italicize a right to freedom, to take risks because someone you loved had died. Just sometimes you behaved totally irrationally when revenge had got under your skin and poisoned your system. Nick was possessed of those very symptoms when he moved away from the antique shop, through a cold night loaded with snow and headed towards the port. The introduction provided by Harry carried as securely as contraband as he made for the river through brightly lit cobbled streets.

Groups of Turkish *Gastarbeiters* smoked in doorways marginally lit; fathers doubled by manual work and tall fiery sons probing Nick's intentions with wide hostile eyes, questioning his right to be in their territory. I'm passing through, don't worry, Nick's body language declared. His head bowed, his hands gripping the lining in his pockets as he read everything around him; the starched washing airing out of high windows, a violinist's inflamed melancholic practise chords drifting away. At a restaurant open until four a.m., customers formed hazy dark profiles at round white damask covered tables. He strolled by a cinema showing Turkish films with unpronounceable names and gory segments on lurid billboards. Distance required; don't stop, don't tempt fate. He walked fast to the edge of the Reeperbahn and the Casino Brazillia, a mock Gothic castle with a fortified door.

He pressed a buzzer and a door slipped its catch, an electronic invitation into a reception styled on Brazilian themes. Panoramas of Rio were screwed precisely down bare brick walls and he stood by the largest, Christ on Corcovado Peak by a door without a handle and a house telephone on a clear glass cube. Over it a printed proclamation: DIAL 400 AND WAIT. He obeyed and heard a badly played samba then a nasally 'Yes?'

'A friend of mine recommended the tables here,' Nick said loudly, drowning out the digital band.

'The name of your friend?'

Tell them Herr Norkus recommended the place; he's a big player in Hamburg, carries weight, Harry had told Nick. 'Herr Norkus,' Nick said without hesitation.

'Wait please,' advised the voice, the line going dead.

The eye of a closed-circuit camera picked up his scent. Body heat, infrared censors? The technology of control, and he'd no idea who was deciding how valid his claim to be a friend of Herr Norkus really was. One nice big smile; show off your remaining teeth they might be discussing how to knock down your throat. What cover did you *use* Sally? Our fifteen minutes of fame, two shadows in need of a home. When the door opened it let loose a fast Latin beat and a twenty-year old groomed to wear an evening suit he'd already outgrown. Clean shaven and smooth skinned, he walked stiffly as though a shotgun rubbed against his thigh.

'Herr Norkus is a valued member,' he declared, doubting if Nick ever would be.

'He said that I would enjoy your hospitality.'

'That is true,' he smiled but didn't appear happy. 'We are not one of Hamburg's most exclusive casinos, but confidentiality is our ultimate aim,' he said with gravitas, guiding Nick down steep carpeted stairs. How many people have had accidents here? Nick wondered, a nasty fall, a broken neck? Anything violent arranged within reason.

The attendant produced a registration card and looked bored by the routine, manoeuvring it aesthetically on a polished steel and smoked glass desk. Carefully he explained which lines should be filled in. When Nick had lied in ink signing himself as Herr Greiz, the attendant recited the menu of the casino which covered three levels. The first devoted to mini roulette, blackjack and baccarat, the second a cabaret show based on the Rio theme, the third an informal bar where guests if they so desired, could select a companion for the evening. He yawned while Nick decided.

Nick chose the bar as a starting point.

Curling in a crescent in a lighter shade of red, the bar surrounded a sunken dance floor that Nick crossed self-consciously, his back exposed to whoever he supposed had been told to watch him. A waitress pushed through the crowded tables; she wore no top, her small breasts shining in the house lights. Setting a paper roundel and a glass of champagne in front of him, one of her breasts brushed his left cheek.

'With the compliments of Herr Blümhof,' she smiled.

Was he being offered her or the drink? 'He is very generous.'

She shrugged, pouting moist crimson lips. 'He hopes that you enjoy your visit,' she added looking to the end of the bar.

'I will try my best.' Nick followed her gaze.

Short, light on his feet, Blümhof waved over with professional charm. He had a rugged angular face, his hair receding fast above his temples revealed a hint of grey and was immaculately cut. Dressed in a black suit, casual black shirt, his age was a mire of contradiction, though Nick guessed it being nothing above forty-six. He smiled as he walked away, a healer bestowing a cure on the shoulders of a worthy few with one light touch, making his way through a door marked 'Privat', which somehow signalled a CD to play, shaking couples onto the dance floor.

'Tell him thanks,' Nick said sipping the tepid champagne. 'I'd like someone to share my table.'

'You have a preference?' she asked, tired of smiling.

'Franziska, if she's available,' he said, wondering what sort of charms she possessed to unlock the money box. In ten minutes, Nick had a female friend, but it wasn't Franziska. Bubbly and eager for him to spend money, she'd grinned at the barman as she flounced over, her hips swinging playfully all the way. No, Sabine didn't know why Herr Blümhof was so magnanimous to him she laughed, leading him out for a dance. No, Sabine did not know why Franziska was not around. Sabine rubbed herself into his crotch but knew no other answers.

'Tell me about Blümhof?' Nick asked, back at his table refusing another dance.

'Me?' Sabine acted surprised at every question that came her way; a delaying gap to decide whether it was safe to continue. In her twenties, her long flowing Titian hair made her face seem too plain. She'd tried hard to lessen her stubby nose and dimples with foundation and blusher, but it had gone on too thick. This guy Greiz worried her, his attitude, those rugged looks. He belonged to a different group of men who never paid for her body.

'You worked for him long?' Nick missed his own glass out when he poured from a bottle of Spanish champagne Sabine insisted he order.

Sabine giggled, Greiz's serious eyes wouldn't let her rest. 'More than I should, but everyone's got to pay the rent,' she said dreamily, keeping time with the smoochy music.

'He treats you badly?'

'Hey, I didn't say that.'

'My mistake.'

'Fine, who's counting,' she said, carelessly resting his hand on one of her breasts. 'You do what makes you feel good in here. No one's going to say a word. We're all here for drinks and fun.' She sulked when Nick withdrew his hand.

'Get many important visitors?'

Souring her lips Sabine twisted a silver ring round her middle finger. It was fashioned in a belt complete with buckle, and he wondered if it symbolised possession? Of her or someone else?

'We have reserved private areas if you really want to be alone,' she said, raising his glass to his lips. 'No one ever forgets Sabine,' she added, her bare shoulders swaying to the beat.

How many other faces does she own? The voices? The gestures copied from films? He pushed the glass away and she brought out childish shock; a badly made veil fluttering briefly on her face.

'How about visitors who have to be given special treatment?'

Breaking rhythm with the sensuous music she shook her head, topped up her glass to overflowing. She had a sudden relish to get off the table and put some distance between her and this stern Greiz. Impressive looks but too forward in all the wrong departments. She needed a real boost, something to help her relax not cheap champagne.

'Don't talk like that,' she laughed, playfully reaching down and stroking his inner thigh.

Gripping her wrist, Nick dumped her hand back on the table and clamped it there. 'Have you provided any special services?'

She smiled and he had no way of telling if she meant it for real.

'Why don't you forget about this? Let's dance again, drink, get to know each other? No big deal is it? Why worry what others get up to? Relax, enjoy this while you're here, let tomorrow take care of what it can.'

'Is there a place these important guests go?' Nick asked, drawing her near feeling her fear, her resistance. 'What about Franziska, why is *she* so special.

You know Franziska?'

She rubbed her bare arms suddenly cold. Glancing past him along the bar she looked for help or a command; all she got was a slow song that trembled across the floor bringing more groping couples out of their secluded midnight booths.

'You ask too many damn questions, know that? Sure, we have VIPs here. I don't get asked if I object. Maybe they spend all their time on the tables, maybe they're making eyes at different girls. Think I keep a record? You want me or not?'

And while we're engaged Blümhof will be making his checks.

Nick laughed and squeezed her arm tighter.

'Is it Franziska who provides the special treatment?'

Pitching back the contents of her glass, Sabine poured another, not needing to look when to stop.

'If anyone asks, wants to know, I tell them you're not interested in me, changed your mind. Moody, talked too much, got a turn off at the start, your wife and kids got in the way. You married? Got kids?'

'No.'

'Doesn't matter, we'll say your family's the reason. I do this for free okay. Now go, straight out, don't think of coming back. You trouble for sure. Me? I'm making a living and like my face the way it is. Go, walk out like I'm not the last girl in the world. Go, don't even bother to smile back. Maybe I see you when I've finished here. After three, in Bar Z up the street. Maybe I won't.'

A few couples were dancing to a livelier tune when Nick walked through them, erotic promises and grim determination binding them together. On the stairs the young attendant in his badly fitting suit stood reverently to one side, allowing him to pass, no body contact, no force. He guessed those came at a price too.

•••

Bar Z never closed. An oak clad cellar long and dowdy, it bore the scars from satisfying primal requests, its battered easiness accommodated changing moods; for those who wanted to get drunk, or those who just wanted to talk. The colour scheme was neutral brown applied to walls, ceiling and floor. Bench seats and solid pine tables were laid in rows, Nick opting for a spot by the kitchen, next to double swing doors that wafted in the smell of disinfectant every time a waiter sprang through. A coffee machine gargled on the counter, in the corner a Wurlitzer played love songs and forgotten popular hits from CDs. Romantic he thought, drinking his beer. Sabine arrived at three-thirty, her red hair tucked up in a cowl. She grinned at the barman and walked over to Nick, her hips still provocatively swung. In a patch of candlelight from the wooden chandelier over their table her make-up had a worn jaded sheen.

'Changed your mind about some pleasure?' she asked, coyly unhooking the cowl from her hair, throwing out handfuls of curls to dry in the bar's appetising breeze.

'No.'

'That's sad, a real waste for you...for me. Suppose you're the type who want to put the world back on course.' She lit a cigarette with a capricious movement of her hands, the smoke finding its way down through her nostrils. Her eyes jumped every time the door up to the street opened.

'Waiting for someone?'

'Someone with a million and a place in the sun.' She smoked hard, nicotine a replacement for joints, cannabis a halfway house from the serious space powder she'd used to satisfy her craving; crystal transport to keep her mind fuzzy and warm. 'Herr Blümhof knew you were going to visit.' She held her breath, anarchy in her pale eyes, taking him in as a waiter brought over a vodka she drank as a habit. She went for a drink and her hand shook fiercely. 'Blümhof's not such a proto guy, okay, unique as a complete shit. I can talk here, understand?' she explained, her glass hitting the table with a thud.

Nodding Nick admitted that he did, leaving Sabine adequate space to fill.

'I've been clean for six weeks, got myself a place lined up at a refuge.'

Two girls danced together in a centre aisle, blonde and brunette their heads laid on each other's bare shoulders, their high stilettos scuffing to a country and western ballad.

'Franziska?'

'Sure, I know Franziska.'

Tipping back the vodka, she called for another with a vicious wave.

'My best ex-best friend, see. We cried and loved together from a long time ago. A complete friend okay, personally speaking. Crazy, always giving it breath on how she was going to be different. Earn for a year or two, then find the right Prince Charming to settle down with and have kids. Fantasy, nightmare, rubbish between her ears.' She took the fresh vodka off the waiter's tray and took a hard pull.

'She the one who offers special services for important clients?' he asked, estimating how long before the vodka took her out of his reach.

'Who knows,' she said shrugging. 'Maybe, maybe not.'

He was pushing and she was retreating; the harder he advanced the deeper she dug down into her own cocoon. He sipped his beer and got a taint of lipstick from the rim of the glass.

'What's so special about her?' He dropped his tone, aware of the danger of boxing her in, the fear of rejection.

'Franziska, boy was she a chosen one, real VIP golden girl. Franziska, one lucky lady, found her Prince Charming when Blümhof claimed her as his own, but she too dumb to see Blümhof's nothing but her pimp. She worked the same shift as me, and we used to make a team for exclusive VIP work. I was just there to make the pre-party go with a swing. Blümhof has this Russian guy who has to have the star treatment. Anything he asks for is given, no questions, some of it the usual stuff, some pretty crude. I was the warm-up, Franziska the main act.'

'Tell me about the Russian?'

'Regular stinking pig. Sergei Gorshov and Blümhof's crawling all over him, his personal chaperon, gives him guided walks through the Brazillia, letting this pig choose who he wants. Always bragging how he's a big international entrepreneur, got interests in SDF Shipping or something. Hope the pig drowns.'

Which explained the monthly trips made by Buscott he thought. *Decent runs to Hamburg to pick up the goods*, the chauffeur had revealed, but it wasn't just provisions for Sergei's local stores, Nick reasoned; it would be cash for the upkeep of important assets and the other essentials required for spying.

The two girls stopped dancing before the record played out. Back at their table they accused a Korean girl of taking a purse from one of their bags, spitting and hissing she got up to leave when the brunette drew a flick knife. In one slow pass the brunette left a bloody line down the Korean girl's face, only Nick appeared to notice.

'Any idea why he got the special attention? Sergei someone Blümhof respects? Must be a reason?'

'Reason this, Sergei that. You got some fix on him?' She turned up her nose and drained her glass. She knew she was beyond help. Blümhof's rehearsed lines and coaching seemed to be days ago, all forgotten, not used. Maybe now he would finally bust her nose for talking out of turn. What could she do? Greiz was too much to resist, he had a way of making you want to confess, and she wanted very much to let it all out.

'What makes someone like Blümhof respect Sergei so much?' he persisted, competing with the drink to win her over.

'Blümhof enjoys living and Sergei can put a stop to that any damn time he likes. Someone said he represents investors in Blümhof's business from the early days, I can't remember, okay. All I know is Sergei has to have all the care. Best champagne, finest girls. Sergei is important, number one guy. Blümhof takes care of Sergei's interests, Blümhof just does what he's told.' She pointed her finger and pulled an imaginary trigger. 'They got a fabulous arrangement okay. Blümhof and Sergei. They buy and sell girls, they buy and sell things you'd pay a damn fortune for.' Wary, confused, she pulled clear of the table. She called for another vodka her voice shrill.

'And Franziska is Sergei's favourite?'

'Not me, okay, I wouldn't want that pig around me again. My best ever friend Franziska, Blümhof's number one, okay,' she said with a laugh, draining her glass. She yelled again for a refill and the bar stopped to listen. 'Sergei is Franziska's one big lover, okay. You're mixing with the wolves Greiz, know that,' she said.

'When does Franziska meet him?'

'Slow up, okay,' she warned, lighting a cigarette, her hand swiping the match off the box in a crooked swoop.

'You see a lot of Franziska?' he asked, desperate to swing her over the last hurdle before she disintegrated totally.

'That's a pretty dumb question Greiz. I seen her without clothes all the time okay. A double act, two beauties and Sergei the beast, ugly like a horse, stinks like a pig. The best two around, that's how Franziska and me used to be.'

'So, she's not your friend any longer?'

'Who cares? She's Sergei's big lover and she's going to make every day sweet. Blümhof takes care of her. Same message okay. Sergei is special, special, special. Blümhof is a regular creep, okay and I didn't tell you that,' she giggled, way out of Blümhof's control. 'He makes special arrangements, got himself somewhere private for his VIPs and Sergei. Franziska's not dumb okay, she's banked something special for the future, something to make us all happy. I got a part in helping her make it happen, she got a crazy deal arranged, but it's all top secret,' she disclosed with an elaborate wink.

'Those her words?' Nick asked, as casually as he dared.

Sabine shrugged swaying her head, rolling it from shoulder to shoulder in jerky nervous movements.

'Second-hand, but sure, they're hers,' she said, the vodka bright in her eyes.

'Blümhof has other business interests?'

'You're too much,' Sabine told him, with a lopsided smile. 'I shouldn't be talking to you,' she said, the sadness weighing on her shoulders.

'You were threatened?'

'No kidding, Greiz. Tolz told me, okay. Tolz works for Blümhof, thinks he's my boyfriend, okay, but he's still a creep.'

'Where does Franziska entertain her VIPs?'

'Who knows,' said Sabine with a mighty shrug. 'Some place outside town.'

'Has it got an address?'

'Don't get so hot, Greiz, you hear? Maybe Sergei tells Blümhof to take care of you also.' She growled and clawed at him, pretending to be a tiger.

'Is that what Tolz said?'

Humming with her eyes closed, Sabine tapped her fingers on the tabletop stained by years of good drinking. Nick roughly took her wrist and shook her eyes open.

'I don't remember, but they expected you to call,' Sabine said sleepily. 'Tolz...Blümhof... Sergei, they bad men you don't want to get behind you. Who's counting, who cares? You a bad man too, Greiz? You sure you're a friend I can trust?'

He nodded his head not wanting to break her course, waiting with all his patience for her to resume. He even called over more vodka, lit a cigarette and put it between her sagging lips. Alone or in pairs the other girls drifted out, making for their own solitary beds.

'Can you find Franziska for me?'

'Who cares. I'm tired, dead on my feet, another night to get through. I got clients to please. I smile, do the tricks and get paid a cut okay, believe me, that's just fine.'

'Meet me again if you get some news, anywhere, you choose.'

'Jesus, Greiz, you're asking for too much. Franziska, my best friend, here one day and then puff, she's gone. Enough, okay,' she caught herself and seemed to sober. 'Right now, I need my bed and beauty sleep. Sorry hero, that means alone,' she said, putting her hand on his chest. 'Don't get me wrong, I'd like to have you share, but not right now.' Halfway to her feet Sabine paused, dumped herself back down. She took an empty cigarette pack out of the ashtray and blew away the ash. 'Last I heard, this is where my best friend ever met Sergei and her VIP clients,' she said, head down writing, the stiff dark roots of her hair standing out. 'I do this because you're a good guy, okay, I can tell.'

Cramming her hair into the cowl Sabine swayed to the door, gave her favourite waiter a long kiss on his cheek and turned to wave.

'I never told you my number?' he called. As he went after Sabine her waiter collided with Nick at the bottom of the stairs, upsetting a full tray of drinks. Rushing over, a companion joined him, fussing over Nick, blocking him in. There were apologies, many smiles and the offer of a beer on the house from the barman, which Nick politely declined. When he got outside Sabine had a start that he'd never be able to make up. He stood on the step, tearing cellophane off a new pack of cigarettes. Left, or right? Knowing that neither might take him to Sabine and perhaps no route ever would.

By himself on the empty street, Nick's footsteps hammered sharp solitary blows on the cobbles. On a hoarding, a hand had scrawled 'Uli is a Cheat!' Aren't we all he decided, we deceive ourselves from the moment we are born and leave nothing but a trail of broken promises.

Twenty-Three

Before Petra arrived the next morning Nick had washed, shaved and made a cup of coffee that he never quite finished. After setting the shop's alarm he set off guided by Sabine's directions on the back of the cigarette pack, taking a slow train out of Hamburg. The day languid, frozen to its core with low ruffles of mist locked close to the land as copses and farms lumbered into view, stage props appearing through dry ice; Deep Purple, Led Zeppelin, Pink Floyd live on tour, concerts in his head. A journey without an end. The name of a station gracefully slid into view announcing his stop, he checked Sabine's looping writing, Rendsburg; snap, I've won.

Following Sabine's route Nick tramped off into a snowy cluster of khaki brick streets topped by furnace red tiles, a setting for fairy tales or lies. He wished that he'd eaten and never bothered to come. One by one the houses were left in Nick's wake as he shuffled out of town towards the shadows of an enchanted forest where Franziska held a key for Lubov's treasure. The farm crept out of a rise at the end of a beaten track, its bright stepped gables a stairway into the low clouds. A sign severely declared that *Bauernhof am Seeufer* was private property and visitors were not welcome. He walked up the centre of the track between deep tyre ruts partly filled by snow. Downstairs the windows on the main house and its two wings were shuttered by wood panels decorated with fretwork hearts. No one answered him at the front door, so he trudged off looking for another way in, along an icy path wrapping itself round the house, entering an open yard where a solid barn blocked out the watery light. Under its eaves an old woman perched as tight as a rook, a cane shopping basket by her bootees.

'There's no one here.' She made no movement, a small dark dummy with a headscarf to protect her from the wind.

'I'm looking for Franziska.' Nick had to shout over the yard, but she refused to acknowledge him with her eyes. She spat into the earth at her feet, her hands creased like brown oilskin found each other and lay in a truce in her lap.

'A whore, a waste of time.' She cleared her chest and throat, spitting out a solid deposit into the wind. 'Sometimes they keep me waiting 'till the afternoon before they arrive. Three kilometres here, three back. I tell Karl it is too far for what they pay. Everyday picking up their filth, see things I shouldn't. Don't I have enough cleaning at home? Now the idle fool Karl will not know to pick me up.' Slapping her arthritic hips, she rose and turned for home, clutching her basket as she made off down the path.

From the barn Nick brought a clay spade, inserting its edge between the door and surround. A pain surged through his chest as he pulled back on the handle, more pressure than his ribs could stand. The wood splintered with a pistol shot crack, fading to an echo that mixed with the snow stirring in the trees; breaking cover herons flapped across a hard slate-grey sky.

A kitchen that had entertained both sides during the war came to attention when he flipped on a light, reclaiming it from its shuttered dusk. Arranged at its centre a table long enough to seat a dozen officers, its ivy leaf tablecloth cluttered by wine bottles, glasses, plates and cups not cleared from a last supper. With no means of defence except his senses, Nick started on the stairs, making cautious progress into the morning light producing gobbets of weak colour through an open landing window, a silk curtain inching and dancing in the draft. He stood and listened distrusting his ears; sound, someone talking. Nick stayed by the walls creeping along, pausing at each varnished door, the air stuffy with cigarette smoke from hours before. He stopped; he had the door, inside a male voice deep and serious. Nick bundled himself in.

On a chest of drawers, a television featuring a young bearded academic lecturing fervently on mediaeval pilgrimages to holy shrines. The other details he saw in no precise order; an oak wardrobe, tallboy and bedside locker, an odd leather glove on the varnished floorboards along with the contents of an imitation crocodile vanity case; lipsticks, eyeliners and powder. A couple of easy chairs piled with glossy magazines, a pack of condoms and box of tissues. And lastly a double bed and king size duvet in a dreamy blue; a fabric sky complete with fluffy clouds matching pillows and a family of cuddly bunnies sitting playfully around.

Wrapped in this but no luxury package, Sabine still in the clothes she'd worn in Bar Z. Her hair was plastered on her forehead and her eyes flopped around trying to focus. She had everything death promised in her face, the creases and pallor of an overdose victim. Every breath surged in forced unnatural draws, a rasping that he couldn't bear. She had rolled from her back onto her side and her fingers in their desperation to escape what her body suffered, had opened a seam on the duvet.

A sprinkling of feathers trickled down to the floor partly covering a syringe, spoon, leather belt, plastic lemon and disposable lighter. Nick was no expert but guessed that she'd been fed her final fix; a hot shot, not cut with talc or bicarbonate of soda, but a mix so pure it packed a hundred per cent hit she would never forget; her head in the clouds for evermore.

'Sabine,' he sat on a corner of the bed and his weight caused her damp body to roll into him. 'Can you hear me?' Avoiding her red panda eyes, he put his hand on her forehead, the skin grey and thin. She was cold and sent a shiver up Nick's arm. Brushing away lank strands of hair, he tenderly stroked her brow as he would have done for Angie or Tom. Soothing, calming her as the gasps for air lasted longer, becoming spasms and finally stopped with a dry frightening bark. He hadn't been there for his mother's death and Tom's; now he'd shared another, as though someone decided that he shouldn't have missed out on the anger and guilt. Kicked under the bed Sabine's purse, a sturdy leather model that held a driver's licence, ID, loose change, thirty euros in notes and a tatty slip of paper folded and opened many times bearing the message: 'Anke Numa,' in a neat flowing hand.

He turned off the television and took one final look at Sabine and thought dear old little Lubov, what have you got me into? Outside he lit a cigarette his hands trembling, not from fear but anger, then he followed a different route through Rendsburg for good measure, feeling utter dismay as he tried to forget Sabine's dying breath.

By mid-afternoon Nick had arrived back in Hamburg the sleet slowly turning to snow, thick flakes that thudded against the train windows as powdery as moths. Nick sought out a cheap hotel, finally finding one at the top of a dismal alley off Lange Reihe in Sankt Georg. It stood at the back of the main tracks into the Hauptbahnhof and didn't have any views. Cobbled and narrow the alley tapered off into a run of tenements where the evening never fully withdrew, where broken and forgotten bodies slipped in and out of flaking doorways in search of their next fix. The hotel's walls were liberally coated in graffiti, its iron balustrades on the balconies were chipped, their rusting bars sunk into the stone staining it where they touched.

Avoiding the pimp who had a permanent corner in the reception, Nick wove around club chairs and palms that must have been freshly potted when the railway was a mere drawing on an engineer's desk. A clerk in a faded suit appeared when he hammered a quaint brass bell. We've gone backwards through time he thought. I haven't arrived in modern Hamburg, but Hamburg in the Fifties, the sort of port where my father would come ashore for a tryst with one of his young acrobatic lovers because he believed young foreign women had better orgasms; tarts on a braided naval arm.

'There is only our best suite remaining, Herr Greiz,' said the desk clerk, a fabricated smile on his lips. He could have been sixty, a dry dusty relic in a hotel functioning as a brothel. He touched the tip of his moustache, his manicured fingers as smooth in rhythm as a pianist's.

Nick paid for three nights and the suite turned out to be nothing better than a double. Dismal and dark, there was a tangy aroma from its last guest. How long since it had been cleaned was hard to tell, but Nick was determined he'd only sleep on top of the bed and its stained duvet. Dropping his small bag of provisions he'd bought on his return to the city, he abruptly turned his back on his suite. Reaching up to set a telltale on the door, a rib not fully healed sent a stabbing pain across his lower abdomen. Black and red filters altered his vision, a fusion of colour that lasted for two blocks, hardly able to get his breath until the ache in his chest started to wear off. Clouds loured over the rooftops and emptied thick sleet over the port, adding yet another misery to the passing cold faces.

When he returned to Petra's shop it was almost six. She greeted him with a curse for staying out so long, providing a coffee laced with cognac. Then she set about checking he wasn't in any more pain, had he looked after himself, not exerted himself, not felt faint or dizzy; questions he wanted to ignore, pretend weren't for him, wished he'd never mentioned the injuries he'd received in Moscow.

'I'm fine Petra, honestly,' he said. 'Listen, I've found a hotel, it's better you stay clear of me,' he said, not daring a glance in her direction.

'You even think of that and I will lock the door and throw away the key,' she threatened him, her mood ugly.

'Okay, you win,' said Nick, backing down, knowing his mind was all made up, accepting more cognac although the coffee was nothing but a ring in his cup.

'That's damn right, I win,' said Petra, capping the bottle. 'Tomorrow we make some rules.'

'Just what I need.'

'Tomorrow, first thing.'

'Any thoughts on who or what that means?' he asked, passing across the slip of paper from Sabine's purse.

A little self-consciously she pulled on a pair of reading glasses, the arms a funky green. 'This I suggest is a reference to the Numa Theatre. It is a cooperative. And Anke must be connected to it. Problem solved,' she declared, removing her glasses. Then gently scalded him as a dunce for assuming such a mystery could not be solved by someone with Petra's intimate knowledge of the Hanseatic city.

'Okay, so now I leave, or Hans will forget who I am,' she avowed with a theatrical laugh, but her eyes revealed the despair. '*Tschüss.*'

Nick watched her go, her trim figure slaloming through the shop, a hanging bell fastened to the shop's door by a brass bracket tinkling as she left, Petra looking back at him as she closed the door behind her. He gave her ten minutes, set the alarm and slipped out of the shop for the last time. Browsing in windows that he used as rear-view mirrors he sampled prices and faces, checking his back was clean; until in a toy shop painted as bright as a kite, a face appeared once too often. This one of yours Blümhof is it? Moscow maybe, come to finish what they started? He was dressed in a black padded jacket, a beanie pulled down just above his thick eyebrows, and from the way he passed on Nick's movements through his personal coms set, he had back-up not very far away. Too professional for one of Jack Balgrey's irregular footpads Nick decided. And if it's not Jack's or Moscow's, it was someone sending a greeting, letting me know I'm on their turf. But for now, the footpad was solo, a tram length between them and closing.

Ducking into the underground station on Königstraße Nick's return ticket to Bergedorf felt sticky in his hand, the destination was the first button he'd punched on the machine. Warm bodies crowded along the island platform and the footpad came up behind him. Approaching from Hamburg-Central a train decreased speed providing Nick's cue; turning in a fast arc Nick hit the footpad hard in the chest slamming him into his outstretched leg. As the footpad hit the dark tiled platform Nick swooped, his knee pressed into the footpad's chest. 'Thief! Robber!' Nick yelled, pinning the footpad down. A crowd gathered jostling for a better view of a citizen finally making a stand. 'Hold him for me,' Nick ordered a portly white-haired traveller in denim shirt, denim jeans, and leather fisherman's waistcoat. 'Hold him while I get my things,' insisted Nick. Not tempted to refuse Nick's brusque command, the traveller sat on the footpad's chest as Nick threaded his way through the crowd. Slipping through an exit Nick sprinted up and out of the station.

On Königstraße Nick walked against the flow of heavy traffic, mostly trucks meandering towards the port for midnight sailings. The van, an unmarked VW came from nowhere, coming to a stop in front of him. Nick checked over his shoulder as a second VW, this one a SUV pulled up close behind. A single command barked at Nick insisting he should halt. And with the order, he recognised the trained tone suggesting they may not be police, but local spooks, and very probably armed. Aware he was outnumbered he complied, raising his arms away from his side as show of his good intentions. They were young with remarkably seasoned faces, their leather jackets glistening in the passing headlights as they patted him down. While one stood clear of Nick, his colleague opened the rear door.

'Please, Herr Torr, you will come with us,' he said with a tidy smile. 'You are invited to a conference,' he added, gripping Nick firmly by the arm.

The skaters had gone home, and his minders kept Nick between them, walking along a path on the lip of the park's ice rink; around them bare oak and beeches shuffled their branches in the wind. A walkway running out into the centre of the rink had a timekeeper's box skewered into the ice by a single metal shaft. As they escorted Nick towards the rink, their holsters chafed against the inside of their jackets. Reaching the walkway, they stopped, one of them directing Nick forward as though he were about to cross a major road.

'Please, Herr Torr.' And with a firm but unceremonious hand, started Nick down the concrete aisle, a groom without a bride.

'Well, isn't this just a great place for an informal chat?' Jack Balgrey met him, his face red, his cheeks blown out, Jack a spectre that would not let him rest. In the doorway to the box a figure too slight for the night watched them, as though they were playing out a scene for his benefit alone. Balgrey tucked his scarf round his neck and adjusted his stance.

'You should have made it more obvious, Jack,' said Nick, falling in step. 'You could have taken a full page in the local paper or organised a civic reception.' Jack Balgrey, a jaded regular SIS officer winding down his career. Jack a seasoned hand with a stain on his record for having an attitude and a fondness for booze.

Balgrey swung on his heels, his gauche face as heavy as a hammer; his flat nose flared and his eyes had long ago run out of sparkle, his hair thick and speared with grey ended in a natural quiff.

'We don't want to be falling out in front of our host,' he hissed, leaning forward, his face close, alcohol and recent garlic on his breath. 'Just be bloody grateful that I'm here to hold your hand. It's a damn sight more than you deserve after what you did to their boy.'

Stocky and plump he had one of those faces Nick had often drunk with in the Riyadh Hyatt Hotel or a Hong Kong bar; a well-travelled company rep, a boring companion for a long hot expatriate night endlessly bragging of tax fiddles and tales of how to beat the local boys.

'You've saved me again, Jack, pretty soon I won't have a life to call my own.'

'Cut out the funnies, you're well in it and I can only do so much. Now come on and say hello to this nice man who has come all the way from Cologne to meet you. Isn't that an honour?'

Jack's friend from the German internal security service, the Bundesamt für Verfassungsschutz, the BfV, stepped out to meet them. A wafer of a man with an unspoilt face and small intense eyes, he wore practical clothes for the season; a fastidious observer of tradition. he was in his early forties with an overcoat that didn't come off the peg. A mendicant air to him Nick thought, and this is your monk isn't it Jack, your very own confessor.

'Herr Döbeln,' began Balgrey with impressive formality, 'this is...'

'Thank you, I am aware,' said Döbeln, abruptly. Perhaps to make up for this curious style he offered Nick his hand, swinging it out stiffly from the shoulder in one graceless leaden arc, his palm very soft and damp.

'I forgot to ask permission for operating on your patch, sorry,' Nick said without meaning a word.

'That is not the issue,' he replied, a handkerchief swiped firmly across his nose. He had a peculiar stillness to his voice, while his eyes roamed nervously unable to rest.

'Why not speak your mind?' suggested Nick affably, sensing Jack's displeasure, nonetheless.

'Very well,' agreed Döbeln, pocketing his handkerchief. 'What concerns my senior colleagues and myself, is the impact that your hostile actions will have.'

Unimpressed, Nick looked across the rink, engrossed by something far away.

'What terms are you interested in?'

'You flatter yourself,' said Döbeln raising a trite smile, removing his glasses, bending back the crook to obtain a snugger fit. 'You are not in a position to make offers.'

'Why?'

'Be reasonable, there's concern in certain quarters that's all,' Balgrey assured him. 'No one's ruling out cooperation,' he said, fidgeting with his feet.

'This is correct,' Döbeln said very quietly. 'If we were only interested in arresting you, this I could have achieved already. You prefer that I should continue?' he wondered smoothing down his short hair.

'We all have ideals, for Christ's sake. Sometimes we've just to modify them a touch. Let a bit of reality see the light of day, remind us where we're going,' Balgrey urged.

'Thanks for the backing Jack. I'll do you a favour sometime, remind you how it feels to have friends.'

From somewhere out in the port or the river, a large ship blasted a leaving or an inward greeting on its siren; a deep bass echoing boom unfolding in the night.

'It is sensible advice,' confided Döbeln with too much effort.

'And what is the reality?' demanded Nick, squaring up to Döbeln, 'is that open for negotiation?'

Döbeln paused, deliberately concentrating on the precise movement of staring Nick in the eye.

'You can be deported,' he proposed. 'A very simple procedure.'

'That would make me really angry, and you don't want that.'

'Think about it,' urged Balgrey, turning in a circle and slapping his gloves together to fend off the cold. 'We don't need to upset friends,' he added, passing them on his tight circuit.

'If I don't agree?' asked Nick as though this was a natural conclusion.

'Arrest and deportation on the grounds of a threat to national security,' said Döbeln with sad finality, plunging his hands back into his overcoat pockets. 'That will create a difficult scenario for Berlin and London to resolve.'

'What *are* the terms?' he asked almost too dispirited to care.

'In Cologne we have suffered also, as your Service has suffered in the past. From weakness, from poor morale, from betrayal also,' began Döbeln and Nick was struck by the conciliatory tones that only come with rehearsal. 'Our problem is heightened by the future, how we respond to the friction inside Europe which inevitably governs Germany's wider relationships. Allegiances with former enemies is easy to preach, but difficult to pay for. Your findings, your conclusions are to be shared with Berlin and Washington.'

'No.'

'This is not an offer, but a condition. Any cooperation we provide will, of course, require deniability. You should go carefully.'

'You get more bargaining power to support Berlin's realignment in European foreign policy?' said Nick, shaking his head. 'Germany striking under the table deals, forming its own special relationship with Washington, that's very naughty. Paris is going to be mightily upset.'

'This is non-negotiable,' Döbeln warned. 'Requests should be made through Herr Balgrey. Now, if you will excuse me, I have other business.' With a slight nod Döbeln set off down the walkway.

'This is absurd, Jack, just too much.' Nick threw off Balgrey's arm, going after Döbeln.

Filling the exit, a BfV operative barred his way, one hand poised level his holster. Out of breath, Balgrey landed at Nick's side.

'Give it some thought,' he said pulling for air. 'What's the big problem with sharing all of a sudden? Don't we have room to barter? Don't we need friends anymore?'

'Mine are dead, Jack, what's your excuse?' said Nick in a fury. 'You're as bad as Head Office now get off my back.'

'And you're the bloody saint, aren't you? You and your pious cause of doing what's right. You share, you hear. There's no failure in that for Christ's sake.'

Two kids on skateboards came around a path at speed, saw the gathering and changed their minds about going onto the ice without even bothering to stop.

'Who tipped them off, Jack?' demanded Nick. 'Who put Cologne on my tail?'

'The Cousins, who else,' said Balgrey. 'Head Office have been bleating for me to hit the panic button if you showed your face. But I thought I'd give you some distance, what with your wife being caught up in it.'

'That's very decent of you Jack.'

'Look, once London turned our product gathering into a manic obsession with suicide bombers, the Cousins stepped in. As of now, they're Cologne's new best friend. You know how they operate?'

Nick certainly did, and he knew that Harry Bransk was always seeking out avenues to exploit, a merchant who peddled information for pure profit.

'The Cousins are trying to have me run me out of town, that it, Jack?' said Nick, for the first time hearing the traffic; movement without shape, a constant mechanical song hardly ever-changing pitch.

'Cologne are playing it both ways.'

'Maybe I'll just ignore their offer, sod Head Office too, do it on my own.'

'Let's not push at the same button, we could end up with a lot of trouble.'

'Can't have trouble can we Jack?'

'Not at my age.' Jack mulled over a point for a second or two, then ventured a question: 'Know anyone called Franziska?'

'Why?'

'The name's come up in a couple of conversations, all of 'em connected to Wynn.'

'Never heard of a Franziska,' said Nick.

'No worries,' said Balgrey, tucking in his scarf.

'Just one thing, Jack?' Nick asked ready to leave. 'Head Office's request for you to report if I showed up? Who was behind that, do you know?'

'That would be telling, wouldn't it?'

'Secrets, Jack, they'll be the death of you.'

'Of us all, old son, of us all.'

But Nick never replied, pounding solemnly away, the snow gently starting to fall once more.

Twenty-Four

The Numa Theatre was not one of Hamburg's most celebrated venues as it lay so far off the beaten track, in a part of the city Nick's father would have described as bohemian; a refuge for anarchists and those groups of a similar persuasion who refused to swim in the mainstream. Beside double sheet steel doors a woman in her thirties was waist deep in the engine compartment of a clapped-out bus.

'Anke?' Nick asked, taking shelter from the driving snow behind the propped bonnet.

Barely noticing Nick or the weather, the woman grunted at a rounded nut, her spanner continually slipping off. Her faded military overalls were a bottle green, soaked by the snow. Dropping the spanner in the toolbox at her feet, the woman straightened out. Her hair dyed purple was tucked under a beret, and she wore it at a chirpy angle, its crown coated by snowflakes, and for a second before they dissolved gave her the pasty head of a clown.

'Cop?'

'No.'

'Then tell?'

'I need to speak with Anke, it's private. This *is* the Numa?'

'What's left of it,' she said, wiping an oil streak off her nose with a frayed sleeve. 'The place is dropping around us. No safety certificate, no performing licence, no one coming through the front door.' She offered a chesty laugh. 'We owe you money too?' she demanded sharply.

Nick humbly shook his head. 'Where's Anke?'

'Who wants to know?'

'A friend of Sabine's.'

Not certain what sort of friend Nick could be, the woman nodded. 'Go around the side to the blue door, up the steps, watch for the floor, down the corridor and ask for Anke.'

'Thanks.'

But Nick received no reply. The woman, back in the engine, this time armed with a smaller spanner, set about the nut cursing it to the end of the world and back.

The blue door sagged forlornly on its hinges supported by a mop bucket. In a vehement Gothic burst, someone had taken the trouble to write STAGE DOOR, and next to it a poster announced dates in different cities for the theatre group, though half of their forthcoming tour was already cancelled.

Inside, the stale air was full of sound that seeped out from the theatre's guts, and from a radio playing far away, Nick could just pick out Hendrix's *All Along the Watchtower*. At the end of a whitewashed brick corridor damp and cold, tiny bulbs burned dimly, lighting his way to a backstage area, veins of calcified wire tacked unevenly along the bricks. Half-eaten by shadow, a woman in a German Army parka had her back to him, doubled over a wicker basket tugging and cursing, straining at the task.

'Anke?'

She sucked in a mouthful of air and spun round.

'What's it to you?' she spat, pushing by him to yell down the corridor. 'Saskia, do you hear me? you good for nothing slacker. Saskia, you'd better have that lighting gantry down and stored and start on these baskets. I'm not breaking my back for you. Saskia... Saskia, you hear me?'

A cloudy reply came from somewhere in the gloom and she shook her head in disgust. She was in her thirties with long auburn hair and a plain tired face, unremarkable but for its hardness.

'So,' she said swinging past him. 'I'm still waiting?'

'I'm trying to get some information on Sabine. I think she came here for help, she told me she had a place arranged in a refuge. You are Anke?'

'I'm Anke and this is the first step to a refuge, well one aspect of it. The girls come here expecting confidentiality and that's what they get. I'm busy, you'll have to find your own way out.'

With a flick of her head she climbed over the basket leaving Nick no option but to follow.

'Wrong way,' she said, removing costumes from twisted rails with one hand, the other dropping them into a basket.

'Sabine's dead, an overdose,' Nick said. 'And someone else made sure she received the fatal shot.'

'Shit, no way.' She sat heavily on a backless chair and her upturned face had a startling clarity. 'Christ… I mean. Hey, Kerstin, you there?' she called to a thin shadow at the end of the corridor. 'Go find Margitta, tell her it's urgent.'

They shared a moment of reflection together. Nick and Anke, a woman he barely knew; as though Sabine was their best friend, someone they'd known for a lifetime at least.

'She *did* come here for help?' Nick wondered.

'Sure, she was here. We got to know her pretty well. I don't know the date. We get so many coming here for their last chance. Most of the women are sex workers, strippers, showgirls, this place allows them to get involved with drama as a form of therapy,' Anke explained. 'Did,' she added. 'They do workshops here in their spare time and when they think they're ready, move on to a hostel where their pimps and dealers can't touch them. If they're desperate, scared or in danger, they sometimes sleep here.'

'And Sabine stayed here?'

'Who are you anyhow?' Anke asked, as though it was an issue she should have dealt with sooner than later.

'Someone interested in why Sabine died,' Nick said.

Without revealing what she made of him, Anke took a tobacco tin from a pocket in her bib and braces and set about rolling a cigarette with slim fingers that had no colour, each nail bitten square. She struck a match, touched the paper until it flared as the flame hit the seam of tobacco.

'You didn't like her?'

Anke took a long drag, her brown eyes unblinking, scanned Nick's face all the while.

'Sabine was Sabine, I don't have to like everyone,' she explained, the rancour twisting her lip.

Nick watched Anke give a benign smile as if this information was something she preferred not to share.

'She was lost,' put in a sharp voice from behind them.

'Margitta,' Anke called, but Margitta dragged away the basket and Nick concentrated on Sabine.

'You don't think she had the nerve to leave the Brazillia?' he asked, wondering if she might have made it to the refuge if Nick hadn't crossed her path.

'We all lack courage,' said Anke. 'Look at us here. We've all been together a lot longer than we'd like to think, idealists who want to escape. We're not exemplary citizens.'

'Did she ever talk about herself?'

Anke trapped the cigarette between her fingers, took one last draw and put it out with her heel.

'You mean how that caring family of hers threw her out? How she began working as a prostitute at fifteen? Yes, she talked about that in some of her lucid moments.'

'What about her boyfriend?'

Abruptly she rose to her feet, her expression wary, her fists clenched tight pressed rigidly to her sides.

'Just who the fuck are you?' she snapped. 'You ask a lot of pretty sharp questions. You ask them, you ask them...'

'In a very professional style,' offered Margitta's cutting voice. Barely out of her twenties, her head rested languidly on a cast iron pillar; a symbolic display of confidence or a posed piece of performance kept as evidence of a creative soul.

'Meet Margitta,' said Anke. 'Our sometime artistic director, our inspiration, our biggest bore.'

'And our mysterious visitor is who?' she asked with a sneer. 'What is it *you* do? Ah, you never told Babette outside, did you?'

'She never asked, and I seriously haven't time or the goodwill to explain,' stated Nick. And to prove it he locked eyes with Margitta.

Assessing Nick's mood, Margitta batted away any lingering protests she harboured, a woman not used to inconvenience or unnecessary and insignificant distractions. 'What has poor little Sabine done this time?' she asked with a brilliant smile, spreading her arms in a mock stage display of horror.

'She died and she didn't have a choice.'

It was hard for Nick to tell if Margitta's flinch, her sudden movement, was shock at an unforeseen loss or an actor disguising another reason why Sabine was so well remembered.

'How well did you know her?'

'Meaning?' demanded Margitta.

'Relationships, they can be very messy. But I don't suppose that you had....'

'Show him where she kept her things,' said Margitta. 'He'd better talk to Carina.'

'Carina and Sabine... they were friends,' explained Anke, showing Nick down the corridor to a plain door that someone had painted a star on. As soon as Anke swung back the door Nick saw a room stripped to the bare essentials, nothing belonging to Sabine left for the curious to tag and label, no more artefacts dropped on her rush through life.

'I'd warn you that Carina is very sensitive about Sabine,' she said. 'Love can deceive us all.' And with a smile she closed him in, her voice lifting in an order as she went back to the packing.

The room had three metal bunk beds giving it the air of a cell. Bare mattresses, a couple of them badly soiled held no blankets or sheets, just rolled or folded sleeping bags for women desperate to escape men. A sink stained from coffee dregs had a threadbare towel hanging from a tap. Beside an arrow slit meshed window, a tall wide chest with nothing but newspaper as lining in any of its drawers. Upending a cabinet Nick discovered nothing more exciting than a manufacturer's stamp; worn, unintelligible with age. Not hearing the footsteps, he spun far too quickly for his ribs when a gentle cough came at his back.

'Anke said Sabine is dead,' began Carina sadly. 'An overdose?'

Nick read the hesitation as Carina came further into the room. He saw too a flash of recognition as Carina glanced at one of the bottom bunks; memories either good or bad and the discomfort of having to face them.

'Someone gave her a pure fix. I'm sorry.'

'She promised me...' Carina approached a different bunk with reluctance, her stiff shoulders buckling under a shiver. She chose a piece of mattress clear of stain and sat down.

'She wouldn't be a user again?' Nick finished for her. And Carina nodded, holding one hand tightly in the other. 'You knew her well, didn't you?'

'We were lovers,' Carina stated bluntly. 'We meant something to each other.'

'I'm sure you did. I'm only here to help. I want to find the person who betrayed her, who killed her.'

Turned to the window, Carina presented a narrow silhouette against the bright haze cast by the snow. She dragged her feet against the bare floorboards, a tiny piece of grit trapped under one sole scratching the dull varnish.

'Margitta says that you might be police, you might not. You could be undercover or something else?'

'What do you think?' asked Nick. 'You seem to take a lot of what Margitta says as fact. Has it always been like that? Does she make all the decisions for you? How long have you known Sabine?'

Consoled by Nick's change of direction, Carina shook her head and turned from the window, her suspicions momentarily discarded.

'Ten months give or take,' she said sensing Nick's willingness to listen. 'It was good in the beginning before Margitta came on the scene,' she said under her breath. Her tapered face hardened, prepared for another push, another question but Nick, content for Sabine's part-time lover to recount her story, made no other sound. And after this depressing silence, Carina drew out her first meeting with Sabine, forced to talk away the pain.

'She walked in off the street one day. Flashed a smile at everyone and gave me a pat on the head. They all thought it a great laugh, the baby of the company gets the right show of affection. Margitta made it last for weeks, patting my head whenever she got the chance.' Her face dark, consumed by the shadow from the wall, she muttered something to herself and got off the mattress.

'And when she left, you ceased to be lovers?'

Lashing out with a foot, Carina sent an empty tissue box skidding away.

'That's something you need to know? For what? What does it matter?'

'It will help me find her killer.'

'Sabine didn't leave me,' she announced, the anger rushing up into her eyes. 'She left this place and Margitta. She couldn't take Margitta's jealousy any longer. I was lucky to love her, okay. I was maybe the first person that she let make love to her for free. You got enough now?'

Voices reached them from the corridor heading towards them, low then high. Anke and Babette the mechanic, paused at the door.

'You okay, Carina? You want Babette to throw him out? See if he's a cop by the way he lands?'

'I'm fine,' she said waving them away.

'She's the boss, is she?'

'Anke is the Numa,' said Carina. 'It was her idea, she hires and fires, makes all the moves.'

'She decides who gets a second chance, who gets to escape their problems?'

'Better you ask her yourself,' Carina hit back.

'Sabine grateful for the chance?'

Carina glanced at him, suddenly unsure

'She never said,' Carina answered in a sulk.

'Did Sabine ever speak of other friends?' asked Nick, making another long approach. 'Particular friends such as girlfriends, best friends, maybe even boyfriends? Someone that she thought she could really trust. A good friend to talk to?'

'She spoke of no one.'

'Tell me,' insisted Nick helpfully, 'there must have come a time when you discussed the past? A mutual liking for something that let her talk about her friends?'

'Sometimes, when she was down, we'd talk about her life before here,' Carina retorted sullenly. 'We slept together, had a few good times to remember. Does that make me responsible for her?'

'But enough for her to return when she needed help perhaps, when she was desperate, or in trouble? If she had no one else she could trust, or who cared about her. Is that when Sabine came to you?' Nick asked quietly. 'When would that have been? When did Sabine come back here?'

Outside in the snow the bus backfired, spluttered then finally died all together.

Thrown, caught unprepared, Carina did a number of things with her hands none of them a success. Her alert eyes lingered monetarily on this hard stranger, then broke away as Nick returned her stare.

'She told you about being in trouble, didn't she? Didn't she, Carina? She came back here and wanted you to give her advice, a place to run to. Or was it to collect something? Pick up an item that she had given you to take care of for her?' said Nick, glancing at the space in the dust under a clothes rail, a space that Nick knew would match the base of Sabine's imitation vanity case.

Carina feigned disbelief. Her body squared away from Nick revealed nothing of her face, but Nick knew of the misery from the pull and downturn of her shoulders.

'And which side are you on?' she asked, facing up to Nick, though the fight had already gone out of her.

'Sabine's.'

Carina dwelt for a terrible couple of minutes on Nick's answer. At one point she seemed ready to put up some resistance only to change her mind, and perhaps of the options that she considered in that cold disheartening room, the one she had less to fear was placing her trust in Nick. Which she did, in a gentle conciliatory voice that compounded her innocence.

'Sabine came to me, scared, frightened, two months ago,' she admitted, distracted, far away, listening to Babette bellow for help.

'That would be?'

'October maybe,' said Carina as if only a fool wouldn't know. 'I'd heard nothing, nothing from her since the time she asked me to look after her vanity case. Then in October she turned up in a real state, in tears, yelling, asking for the case back.'

'Did she tell you what the problem was?'

'Some friend of hers had got into a mess. But it was going to be okay, made right in a couple of days, no problems, no worries. This friend is in big danger, and only Sabine can do this. This friend has to be saved and Sabine's just met someone who can help.'

'Who was going to help?'

'Some woman, okay, I don't know, and I didn't ask,' she said with spite.

'What was in her bag that was so important?'

'Said it was the key to unlock the money box. I asked her if she'd been using again because she was going through the bag as though her life depended on finding something.'

Which it had done thought Nick, but Sabine wasn't to know. 'What was she looking for?'

'One of those protective postal packets, and I asked what's in the bag, asked her to let me help, take care of things. But she said she didn't want me involved. I must have looked like I thought she had a stash in the bag, so she showed me. It was a DVD and she said it was a private film. I thought she was crazy, but she took it with her bag and told me not to worry, Sabine was going to save her friend.'

'You know this friend?'

'She never gave me the details,' said Carina. 'But I guess it was Franziska.'

Reaching in the back pocket of her jeans Carina pulled out a wallet. From a clear plastic flap, she lifted out a photograph; taken in colour in a photo booth, the curtain not properly drawn because a blaze of light swam across their faces, so they seemed as pale as prisoners. Three faces in rapture, Carina on the swivel seat, a girl squeezed either side; Sabine and a beautiful blonde who cast a radiant laugh at the camera.

'That's Franziska?' asked Nick.

'Sabine's best friend,' said Carina with a smile, 'Sabine's sister.'

In some ways Nick's world fell in on itself at that very moment; not only from Carina's disclosure regarding Franziska, but also at the realisation that the DVD Sabine staked her salvation on would probably contain footage of Franziska entertaining her special clients. Franziska told Sabine she'd banked something for the future, remembered Nick, and Sally Wynn was never allowed to collect it. *I got a part in helping her make it happen, she got a crazy deal arranged, but it's all top secret*, Sabine had told Nick.

'Did she say what she was going to do with the DVD?'

'She wouldn't tell me, only that I had to wait, and we'd all be free.'

'Has anyone else called asking for Sabine?'

'You mean Tolz?' said Carina with loathing and shook her head. 'I knew about her and Tolz,' she admitted. 'Sabine told me, he was part of her past, part of what she was leaving behind. He never dared show his face.'

'And no one else?' pressed Nick calmly.

'A guy was here, but Margitta dealt with him.' Amused or troubled by the recollection, Carina twisted his hands tighter, the black varnish on her nails heavily chipped.

'When was this?'

'Yesterday.'

'And what did he look like?'

'This guy can take care of himself, for sure. Big, stocky, maybe an *Ossi*, maybe more Russian, I didn't pay much attention. He only walked past me and that was enough. His eyes, they don't give you a second chance.'

'No one else?'

'No.'

Carina bowed her head, thought, then finally found a grin. 'We had great times together.'

'She was a good person.'

'But no one knew or cared,' said Carina with a prolonged sigh.

Back outside Nick lit a cigarette. In the alley the bus stood trembling and rattling like a tank as Margitta headed up the company in a shivering chain as they loaded away what they could of the theatre, working all-out under the considerable eye of Anke. Walking up the alley Nick heard her shout after him, a long stabbing call sounding like an insult. Turning up his collar in an act of defiance, he kept going into the thickening snow. I'm the perpetual latecomer he thought, deeply troubled how Moscow was on the trail of Sabine so quickly.

At an Aldi store on Eiffestraße, Nick browsed the salads and cold meats, buying some meagre provisions to take back to his hotel room in Sankt Georg. He knew she hadn't been there when he entered, but now she was waiting outside the store for him when he left; pretty and deadly serious, a slim woman in her thirties, she'd pure clear skin and hair mowed close to her skull. She wore tight jeans, combat boots, a ski jacket and the same smile he remembered from shared operations. Setting off from where she'd taken up position, Erika carried off a classic brush-contact drop, a folded square of paper pressed into Nick's waiting hand so deftly that he hardly felt it land. Erika, one of Ernst Sargens' team; a private consortium made up of specialist ex-intelligence and military officers who had proved their value with Nick and CO8 in the past. Erika's background was with the *Bundesnachrichtendienst*, the German equivalent of the Service. Taking to what any curious observer seemed a cursory check of the provisions in his carrier bag, Nick noted the address on the paper.

● ● ●

Once it must have been a prosperous block built of solid stone cut fine, trimmed with matching delicate ribs; now it had a layer of grime that the brightest of days never penetrated. It housed bars where old anarchists came to drink; alongside bookshops that dealt in the political, and mysterious shops that took orders by arrangement only. He counted off the turnings and knew that she was waiting for him. In the entrance to an alley, a young woman watched him arrive, her gaze lingering in the street as though something kept it permanently there. In trousers, leather jacket and dark practical boots, she retreated as Nick neared. He thought she called his name, but when Nick looked, she had her phone pressed to one ear and never acknowledged him. One more of Ernst's operators? Nick wondered, like Erika, and most probably a dozen others he hadn't spotted.

Slipping her phone into her pocket she approached Nick with a measured walk both surly and independent. Wastefully thin she had hair dyed a vibrant red, a keffiyeh around her neck. She watched him with the arrogance of a student radical, and in the 1970s she'd have supported the Red Army Faction, he thought.

She issued a series of directions, never seeming to move her lips, and he obeyed them to the letter. He moved on into the first courtyard and kept going. From a maze of tenements, a symphony of voices boomed out as though trying to prove a point. Nick moved quickly through two more courtyards unchallenged. He kept going until he spotted a row of grain silos reared over the rooftops, silver bullets aimed at a pewter sky, and crossing a swing-bridge he entered an alley recovering from the night. At the end of the alley the light ran out altogether, and he descended a narrow flight of steps into a final courtyard strewn with cans and rocks. It resembled a battlefield waiting for the dead to be added in strategic places, the final touches to complete the tableau. A group of kids with swollen eyes and pale skin swarmed round him, asking his name, his purpose, pulling his sleeve, touting for their junkie sisters or mothers.

Nick pushed through not speaking, and a stone hit him squarely on the shoulder. He didn't look back; going on towards a blighted tenement struggling warily up in the frail light, the remains of a crude barricade blocking its entrance, a motorcycle without wheels and the bodies of supermarket trolleys stocked with rubble. Climbing over them he waited for the next stone or fist to land. On concrete stairs starved of light, he smelt vomit and trapped smoke from a previous fire lit to cleanse or repel unwanted callers.

On the top landing there were a dozen doors, most of them boarded along with the windows, the last two without padlocks. From one, a young squatter with reserved eyes followed Nick's progress. When Nick drew level, the door slammed and music started up, pounding through the slab walls in their own decadent beat. I am the intruder he thought, knocking loudly on the last door, I represent all in life that there is to hate. Dominik greeted him, another of Ernst's troops on loan, in jeans and T-shirt, his blond hair short and tufty.

'Long time, Nick,' he said kicking the door shut and sliding the bolts. 'Welcome to our nice little place, all the comforts of home. It stinks, Nick, but we're happy to be here.'

They were in a long, confined hall plagued by the damp. A ship's barometer showed fair on a wall shedding its scrolled paper, and mould covered the woodwork in a rash of black spots. It might have belonged to a dozen students or squatters Nick thought, Harry would have seen to that, put word about, even bribed the young killers in the courtyard. Nothing had the permanence of a residence. In each room as Dominik conducted a guided tour, he found the impermanence of spying, the litter, the throw away artefacts of life taken a day at a time. A couple of ex-army issue blankets divided off the lounge and Dominik escorted Nick through it like an honoured guest. Sat at the window Erika waved without bothering to turn, her attention locked through a pair of binoculars mounted on a tripod providing security.

Opposite her, Juergen, another of Ernst's happy troupe sat on a cracked leather couch that someone had disfigured with permanent marker, drawing graffiti of a very sexual nature; crude bodies in basic poses, and the same theme had been carried down one wall in felt tip, but here the bodies had bled in the damp. This is the sum of my team to take on Moscow thought Nick, a collection of specialists borrowed from Ernst, plus Danny and good old Harry Bransk.

A net curtain ran across the window threaded on a piece of wire hooked on nails cutting down the glare, damping the reflection for anyone outside showing too much interest.

'There's a number of targets that we need to keep under surveillance,' said Nick, when Freja, an expert on the acoustic stealing of sound appeared with coffee in stainless steel mugs.

'How do you want us to run it?' asked Dominik.

'Static and mobile,' said Nick, revealing the targets for surveillance including Jack Balgrey. 'Changes of clothes and personnel, images where possible.'

'Ernst told me to confirm with you that he is already making provisional preparations in Winterthur,' announced Erika over her shoulder.

'I'll call him later,' promised Nick

Stretching out as though relaxing on a beach, Juergen rubbed the warmth from an oil heater into his fingers. His left hand first then his right.

Suddenly the room became too much for Nick, the heater with its noxious scent, the anticipation of imminent action.

'Let's go over our plan of attack,' he decided.

Twenty-Five

A taxi had collected Nick and driven him through Hamburg as though they were heading for a fire. Waiting for him, a small reception party grouped together on a remote quay off Roßdamm; Jack Balgrey and standing aloof, Döbeln. Jack's struck a deal behind my back, promised the BfV everything, Nick decided, paying off the taxi that had ferried him here in response to uncle Jack's quixotic demand.

'I was ready to give you up,' Balgrey said as Nick ambled up.

'Döbeln taking you out for a midnight feast? A few glasses of blood before you get back into your casket?' Nick said, the cold working on his fingers, no feeling at all; just numb as though his dentist had practised injections on them.

'No wonder Moscow were glad to see the back of you,' growled Balgrey.

'Sent you on a training mission, Jack? Come to see how us pros do it?' Nick taunted him. For Head Office always seemed to cast a shadow on CO8 operations, trying to muscle in; turn assets, make their own bed without lying in it.

'You're not even in the same league,' laughed Balgrey.

'Which one would that be? The one reserved for losers you're always top of?' snapped Nick as Döbeln stepped smartly forwards.

'We have business to attend to,' he reminded them officiously.

Nick truculently faced Döbeln and shook his head. Under the branched stems of a crane, the BfV's man cast an imposing presence, the grey suit, the unbuttoned overcoat, the red scarf; all stirring Nick's memory of cold Cologne mornings when the liaison partners were summoned to attend counter-terrorism briefings to clarify the latest pattern analysis, as they used to term it.

'This way,' proposed Döbeln setting briskly off, padding towards a long low morgue of grey brick; a squat building damp from layers of snow, a building not requiring windows because the river police post next door had all those.

'Could be Oskar, could be a mistake,' stated Balgrey, a stage whisper.

'How did *he* get involved?'

But Balgrey never replied, only glared as they strode on. Oskar the fantasist; Nick remembered him well, a freelance journalist working out of Hamburg who always fancied himself as a spy. A loner who used maps, travel guides, magazines, newspapers, internet global security sites, even declassified CIA documents to manufacture his own fake sources and worthless intelligence. His very own secret bricolage that he believed would buy him entry into the secret world. No one ever took Oskar seriously and Nick couldn't understand why Jack suddenly would.

'Best behaviour, remember,' Balgrey hissed. 'Or they'll put you on the next plane home.'

Together Nick and Balgrey entered through swing doors held by crooked springs. Official edicts in gruesome colours warning about rabies and a dozen other infectious way to die hid the cracks in the reinforced glass. Then the smell hit Nick in a sickly rush, river and formaldehyde in a lobby spotlessly clean with polished floor tiles in sea green, reflective cream walls and a dozen stacking plastic chairs with red seats and back pads.

Two river policemen were dealing with a Chinese captain, one of them peeled away and came forward; the end of his shift in his eyes, reporting to a weary officer in plain clothes, taking him to one side, words low, confidential, a mouth close to the detective's ear. 'Sailor... Filipino... missing for a watch... stabbing.' Nick picked up the basics, a radio drama with the sound a tad low. Busy night in the morgue he thought, as an interpreter came with a jug of water for the captain. Through an opened office door Nick saw a pathologist in cream boots and a blue patterned hat swing from the hip, answering a question from someone farther back. The calmness and ordinary way these people went about their duties made Nick uneasy. Balgrey shrugged at him, another routine to be completed, nothing more taxing than filling in expenses.

'Gentlemen.' Döbeln cleared the little sad group writing up murder details. 'Please.'

In fast lurches he sauntered into an office laid out for administration containing four desks of grey metal arranged in a square. At one, a middle-aged clerk in a white coat retreated into her seat when Döbeln perched on a corner of her desk. She had a flushed face, shoulder length hair missing a wash, and hesitant eyes behind hornbeam glasses; all of her crushed low into a defensive ball as Döbeln loomed over her. Entering their visit, date and names in neat capitals, her pen nib crackled louder than a welder's torch. She gently folded the ledger closed and invited them down a passage where fluorescent tubes hummed and stuttered.

Embarrassed, uneasy, Nick concentrated on the floor tiles noticing how the colour was derived from masses of individual flecks, counting them as they went. Three hundred and eighty tiles in all, before they gave way to carpet in a viewing room, nothing more than a hot cubicle sprinkled with plastic flowers and potpourri in plain wide lipped bowls. She asked them to wait and clumped out, letting the formaldehyde in. Balgrey flopped in a chair his face a shield, no sentiment showing or permitted. This wasn't right decided Nick sitting back; Oskar working for Jack?

'How did he die?' Nick brusquely asked Döbeln, draped in a chair opposite Balgrey. They were waiting for the show to begin, the body to be drained, a dab of foundation added, holes stitched and darned.

'Not pleasantly, I think. A body in the water carries so many disadvantages.'

'Being dead's a bonus then,' mumbled Balgrey.

'Perhaps working for your Service did not help,' Döbeln declared plaiting the spare ends of his trench coat belt, tying them, flapping them. 'He was vulnerable, yes?' he asked, throwing a glance at Balgrey. 'Maybe you exploited him too much?' He sprang out of his chair with a sudden thought, attending to something at a small window set in the wall everyone tried to avoid.

'Nice one,' Nick said to Balgrey. 'Nice touch, Jack, upsetting the local angels.'

'Not guilty, no connection, hands spotlessly clean,' Balgrey confessed with a smile.

As a diversion Döbeln and a morgue attendant conversed through the glass, a flurry of waves from this side and a gloved thumbs up from the other. What are they, wondered Nick, the warm-up team? Wafting in, the woman clerk produced a clipboard from the folds of her white coat. A master of ceremonies with a shy greasy curl trapped between her spectacles and her brow.

'Who is going to identify the body?' she asked.

'He is,' said Döbeln and Nick in the same breath.

'Very well.' She tapped reprovingly on the glass, attempting to wake a guest who'd overslept.

In one busy dash Balgrey was over at the window staring in. Craning his neck from different angles he took his time, nodded once as in a goodbye, turned and said, 'I *think* that's him.' Handing him a biro, the clerk pointed on her clipboard where he should sign and signalled the curtains to be closed again.

'If you wouldn't mind,' said Döbeln to Nick when Balgrey had retaken his seat. 'I would like to be absolutely sure.'

Nick caught Balgrey's eyes and Döbeln's mealy little stare as he moved up, both watching him suffer in their different ways. The nylon curtain whisked away for a second time. I name this body... He stared through the viewing window; his mouth dry. Shrouded from the neck down, Oskar lay on a chipped enamel trolley. Shrivelled and crinkled his face still had a rugged dignity, one he'd seen collapse into a smile, flare into a temper or look just plain childish. In some countries they stitched eyes closed after they'd been emptied by bullets; but here they'd no need with so little of Oskar left. An uncanny tint covered Oskar's peeling deflated flesh where propellers hadn't mauled it. What's the rest of the body like if his head's this bad? Very nice, wonderful, someone will be able to tell his ex-wife that he looked at peace. Colours and texture of corpses, he'd had the full range since that night on the highway in Russia.

'It's Oskar.'

Out of her pocket the clerk took her biro and hoisted the clipboard forward for Nick to sign, as though she needed his autograph.

'He was married, yes, had children?' Döbeln enquired, knotting his belt for the hundredth time.

'Split up, she threw him out,' said Nick, remembering how Petra had to routinely fend off Oskar's advances as he bluffed and charmed her that he'd something valuable to sell. 'They had a couple of children, two I think.'

'Is this her?' Döbeln asked, taking a photograph out of his pocket. 'Have you met her?'

Was it official procedure that they could only view one corpse, as though two would be too much? wondered Nick. He took the police photographer's profile of the dead waitress who'd served him at his table before Sabine entered for her big scene.

'Never seen her before,' he said.

'How about you?' Döbeln asked Balgrey, taking the photograph from Nick and passing it on.

'Presume she's one of Oskar's sources,' suggested Balgrey. 'But don't quote me on that.'

'How was she killed?' asked Nick.

'They were recovered handcuffed together,' Döbeln disclosed.

'Poor sods,' muttered Balgrey, his eyes dark and nervous. 'Finished? Done our duty?'

No more hot leads for you to fabricate, Oskar, thought Nick as they made their way back to administration, a fast procession returning to the living. Nick and Balgrey waited while Döbeln formally closed the proceedings, a private affair conducted in a hush, the clerk smarting from the impropriety of having two unofficial witnesses there.

'Sign here,' Döbeln said to Balgrey, his finger pointing to the first box on a thin wad of four forms.

On a metal desk under a map of the port, all Oskar's clothes and possessions sorted into piles beside a clear evidence sack and an inventory sheet still to be completed. As Balgrey added his details, Nick slid a long metal key fob with the name of a rooming house stamped in red towards him.

'You also,' called Döbeln and as Nick added his name, the fob was already securely in his pocket.

Outside, Balgrey shot Nick a contemptuous glance as the port wandered on, ignorant of one small tragedy and loss. Nick thought of Oskar and the time he claimed to have a hot Middle East contact, only it turned out to be his brother-in-law; now that was cheek, a real headache for Petra to untangle.

'What's that?' Balgrey demanded, as Nick mumbled something to himself.

'A farewell,' he explained, absently. 'For someone that I pretended to know.'

'Didn't rate him, so I wouldn't know.'

At a slipway they ran out of room to walk and the port purred on, one loud animal hidden in the snow filled air. Döbeln left the morgue in a hurry, a man coming from a restaurant, testing the night air and scanning for a taxi. He spotted them and trotted across.

'What's the official verdict?' Nick asked weary and weak, tired heavy patches under each eye.

'A stabbing, they both had stab wounds, but probably drowned. Waste metal was used in their clothes as weights, but so many vessels in the port create a whirlpool, a spa. Everything is pushed to the surface eventually.' Döbeln said as though he didn't entirely agree with the theory. 'I have more details to attend to. Please excuse me,' he said, trekking off across the quay's frozen expanses to his car.

'We need to talk,' proposed Balgrey, 'away from interruptions,' he added, nodding to the morgue before setting off for a quiet corner of the quay followed by Nick.

'You ready to explain your involvement in this to Head Office?' Balgrey demanded over his shoulder as they moved to the quay's tip. 'Because I'm not covering for you.'

'Meaning?'

'Oskar,' spat Balgrey. 'Come on, it's too convenient how he and his source were neatly terminated after you turn up on my patch.'

'Coincidence,' retorted Nick.

'Really? Don't expect Head Office to believe that cobblers if I don't,' insisted Balgrey turning, his rugged face thrust forward at Nick. 'Another exclusive CO8 operation is it? You're not an elite, you're a rabble, a fucking nuisance.'

'But *we* didn't get Oskar killed,' yelled Nick pushing Balgrey out of his face. 'Someone was so desperate for a piece of the action they scraped the barrel dry with Oskar.'

'Well he never invited me to the ball, and if it wasn't you, he'd found himself a partner. Oskar never danced alone,' Balgrey avowed.

A silence divided them and took them apart as the wash from a pilot boat patted the pier below their feet. Wheeling around, Balgrey squared up to Nick. 'Don't expect me to protect whatever devious game you're playing,' he warned. 'I'm not risking my neck without a sight of the action. Not think I'm owed even that?'

'Join the queue and you're owed zero.'

'Never was one for queueing, old son,' Balgrey flung back. 'I'm skipping to the front so I don't miss out.'

'Go to hell, Jack,' said Nick, lighting a cigarette.

'Lift into town?'

'Go to hell.'

'See you there,' laughed Balgrey, striding off.

A motor scooter with its throttle jammed madly back, came too fast across a chained bridge separating docking basins. Flicking his cigarette into breaking waves, Nick looked around. From the shore a dusky tint deepened shoals of snow, and a thousand different noises bubbled around his head; cars, trucks and generators, thrashing engines joined as one. Minibuses in shipping line colours discharged solemn faces for the voyage out and sped off. And how far will I have to go to find Lubov's gold? Nick wondered, watching a police launch churning through the Elbe, riding propeller surf from tankers and cargo ships coming into the hafens of Steinwerder with the tide. He felt in his pocket, his fingers closing round the metal key fob and made his way off the quay in the falling snow.

A couple of metres up the road he took a taxi from a rank of Mercedes used by seamen with the same frequency as liberty boats. Drained, yet alert with a sense of urgency, he rode silently into Hamburg; swept up along the Kohlbrand Bridge, then plunged under the river on the E45 autobahn. Nick with another dead face to remember and Hamburg didn't even care, a city of traffic and human pleasure too busy to even slow down for the loss of a minor player named Oskar.

•••

From his obsessive, and as it turned out to be, deadly fascination with all things espionage, Oskar had taken to practising the tradecraft of real and fictional spies he'd studied on film or read about, and had turned into a man continually on the move. To keep clear water between him and his imaginary opposition, he stayed for a couple of months in small hotels, paying up front, conscious of every footfall outside his door. Though his real reason for this elaborate subterfuge was that his wife had given him no option when she discovered he was having a string of affairs with women he'd duped into believing he was a secret agent. A woman of strong Lutheran conviction, his wife cast out his clothes onto the street rapidly followed by Oskar. Since then, he'd been hiding from her lawyers and the last address he'd taken was on the key fob in Nick's hand; a rooming house on Molingstraße, its number faint after years of passing from hand to hand.

A caretaker was hunched over a laptop in his foyer booth when Nick strolled past, lifting his eyes only for a second. A seasoned veteran of knowing who to challenge, who to admit, he concentrated wisely on his night-time entertainment.

Locking himself in to Oskar's final sanctuary, Nick surveyed the wreckage. Across the carpet a deep earthy brown strain similar to blood, though once on his hands and knees Nick discounted it as human and thought it more probably wine, confirming it when he rolled out the empty bottle from under the bed. As he straightened, brushing fluff off his knees, long quick steps stomped towards the room. He checked his breath not moving, his back against the wall. A key scraped in a lock opposite followed by a racking cough and a door slamming with a decadent bang.

He followed a path already set away from the wardrobe; a pair of jeans outstretched on the floor, one leg bent ready to sprint; socks, boxer shorts and a Press Club tie scattered in an uneven line. Eliminating the items as evidence of an unprofessional search, Nick went over to the washbasin and medicine cabinet screwed off-centre onto the wall. Razor, soap and toothbrush were dumped around a sliced open tube of dental paste. There was a power lead for a laptop, but Nick couldn't find it and knew it would be gone.

On a table used as a desk, Nick went through Oskar's homework in the form of magazines, maps and printed documents from a dozen security websites. Spilling from a laminate wardrobe, pairs of shoes ripped from their soles, collars and shirts torn clean to the seam. Sifting through other bits and pieces, part of his mind searched, and another part listened for the return of those who'd made a mess of Oskar and his room. Rung to be warned by the caretaker that he had a stranger nosing around, not a resident but someone he hadn't seen before. Come quick and you'll catch him.

And they might be on their way right now for all Nick knew. He moved faster, his hands picking up an unswerving rhythm. By a broad window he stopped. The view didn't interest him much, a plain standard paved square a few floors below didn't exactly take his breath away, but the red window box drew his attention. The room's light had picked something out in the compacted soil and clumps of weed. He wrenched back the clasp easing up the window and took a closer look. Of course, it could be anything; foil, sliver of glass, anything bright would glint in this light. He scraped back the soil and lifted out a biscuit tin; oblong and new, not buried for very long. Carrying it over to the bed, he noted how its price tag was blistered and so too was its enamel.

Placing it on his knees Nick eased off its top emptied strips of paper, and folded squares of newsprint until he found a dead pigeon that stank to high heaven. Tipping the pigeon out, there was another bed of paper; beneath it a sealed postal packet inside a plastic bag. Thumbing open the stuck down flap he shook out a DVD. And Nick sat there holding what Sabine had died for and Sally Wynn was fatally prevented from retrieving. And poor Oskar for once had something that could really have made him into a legend, turned him into a genuine living and breathing secret agent as Harry Bransk's contact; Oskar and his latest girlfriend from the Brazillia never realising how badly they'd get burnt.

From the way the room was searched and how Oskar and his friend were dealt with, Nick knew it wasn't Moscow's style, but Blümhof cleaning up for his good friend Sergei. At Oskar's table Nick found adhesive tape and a thick black marker pen. Resealing the postal packet, he wrote FEO – For Eyes Only – adding Rossan's name in capitals below; before quickly checking the room for anything else he might have missed. As he pulled Oskar's door closed after him, a racking cough followed him down the corridor, the postal packet snug in his pocket.

Twenty-Six

From the rooming house Nick took a taxi to the Neederdorf Grill on Deichstraße, delivered by a chubby round driver with nail brush hair who pulled up with a suicidal lurch for the kerb. He found Jack Balgrey at a corner table and joined him without an invitation. Keeping her distance at a banquette by the door, Erika didn't even raise so much as an eyebrow in Nick's direction as he walked by.

'Drowning your sorrows, Jack? Been a pretty rough day back at the old import and export business has it?' Nick asked.

'Piss off, can't you see I'm busy.'

Jack had ordered his second bottle of house red and Nick helped himself to a glass, his first long sip ran sleepily through his body.

'That's not the way to treat an old friend. I thought we could have a few drinks together, our way of saying goodbye to Oskar.'

'Really,' grunted Balgrey, topping up his glass.

'Did you forget to mention that Oskar was working for Harry Bransk?'

'Piss off, old son, do us all a favour.'

Stranded on a small stage in a corner, a comedian finished off his routine, and a pianist started on a standard repertoire of cocktail songs. Polite laughter and candle smoke, a happy melee as office parties unwound preparing for the festive season and compulsory family reunions.

'Your tradecraft is slipping Jack,' offered Nick. 'Seems to have gone a little rusty,' Nick added. 'I heard a rumour that Hawick was in town, that you and he had a tête-à-tête.'

'Someone's pulling your chain, load of old guff,' blustered Balgrey. 'The Deputy Chief wanting to meet with me? Pure cobblers, one hundred per cent cobblers.'

'Yesterday, *St. Pauli Landungsbrücken*,' said Nick, pushing a photograph captured by Erika and Freja across the table. One clear black and white image from a series taken in front of a ticket office offering harbour tours; framed against the impressive backdrop of the free ancient Hanseatic port, Jack and Hawick neatly caught cold.

'Chance encounter, one in a million,' suggested Balgrey, sliding the photograph back.

'Don't get me angry Jack.'

Glimpsed through the grill's full windows, a row of pretty merchants' houses gleamed in the night. They offered ample distraction to pull away Jack's thoughts from having to explain, though by now he realised there could be no more evasion, and his wayward stare as good as saying he knew he'd no escape routes remaining.

'Putting pressure on me wasn't he,' Balgrey stated pouring more wine, in desperate need of an anaesthetic. 'Hawick was implying that my pension would be well and truly crapped on if I didn't comply with Head Office's wishes.'

From Jack's grim expression, Nick read a sense of hopelessness, a severance of another bond with his past. 'What do Head Office want?' asked Nick.

Glass cubes held small round candles, and Balgrey's heavy face was covered in licks of dancing light. 'Your every move, who you met with, what you planned, even probably what you had for breakfast knowing Hawick.'

'And how are you expected to do that?'

'I have my ways,' said Balgrey with a seasoned drinker's sly wink.

'Would that include our mutual friend Harry?'

To what extent Harry Bransk featured in Balgrey's operational equation seemed to require a further stimulant, and another bottle of wine was duly ordered. He made the wine his focus, a quarter of the bottle gone on Jack's lamentations of his career shortcomings, his fragile marriage and uncertain future. They had the corner to themselves by an open fire, the flames reflected on oak panels as dark as ebony.

'Harry's been on the payroll since day one,' admitted Balgrey, sullen, not bothering or caring to lift his eyes from his glass, turning it round and round on the tablecloth. 'He's another one to add to your list of certified double dealers. And you can thank Head Office for the intrusion,' he said, a sneer flung in no definite direction.

'Who authorised all this? Who's running the show, Jack?' Nick asked, politely.

'Comes under the eagle eye of a Special Operations Directorate they've had running for a while,' Balgrey moaned. 'His Hawickness with Blackmore and Stratton all peering over my shoulder.'

'Head Office has put you in an impossible position,' said Nick.

'Strung up by my balls,' growled Balgrey. 'You don't know the half of it.'

'But you don't have to take it lying down, Jack.'

'Really, and how do I do that?' Balgrey flared, glass in hand. 'Got a solution for your uncle Jack, have you?'

'As a matter of fact, I have,' said Nick, sharing out more wine. 'From now on you're working exclusively for me.'

'For you?' Balgrey laughed, his heavy shoulders rocking. 'I thought I was doing that already, old son. Giving you a lead on Oskar. What was that, a dream?'

'That was you doing as your man from Cologne suggested. Working for me might just keep you alive long enough to collect your pension,' said Nick, looking over his glass at Jack. 'You can start by arranging a meeting with Harry, your usual routine, nothing to alarm him.'

'What if I don't want to be part of your team?'

'That's not an option you should even consider,' said Nick

For the first time since he'd sat down with London's representative for their chat Nick smiled but it wasn't what Balgrey regarded as friendly.

'I want this to go priority to Head Office, tonight, for Paul Rossan only. Oh, and Jack, if there's so much as one of your smudged prints on the material inside, I'll break every one of your fingers,' Nick promised, sliding the postal packet from Oskar's across to Balgrey as he rose to leave.

• • •

Mid-morning in Hamburg and Harry Bransk stoically waited for Jack Balgrey, kicking his toes against the polished floor in the *Kunsthalle* on Glockengießerwall. Harry displaying total concentration, affecting knowledge that he didn't have. His hands rammed up to his wrists in his pockets, his head tilted at an angle pointed at Friedrich's *Wanderer*. He hardly shifted his gaze as Nick came softly to his side.

'You haven't been straight with me, Harry.'

Faster than Nick anticipated Harry darted off, only for his exit to be blocked by a guided party entering from another gallery. Without ceremony or a word Nick took Harry's arm and walked him quietly away, setting out on their own exclusive tour.

'On my honour, Nick, I don't know what you're talking about, okay,' Harry complained in a whisper, arms outstretched to emphasise his case.

Nick sighed. He could smell Harry's potent aftershave clinging to the purified filtered air around them; Finnish, aromatic, tossed on with liberal goodwill.

'Jack tells me you've been working for him from the moment I arrived.'

'Nick, I need my regular clients okay, you come through once every now and again and I work with you. It's a question of supply and demand, of me earning enough for a decent cut to feed the family.'

'You haven't got a family.'

'I was talking metaphorically.'

'That include metaphorically selling me out?'

'What you mean?' Harry demanded, deeply affronted. 'I'm working my fingers completely to the bone on your case. Nick, okay. Toiling on your behalf, and I break off for this? Jack made it sound like some damn catastrophe.'

'It is. They seemed to be expecting me at the casino,' Nick said, steering Harry on a new course. 'Who got to hear about it? Care to tell me that, Harry?'

Angry, close to revolt, Harry cut in front of Nick ready to stop him by force. But Nick drew up by himself without a trace of familiarity on his face.

'Nick, what is it with you?' pleaded Harry. 'You had a tough reception, that it? Okay, I appreciate the casino was not going to be a piece of cake. But I swear on everything I love, okay, everything that I own, I swear on all of it, that I don't tell a soul.'

'Was Oskar making arrangements for my officer?'

A school party advanced on them streaming through from one idiosyncratic block of contemporary art as a finale to their tour, a couple of children mocking a set of black plastic shapes until a reproach from their teacher cracked louder than a whip.

'Sure,' agreed Harry as though he'd just had personal confirmation.

'Oskar's dead, so is his girlfriend. An escort from the casino told me Blümhof knew I was coming, I had to be dealt with. She's dead too.'

Harry's face was set like stone, nodding once that he'd received and understood. Though how far Nick had been involved in the deaths, Harry for reasons of personal safety was not prepared to follow-up. 'Someone else tipped them off, obvious,' said Harry with an awkward smile.

'That's good Harry, I like that.'

Moving without routine or by a route suggested in the catalogue, they took cursory interest in the art strung up about them on the walls; passing quietly from one century to another sublimely unmoved as one 'ism' replaced its detractor.

'It's bad for business, Nick, I get you killed, my reputation takes a dive, huh?'

'You trying to sell some material onto another interested party? Such as sharing details with Jack about Sergei's trips to Switzerland?'

They stopped in front of Makart's *The Entering of Emperor Karl V. in Antwerp* and whether Harry shook his head at the attack on his probity or sheer scale of the painting, Nick couldn't quite tell.

'Nick, I swear, I have no other deals running. Jack doesn't have a glimpse of the Swiss connection, okay. Frankly Nick, this between me and you, okay? Jack's happy to bump along the bottom until he retires. And besides, he pays peanuts. Listen, I made all the arrangements as requested. You got inside the casino, and you've got a place for the team in the port. Now I'm taking some pretty damn big risks for you considering the people you're chasing. That not good enough, huh?'

'One last chance, Harry,' offered Nick.

'Sure,' said Harry. 'One chance is all anyone needs. You paid for a gold standard service and Harry is nothing if not totally focused on client satisfaction. So, what Nick wants Nick receives, gratis, no extra fee, on the house.'

'So how about earning what I'm already paying you. I want an up to date location for a Blümhof employee called Tolz.'

'He's crazy, a complete cuckoo,' offered Harry.

'I don't want a psychological assessment, I want a location.'

'Sure, I was just adding background.'

'I'll need a car and a 9mm, both clean, both untraceable.'

'No one will know they were ever made,' Harry promised, his hand providing a magician's flourish.

'Remember Ernst?' Nick asked.

'Sure, he's totally committed, I worked with him before.'

'Well, you're going to work with him again,' said Nick, handing Harry a train ticket for Zurich. 'You leave this afternoon and Ernst is going to make sure you behave yourself.'

'No problems Nick. Me and Ernst, sure, we make a good team.'

'You don't want to let me down, Harry.'

'Okay, sure, Nick, relax, I'm now officially on the team. I don't want you to start getting jumpy.'

'Harry, I don't get jumpy, I just get mad.'

'Sure, I remember,' said Harry with a grimace. 'Count on me Nick, Harry can be relied on to deliver. Five-star treatment okay, I'm totally devoted to our partnership for sure. You worked with Harry before, remember. You think there is some other way, just let me know. Sure, we got to look out for each other, we a pretty talented pair for one thing. Basic rules okay, but they work just fine.'

'Basic rules, Harry.' And far from convinced Harry would keep any of his pledges, Nick walked away.

•••

After a restless night worrying he'd overlooked some key aspect, Nick slipped out of his hotel with extreme caution. The early morning snow thick in his face, the time not yet quarter to eight. On an underground car park close to the Reeperbahn, the lower deck was empty as he dragged his feet through the slush melted in heaps at the bottom of concrete stanchions.

In front of him, the Passat was waiting as Harry promised. Nick switched from one bay to another, weaving low in the shadows; running out of the artificial daylight to the car, its bay deliberately darkened, the bulb smashed, its filament hanging in a question mark. Crouched by the bonnet splinters of glass cracked under his heels. He found the keys double taped inside the front bumper, the documents and licence tucked up behind the sun visor. When he tried to push back the driver's seat, it jammed on a paper bundle that tore as he tugged it free. Wrapped in pages from the *Frankfurter Allgemeine*, a 9mm Heckler & Koch lovingly oiled. He pushed it in the glove compartment. The engine started first time.

Left and right, glancing in his mirror, Nick set out driving northwards already decided against the autobahn, the window down, the cold smarting his face. On the horizon a barrage of cloud running in the opposite direction; in his mirror Hamburg disappearing fast, its green turrets, tiles and modern glass towers twinkling and sinking without a trace. A December mist hung over the fields on a morning still incompletely formed, a cautious sun pushing for its first showing. Through the villages he kept the speed down, his anger burning like a slow fuse, the cold fierce, unrelenting.

In Kiel he bought a carton of Camel cigarettes, two large mineral waters and a bottle of the strongest vodka he could find from a convenience store. From a twenty-four hour pharmacy, Nick selected a box of glucose and condoms, the counter assistant never engaging his eyes. He paid in a hurry and drove northeast, across a featureless land rolled out as flat as it would go.

Going north, a couple of weeks shy of Christmas and no bright star showing him the way, only the lights of houses in protective clusters huddled behind sea walls shone brightly. Holding the car against the sandy wind he headed on, folk songs on the radio, a festival filled by childish fluted voices. Laboe came and went, its U-boat welded to crutches and its brick conning tower of a marine memorial craned eagerly for the sea. Curling inland, the road whisked him on and on, an outcast searching for somewhere to call home. And by some geographical trick, the Baltic waited for him again at the end of an exposed finger pointing accusingly at Denmark.

Tapering away in a ragged scar, the road skimmed the back of a hill, its crest marking a high point above the desolate beaches. Nick left the car by a wavy ridge of sand craters and dunes forming the ragged edge of a tree line, a small plantation spreading sleepily up and over an outcrop. A freak of nature, a bump not flattened and stripped clean. The isolation made him feel totally at home and Nick worked quickly, pouring out three-quarters of the vodka and added mineral water. Carefully, he added a measure of glucose powder into a condom and tied it securely at the neck.

He walked on the sea wall, as out in the channel steerage buoys flashed at him, one big eye then another as incoming ships brighter than palaces headed in from the open sea. A girl in her twenties lugged two rubbish sacks up the pontoon from a motor cruiser. He watched the awkward sway on her hips, the strain tell on her arms as she tossed the sacks into a battered skip below the wall. She had a mass of pale blonde hair and freckles waiting for the sun. She glanced curiously up at Nick.

'You lost?'

'Admiring the view,' Nick shouted in return.

'Why not, it's free,' she laughed and was gone.

Alone again, the cold wrapped itself round Nick's fingers as he checked the magazine. Satisfied, he tucked the H&K into the waistband of his black cords, barrel down in the small of his back. A ghostly silhouette of a ketch motored through the channel; its engine light and soft, overcome by a scudding swelling tide racing over a sandbar. The coast was a dark thin line of stillness and peace, the only light came from the hill, a pale glow. Tolz was at home. He climbed up the headland avoiding offering himself as a premature target, his ascent left and right, never straight. Crouching between fallen branches ripped off in a storm, Nick saw Tolz's motor home in an uneven clearing levelled by spars, wooden staging boards making a temporary walkway over the sandy earth. Parked next to it an expensive SUV facing down the track, ready it seemed for a rapid escape.

Thirty, forty paces down the boards and Nick had made enough noise to know he could only go on. A motion sensor spotlight fused him to the top of aluminium steps, the muscles in his arms tightening. Nick hammered on the door and its skin buckled under his fist; a sprinkling of twigs and stems from a startled bird in overhanging branches clattered on the motor home's roof.

'Tolz, Tolz, you hear me?' Nick shouted, not sure where to direct his message. 'I need to talk. Tolz?' He beat on the door again, holding up his offering.

The latch turned and the door opened wide enough for him to squeeze in, right into the twin tubes of a shotgun locked onto his chest.

'Close it, my man,' Tolz stepped back giving his visitor all the room he needed. 'Show me,' Tolz swung Nick's carrier bag with the shotgun barrel. 'Empty it,' said Tolz, indicating a spot on the table for Nick to place the cigarettes and vodka.

'It's a show of good faith,' said Nick emptying his carrier.

'Now let's see if you're clean.' He waved the shotgun to show how Nick should raise his arms and spread his legs. Tolz patted Nick's sides and pockets without any skill, missing the H&K in the small of his back. 'What's your handle?' he demanded, prodding him into the centre of the van. 'Your birthday tag? Many happy returns who?'

'Greiz.'

The interior looked as though it had been searched and never put right; dirty cups and plates were stacked in uneven piles on a stained carpet. This is how it always is Nick thought, Tolz is too high to notice. Twenty-six? Seven? And he's hooked with a bad craving, needing the heater full on, circulating the smell of grease from meals cooked for speed. He went where the shotgun sent him, to a bench-divan. Tolz swayed by the cooker, the shotgun balanced across his forearm as his free hand unscrewed the cap of the vodka bottle.

'You're the bad man, Greiz, that right, that your gig?' He talked as though a hand were applying pressure to his larynx, strangling him slowly. He gulped at the vodka and some ran wide of his mouth, a dribble cascading down his unshaven chin, dropping onto his faded white T-shirt dedicated to saving whales.

'I hear you're a friend of Sabine's?'

'Trouble, first-rate bitch.' He shook his head and a coil of greasy hair skidded and smeared his round wire glasses. A pastiche of a 1960s student refusing to reform, his hair ran to his shoulders, a thick Left Bank moustache worn as a token of intent; symbols of a lubricious life lived in hustling for the next plunge of the needle. 'Greiz...well, well. Blümhof said you might make a visit.'

'He was right.'

'Sure, he is, Blümhof's cool. Now my man, it's time for a smoke before I leave, I'm already late,' said Tolz.

With one hand Nick tore the cellophane on the carton and lifted a pack of Camel cigarettes out, laying them carefully on the edge of table. Tolz pounced, the puncture marks down the inside of his arm as livid as insect stings.

'How was Sabine trouble?' Nick asked as Tolz continually sniffed.

'Shut it! No more fucking chat,' he raged and pushed the shotgun forward. 'I'm a peace-loving guy, Greiz,' he said breathing fast, sounding ready to short circuit. 'But you've screwed that up.' He pushed a holdall part full out of his way with a cowboy boot that had a scuffed toe. 'Blümhof is not pleased, he's not a guy to cross.'

'Did Sabine cross him?'

'That bitch crossed everyone.' Tolz had smoked the cigarette half through with long nervous draws. He flicked the ash in the tiny sink where it stuck to a pan coated in fat. 'Maybe I'll get my reward for taking you out, my man.' Tolz brought up the shotgun. Stretching his neck to the window he listened, an ear close to the glass that transmitted nothing but the groaning of branches over the van. 'You're a threat, big bad threat. Yeah, number one wanted man. Gold star, Greiz, gold star for me if I take care of you.' The cigarette, burnt out between his lips, flew into the sink after the ash. 'A main man is having to come and remedy all the problems you caused. Blümhof and Sergei's beautiful operation is going to have to fold. They not happy, they want you to suffer Greiz, suffer real bad.'

'Who is coming?'

Tolz stared at Nick as though he were a hallucination. 'You're not listening, man. Sergei's main man, the one who gives the orders.'

'When?'

Drinking from the bottle, Tolz's mind tried to organise and recoup his plans that Greiz had shattered. Hissing on a bunk built up over the driver's seat the gas lamp was getting into his senses, leaking into the nerves, blocking his thoughts. Any second and he'd blow it out for good.

'Look Greiz, this isn't personal. Only I've got to consider my future.' He drank harder, trying for a quick hit from the booze.

'Where is Sergei's boss going to meet them?' Nick asked again, and held his breath, worried he would never have chance to reach the H&K digging into his back.

Going for more vodka, Tolz changed his mind. A swing of mood and his eyes took on a distant stare. 'You think I'm dumb? You're more crazy than me. What you got to offer? You got something good as a starter for our deal?' he asked, his voice all high-pitched notes. A thin grim line on his lips composed a goodbye smile.

'Something to let you forget that I called. Relaxation, while I walk away,' Nick proposed, and in slow motion brought out the condom. 'Free, a favour from me, Christmas come early.'

In disbelief Tolz waved the shotgun and Nick held up his hands. Sweat streaked Tolz's face, plummeting in steady droplets to soak the whale on his chest. Balancing the shotgun in one hand, waving it determinedly at Nick's head, he laughed and grinned, now more than ever totally unpredictable. He stuck out his left arm for the condom. Nick came off the bench seat fast. His head down, the heat off Tolz and his stinking odour right in his face. Tolz squeezed the trigger and the pans in the sink took the full force of the cartridges, bouncing, flying through the van. One blow put Tolz on his back and Nick landed on him, his knee in Tolz's throat. He slammed the H&K into Tolz's beating temple; Tolz screaming he was blind, screamed and yelled until Nick jammed a scraggy piece of towel into his hand.

'You never got around to the important details. Where is the meeting going to be held?' Nick yelled, retrieving the shotgun and tossing it up on the bunk. He poured vodka onto Tolz's scalp turning the blood pale. 'I still want to hear?'

'Bad, I'm hurting bad,' Tolz groaned, bending the crook of his glasses over his ear one handed, the other clamped the towel to his wound. 'A couple of snorts, medicine, make me complete again,' he pleaded.

'Try it,' said Nick and threw the condom down to Tolz who bit open the knot, licked his finger and dipped it into the powder. 'Wise man, a bad trick you've pulled,' he said, the glucose running through his fingers onto the filthy carpet. 'Bad man, Greiz.'

'Where?'

'Place owned by Sergei and Blümhof.' Weary, unable to stop his nose running, he tipped his head back and closed his eyes.

The vodka finally caught up with him and the cold sweat thinned out. Emptying all the vodka over Tolz's head, Nick watched as the torrent ran down his face, hanging in the thick moustache that Tolz licked with real desperation. Nick smashed the bottle into the table. 'Where?' He lifted a pan out of the sink loaded with dregs of food and oily water. 'Tell me?' He emptied it slowly over Tolz's bowed head.

Spitting it out, sitting straight up, Tolz shook it off in a fine spray. 'They got themselves a boatyard close to Blankenese, uses it to import and export things, bad things, good things. The main man is due to call soon, in a day, a couple of days. I don't know, he didn't share the details with me.'

'Great, now move, get up, move.'

'You mad? You crazy? Where?' Tolz stared up at Nick, one scary monster too many. One of those weird creatures he'd had dealings with before; shapeless forms that came looking for him from a planet with an inky cold moon. He blinked but this one wouldn't disappear and the more he looked, the more real it became.

'Move it.' Nick stood clear as Tolz grappled with his legs, useless funny pieces of skin, bone and muscle that he didn't quite know what to do with.

A prolonged burst of automatic rounds came from the treeline, rupturing the motor home's panels. Nick threw himself forward towards the driving compartment as Tolz's body twitched and jerked. Rapid fire spraying the cabin; glass, metal, fabric and wood flew around in swirls of dust. The noise piercing, as though Nick were inside a metal drum some demented half-wit was determined to beat flat.

Hugged down on the musty carpet Nick clambered over the front seats, pushing himself flat into the footwell. Reaching up Nick opened the passenger door then bundled himself out, rolling, clinging to his drawn pistol. Hunkering down by the wheel arch Nick waited.

A full minute passed before Nick heard feet crunching over the debris inside the motor home pause at Tolz and move towards the driving compartment. Raising his pistol, Nick's aim traversed with the footfalls. Bracing himself Nick fired in rapid succession, aiming high then low, sweeping along the panels. There was no cry of pain just a dull heavy thud. Nick reloaded and slowly straightened up.

Slowly he eased open the motor home's main door, entering not at a rush, but a foot at a time. Nick moved forward his pistol levelled at the prone figure lying by the front seats, blowing frothy red bubbles, his fingers itching for an assault rifle Nick kicked out of reach. The face he vaguely recalled; one of the drunks he'd passed on the stairs on his way to Vrangelya's apartment. Nick wiped his mouth with the back of his hand as he looked around; the interior was trashed and so was Tolz: a soft toy ripped apart. Drifting through the air, dust and fragments settled on the wreckage. Stepping through the mess, Nick dropped into a hunched ball on the motor home's step, drew up his knees and rested his head on his arms.

Twenty-Seven

After landing at Zurich airport Nick took a local stopping train to Winterthur, slowly starting to doze, his mind swimming with various possibilities that offered no clear solution, only a host of complications. With his eyes still hazy, Nick stepped into Winterthur's Bahnhofplatz and a hail shower. The cold night chilling him to his core as he fed in a handful of francs and dialled from a payphone under the station canopy, a brief call declaring his arrival. Returning the handset, Nick made a show of searching for a second number on a scrap of paper. In the square a trolley bus lurched along, blue sparks spitting from the overhead wires in the moist air. From a bar opposite, the heavy beat of a disco thudded like mortars as a police car toured slowly through the square, turning by the Migros Grocery store, and Nick felt the dryness settle on his lips.

The cold ran into his hands as the car took forever to pass, the policeman glaring into the night, his blond moustache as bright as his badge of office. Ring, Ernst, ring, he urged, working on five separate excuses in the empty minutes before Sargens returned his call. And after the brief exchange of more clear code merely confirming details, Nick, dead on his feet, secured a room in the Station Hotel using yet another discoloured smile as the clerk made an epic of booking him in, of offering the menu even though the restaurant had closed.

Depositing the bare minimum that he carried with him in his room, Nick hurried out again a different hotel in his sights. This one the Hotel Wartmann where outside a sign swung as if on the gallows; toiling under its message: *Haldengut Bier. Echt gut Haldengut.* Inside they were waiting for him in a private room behind the hotel's main bar; Bransk and Ernst Sargens huddled together like Horatio and Marcellus waiting for the ghost. The room had no windows and the biggest cowbell in Switzerland slung behind the door. The hot air reeked of leather from the tack hanging off the walls, bridles and halters and the odd saddle. On their table a candle flame spluttered in the heady air, licking the inside of a clear glass cup on a sandstone base. Ernst rose to greet him. Stocky and dark haired he had a gypsy tint to his skin that some women adored; his broad smile had the makings of a handshake all its own, but they still made a formal greeting.

'Nick, Nick, but this isn't a day too soon. How are you? My boys and girls I loaned you, they behaving?' Ernst smiled, on his feet and sprinting nowhere. 'They should, they get paid damn enough.'

With one of Nick's hands clamped firmly in his own, Ernst pumped it up and down as if he was parched and badly needed water from a well. Thirty-nine and he spoke with a dignity and formal kudos of a sixty-year old. Ernst Sargens, ex-German special forces, a respected member of the *Kommando Spezialkräfte*, the KSK. Sargens appraised him. Nick the serious Englishman he'd adopted, cared for and protected on some dangerous missions, a surrogate brother not of Christ or crime, but the good time.

'It's good to see you Ernst,' said Nick when they had settled at the table. 'It's been a long time.'

'Too long,' replied Ernst, saddened by the fact. 'This I know is personal Nick. A bad business. Harry has told me the details. We do all we can to help.'

A waitress brought a third coffee to the table without it being ordered, grinning angelically at Ernst.

'Appreciated Ernst,' said Nick, and out of embarrassment stirred his coffee.

'Then we start,' decided Bransk after an uncomfortable minute. 'This is the lay of the land, Nick, okay. A rough outline and no more. It's almost Ernst's backyard so he can run you through it.'

As a preliminary gesture that marked all of Sargens' briefings, he offered his cigarettes; the smoke remaining over their heads in a dense pall, clashing with the smell of cracked leather and food.

'I would say then, Nick, if you don't mind,' opened Ernst. 'That all the indications point to us carrying off a successful operation if you wish, nothing too complicated here, we've plenty of options to get at our target,' he concluded, handing over a package Danny Redman had delivered from London on behalf of Rossan.

By five the next afternoon they had as they say, walked the course.

Römerstrasse was a long wide avenue built for prosperity, a pretty enclave with a view of the hills. An oasis of villas, each an individual statement, each one grander than its neighbour, each isolated behind walled gardens and electronic gates. The light had faded, slipping by them in an ebbing tide, a dull uneven gloom creeping into its place. Bare rowan and ash branches flailed in revolt as welcome home lights turned the drives into morning. A winter finality marked the day's close; a bitterness that stayed on Nick's skin, causing him to shiver for much of the walk.

'That's our friend's.' Ernst pointed to a villa over the road, heavy with rococo charm. 'It's been in his wife's family for years, bought as an investment. Left to her by her father, who made millions from his very impressive insurance company in Zurich. She's quite a wealthy lady in her own right, our friend did his homework for sure. He's landed on his feet since he married. The flat over the garage is for domestics, a live-in couple who do the cleaning, cooking and gardening. Our friend has four kids, but only one still lives at home and they just converted part of the garage into a sauna. The back is a nightmare, Nick. Fountains, statues, you just can't move at night without risking breaking your neck. There's even a grotto but that's used for the Dobermanns.'

'There was no way we could make an approach to him at home,' Harry explained, as they came level with the gates. 'He has the place well stocked. Pressure mats, beams, only a fool would make a forced entry.' As if to emphasise the point, a large dog made a charge down the drive.

'How's he going to respond?' Nick asked. 'What's his background?'

Looking handsomely around, a man born for the moment, Ernst presented the harvest of some very delicate research.

'We're awarding no prize for good behaviour here, Nick,' he said stiffly. 'Our friend comes from a solid family in Berne, well connected, the right side of being rich, very presentable, friends and uncles in the right places. He joined the bank with a decent degree in economics. With his connections, he was meant to be heading for the top, but he never did. All at once he's a high-flyer with broken wings, got a sideways tilt to their new branch here in Winterthur and never looked forward since.'

'Reasons?'

'Family scandal. Nephew got busted at the border with a van packed with hash,' said Harry. 'It wasn't for personal use and the bank are very hot on their corporate reputation. Our guy got caught in the fallout, and if the bank took that line then, Jesus, this time they'd crucify him.'

'I suppose they would,' agreed Nick.

'Nick, listen to me, okay. He is our man, for sure. A small-town climber, respected family. Loyal, shakes all the right hands, goes to church, walks the dogs. He's so dependable, they built the damn bank around him, know what I mean. He's been here so long he's trusted to the hills and back, just the sort not to attract any attention. On the surface he's a pillar of the community, but below the surface, well, he's a dirty boy. His weakness is the owner of a boutique dealing in designer jewellery. He met her at the local tennis club, his wife doesn't enjoy physical sport. Our guy adores his girlfriend, and she's also the best friend of his wife. He's a loser. Nick, a loser all the way.'

'Do we have enough to turn him?' wondered Nick.

'We got plenty of fuel,' Harry revealed. 'Enough for a basic final demand, Nick you understand, but we got more if we need it.'

'We have plenty to open him up,' Sargens added, his face acute, alert, glistening in the passing headlights.

'Totally?' And Nick became aware for the first time of the completeness in Ernst's and Harry's vigour.

'Totally, as in nothing to lose, Nick. To look at him, you'd think this guy was flame proof. If you didn't know his history, you might think he going to be a sure hit for husband of the year.'

'What do we have?' Nick asked.

'This guy is living beyond his means, buying a new place for his mistress to live, plus all the money he's throwing at keeping his wife and small brood happy, and the only way he can be doing this is by offering favours for someone and taking a payment in return,' disclosed Harry.

'Your decision,' Ernst proposed.

'I don't see what other choice we have,' Nick said finally. 'We'll take him.'

The sky began to clear. There was going to be a frost, Nick felt the chill sharpen as headlights passed them in a rush to get home.

'It's got to be outside then?' presumed Nick. 'Our best chance will be in the open?'

'We shouldn't have any problems,' pledged Harry. 'Ernst's put a good team together.'

'My boys and girls are good, Nick, they've all got previous experience, know the ropes, know what's needed, you worked with some of them previously. Anja cut her teeth with the military. Liesel and Ursel, they're fine, can take it.'

'Backup?'

'All reliable,' Ernst assured him. 'Markus and Ignaz are steady, not likely to get shaky. Lukas is the driver, he can handle whatever comes his way.'

They were strolling side by side, Nick and Ernst divided by their thoughts, Harry forever concerned about security dawdled at their heels. Why do we always end up plundering another life? Nick wondered. Lubov died at one end, the traitor is waiting at another. How many lives will need destroying in order to make the traverse, to get safely across? he asked himself.

●●●

The house in Goldenberg was new, typically Swiss, a split-level chalet with a flagpole for National Day. It stood behind the Kantonsschule and it had all the conformity to make it anonymous, thought Nick from the van. They were parked on a corner, Markus flicking through the morning paper, Nick a clipboard on his lap. At eight o'clock Klara Tanhoff began her journey. Her Fiat sparked first time; its newness impressive as she drove on by. At the junction with Rychenbergstrasse she stalled, and Nick had a heart stopping couple of seconds until the engine came back to life. Over gunning it, she turned left by the *Musikschule-Konservatorium* before turning down into Winterthur, the morning overcast and cold, a thin mist stuck to the wooded hillside, deep cloud shutting out the sun.

Markus, a man of habit, waited exactly fifteen minutes before driving up to Tanhoff's house as on previous mornings, down the van's side the name of an electrical contractor dreamed up by Ernst, and a telephone number manned by Ursel in case anyone should ring. A rough key needed firm pressure, taking no more than a couple of twists before the door swung in. She has a few friends, Ernst had declared. Lives by herself and only has the one visitor who treats it like his second home. She never uses the front door; she keeps it chained and comes out of the back. Entering on Markus's heels, Nick found the kitchen still warm, a smell of fresh coffee roaming in the air, but Nick couldn't see a cup or mug. In the dishwater he told himself and checked to satisfy his curiosity. The machine was empty leaving him unreasonably disappointed, as if finding an ordinary cup might have given hope that Klara Tanhoff really existed.

'The power is off, and the phone is dead,' Markus told him, unpacking his case, laying out the instruments clean enough for any operation. 'She never leaves a thing out of place. You would think that no one lived here, except for the audio and video.'

'Yes,' agreed Nick, watching Markus go to work, surgical gloves on his eager hands.

Unplugging the kettle, Markus removed the socket cover retrieving the room transmitter. With a satisfied smile, he returned the original cover and screwed it back in place. It is so easy thought Nick, stealing pieces of other people's lives; power sockets, telephone sockets, even the adaptors used for Christmas lights could carry away conversation.

'How many rooms did you wire?'

'Each room,' Markus answered, his nimble fingers extracting two black micro wireless devices from a table lamp. 'This is easy, yes. She has no knowledge, no friends to make a sweep, so I can afford to be generous. A main transmitter for sure, then I also provide a backup. Two to a room, no failures, the full story nice and clear.'

Weary, tired and irritable, Nick moved on.

Upstairs he found the same sterile scene; bleached floorboards supporting furniture cut to a simple pattern and finished by hand. Below in the living room he heard Markus scratching at a wall socket, as frantic as a mouse. In the bathroom, flying fish embossed on the shower screen dripped silently into a white plastic tray. He smelt a delicate fragrance; perfume or soap, he wasn't sure. Tanhoff had nothing of value he decided, as Markus somewhere above, cheerfully whistled as he collected his precious transmitters and cameras. She has a lover who brings nothing but himself; for there were no touches of him here either, no second toothbrush, no shaving set, no large bathrobe behind the door.

Across the landing built as a poor minstrels' gallery, Nick came on the main bedroom where a double bed rested opposite the window, its quilt matching the walls in their blank whiteness, a statement of virtue that failed to impress. I am becoming an expert on bedrooms he thought, remembering Sabine's. On his hands and knees, Markus replaced the original socket for the bedside lamp.

'The quality of sound could be better,' Markus said, finishing off, packing his case. 'Not too bad, you should have a close-up or two,' he said, handing Nick a laptop, the audio and visual footage uploaded from what he'd picked up on the receiver and feeds in the back of his van.

'Just as long as we have his face,' said Nick to Markus' departing back.

Hung above the bed a solitary picture one of them must be able to see when they made love; a print of a desert island, the sun just rising or setting, a dream or illusion? wondered Nick. Klara's joke perhaps? He looked to find an earring, a book with a page turned down, some loose change, even dust, anything to give Klara Tanhoff some shape; a reference that he could attach to her sullen face and make destroying her lover easier.

Standing back from the window Nick saw the Volvo arrive; a black estate with false plates and Ernst driving. A shot of pale sun broke through the clouds scorching Nick's face through the glass. Casting glances along the block, Ernst conducted the removal of a broad figure out of the estate, a bodyguard protecting an important guest. The man appeared to be in a shock, pale and ill, either that or they've hit him too hard thought Nick. Liesel linked arms with the man, his immaculate dark grey suite out of place, unnatural against Liesel's tight jeans and sweatshirt; Anja and Lukas bringing up the rear, bags of shopping for cover.

A BMW drew up behind the Volvo with Ignaz at the wheel. And what could be more natural than for Klara Tanhoff's lover to park his car outside her house? If Nick required proof that any of the neighbours should show customary Swiss zeal and inform the police, he had it at that precise moment. Two mothers wheeling prams passed the cars, neither of them offering so much as a second glance. Downstairs Nick heard raised voices, and someone put a CD on; a little music for the friends of Klara, that is not unusual either decided Nick. Then the footsteps on the stairs, slow, assured, not a hangman's coming to measure him for the drop, but Harry Bransk, actually smiling, the biggest smile of his life. Red in the face, the smell of a fresh Swiss morning on his jacket, he grinned broadly, bringing personal thanks from an ecstatic team to their elected coach.

'No problems?'

Harry shook his head without losing his grin. 'They're one of the best teams I've worked with.'

'No worries about witnesses?'

'A dream, total team effort, we took him clean,' said Harry.

'Then we should be fine,' said Nick, appreciating that without Ernst, Danny and Harry he'd be playing to an empty house. 'I think it's time that you brought up our guest,' said Nick, checking he'd everything ready.

Escorted up by Ernst and Lukas who actually had to pull and push, Jürg Mauer chose to stay with his back to the bed. That's fine, I know where you're coming from, facing your own lust in front of strangers isn't easy decided Nick. Mauer remained by the window, a burly figure with a wise face and dark thinning hair. The looseness in his shoulders stiffened as footage of him and Tanhoff played on the laptop set squarely on the bed by Nick, the hissing clearing to Klara giggling and groaning as Mauer asked if she wanted more. Fake sounds of joy, a straight playback of regular bedtime action spreading through the room, the unmistakable sweating face of Bauer clear and visible as his mistress rode him. Whether it was Klara's clinical performance, Mauer's enthusiastic grunts of pleasure or pure embarrassment, the branch manager of a respectable Swiss bank suddenly awoke as though coming out of a dream. Ashen faced he threw the laptop against the wall, shattering it with a bang.

Nick glanced unconcerned at the wreckage.

'We have additional footage,' said Nick, raising his eyebrows.

'You are crazy,' Mauer stormed, fluently switching on his English. 'You are all mad, animals, thugs. I am a Swiss citizen and you are making a grave mistake if you believe you can avoid justice for kidnap and abduction. I am Herr Mauer. I am employed by a bank with considerable influence. You will be pursued, every one of you prosecuted. You are fools to think you can keep me.'

Lunging forward at Nick, Mauer only gained a couple of steps before Ernst and Harry restrained him, whilst Nick the object of his rage, remained unmoved on a corner of Klara's bed.

'Don't touch me, get your filthy hands off me,' Mauer snarled, more in exhibition than threat. 'Is this the way to treat a man of my position? Answer me? Do you understand justice?'

'We all understand justice, it's the interpretation that's difficult to define,' suggested Nick, fixing Mauer with resolute eyes. 'Now, please, sit down and listen.' Nick waved his hand for calm, in perfect control.

Once more Mauer erupted. 'Who do you think you are dealing with? So, I have a mistress, who will care about an extra-marital affair in the twenty-first century,' he said brightly, finding a seed of hope, his confidence returning.

'Paid for by Moscow.'

'Moscow... Moscow. Where is your right to make these accusations?' he blustered, rising to his full height, Ernst and Lukas promptly at his side. 'If you leave now, I will forget that you even tried to blackmail me. That is my option, that is my deal.'

'Whether we leave or stay, it is highly probable Moscow will seek redress... revenge,' said Nick reasonably. 'It will be assumed that you have told us many privileged things.'

Taking measured steps to the window, Mauer studied Nick as though he needed more persuasion. 'I am a man of substance,' he declared indigent once more. 'I am in receipt of a considerable salary, I have invested wisely and this,' he said with a wave of both arms, 'is my reward, an investment. Moscow,' he snorted, 'has nothing to do with this or me.'

'Innocent people have already died to prevent us reaching you,' said Nick. 'What is Herr Herzel going to think when he learns we have interviewed the manager of bank where he makes monthly deposits at your branch? How is it possible Herr Herzel can hold an account? A non-resident using false documents, yet he obtains an account, and one which isn't subject to high deposit limits and high fees? What reason would Herr Herzel have to hide his identity? Perhaps it is because he is Russian? Perhaps it is because he is an intelligence operative? Herr Herzel, or as you may know him, Sergei Gorshov, will assume that you have disclosed many private details. You are at risk, you should not forget that.'

As Nick spoke a gradual change in manner overtook Mauer. The colour in his cheeks was gone, and visibly shaken, his composure had withered. A man faced with such devastating evidence had no easy decisions to make and Mauer was no exception. He floundered for something to say, his heavy eyes looked first to Lukas, then Ernst, coming at last forlornly to Nick.

'This is a lie, totally untrue.'

It was the final protest and they all knew it. Uttered flatly without any conviction or feeling, it was an act of defiance that even Mauer had no faith in.

'Why not sit down,' offered Nick. 'We have evidence of the movements of a funding stream from Moscow to Panama. From there it goes through a number of shell companies before arriving in Hamburg. And from there, well, you are fully conversant with the arrangements. It would be better for your safety, Herr Mauer, and those you care about, if you cooperate. I give you my assurance there would be no reason for Frau Mauer or your banking colleagues to witness your performances with Klara, or of your other indiscretion in Hamburg. If you cooperate fully, we can speak on your behalf if you request protection.'

'Lies,' he complained feebly, accepting a dressing stool provided by Ernst. 'You are crooks, thieves, nothing more,' Mauer grumbled, turning unhappily from his own reflection in the dressing table mirror.

'I will give you five minutes to make up your mind, cooperate with us, or take your chance with Gorshov, your wife and the authorities here. You agree to work with us, and I ask for nothing more than total commitment.'

'Commitment,' he repeated loudly, an oath. 'If I do not adhere with your demands, I will lose everything. If I lose everything, what commitment is that? Everything lost.'

'Everything, possibly your life, maybe the lives of your family also,' Nick told him. 'Gorshov's superiors will know very soon that he has been betrayed, and there is nothing I can do about that.'

Downstairs the music was getting higher followed by laughter. The more noise you make the less attention you create; fact of life thought Nick, noise gives assurance that you're invited, welcomed and not a prying thief. In Klara's bedroom they were in a different world; isolated, waiting for Mauer to make his decision. Which he did, drawing a huge breath to commence his heroic tale.

'My bank arranges conferences for all its managers,' he began. 'The purpose is to review banking policy, the implementation of new regulations.' He glanced up, touring the faces around the room, considering whether he should continue, which after a hesitant pause he did. Nodding at the conclusion he'd reached, Herr Mauer, drew out the sorry details of his entrapment. 'Previously the conferences have taken place in Paris, London, Stockholm, many different countries. This one was due to be held in Berlin, but some complications concerning the venue occurred, so it was relocated to Hamburg. The conference was neither too onerous, nor too tedious,' he admitted with typical Swiss candour.

'In the bar of my hotel I was approached by this Herr Herzel, this Gorshov, this... this imposter. We discussed many topics and told me he was celebrating a very generous win from playing roulette. I am not normally a man who gambles,' he declared piously, 'but he suggested I might enjoy a visit to a casino.'

'The Brazillia?' Nick intervened when Mauer lapsed into silence.

'Yes, the Brazillia.'

'Please, Herr Mauer, do not omit important details,' Nick officiously reminded him.

Accepting the censure with a strict nod, Mauer rallied himself for his next disclosure. 'We enjoyed more drinks, I played a little roulette, made modest wins at blackjack. The floor show was perhaps too risqué, but enjoyable. The imposter introduced me to a very charming friend, her name was Franziska...' At this critical juncture, Mauer shook his head, took not one, but three deep meaningful sighs.

'Intimacy took place,' Nick said very gently. From sequences Rossan had recovered from the DVD and forwarded to Nick, the additional company of Sabine was a revelation Mauer didn't feel inclined to admit.

'Yes,' Herr Mauer eventually conceded, 'we enjoyed intimacy. I thought nothing more of it until a month after I returned home. The imposter makes an appointment to see me at my branch. I was surprised, naturally, but the explanation he provided appeared quite logical. He disclosed he was in Switzerland on business, which is very natural. Of course, I didn't realise I was the purpose of his business. He showed me a recording of my indiscretion he had on his phone. He proceeded to outline how I, and my branch, would assist him in certain financial transactions. There, that is it,' he said with an air of finality.

'I appreciate your cooperation,' admitted Nick graciously. 'However, there are particulars we would like clarifying,' Nick suggested. 'Not the monthly deposits made by Gorshov...' here Nick took a deliberate weighted pause, 'but how those funds were used?'

His head hung low, Mauer nodded in principle.

'And unless you are willing to give me your full assistance, your bank will be informed immediately.' Nick waited for the censure, the victim's last attempt to convince himself he was in no position to reject the reasonable offer. 'I really need you to make up your mind.'

Mauer hesitated for a moment before venturing his opinion. 'You are a fool, you're a lunatic,' he decided. 'You cannot protect me from the sort of people you refer to... spies... criminals... murderers.' And before anyone could prevent him, he had lurched over to Nick and tapped him on the shoulder. 'They can get to me as easy as that.'

'Sit down,' Nick snapped.

The music lifted again, the floor vibrated and Mauer lost his concentration briefly. 'Keep it reasonable,' Ernst shouted from the gallery returning with an apology on his face and resumed his vigil by the window.

Mauer stared unflinchingly ahead, his grey eyes resentful at his plight.

With a shrug, he folded his arms across his chest. Perhaps determined the whole world should take a share of the blame, Mauer retreated into silence.

Sensing the momentum slipping and Mauer's resistance increasing, Nick slapped the palm of his hand on the bedside table, rocking the lamp. 'We need answers, not tomorrow, the day after, but now. I need to know if you're going to provide me with those answers?'

A prospect so daunting that Mauer screwed his silk handkerchief into a tight ball, a move Nick recognised as clear as signal as he might have wished for, that Mauer had finally lost his inner struggle.

'What a fool to pay twice over for stupidity.' He covered his face and reflected. 'Please, what is it you require exactly?' asked Mauer, lifting his eyes to Nick in one last open appeal.

Markus brought them coffee, three small cups and a pot that gleamed from never being used. Mauer listened in a rapt silence as Nick outlined how that one monthly special payment was the only stumbling block to Mauer avoiding personal ruin.

'It's important that you're totally frank with me,' Nick added as a warning.

Staring blankly at Nick, a slight frown of suspicion puckered Mauer's heavy brow. Slipping off his jacket he folded it neatly and laid it by his feet, loosened the knot on his tie, unbuttoned his collar, a man about to play serious poker.

'This monthly deposit is really a very straight forward transaction,' Mauer admitted.

'Perhaps you would share this with us,' Nick suggested.

Returning a thin smile, Mauer explained. 'Part of it is held in a numbered account, the rest is for the maintenance of an isolated property on Fehmarn, this you understand is a German island. A large house with many acres of land on the coast near Puttgarden,' Mauer stated, with no qualms, no hesitancy and no compunction in revealing the scope of his deception.

'And ownership of the property?' Nick observed casually.

'For this I had to be inventive,' he disclosed with immodesty. 'A company was formed and registered in Klara's name. The purchase of the property was completed many years ago and did not even make a dent the sum deposited to open the account. With such a balance we could have bought the entire island,' Mauer laughed.

No one else so much as smiled along with him, and here Nick noticed a visible change come over those in the room; we have uncovered Lubov's real treasure he thought.

'The name of Klara's company?'

'Hämvis GmbH. And it also owns this property,' he disclosed, lifting both hands as if in prayer, but his only consideration was to draw attention to the house he'd purchased for his mistress. 'For this acquisition, I wisely used the cash gifts provided by the imposter.'

'The numbered account is still active? Have there been withdrawals perhaps?'

Whether he was aware of the importance of Nick's question or he'd begun to enjoy the limelight, Mauer made an inordinate fuss of remembering. Finally, when it seemed Nick was in danger of beating it out of him, Mauer nodded. 'It continues to receive a monthly deposit, but not one single dollar has been withdrawn. The account balance is substantial, extremely healthy. With such an amount I proposed investment strategies to the imposter, but he refused. He insisted his friend would not be interested and it occurred to me, this friend does not want to draw unnecessary attention to their activity,' Mauer said, swallowing hard, because he appreciated just as everyone else in the room did, that at that very moment he had just walked out of the shadows into the light.

'And the name of the account holder?' Nick asked, suppressing his impatience as Mauer started to dry, needed nudging along.

'Kristina Mörtviken,' Mauer confessed, and the knot of silk went from hand to hand. 'The name is Swedish I believe. Naturally I am careful when the account is opened. Practise subterfuge, a slight of hand here and there regarding documentation. But the imposter would have it no other way,' Mauer stated.

'The property on Fehmarn is leased to the same person?'

Closing his puffy eyes, Mauer played out his remaining moment in the spotlight until Nick again quite bluntly demanded the name.

'No, it is leased to Druyer GmbH, a Hamburg company, it has diverse interests I believe.'

And Nick refused his quite natural instinct to reveal his surge of anger, his justified sense of disbelief. Visualising instead, Jack Balgrey as the sole representative of Druyer GmbH, servicing a property belonging to Moscow. Jack and his company, a wholly owned subsidiary of the Service; which did indeed have diverse interests, though not one of them should have included being employed by the GRU.

'You have been extremely helpful, Herr Mauer. There are, however, a number of procedures we need you to undertake. You will assist us in closing the accounts you have discussed and transfer the balance to an account my colleague will provide. My colleague will also require a complete record of all transactions made by Gorshov,' said Nick, nodding in Ernst's direction.

'You ask too much of me,' Mauer protested. 'What about my safety? How can I protect my family? And Klara, she will in danger.'

'You would not have been permitted to live beyond your usefulness, your knowledge was always going to be a threat,' said Nick and paused as Ernst came to his side, a whisper in his ear. 'I understand, no problem,' Nick said to Ernst and turned back to Mauer. 'We have an agreement with the Federal Intelligence Service for you and your family to be relocated to a safe house.'

'But now, this very moment?' Mauer said, reaching for his jacket. 'You want me to leave immediately?'

'Exactly.'

'I have commitments here, friends, a reputation, a very good life.'

'I'm not forcing you to leave, but Moscow do not tolerate betrayal.'

'Yes.'

Already thinking through his options, Mauer had a sudden afterthought. 'What of Klara, where is she? What have you done with her?'

'She is safe, she is being looked after by the FIS and I understand she has accepted an offer of a new identity, a new life.'

Suddenly the party broke up, the group departed as quickly as they arrived. Silently, with no farewells on the step, no goodbye kisses, Liesel and Lukas made a final inspection before Markus locked the door returning the house to its limbo. With quite enough things to concern him, Nick refused to return to Winterthur by car, opting to walk, allowing himself a chance to go through his remaining objectives.

Twenty-Eight

Three in the afternoon and already it was dusk, the road out of Hamburg taking Nick in a new direction. Sleet turning to snow bumped against the Passat's windscreen as he drove on into Blankenese and tucked the car out of sight close to the Elbe, the hollow melodic notes of a channel buoy tolling in mourning as he walked away. Following the river line Nick climbed past chalets built for the view, taking a stiff assent up the *treppes* that drained his legs. Through long windows, oblongs of honeycomb light spilled onto the snow by his side; nothing else moved other than a dog padding its way home through an empty square. Over the hillside a mist thinner than silk blew and billowed through the pine trees, and rounding a corner everything fell away; houses, trees and hill. On the horizon Hamburg burnt under halogen, a beautiful orange coming from generated power and not Allied incendiaries.

Slipping and scrambling Nick started down a harsh steep path leading out of a canopy of branches strung with outdoor lights, their coloured bulbs bobbing in the wind giving off a numinous glow. Without warning, the path spread into a clearing and he was facing the river. Around a tiny inlet of unequal sides, grocery stores, ships' chandlers and restaurants were dark and closed until next season when fair weather sailors would arrive. In the shadows, Ernst Sargens hunched up tight against the cold began impatiently waving with a torch, a father calling home his wayward son.

'We thought you weren't coming,' Sargens said, his heavy jawed grin replaced by a sombre look. 'Danny was getting concerned.' They shook hands and as an added touch Ernst embraced him, the torch digging into Nick's arm.

'They're doing a fantastic job, Nick,' said Ernst ushering him along.

'Since Switzerland the boys and girls are glad to be involved. We want to be there at the end, to help him wrap it up, they told me. They're good Nick, they're committed.'

Snow stood in soiled heaps at the roadside and a thorough frost gave it a slick sheen as Ernst crunched through it, jogging up concrete stairs to the second level of holiday apartments; three rooms and a dining kitchen, furniture out of a box. Ernst had paid for a month explaining to the letting agent he and his crew were here to try out a racing yacht, a breakthrough in design, a commercial secret. The agent couldn't have cared if they were planning to dam the river so long as he got his commission, and the deal was signed; nothing would pass his lips the agent promised, they'd have to torture him first. Ernst without a flicker of a smile told him that could be easily arranged. And Ernst's team had decamped from their original grubby squat to concentrate on Blümhof's boatyard, no doubt much to their fellow squatter's relief.

'There'd been no activity since we set up,' he said ushering Nick to a picture window to admire the view. 'Then yesterday, bang, we had arrivals.'

At the far end of the small inlet as though distanced through shame, Blümhof's boatyard sprawled raggedly over a sloping shore. Nothing more than a melee of sheds and buckled canopies over unfinished hulls, all of them waiting for a final touch Nick reasoned they would never receive.

'We've assembled this from the faces Erika caught when they arrived. Where possible we have cross-referenced them,' Ernst explained, leading Nick to a rear wall.

A series of photographs were taped on the wall alongside a panorama of Old Hamburg, elegantly done in watercolour from across the Außenalster. Some recent, the work of Erika, others were file copies in black and white taken at night, some dark and grainy the result of low light and high ISO. Nick didn't even want to guess how Ernst had acquired them; a who's who of Moscow's remaining players Ernst had assembled in a genealogical tree covering a sheet of A3, with names and flow arrows added in different colours.

'Not bad, Nick, a good job, yes?' said Ernst touching each image in turn, applying names to faces. At its head one severe and stiff face that Ernst identified as GRU General Evgeni Kasimov, beneath him the sullen pout belonged to Sergei Gorshov, whilst farther down in the order of merit, Franziska and Blümhof, and in last place, a face belonging to dark streets;

hard, intense, a legman who Ernst named as Shikovo.

Exactly what role did Gorshov play in Angie's murder? wondered Nick staring at the Russian's surly features. 'He's the key player,' said Nick, tapping Gorshov's image.

'The female, we cannot decide why she is here?'

'Anything's possible,' sighed Nick, moving over to the window standing back in the shadows, staring at the boatyard until his vision blurred. 'Can we take them?' Nick wanted to know, rubbing his eyes.

'Say the word Nick, everyone is in place. Your show right down the line, your word. Say when.'

'Go,' Nick said with quiet determination. 'We go Ernst, it's a green light.'

Talking into his radio, Ernst relayed his orders and Nick ran after him down to a waiting Mercedes.

'It's going to be fine,' Ernst assured him, pulling on a dark balaclava that he rolled down round his neck. 'No problems, Nick.'

'There never are,' he answered, only too aware of the danger.

Fine specks of snow swirled looking for somewhere to land, drifting aimlessly in circles as Ernst drove round the block parking opposite the boatyard gates, cutting the engine and headlights. Now they had ringside seats with a chance of seeing blood. Ernst grabbed another balaclava off the back seat and dropped it in Nick's lap. Very nice, now he was really one of the team. The traffic had all but dried up and a pale light struggled in the thick white air when Lukas brushed by, dragging himself off up a frozen bank close to the Elbe where trees grew to no great height, bent double by the wind. Coming the other way Erika and Markus argued, their breath bursting in angry white puffs. Two missing? Nick twisted in his seat. Ignaz and Danny as a second entry team? Uncertainty and fear, a rush of nerves that he'd unleashed a diabolical force; Dr. Frankenstein unable to control his monster.

'OK, Liesel,' Ernst in conversation with a voice sounding miles away. 'Take a good look round on your way in to check for opposition, count the cars.'

By the crooked trees, Lukas stooped to tie a lace on his combat boot, Erika and Markus were clinched in a kiss by the gates and everything ran at normal speed. Parked just inside the yard Nick saw a Land Cruiser resting in weak light coming from a stockyard pole. An off-roader's dream with tinted windows, blocked in by Freja and her Volvo estate.

'She can cope, Nick, no doubts. Freja can make it happen,' Sargens said, tugging up his balaclava.

This is worse than taking a jump from a plane Nick thought, easing his own woollen helmet on. His body jerked as Ernst's radio crackled which might have been the cue for stage effect smoke, a charge and Danny's H&K slaying everything in sight. But it only brought an absurd stale pause, normality and ordinariness damping the tension, allowing Freja to prop up the Volvo's bonnet and peer into its guts; bent from the waist as if she'd been frozen halfway to touching her toes, her blue jeans tight across her rump.

'We've one chance,' Nick said, and somehow, he thought, we might just pull this thing off. Shaking her head Freja bent further into the engine. They must be blind, or she's not their type.

'We've a response,' said Ernst, making it sound as though someone had replied to an ad on a dating website.

Out from a clapboard office a figure came to check the obstruction, thumping down three steps to get a clear look. Ernst passed Nick a night scope and a fudged shape took on proportions that Nick could claim belonged to Blümhof. A flare suddenly exploded in Blümhof's hand and Nick realised it was a match intensified by technology. He handed the scope back to Ernst and Blümhof's cigarette became an ember. An incomprehensible yell from Blümhof brought Freja out of the engine. She gestured a helpless look, venturing into the yard to meet Blümhof halfway.

'Move it, get it out of here.'

'But it won't start,' said Freja, striking her fingers through her short hair in apparent frustration.

'I don't care. I don't want to know. Move it.'

'Come and try, have a look. Maybe I've not checked something,' said Freja.

'Me?' said Blümhof and tossed the cigarette over his shoulder. 'There will be a fee if I get it started, are you prepared to pay?'

'Depends on what sort of job you make,' laughed Freja as Blümhof admired her figure all the way back to the car.

'Turn it over,' ordered Blümhof. Freja obliged and the engine went through its preliminaries but never fired. 'Battery's dead.' He got out from under the bonnet and froze. Freja's H&K P9S pointed at his head, not his heart.

Erika and Markus hit him at speed, and he put up a minimum struggle, his head bagged, his wrists cuffed before they dragged him away. Through Ernst's open window Nick heard two rapid rounds emptied into the night. Ignaz and Danny lurking, a trap set and by the sound, already sprung. A terrible pause then figures suddenly running.

Screaming orders into his radio Ernst stamped on the accelerator and they humped over the pavement, crashing right through the fence. Uprooted posts and wire stuck under the car sent out a shiver of sparks, the muscles in Ernst's hands taught and solid as he fought with the yammering wheels. Throwing the car around a corner, they skidded into a hull and took it straight off its wedges smashing a headlight, the engine screaming wildly. They missed Lukas by inches. Rolling over and over in the snow in front of a motor cruiser stripped to its ribs, Danny and Shikovo not playing but intent on serious injury. In the pillar of headlights Gorshov sprinted away from the rear of the office.

'He's mine,' Nick shouted, out and running before Ernst could even shut off the engine.

Nick landed with a crump that rearranged his senses. Pools of darkness and pools of ice under his feet, his legs pounding away under him that he couldn't regulate. Ducking under a hull, a length of anchor chain crashed past his head, cracking and splitting a fibreglass mould. Gorshov swung the chain again in a flail, crunching into Nick's shoulder. He parried Gorshov's lashes with a boat hook driving him back. With both hands Gorshov hurled his chain, scrambling clear over a racing yacht's cockpit. A dull drumming ahead as Gorshov, slipping and dropping, pounded across a column of icy oil drums close to the yard's fence. Nick ran, drove his legs harder, his snatched breath giving off shrill whistles. Vaulting a hurdle of masts, he lunged. One of Nick's hands in mid-air, curving, falling and snatching at Gorshov's legs. Dragging him off the wire, Nick punched. Venom. Anger. Frustration. Blows to Gorshov's body and head. A fine spray of blood and sweat bounced off the Russian as he shook Gorshov to his feet.

'London... who gave the orders for the preventative measures? Who targeted the woman for execution?' He slapped Gorshov into paying attention, take the stupid grin off his face, pay his respects for the dead. 'Who gave the order?'

'Go fuck yourself,' panted Gorshov, touching a corner of his mouth. He glanced at a trace of blood on the back of his hand, then stared defiantly at Nick.

'Did the asset in London know?' Nick screamed, two severe punches rocking Gorshov's head.

'Fuck you...,' the Russian ran out of breath, and his chest squeaked as he gasped for air. Shaking his head, he clutched at his chest as though he needed to get it open and do some urgent work inside there. He tried speaking but his voice had been lifted out and there was only a strange hollow echo left.

Nick slammed Gorshov into the fence.

'... targets... you... her....' Gorshov took a break between words, a lull to recharge his lungs.

'That so,' said Nick.

Grabbing Gorshov by his collar he hurled him into a catamaran, his head hitting the boat's skin with a sickening thud.

'On your knees,' yelled Nick, kicking Gorshov off his feet. The cold night staining his skin reminding him of Sabine, he stood panting and sweating, a fighter waiting for the next round.

Gorshov moved every muscle in his face, a rushed check through his nerves ending with an outright laugh. Nick unzipped his jacket, withdrew his pistol and pressed the barrel into the nape of Gorshov's neck.

'Do it...' Gorshov hissed. '...save Tazi the effort...'

'I've got better things to do,' spat Nick, stepping away as Freja and Erika arrived.

The adrenalin firing Nick gradually subsided, a sluggish return to something close to a normal. Waiting for him inside the yard's office Ernst paced backwards and forwards, stepping over Ignaz's legs as he sat on the corridor floor cleaning his H&K; obsessive wipes up and down the smooth barrel. Groans from Gorshov rhythmically kept time with Ignaz's polishing; sullen and sulky, concentrating on his task.

'They're all accounted for,' Ernst said, avoiding Nick's simmering eyes.

Cuffed and sitting on a pile of hessian sacks, Evgeni Kasimov calmly watched the drama unfold.

'You appreciate that I will claim full diplomatic immunity,' Kasimov declared, his voice hard but sounding as though it belonged to a shadow.

'Don't speak to me again,' Nick warned him, walking off.

In a storeroom Freja and Ursel were taking care of Franziska, kneeling each side of her on a thick mattress, helping her dress. She visibly shrank as Nick came in.

'You have nothing to worry about,' he said, a clumsy knot to his voice.

'You are safe. Blümhof is an animal,' he added, seeing for himself the depth of her beauty, the reason why she'd become the preferred honeytrap bait.

'They threatened to kill her,' Freja said with a narrow smile.

'They would,' he answered, going through into a small office.

The office was painted a dull brown with a stout ledger desk taking pride of place under a window. Blueprints, newspaper cuttings and steerage charts were pinned in no order on the walls, a pot-bellied stove gave the only warmth dropping ash into a split pan. There was a smell of cigars, cheap aftershave and cooking more than a day old. Nick however had no surge of excitement, or righteous justification or even cathartic release; which given the circumstances might have been appropriate. Instead, he paid much attention to a sepia print coming away from its frame. Young faces discoloured over the years turned brown, given a hard edge, as though their skin were leather. A group of them arranged stiffly at the stern of a yacht about to be launched. From its mast, tails of bunting were caught in a breeze that would later carry the scent of war and death. The waiting is almost over he decided, heading out into the yard.

• • •

Nick drove away from the river into a plantation of saplings as slender as nails, a snowplough lumbering up the road behind him as he made a tedious journey back into Hamburg and Druyer GmbH. The company had its registered base in a small suite of rented offices behind the solid Gothic-styled brick walls of a former spice warehouse; its jutting gables and towers climbing high above Pickhuben, marooned between canals in the port's Speicherstadt district. Besides Jack Balgrey's quite spacious office, there was a small anteroom for Lucy, a Service administrator and behind secure metal doors, the comms room run by Euan, a bookish thirty-year old who longed for an exotic embassy posting with a communications room larger than a cupboard.

But as Nick patrolled outside that evening, only a single light burnt in Balgrey's office on the third floor. Headlights streamed past Nick as he rounded the back of the warehouse, the city running up to full flood as commuters and shoppers poured towards the autobahn and suburbs. Rolling in along the canal a fine web of mist clung to the freezing air. Come on, Jack what's keeping you? Nick walked off the cold in his legs, fifteen paces each way never moving from the shadows, not stepping near the security camera's infrared cone. The Skoda had a coating of dust and dried mud down each wheel arch and was the dirtiest in the car park; a burgundy estate Jack Balgrey finally approached at a quarter past seven; careless, not checking the shadows.

Whipping round too late as he opened his door. Balgrey never saw Nick strike. A low punch in the small of his back followed by a firm hold around Balgrey's flabby neck.

'It's time we talked, Jack, time we talked about a house on Fehmarn. Time we talked about you working for Moscow. Time we talked about everything,' Nick whispered into his ear. 'We're going for a drive, Jack,' he ordered, releasing his hold.

'Come on, Nick, what's the hell's eating you?' groaned Balgrey clutching his side, his breath drawn hard into his chest gave wheezy lunges that rocked his body.

'Get in,' ordered Nick, holding open the driver's door.

'I don't know what you're talking about, but you've done damage, old son, that's what you've done,' he whined as Nick slipped into the passenger seat. 'What do you say about a proper grown-up chat before you do me a permanent injury?' His back curved away from the seat too brittle to be straight, his unblinking eyes observing Nick's fierce stare.

'Drive, Jack, because we don't want disturbing, do we? You follow my directions. Now drive.'

Closing his eyes, Balgrey shifted his body in the seat. Steph was right, Stephanie his wife was never wrong. Too old, too slow, not sharp enough for a tough operator like Torr. He should have thrown in the towel years ago, taken a pub in Dorset, a free house with passing trade and a tasty barmaid to ease the winter nights. As long as they had somewhere for Steph's bloody precious dolls, they'd be fine. Starting the engine, he clumsily mistimed the gear changes and drove with an intensified alertness; traffic lights, festive lights, colour and bloody pain. He teased himself with a clip of how he'd bolt for it, taking his chance at a red light. Glancing at Nick's face set tight next to him, he swallowed his plan concentrating on trying to memorise the route, anything to give him hope. Ten years too late for anything remotely heroic against someone as good as Torr.

'This really necessary?' he demanded, as Nick made him cut a corner and park in what must have been the darkest spot in the city near the Altona fish quays.

'Out.' Nick pointed him towards the door. Jack Balgrey, our man in Hamburg; approaching fifty and never going to change. A career dogged by mishaps, poor decisions and the one drink too many, Jack's mind running on dreams of his retirement, the fuel for a lack of imagination. 'Out.'

'Steady on, Nick,' he protested, untangling himself from the seatbelt, his door elbowed open.

'Move, Jack, we're running out of time.'

Nick shoved him forward down a long cinder track, its surface churned by years of wear. It led into a gorge of factory walls covered in moss and green streaks, melting snow spewed from smashed gutters.

'How long have you been Moscow's stooge? London aware of the property you manage for Moscow?' He jabbed the swelling chest with his finger and Balgrey stumbled backwards into a cobbled loading bay. Falling, he crumpled saturated cardboard boxes and smashed a couple of empty bottles. 'Come on Jack, lost your tongue?'

'Look, whatever you think I'm responsible for, there's an explanation. Before you do something stupid, hear me out,' he urged. Puffing and blowing he got onto his feet. 'I'm one step down to retirement here. I'm ignorant of what anyone's got up their sleeves. It's a shoebox posting, and I jump when Head Office tells me to jump. I send the crap Petra thinks is gold, but that's about it. Moscow... not in a million years.' He shivered and pulled his coat together. His fingers trying to fasten the buttons that had burst free as he went down. 'I'm an outside interest as far as Head Office are concerned, someone who never merits a second look.'

'Come on Jack, you were working late this evening. What's all that about?'

'End of year accounts, London want 'em filed by yesterday.'

'Part of your duties to be a caretaker is it Jack?'

'Don't know what you mean.'

'Let's begin with the house on an island not a million miles from here,' Nick suggested.

'The place on Fehmarn?' Balgrey asked, genuinely puzzled.

'The very same, Jack. Explain about the arrangements you have with a Swiss property outfit for the upkeep of the house.'

Balgrey laughed but it was only nerves, the type when someone is caught red-handed, a natural mechanism for defence.

'Hear the river Jack? Not far to walk is it? Out on your own they'd say, meeting who or what they wouldn't know. Only assume that you must have tripped, gone into the water swallowed a lot, bobbing up and down in your heavy overcoat. Alive, just, thinking of someone you care for until along comes a passing ship. Death by drowning, Jack, that's not a way to retire. Tell me about London, Moscow and the Puttgarden house? Save getting yourself wet, Jack.'

'I'm with you, old son, I'm walking up the hill fast, I comprehend.'

'About the house?'

'Came as part and parcel of the posting,' said Balgrey, 'another routine that I had to tick the box for. Look, whatever mischief you think I've been getting myself into was already here when I arrived,' he said, his flaccid throat quivering.

'Now you've got that out of the way, how about telling me the truth before I lose my patience? Come on Jack, spit it out,' Nick hissed, his nose almost touching Balgrey's. 'Tell me about London, you doing your bit, Moscow and the house? What's the arrangement? I'm losing confidence in you. I'm sorely tired with people not cooperating.'

He'd run, he bloody well would. A couple of times Balgrey's leg had twitched in a sprinter's nervous longing as he out manoeuvred Torr in his mind, but where would he reach? Out of condition and not in Torr's class, he'd get nowhere fast.

'Look, this isn't going to do you any good,' he said, going for some of the guff he'd ladled out over the years.

'The house, start with that.'

'You're crowding me, I've a lot of face to lose if all this comes down about my ears.'

'You?' Nick flung out his arms, turned in a half circle of fury and his composure went. He swung hard and Balgrey sank to his knees in pain. 'You've not even started to hurt yet, Jack.' He dragged Balgrey to his feet and stood back. 'Answers.'

'Hamburg was a smack in the face, a don't thank us posting to nothing more than a backwater post office,' Balgrey wheezed. 'I have a couple of years to run before early retirement and for that reason Head Office couldn't work out where I should spend my winding down tours. Square peg and round hole syndrome, old son. So, when my predecessor managed to drown himself on his annual scuba diving trip in the Maldives, Personnel had a solution to its problem of what to do with me. My routine old son, is to sit tight and do what I'm asked until the hands reach the hour for me to pack up and go.'

'The house Jack?'

'What is there to tell?' Balgrey shrugged and finally thought it safe to straighten up, his hands off his knees facing one bloody dangerous Nick Torr. 'The house was all part of the mundane and not very exciting in tray I inherited from Partington when he failed to surface from the Indian Ocean in the same condition as when he entered it. There was the usual watch list, potential contacts, potential spooks and one grand coastal pile on Fehmarn, for the Hamburg officer to provide adequate care and upkeep of, lock, stock and barrel, including a bunch of keys. Another Druyer asset I had to manage, so what, it was cosy for everyone.'

'Didn't you find that odd?'

Swabbing his mouth with a handkerchief, Balgrey bent and straightened once more, forcing air inside his lungs. 'Why should I? I presumed it was just another safe house, one of the many that we have salted across the globe.'

'And if I asked you nicely about Partington, you'd be able to give me all the details?'

Balgrey laughed right in his face, rotten breath and serve him right. Nick Torr, the hero on his white flaming charger. 'You're sounding obsessed, old son.'

'How long had Partington been in Hamburg?'

'Ask Personnel.' The handkerchief swabbed again, the brightest object around.

'I'm asking you, Jack, and this is your last chance,' said Nick, taking a step closer. 'How long?' Tense, Nick was ready to adopt a much tougher approach. 'Well, Jack? Sink or swim?'

'Off the top of my head, no firm date. I'd have to check,' Balgrey disclosed, ramming the handkerchief into his pocket.

'Approximately, Jack, you can manage that.'

'Six... seven years.'

'Did you visit the house?'

'Once or twice a month as per standing orders and no, there wasn't a bunch of squatters in there. I just did precursory checks inside and outside, made sure there were no problems and on the odd occasion that a job needed doing I got local trades in, paid up and sent the receipt to Switzerland,' Balgrey said. 'Good old Jack, never let anyone down.'

'So help me Jack, you expect me to believe that someone with your experience never queried why a Service safe house had its upkeep paid for by a Swiss company? That you weren't required to call in our own trades for maintenance? Come on Jack, you're beginning to disappoint me again. You know Head Office is all about accountability, Jack, don't you? Every penny scrutinised by accounts, no wastage, no overspend.'

Balgrey forlornly squinted around, looking for a way out or help but there was nothing forthcoming. 'All right,' he confessed, 'I was informed that it was a joint venture between us, the Swedes and Cousins called Operation Five Star Delivery, funding was a three-way split, hence the Swiss company as a front. As the nearest station, Hamburg was tasked to maintain and care for the place, two trips each month to check its condition and any problems we had to sort locally.'

'Who briefed you?'

'Group hug from Hawick, Jane and Blackmore wearing their Special Operations Directorate hats.'

'Why the isolation from Head Office?' Nick wondered, but he already knew the answer.

'It's a sort of half-way terminus for anything coming in from Eastern Europe, particularly threats directed at the Balts by Moscow rattling its sabre on their borders. That's the truth, the whole truth and nothing less or more.'

'How does it work?'

'The house is used to meet an asset. Nationality and value weren't disclosed. Us, the Cousins and Swedes take it in turns for a heart-to-heart, no fixed and fast dates and that's why it's checked religiously twice a month.'

'Then you do what?'

Jack Balgrey, for the very first time that evening, and quite possibly even in months, shook his head in complete honest ignorance.

'You report to who, Jack? Who do you tell it's clear, all tidy, ready for action, who do you tell?'

'Had to go through RUS/OPS, personal for Parfrey.'

'And the arrangements were handled exclusively by RUS/OPS? Well, Jack, that it?' proposed Nick.

'Far as I know, and I didn't know who made the decisions,' said Balgrey agitated. 'I'm this close to signing off and it isn't my place to question policy. I'd be hauled back home and let go. "Thanks Jack old thing, very nice what you've achieved, nothing fantastic, but solid stuff, now bugger off and collect what little pension you've got coming to you." Me, I'm just content minding my own business, don't want to rock the boat, nothing wrong with that is there?'

'Why should you, Jack, what's wrong with being Moscow's cut-out?'

Wiping his lips with the back of his hand, Balgrey had a sudden realisation. 'I've been right royally stitched up, haven't I?' he stated, as though someone has just illuminated a very dark highway and he could now thankfully see his way home.

'We all have,' Nick answered.

'Christ, I had no way of knowing,' he admitted, his mouth and throat dry.

'You weren't meant to, no one was,' explained Nick. 'Anything special about the house, Jack, anything you noted?'

Balgrey, for once not playing for time actually had to think, his pudgy face grimaced in concentration as he went over the interior in his mind. Pulling together an inventory of each room, he considered what up to then he had taken for the mundane, seeing everything in an entirely fresh perspective. 'Place always reeked like a perfume counter,' he ventured slowly, 'odd now I come to think of it.'

'What else? Come on,' Nick encouraged him.

'Anything, old son, anything?' Balgrey wondered, not sure what Nick wanted.

'Anything out of the ordinary, anything that caught your eye.'

'Difficult to say, one safe house is just like another, except…' Here Balgrey perhaps recognised for the first time what Nick was striving to find; the anomaly that betrays the over confident, the ordinary that when read differently yields the extraordinary. 'The main room seemed too personal, little objects, more like souvenirs really, dotted around.'

'Where from? Can you remember Jack?' Nick asked with an intensity and passion in his voice that was both threatening and fearful all at once.

'Not all of 'em, old son, think there was stuff from Nairobi, Stockholm, Moscow, Washington, Berlin and London. Pretty odd choices if you ask me, not stuff I'd class as important.'

But someone had very valid reasons thought Nick. Someone reaffirming a commitment. 'I need your comms room,' Nick insisted, his mood now determined.

'Whatever you say, Nick, lead and I shall follow.'

Which is exactly what Nick opted to do. In Jack's communication room Nick composed a cable on the secure ARRAMIS system for the CO8 duty officer, classed priority and for the immediate attention of Rossan alone, requesting a name check on passports and visas bearing any traces on Kristina Mörtviken. He then drafted a separate cable for Rossan again, classification ULTRA, that asked for verification on Service worknames consistent with postings in Nairobi, Stockholm. Moscow, Washington, Berlin and London. When Nick had finished, Jack with a growing sense of relief showed him out.

'Is that it? All you want? Free to go, am I? Forget you've ever seen me. Let a failure get back to his wife?'

'For tonight.' Nick held out his hand, and Balgrey came forward to take it. Instead of reconciliation, Nick slammed him against a doorpost. Unable to move, Balgrey winced as Nick's face came within an inch of his own. 'Our arrangement is private Jack,' Nick said. 'You don't need to discuss our joint operation with anyone.'

Wistfully nodding, Balgrey hung his head and shuffled along towards his car.

Twenty-Nine

The girl wore her golden plaits like campaign medals as she strode purposely up Hamburg's Neuer Wall. Not displayed on her chest, but falling evenly down her long back, over a velvet collar on a Sunday coat, a coat old fashioned in its cut, held by a row of double buttons and gathered round her tapering waist. It reminded Nick of the coats worn by his aunt and her sisters, refugees on painful photographs; a whole family album of them documenting his German mother's exodus across Europe. Now of course like so many contemporary phases of fashion, retro was 'seriously in' though there were some things from the past better left undisturbed. In front of Nick the girl walked with assurance, her route predetermined while he had nothing to occupy him except keeping her in sight.

Nick kept his steps brisk and short beneath the hooped splendour of festive lights as Hamburg began to prepare for the night. Demurely, her held high and proud, the girl wove through warps of women laden with children and bags. *You follow Rosa, everything's prepared*, Harry had promised Nick. To hell and back if it proves Lubov correct, vowed Nick, though he only had to go as far as the Wilhelmsburg district. In some major cities there are certain areas, perhaps consisting of a street or two, where the fieldman instinctively adjusts to a change of atmosphere; a menace in the air, a sense of knowing that somehow you have crossed into unknown and unfriendly territory. And Nick had that now, trailing right after Rosa into a café rooted right under a Second World War concrete flak tower that guarded nothing more strategic than a children's playground. Picking her seat with deep concentration, Rosa stared out across marble-topped tables as dull as headstones.

No eye contact Harry had said, let Rosa make the moves; only she has gone to sleep, she has forgotten Nick thought, trying to catch her wilful gaze. Decorating the walls were patchy relics of circus life. Posters from a different age were framed big and small, along with tickets, a whip, and suspended from the high 1930s ceiling, a trapeze the owner had once spectacularly performed on. As Harry predicted, Rosa ordered a coffee. 'When she has finished Nick, she will ask you if you have a pen she can borrow. She will accept your pen and tell you a destination.'

Except none of what Harry promised actually happened. In the middle of ordering his own drink, Nick watched as the whole performance went to pieces. A waiter crisp with authority, a starched towel across his forearm, bent to Rosa, spoke then fell back smartly. Holding his cheek, he yelled and swore as Rosa stood to aim another slap with her open hand. A couple of regulars sat immobile as the screams reached full pitch. The table upended, scattering the cup and menu. More staff appeared, the trapeze swinging furiously as they passed.

In the melee, a heavy hand pulled Nick sideways, dragging him away through empty tables into the kitchen. A precaution, a thin boy in chef's whites assured him. Nick dug in his heels. From what? From whom? From those following you sent by Moscow, the thin boy answered as Nick was tugged roughly by the arm; out into the cold evening air that pushed frantically into his face. Into the back of a Renault box van; nudged forcefully from behind, Nick struck his head on a door pillar and instinctively felt for blood. Thrown head over heels as the van drew sharply away, Nick lay perfectly still amongst a collection of laundry sacks.

Stabs of orange light came in quick succession through the van's rear window, prison bars of amber flashing on his outstretched legs. Moscow all over again Nick thought. Cold off the floor seeped through his coat and Nick slapped a couple of laundry sacks into shape forming makeshift cushions and began to replay key segments of Moscow's cunning strategy. A moment of quiet reflection before the madness began. After his meeting with Balgrey, Nick had kept his own counsel, preferring his own dour company as he awaited Rossan's response. Moving between hotels, never staying longer than one night, Nick always paid cash in advance acutely aware that he had made himself a prime target. Leaving himself an exit, planning a route, he experienced once more some of the urgency he had known in his early days of front line operations. Now a different nervousness gripped him, a state of heightened anticipation and clarity, as well as the depression. Unshaven, eating only when he had to, when the weakness threatened to keel him over, he had become a creature of preparation. Long hours only punctured by the waiting.

As he lay there atop the laundry sacks, Nick had a sensation of it all being a dream, of having no real concept of how it all had begun, or why so many had perished as he followed Lubov's trail for the treasure. If he'd also demanded of himself a truthful assessment of whether he'd succeed, his answer would have to be that he couldn't be sure. There were too many unknown factors in the equation. Had Rossan actually succeeded in carrying out Nick's bidding, had he matched the souvenirs from the Puttgarden house with a face? Had the offer of opening a dialogue with Moscow been rejected? Asking himself a further rhetorical question of how much could go catastrophically wrong? Nick again had the answer – plenty, reminding himself that Rossan had not only Bailrigg to convince, but Moscow also. And if Rossan... But Nick didn't want to dwell on that particular 'and if'.

But waiting had always been an occupational hazard that stunned the liveliest senses, so that months and years seemed to have passed after Nick and Foula had set out for Moscow. Since then, Moscow's main asset had always been a step ahead, and Nick sorely wanted an answer as to why someone would allow innocent people to die to protect their treachery. Right now, he wanted that answer more than ever.

The van pulled up sharply flinging him into the partition behind the front seats. Cold air swam into the back and the driver's voice insisted he didn't move. Edging up to the back windows he pushed his face tight into the corner, giving himself a broad view through the glass, watching as the front passenger set off alone. On each corner of the market square four braziers caged in roaring flames, seasoned wood spitting in the heat, black tails of smoke corkscrewing over red roofs and families in small groups, chocolate for the children, plum brandy for the parents. Nick's eyes wandered through them; a stranger come to steal their joy. Pulled open with a dry rusty cry, the back doors brought in a handful of sleet, a familiar greeting and Danny Redman dressed in black.

'From Rossan,' Danny said, passing across a thin envelope as the van set off.

As Nick reached forward for Rossan's response, Danny saw his fingers hesitate for the briefest of seconds before he snatched the envelope off him, ripping open the flap as though an inner turmoil, a craving, consumed him. Nick, his head dipped low, read the single sheet of A4 paper in the murky van's light, grunted at the end of the page then scanned it again more quickly; nothing coded just all the facts presented clear – dates, locations and a name. When he'd finished Nick tucked the paper and envelope into an inside pocket. His eyes, noted Danny, were ferocious, his mood dark, murderous even; staring so intently, that Danny later swore that Nick could see right through him and the side of the van.

'Rossan also said to say that we're on,' added Danny, though because of his mood, Nick might never have heard him.

Thirty

End of the line, full circle reached, and Nick was at the point of no return as his team of irregulars took up their positions on the island of Fehmarn. He snatched at his parka hood, losing a running skirmish with the freezing Baltic gusts storming in off the sea. This is it here and now, this is where he finally laid the ghosts to rest: Angie, Sabine, Lubov, Wynn, Lister, Parfrey and God forgive them thought Nick, all the others who the London traitor had condemned to death over the years. He swung away and glanced off to his right, not bothering to look up at the house's windows facing Puttgarden's small square.

He knew he had an audience tracing his every step, standing there with all the lights off: Hawick, Blackmore and Jane with Rossan holding their coat tails, come as official observers for a joint operation. What operation they had demanded? The culmination of a Langley led adventure Bailrigg had explained, in a thoroughly bad temper when he briefed them collectively the day before. Something the Cousins had simmering for a while when it unexpectedly came to the boil, but the Cousins had overstretched their resources. 'So, they've had to go cap in hand asking for assistance, which means Cologne have cleared the way and Torr and some freelancers are making up the numbers, coordinating the final stages.' Bailrigg announced as though it deeply pained him. Exactly who or what the Cousins had landed Bailrigg kept vague, stressing that with Washington, London and Berlin holding hands on the outcome of what had been touted as a high value catch, he wanted them present to make sure the Service wasn't palmed off with left-over scraps.

As invited spectators, the guests from London had taken their positions in the house, a fine old property bordering the square, its roof pitched unevenly towards the street, its bright shutters pinned back against white rendered walls. Smeared by sand urged off the shore by the Baltic, its windows were coated in a fine brown film giving the square an old-world tint. A seasonal residence belonging to a senior civil servant from Berlin that Döbeln had secured for the operation, which Nick and his tireless team had worked solidly without a break to prepare for the forthcoming show.

Upstairs in one of the bedrooms Ernst had set up his electronic toys and sundry equipment on a dressing table lovingly treated to furniture wax. 'Basic, but fine, enough for our needs for sure,' Ernst had assured Nick, checking the equipment the previous afternoon. Danny hoped it would also be enough, because in Nick's absence, he had been delegated second in command and part of his duties including briefing the senior officers from London. Which he had done, by firstly standing with Jane as they watched Nick circle the square and disappear.

'Does Nick seem his usual self to you?' Jane asked casually, turning from the window her sharp eyes locked on Danny.

'When isn't he stressed or concerned about an operation,' Danny admitted. 'Everything's up in the air. Organising this firewall around the joint reception party has been manic. Too many cooks and all that.'

'I can imagine.' Jane hadn't taken her eyes off Danny. 'Do we know what sort of deal the Cousins have brokered?'

'Something Langley has cooked up with us, and Cologne's stirring the pot,' said Danny, following Nick's script to the letter, though with the amount of culinary references it ought to be have been a recipe he decided. 'Nick's handling the reception and he's keeping everything close to his chest.'

'He would,' agreed Jane.

And Danny had used the same script for Hawick and Blackmore without deviation or variation, delivering his lines without so much as a hiccup. After that, Danny disappeared from the stage, his role completed, and as Nick had stressed, if everything fell apart, there was no reason why Danny should be caught in the fallout.

Now, with their teams split between the square and the ferry terminal, Nick and Ernst did one final check and returned to the house with nothing before them but the night. A sullen moon had slipped behind heavy cloud and the darkness glowered over Puttgarden like the advance of a hostile force. The darkness had crawled across the frozen plain seeking them out. It's the night making fools of us thought Nick, come all the way from Moscow for its revenge. Nearby a dog barked a lonely call that ran through the square as Ernst once more monitoring the airwaves, called out the time; Nick noting the taut voice, feeling the same tightness constrict his own throat. Outside a lively wind picked at the mounds of hard snow, kicking specks of white into the air where they shone for a few seconds and went out.

On a tall stool borrowed from the kitchen Nick sat by the window, a group of kids wandering across his view obscuring a Volkswagen camper, three boys and a girl joking and playing about, pushing and jostling their way to a corner of the square. The exchange is not going to happen Nick panicked in a wild moment of doubt, the waiting, the suffering, the dead along the way, all would be for nothing, a useless epitaph for failure. For Nick felt nothing of triumph or achievement, merely the empty longing of someone who has had a glimpse of the future and can only helplessly watch it vanish. A big new estate laboured through the frozen streets before pulling over for the kids to climb in. Twisting to follow the red tail lights, he thought it's all been called off and we're the last to know, Moscow has broken its end of the deal. He turned to the camper again in the middle of the square where it sat at rest in a stark crater of light. Sitting up front was Markus; his hands on the wheel, clearly visible from a distance, while lying on the floor in the back Freja and Liesel had their weapons trained on Gorshov. Who, far from being what Roly dismissed as *a minnow, nothing higher than an enabler offering B&B to the serious players passing through*, actually turned out to be a fully paid-up GRU colonel of some substance, and rather more important than anyone gave him credit for.

'Everything okay?' asked Nick at the window as Erika walked in, and down in the square Lukas trailed off out of sight. 'Where's Rossan?'

'Having a conference next door with the three seniors. Not to be disturbed, all of them deciding on procedure.'

'Good,' said Nick.

Around Nick a haphazard stock of equipment stacked in no necessary order, a covert intelligence team's wares packed for a busy night's work. Radios and receivers, tool rolls and hard cases holding electronic devices – binoculars, night scopes, all the assistance specialists would require for the covert surveillance of an exchange. Was this how other memorable failures down the centuries had commenced? The commanders sitting and fretting before a battle? Croesus, Harold, Richard III, all of them camped close to the battlefield which in a matter of hours would be the scene of their destruction and humiliation. Watching, waiting, hearing distant sounds of the enemy and seeing the flames from their campfires and the bark from their dogs of war. Did they also put on a smile and a mask of courage as they tried to conquer their own inadequacy and fear? he wondered as Ernst joined him, chatting on his radio to his boys and girls in the square and the watchers by the ferry berths.

'Why's Balgrey so late?' Nick asked no one in particular, panning a night scope along the road remorselessly flowing on and up from Hamburg on the E47 through Heiligenhafen to this skinny island peninsula where it dribbled into the sea. Ernst pacing behind him, the king of the airwaves, everyone's friend of all time, Ernst and the wonders of modern technology.

Nick let his mind drift, following the crying wind as it plucked at mounds of hard snow, flicking specks through pyramids of light shining from the street lamps. In this mood Nick reminded himself that he was doing this out of duty for his country; that he agreed with Orwell on the concept of patriotism as being devoted to a nation, and its way of life rather that nationalism which was utterly divisive. And if that was too deep, too patriotic, Nick would have provided a popular analogy, that all his life he had refused to cross to the dark side because he despised what it offered, what it turned individuals into.

'Coffee?' asked Ernst. Not getting an answer, he poured boiling water over the granules in three mugs.

Watching wind and snow was a tiresome game, a countdown to destruction or humiliation that didn't improve Nick's inner gloom, less so when movement caught his eye. A figure crouched into a low run moving so fast it could have been mistaken for a shadow. Then it was no more, swallowed by a thick group of sturdy elder trees swaying and bowing by a Protestant church monopolising the town and square, easily outgrowing the trees with its steep straight corners and a high box tower.

'It's going to happen, Nick, no problems,' Ernst reassured him. 'Jesus, you're making me jumpy, have some coffee,' he insisted.

'Why don't we pull Anja off the ferry berths to boost numbers by the vehicles?' Nick said, his binoculars swinging up and down the square.

'Hey, think some of the time, Nick, please. The Ferry is due any minute,' Ernst said, shaking his head as he looked at Erika.

It'd be no use trying to reason with Nick at this point, realised Ernst.

He'd also lived with this tension before, when the final round of surveillance actually takes its toll, even with experienced guys who one moment are calm, the next they're ready to blow. On his radio an atmospheric hiss played up and down a scale all its own.

'What time is the last sailing?'

'This *is* the last sailing from Denmark,' Ernst said, rolling his coffee around the walls of a thick mug.

'Balgrey will show,' Erika said, conciliatory, trying to damp down Nick's fuse, bring him back from the edge.

'Does everyone know what we're doing?'

'Actually, I tell everyone we're here for a vacation,' said Ernst. 'Nick, listen to me, please. Everything's going to be fine. I told my boys and girls they could have it rough. They know they're not here for the view. Isn't that right?' he asked Erika.

'Sure, we're not kids.'

Consoling himself Nick counted the cars in front of a hotel opposite, eight assorted makes including the camper, and parked strategically nearby, a second-hand BMW four-by-four, containing Dominik.

'Everyone knows the fallback?' asked Nick.

'Nick, please,' cried Ernst in total exasperation.

'I was only asking,' said Nick, marking off reference points, dividing up the square into areas of risk and threat as snow careered down, see-sawing romantically on the town.

'We may have a problem,' said Ernst, cranking his head from his radio. 'Markus reports that he's already sighted opposition.'

'That's too early, not what was agreed,' snapped Nick.

Holding up a hand, Ernst spoke rapidly into his mouthpiece then pressed to receive. 'He thinks Moscow have people in place, okay. They may be observing, they may be rogues.'

'That's wonderful, Ernst. How long have we been making sure this exchange was going to run to our schedule?'

'A small problem, Nick, okay.'

'No, Ernst, it's a big problem. We've got uninvited guests out there and we don't know whose side they're on. Go find them, Ernst,' insisted Nick. 'Erika you reinforce the team in the camper.'

'We've action, the ferry's berthing,' Ernst announced his radio chattering away. 'Ten minutes before they roll off. I'll take care of it,' promised Ernst, spinning on Erika's heels and heading for the door.

I should have asked Döbeln to quarantine the town thought Nick; passports required, a full ten-year history, positive vetting to get in or out, of course I should. This is Tazi, the man who doesn't answer to any directorate muscling his way in. Behind him Nick heard the door open, glanced over his shoulder and saw Jane come slowly to his side.

'Things not going to plan?' she asked, her voice low, strangely disinterested.

'I'll get over it,' Nick answered, his attention elsewhere. 'Where's Teddy, Roly and Paul?'

'Still squabbling over whether it's us, the Cousins or Germans who get first bite. I gave them my opinion,' she said.

'You always do,' said Nick slipping out the card with its message versed in Latin, the one he'd taken from the side of Angie's grave. 'Meant to thank you,' he added snapping the creased card down in front of Jane.

Without answering Jane lifted it, stared at it for a moment before passing it back to Nick. 'I didn't think you'd know it was me.'

'It's the small details that always matter.'

Years impersonating minutes, Jane's regular breathing by his ear, her perfume running down losing its appeal and power. Cars with Danish plates were rumbling through the town off the ferry, Ursel and Anja supplying a running commentary when the first foot passengers appeared over the bridge. One chance and it's going to be tonight or never.

'A Nissan minivan, red, two up front,' Nick relayed Ursel's words to the camper and BMW. 'Do you receive? Should be coming over the bridge around now.'

'The Nissan has company, all the way from the ferry. Mercedes, Danish plates, three up. Two front, one rear,' Anja reported.

Distorted voices answered in relays, booming round the room in a wide echo. Gothic clock bells clanged in the church tower; timing Nick would never forget. The Nissan sped into the square throwing up sparks of snow from under its wheels, stopping behind the BMW, becoming its very own shadow as a large Mercedes fresh off the ferry drew up across the square.

'Senior members of the opposition,' Erika's crackling voice said. 'Definitely.'

Pulling slowly into the square came a rugged Ford Expedition complete with tinted windows, good old Jack Balgrey's arrival creating another flurry of radio traffic piped into Nick's ear. It also brought Blackmore, Hawick and Rossan into the room after hearing and seeing for themselves the scenes unfolding from the monitors feeding the action directly next door.

'Must *we* always be so tardy?' demanded Hawick, shrugging his coat onto his shoulders, tucking his scarf inside his thick lapels.

'Do we know who's going to be in the bag?' wondered Blackmore, already dressed it seemed for a brisk evening stroll. 'Thought the exchange was low key?'

'I think Nick may have other plans,' said Jane remotely.

For Nick, intently staring from the window an immediate answer didn't seem pressing.

'Positive ID from Ernst on the Nissan and no one moves until I say,' said Nick into the radio.

'I wouldn't think anyone's in a hurry,' said Rossan, comfortable on a chair at the back of the room.

By the church bare branches waved and cavorted in quick rhythm set by the wind, but it wasn't their dancing Nick noticed, but a GRU operative climb out of the Nissan and take up station as he surveyed the square.

'Time to go?' Hawick and Blackmore asked in unison, and without waiting for a reply they were already on their way down to the square.

Sliding back the camper's door Erika and Liesel signalled their pledge, their token of good faith by illuminating Gorshov's face with a flashlight. Nosing forward the Mercedes made a pass, its headlights yellow plumes showing up the spreading snow. Reversing past the camper, the driver of the Mercedes craned to look inside. Uncertain, one final decision, this the big one thought Nick. You make your mind up if everything's legitimate, if I have kept my end of the bargain reasoned Nick, then you must jump one way or the other.

'He's not sure,' breathed Jane.

'You okay?' Rossan asked her.

'Why shouldn't I be?' she curtly demanded.

'Twenty, thirty seconds and we are going to make the exchange,' said Nick into the radio's mouthpiece. 'Everyone ready to go? Is that a yes, Ernst? Did I hear you confirm?' Ernst approved and Nick swallowed. 'Dominik, you confirm?' And Dominik did.

Coming full circle, the Mercedes drew up a good forty metres short of the camper. Out of the house and crossing the square slowly, Blackmore in Hawick's footsteps. Nick had a stomach cramp as he watched for any signs of a problem, his thoughts running so fast they smeared and caught hold of each other. Snow blanking out the windscreens of cars parked in the square. Idling, its exhaust billowing in the icy air, the Mercedes stood ready in position so its rear seat passenger would have a grandstand view as the disgraced officers made an undignified run for home.

'Let's go everyone,' said Nick, ushering Jane and Rossan out of the door.

In the square an agreed routine saw Gorshov escorted from the camper by Markus, Freja, Liesel and Erika, their warm breaths punching holes in the minus air. None of them carrying bags and suitcases bearing gifts, but a hope that they would be received warmly on what was after all, Christmas Eve. Then out of the Ford came Jack Balgrey, holding open the rear door as General Evgeni Kasimov stepped neatly out into the snow, the 'main man' as Tolz described him.

With Nick's chips clearly piled high on the table, it became, as Rossan would later describe, a tense second and a half as the Moscow contingent made their minds up if they were going to play or cry broke. To Rossan's sheer relief as well as Ernst and his team, the rear door of the Nissan swung open and Irina Dezhenka, better known to Nick by her workname of Kristina Mörtviken levered herself out.

'Nick what have you done?' said Jane, her voice alarmed, her hand touching his, her skin freezing as they took a slow diagonal route across the square.

'Shame Gav couldn't be here,' said Nick. 'Wonder what he'd have said when he saw Katrina again?'

Striding into position, Balgrey took the front with Kasimov dutifully at his side. A metre remaining to be covered between the two opposing teams as Irina stepped ahead by herself, perhaps out of disgrace, and she seemed to be searching about her for a familiar face. Kasimov on the other hand had a tough spring to his steps, his eyes level and set, never varying his gaze from straight ahead as though off to war. On their walk from the camper, Markus and Erika flanked Gorshov, and as they neared the Mercedes, a rear door was flung open. A thin figure in the rear of the car twisted to gain a better look, maximising his position to add his own form of humiliation and displeasure to the returning GRU officers.

Snowflakes stuck to Nick's face, clung to his hair as he scanned the square a sense of fulfilment slowly rising.

'It's a trap,' screamed Jane in Russian, darting towards the Mercedes.

Nick on her heels dived in a rugby tackle bringing her down. Screaming Jane's name, the rear of Irina Dezhenka's skull disappeared as a high velocity round struck her mid-centre in the forehead. Dropping in a heap, her knees hit the hard snow, splaying out and buckling as the rest of her bounced, unfolded in a bundle.

Noise from a dream seemed trapped in Nick's head; slow, slurred, a high-pitched scream, a record played on the wrong speed. A second shot cracked, then a third as Nick lost his grip on Jane. The severe kick in his back jerked him forwards. Nick locked in a capsule of pain and sound containing the Mercedes engine racing, more yells and screams all at a volume he couldn't control. He tried lifting himself and did. He crouched and saw the Mercedes door slam closed as it sped off without Kasimov, Gorshov or their London asset.

A serious bruise was growing in Nick's back from a vengeful kick, delivered by Jane as she viciously set about him. Punches and desperate slaps delivered as she screamed and spat at him for being a bastard. 'Why?' she yelled her fists aimed in tight swings at Nick's head. It took Rossan a good half a minute to haul Jane off and he had to accept the help of Erika, Liesel and Ernst to restrain her.

'Why Nick, why Irina?' Jane demanded the snow clinging to her hair.

'Do you really need to ask?' Nick said staring straight into her eyes. 'A means to an end. The same as Angie was.'

'I had no say in it,' she screamed.

'But you knew about Lister and Parfrey,' Nick retorted angrily. 'You exploited Parfrey and she unwittingly gave you Lubov. Parfrey even sacrificed herself because she thought you loved her.'

'I had no choice, Nick, believe me, no choice,' she shouted.

'Everyone has a choice,' Nick raged. 'You let them murder Angie and you let them murder Juris Valgos, you even planted his phone in my house for them. Everything you did was to save your own skin,' he shouted turning his back.

When they'd led Jane away with her hands tightly cuffed, Nick kicked out at a pile of heaped snow. Forgive me Angie, but I had to make sure that you did not die in vain. Around him, blue lights appearing as Rossan and Döbeln supervised the packing away of the Russian dead; Jane's lover and handler Irina, Kasimov and Sabine's hated Gorshov. In all the rumpus and confusion, no one paid much attention to two figures working their way through the trees by the church, walking quite calmly, their weapons broken down, carried in neat blue holdalls.

•••

As the weeks passed following Jane's exposure as Moscow's loyal acolyte, there were no confirmed sightings of Nick. Instead there were the swirling mists of speculation, reports from the side-lines by those who professed intimate knowledge of the Service, though none were its in employ. These were the partisan spectators of Whitehall, who in a particular capacity brushed up against the Firm's hem and considered themselves connected.

Rumours circulated on how Nick, having lost the capacity for sound reason like Ahab chasing his whale, had embarked on his own murderous vendetta, starting with the hunt for the mysterious Tazi figure in Moscow. Which made Hawick's rush to have a full complement of Mortland's Regulators guarding his home perfectly reasonable they sagely agreed. Others, insisting Nick was utterly broken in mind and spirit, related how he had abandoned the land for the sea, devoting himself to a voyage of rediscovery on a lonely voyage aboard his yacht. The more imaginative had him clearing landmines for a charitable trust or sinking drinking water wells in Africa. A couple of devious minds swore they were in possession of evidence Nick was selling his services as a mercenary.

It was perfectly accurate that he hadn't been seen anywhere near the Mad House, nor had his shadow come within sight of Head Office, but that was because C had granted Nick extended leave. In any case, everyone had their heads down awaiting a savage cull which was said to be imminent, so it was a case of staying low and hoping the shell exploded in someone else's trench.

If anyone had bothered to make the effort, Nick would have been found at his Devon sanctuary, slowly healing his mind and body in his beloved retreat. As part of Nick's slow recovery, he completely gutted the cottage, removing all traces of Jane. Everything tainted by her went into a skip, as Nick merciless in his own final act of cleansing, undertook a redesign of the interior, his personal suture; books, rugs, furniture and paintings discarded without a second look. Replacing them with a style he could honestly call his own; furniture and fittings, all antiques to go with renovated bare floorboards and simple rugs, a sofa and chairs to curl up on and forget you're alone.

To lessen what Angie's interior designer friends would have called the chromic diffusion between tint and shade, what Nick knew to be bare emulsion walls, he hung original photographs and paintings themed on the sea. He added a modest oak kitchen while he was in the mood for change, with upstairs treated to a bathroom half panelled and tiled, and his bedroom refreshed with a double bed that he did not intend to share with anyone ever again.

Nick knew that he would never be allowed anything so close to total closure from the events that he had set in motion, beginning with the attempted extraction of Lubov from Moscow. He realised that eventually there would be something to shatter the spell of normality and return him to the world of dirty work, which occurred one midweek afternoon. Nick had fallen asleep stretched on the sofa, a copy of Joyce's Dubliners had slipped onto the floor creasing a couple of pages, whilst in the corner, the television silently played some inane repeat. Stumbling awake at the car's crunching on the gravel, Nick reached the door before a contrite Blackmore could knock.

'Hey ho, Nicholas Torr, I presume,' declared Blackmore his voice wound high, demanding Nick get his coat right away, for Roly had an urgent desire to take in the sea air, repeating the demand as though to a child. So off they set into a splendid crisp afternoon, enjoying the lazy sun until the long-off dusk came in its place.

'Can't hide away down here for ever, you know,' Blackmore said, admiring the view over the Channel from a headland path.

'I'm not hiding, I'm waiting for my Accountability Board review.'

'Good, fucking luck with that. Could be months before we see a glimmer of normality. Blessed be the meek. Hawick's positively rolling in the shit, loving every minute of it. But he's not about to kiss and forget with you. You assaulted him and he's determined to have you pay homage, grovel and plead forgiveness.'

Refusing to be drawn by Roly's wily assessment, Nick simply laughed, his face turned to the sea.

'Redman sends his regards by the way, he's back on duty, returned to the fold, Paul and I made sure of it.'

'He should be.'

'Given any thought who had their finger on the trigger? Moscow insist they're not culpable but haven't protested at their loss. Three nil to us was it, Nicholas?'

For a moment he seemed to have detached himself from Roly, his surroundings, as he replayed the post-operational debriefing on Fehmarn. A number of points were covered; one of them being the identity of the individual in the back of the Mercedes. According to Erika who exchanged glances with him, he was a thin, pauper looking figure, as insubstantial as a phantom with such a murderous stare, it raised goosebumps down her arms.

'Tazi,' snapped Nick.

'He's turning out to be a right menace, isn't he? What was he up to? Casting a critical eye over his chatelaine, our very own darling Jane? Measuring you up?'

'A display of his power, as retribution,' answered Nick. 'A declaration that *his* directorate will not countenance failure.'

'And what directorate would that be?'

Ignoring Roly's drift entirely, Nick brusquely retorted: 'They broken her yet?'

'Not a chance. Jane Francis Stratton's playing games, all "no comment" interviews.'

'How's she taken it?'

'Wonderful, how do you think? She's full of bravado, spite and malevolence of course. Keeps telling us that we can lock her up and throw away the key now that she's lost her one true lover Irina. Other than that, not a meaningful tweet,' confirmed Blackmore, striding off.

'What *have* you got?'

'Nothing of substance. From the trail you opened, we know Irina Dezhenka crossed paths with Jane and did a very expert number in wooing her into Tazi's fold. Where, why or when, she ain't telling. Irina has been her lover, mentor and handler ever since,' said Blackmore, refusing to look at Nick, his eyes fixed remotely down.

'It was before Dezhenka did her number on Gav in Latvia,' said Nick, his mood suddenly savage, his eyes fiery.

'You're bound to feel angry, it's natural.'

'Is it?'

'If you hadn't stuck at it, think of the damage she'd have wreaked. Promotion? She could have had a realistic shout at becoming our wise and respected leader.'

'Hasn't she done enough damage?' Nick retorted.

'None of us saw through her, so you can't blame yourself,' Roly advised, trying to sound upbeat himself. 'We're just the pilgrims in this life who sometimes find ourselves going in the wrong direction, that's all. We all should have spotted her rotten core.'

'That it, Roly, we all just get back into our normal routine?'

'World's not a safe place, Nicholas, don't believe anyone who tells you otherwise.'

'She wasn't the only one, you know that.'

'Oh, I reckon Tazi must have planted others, maybe some who are far more important than our Jane Francis Stratton. Hawick's had a new broom to all floors, your little outpost too, found nothing but officers long past their sell by date in *his* opinion. Had quite the rampage our Teddy has, culled anything and anyone who didn't sit pretty with his thoroughly modern agenda. Everyone left standing has been assessed, treble-vetted, and I'm told that includes you. So we can claim to all concerned that we've had a bloody thorough spring clean, humans and systems.'

'It's come at a price though hasn't it, Roly?' retorted Nick, turning for home.

'And you've paid in full,' declared Blackmore, slapping Nick on the shoulder.

Yes, yes, I have, decided Nick, I'm the survivor who's walking home to a life without Angie. Bringing up his collar, he shoved his hands into his pockets and trudged off at Blackmore's side.